THE MAKING OF A HIGHLANDER

ELISA BRADEN

Copyright © 2020 Elisa Braden

Cover design by Dar Albert at Wicked Smart Designs

For more information about the author,
visit www.elisabraden.com.

ISBN-13: 978-1-950805-05-1

CHAPTER ONE

September 30, 1825
Glenscannadoo, Scotland

"Did you wear it betwixt yer bosoms, as I instructed?" Mrs. MacBean's squint was an accusation of imbecility—one Annie Tulloch did not appreciate.

Annie tossed the foul linen pouch on the old woman's table. "I could tuck it betwixt the cheeks of my arse, ye daft crone, and the result would be the same. It doesnae work." She planted her hands on her hips and nodded toward the silent, pale boy by her side. "He's nae better."

Mrs. MacBean shook her peppery head and pursed crinkled lips. "The sage mightn't have been strong enough. 'Tis best to harvest during a new moon."

"It smells like stew cooked in a chamber pot."

"Aye. The mushrooms are a wee bit pungent. Mayhap I used too many."

"Mayhap ye ingested too many."

"Och, I havenae done that in ages, lass. The first time ye wake up naked with a goat, shame on the devil. The second? Shame on ye."

"You havenae the foggiest notion what you're about. I'd have better luck beggin' a remedy from Ronnie Cleghorn."

"The simple lad who gnaws rope when his father isnae looking?"

Annie raised a brow.

Ordinarily, Mrs. MacBean's milky left eye tended to wander. Now, it twitched with annoyance. "Listen well, lass. I've lived three of your lifetimes in the mists of these lands." She swept an arm around her dingy hovel strewn with old books and dried weeds. Slapping a cobweb from her sleeve, she continued, "Ancient knowledge runs in my blood. My mother's mother's—"

"Mother was a seer," Annie finished, rolling her eyes. "Aye. So ye've claimed. Over and over—"

Sniff. "'Tis true."

"—and over until I'd prefer to eat whatever foul substances you stuffed in that pouch than to hear the tale again." Annie glowered. "Perhaps after four generations, your blood's weaker than an innkeeper's whisky." She glanced down at Finlay, who hid behind her hip. His blue eyes were shadows. His wee hand clutched his middle. Her own middle twisted as dread gripped hard. "But it's plain you cannae help him. Nor me. Just admit it."

The old woman's glare gentled into sympathy as her good eye roamed Annie's expression. "Ye mustn't fash yerself, lass. We'll discover the cause of the laddie's affliction."

"He needs a cure. I'm wastin' my bluidy time with ye."

"And who do ye suppose would offer better, eh?" She scoffed and blew her nose on her woolen sleeve. "Go on, then. Beseech the laird's surgeon." The old woman's sarcasm burned Annie's aforementioned arse. "See how much he can tell you about it. 'Course, he'd have to acknowledge the lad's existence first. Trouble, that. Mayhap the priest—"

"Oh, for God's sake."

The old woman's expression darkened. "Precious little that priest does for God's sake, lass."

Annie turned and paced to the open front door of the cottage, her chest squeezing. Something was wrong with Finlay. He'd grown increasingly silent over the past year, shadowed and absent and frail. Annie had tried to coax answers from him, but he couldn't explain what was wrong. The only one who might know how to fix him was a woman whose sanity was in greater doubt than Annie's.

The old crone was an outcast. She'd been forced from her home by her former laird to make way for more profitable tenants—namely, sheep. Several years past in a fleeting mood of generosity, Glenscannadoo's laird, Gilbert MacDonnell, had welcomed such castoffs as Mrs. MacBean.

The foolish popinjay could scarcely pay his own mortgage and had long ago sold most of his lands to settle debts. But the Laird of Glenscannadoo fancied himself quite the paragon of Highland courtesy, so he'd invited Mrs. MacBean to live at the edge of the village in a cottage no one else wanted, a castoff woman in a castoff house doling out herbs and midwifery to villagers who called her a witch.

That woman was Finlay's last hope—the only hope.

Annie's stepfather and two of her stepbrothers had helped repair Mrs. MacBean's roof, rebuilt the hearth, and reattached the door. In return, Mrs. MacBean routinely made liniment for Annie's stepfather's aching joints, and carved ugly trinkets she swore would bring Annie's stepbrothers "wives to please yer very soul."

Mrs. MacBean owed a debt to Annie's family, and the MacPherson men tolerated her gestures. Annie was not a MacPherson. The woman owed *her* nothing. And yet, she'd been kind. She'd seen Finlay, *acknowledged* Finlay, when no one else did.

Feeling the laddie's cool, dark hair slide through her fingertips, Annie sighed and leaned against the open door, trying to stifle the fear that clutched with a cold, relentless grip.

At midday, the sky was like iron. Drizzle had started up again. Had it ever stopped?

She gathered her plaid tighter around her, folding her arms across her chest and watching mud deepen along the lane. "Have ye enough bread to see ye 'til Wednesday, Mrs. MacBean?" she asked over her shoulder, eyeing the basket of loaves she'd brought.

"Oh, aye," came the vague reply. "I'm obliged to ye, dear." The chair near the fireplace creaked its familiar groan as the old woman sat. "The brown book with the acorn on the spine might say somewhat about spiritual afflictions. Now, where did I bury that one?"

Annie caught Finlay's gaze and crossed her eyes. He glanced toward the muttering Mrs. MacBean and smothered a laugh.

"We'll return in a few days, then," Annie said, plucking her hat from the hook.

The old woman scratched her head. Then her leg. Then her elbow. She stood and searched beneath her cracked wooden chair.

Annie raised a brow at Finlay, who shot her a crooked grin. She was pleased to see it. He'd been so unwell of late she'd begun to despair of ever seeing that Fin Grin again.

Perhaps this would be one of his better days.

As she left the cottage, he remained tethered to her side. She tugged her hat lower, cursing the sullen rain and the wilting brim. She'd inherited the worthless thing from her stepbrother Broderick, who'd inherited it from her eldest stepbrother, Campbell.

Blasted MacPhersons had heads the size of washtubs.

Huffing as she resettled the hat on the back of her head, she added four strapping stepbrothers to her silent cursing and tromped through deepening mud.

Down the lane that ran from the foothills along the loch toward the village, two MacDonnell women lingered outside a tidy cottage. The younger Mrs. MacDonnell resettled a bairn on her broad hip and grumbled to her mother-in-law, "Cousin Dougal says work at the kelp beds has dried up. Next, I expect he'll be bletherin' about Canada again. That wife of his, no doubt. Glaswegian tart." The bairn fidgeted until his mother pinched his leg. He whimpered but stopped squirming.

Grisel MacDonnell was Annie's age, four-and-twenty, and already had four wee ones. Annie pitied those children. Grisel had a spiteful temper. Two of Annie's scars had come from her teeth. They'd been lassies no bigger than Finlay when the injuries occurred, but still. Spiteful.

The elder Mrs. MacDonnell glanced up at the rain. "Warned him, I did. Naught remains in the coastlands but seabirds. Canada might offer better prospects."

Grisel's full lips twisted. "My fool husband says the same. Mayhap we should all board a ship, then." Her gaze snagged upon Annie. "Christ's blood," she hissed, shifting her bairn to the opposite hip and backing toward the garden gate. "'Tis Mad Annie. She's been to see the MacBean witch again."

Her mother-in-law spun with a darting, wary stare in Annie's direction. "Best get inside," the older woman muttered, gesturing with nervous fingers. "Out the rain."

A devilish impulse took hold of Annie. She caught Finlay's eye.

Ah, there was that Fin Grin again.

She winked then whispered, "Watch this." Spinning mid-stride, she began walking backward as she passed the two women. She extended her arms, letting the folds of her plaid drape like wings. "Och, 'tis the rain that delivers the curse, Mrs. MacDonnell."

"C-curse?"

"Aye. Dinnae ye feel it?" While the two women watched with saucer eyes, she raised her arms above her head as though calling down the powers of heaven. Her voice dropped to a thrum. "Whosoever causes a bairn tae greet an' wail shall suffer the selfsame miseries twelvefold. Beware. Beware. *Beware!*"

Grisel's ruddy skin whitened with each "beware." She frowned at the tear-stained bairn on her hip then eyed Annie with disbelief.

Annie didn't blame her. If she were the sort of mother Grisel was, she wouldn't want to believe in retribution curses, either.

Fluttering her fingers for added effect, Annie didn't have to tell Finlay to join in the fun. He crossed the lane and tickled Grisel's back. The woman shuddered and paled further. Finlay darted back to Annie's side, covering his laughter.

The elder Mrs. MacDonnell ushered her stricken daughter-in-law through the gate as Grisel stammered, "D-does it seem colder of a sudden?"

As the women scurried inside the cottage, Annie chuckled, ruffling Finlay's hair. "Ah, that trick never loses its shine, Fin. Well done."

They continued into the village square, a rather grand description for anything in Glenscannadoo. In truth, it was an irregular, roughly cobbled strip bounded by a single inn, three taverns, and five shops. At the center towered a statue of a MacDonnell laird. Annie supposed it was meant to represent Gilbert MacDonnell's father, but the likeness was far handsomer—and assuredly had more sense—than the man she remembered. He stood proudly in a kilt, cap, sporran, and brogues, gazing over haggard rooftops toward Loch Carrich. One hand rested upon his sword as though prepared to battle beside Bonnie Prince Charlie for the honor of his family name.

And he was that foolish, she thought, sniffing as she passed through his shadow.

Finlay clung to her side as they entered the haberdashery, but the moment her laddie spotted the tartan display, he drifted toward the colorful bolts of wool at the rear of the shop.

"Dinnae go far," she murmured.

He gave a distracted nod and continued on.

Behind the counter, the portly Mr. Cleghorn glanced about his empty shop and shot her a suspicious frown.

She ignored him to peruse the skeins of thread. Plucking a fine ivory and a rich blue, she bent to consider the greens on the lower shelf.

"Ye're puddlin' my floor, Anne Tulloch," Mr. Cleghorn grumbled.

Annie glanced down to where her plaid ended and her trews tucked into her boots. A cascade fell from her hat's brim. "So I am," she said, feigning surprise. She swiped a finger across one of the shelves and held it up so he could see the grime. "Seems somebody should introduce this place to a bit of water now and then."

"Do ye intend to buy that thread or steal it?"

Knuckling her hat back, she replied, "Well, now, I didnae reckon you'd be amenable to thievin', Mr. Cleghorn. Generous of ye to give us an option." She pretended to weigh the skeins between her hands. "Pay or steal? Pay or steal? A pure dilemma."

"Wee harridan. Ye'll nae steal from me."

Grinning, she called, "Hear that, Fin?" Her laddie turned. "Mad Annie isnae merely mad, but a thief in the bargain." She glanced down at the wet spot around her boots. "A proper storm come to drench the haberdasheries of Glenscannadoo."

Cleghorn drew back, his expression edged with fear. "Who are ye talkin' to, lass?"

Disgusted, she plucked a green skein from the lowest shelf and stalked to the counter. "Add these to Angus MacPherson's bill," she snapped.

"Yer stepfather didnae approve—"

"Angus likes his shirts mended. That's all the approval I need."

Cleghorn frowned until his shaggy brows knitted together, but he didn't argue further. Moments later, the bell above the door rang. The next thing Annie felt was a collision in her lower half.

"Ooph!" She twisted to see freckled arms hugging her waist and a mop of russet against her hip. The lad's hair wasn't quite so fiery as her own, rather the color of autumn leaves. But his smile warmed her better than any hearth. She chuckled and stroked rainwater from his cheek. "Ah, 'tis glad I am to see ye, Ronnie. Only this mornin', I was sayin' how one of your smiles would cheer this pisser of a day." From the corner of her eye, she saw Finlay approach. "Isnae that so, Fin?" He nodded and Ronnie laughed.

"Ronnie, leave go," Mr. Cleghorn grumbled to his son while penciling her purchase into his shop accounts. "Miss Tulloch must be on her way."

"Must I, now?"

Cleghorn glanced up with hard eyes. "Aye. Ye must."

Ronnie's arms slid away with his usual reluctance. She glared at his father a moment before kissing the boy's russet head. His smile faded into mild confusion. Finlay distracted the lad by waving him toward the tartans. They raced off together while Annie leaned close to the shopkeeper.

"The youths in this village knock yer son flat on his arse for the sport of it, Mr. Cleghorn. 'Tis a wonder he isnae skinned elbow to knee. Ye might consider such things when ye're deciding his friends for him."

"He has enough troubles," came the accusatory answer. "He doesnae need yours."

Galling, but likely true. The lad was simple—a pure delight, of course, but *different* and, therefore, scorned. Being friendly with Mad Annie Tulloch wouldn't help matters.

"Go on with ye, lass," Cleghorn said. "Yer stepfather will be wonderin' after ye."

"Wonderin' after his dinner, perhaps," she muttered beneath her breath. She formed a pocket in her plaid by tucking a loose corner of the blue-and-green wool into her belt. Stashing her thread inside while Cleghorn disappeared into a storage area behind a curtain.

The bell rang again just as Finlay showed Ronnie a favorite trick: making a piece of rope appear in the boy's hand. As usual, Ronnie collapsed into giggles.

A man entered, pausing to glance about the shop. Bearded. Tall. Dressed like an Englishman.

Because he *was* an Englishman—the only one in Glenscannadoo.

Long strides carried him past the first row of shelves. He removed his hat—an Englishman's hat, once fine and black, now gray and tattered—and raked a hand through sun-streaked brown hair. Mist decorated his shoulders, which were at once lean and powerful beneath his black coat. He plucked up a bolt of linen, a tin of buttons, and a pair of shears.

His motions were efficient. Decisive. The Englishman often moved with purpose, she'd noticed, as though he didn't bother expending effort until he'd locked upon whatever he desired. Then, he pursued his quarry as though nothing else existed.

Amusement quirked her lips as he laid his purchases on the counter. "Ye'd do better buyin' oiled canvas, English," she advised. "That roof of yours cannae shelter ye from a bird's wayward shite, never mind the rain." She flicked the fine linen with her finger and looked him up and down. "Petticoats'll flatter yer bonnie figure, no doubt. But they're bluidy useless against a Highland winter."

His mouth twisted, not precisely a smile.

But, then, she and he weren't precisely friendly.

Hazel eyes flickered over her. "Miss Tulloch."

"Mr. Huxley."

"How is your father? Feeling more amiable, perhaps?"

She chuckled. "Stepfather. And ye know better than most Angus isnae amiable, even when the sky is shinin' rather than pissin'."

"Pity." His attention wandered toward Cleghorn, who'd emerged through the curtain and gone to remove a piece of rope from Ronnie's mouth. "He should take my last offer."

The lines around John Huxley's eyes suggested he'd once been a laugher—or at least a grinner—but she rarely saw it. For any Englishman, being trapped in the nether creases of the Scottish Highlands might do that, she supposed. He'd also spent the past year battling over property rights with the stubbornest Scotsman ever to don tartan. That would put anyone in a foul temper. Still, this was the same flat, cynical look Huxley had worn since arriving in the glen summer before last.

He'd come to claim land left to him by a friend. The property, which abutted MacPherson land, shared commonty rights to the loch in the neighboring glen.

Thick woodlands, abundant deer, clear streams, and access to the loch for swimming and fishing made Huxley's land an ideal hunting property. Annie imagined the Englishman could demand a fortune from some fancy English lord, were Angus agreeable to settling matters. But he wasn't.

As things stood, Huxley couldn't legally sell until the dispute over the commonty was settled, and Angus would only settle upon terms if Huxley agreed to sell the property to him. Huxley had promised his dead friend that he wouldn't sell the land to Angus MacPherson.

A year later, the stalemate hadn't yet broken.

Occasionally, John Huxley would pay Angus a visit, handing Annie his hat with that same calm, weary expression. The two men would argue a bit before Angus told him where he could stow his offer. Then, Huxley would leave. Each time she saw him, his beard was a little thicker, his hat a little grayer.

But his expression never changed. She sometimes wondered what had made him so bone-weary—apart from Scotland's inhospitable weather.

Now, she tilted her head and rested a hip against the counter. "Ye're stubborn as he is. Why not sell to Angus, eh? Ye could return to London, or wherever it is ye come from. Have a proper roof. Have a proper hat." She scanned his face, noting the beard could use some trimming. Having seen the man bare-faced, she wondered if he'd grown it to disguise his preposterously handsome features. His eyes remained visible, of course, so it was a wasted effort.

That hazel gaze returned to examine her. "I shan't be selling to Angus MacPherson." Although he said it without heat, she heard the weight of the surrounding mountains in his words.

"Why?"

"I vowed I would not."

She scoffed. "Ye promised an auld, jealous fool that ye'd spite the man who 'stole' his bride. Lot of male nonsense, if ye're askin' me."

"I don't believe I was."

Sighing, she conceded the point. "Fair enough, English." She patted the bolt of linen. "Dinnae forget the thread." She plucked the ivory skein from her makeshift pocket then held it up in feigned surprise. "Och, no. Appears I've nabbed the last of it." She clicked her tongue. "A pure shame. Yer petticoats willnae be so fine, after all."

His lips twitched briefly inside his beard. "You might be surprised, Miss Tulloch. I've a way with petticoats." He glanced down at her trews. "I see you're still developing similar talents."

Other lasses might be insulted, but Annie merely brushed the haphazard folds of her plaid and laughed. Had she been wearing it over skirts, the blanket-sized length of wool would be a proper *arasaid*, as other Highland women wore. But she hadn't the patience for muddy hems and flammable layers. Too much work to be done. "Ah, ye amuse me, English. I must say, ye do."

He huffed—nearly a chuckle—and donned his hat. "Give my regards to MacPherson."

Cleghorn came to take Huxley's coins, and Annie took her leave, waving Fin over to take her hand. Outside, beneath the shop's eave, she paused. Huxley exited behind her and strode across the square to his cart. Her eyes followed him then caught on the two men standing near the MacDonnell statue. One was garbed in bright tartan, the other in refined riding clothes.

"Lord," came a whisper from her side.

Her heart thudded.

Finlay hadn't spoken in weeks. Was this a sign he'd begun healing?

Her eyes flew down, only to find the effort of a single word had cost him half his color. Worry sank its claws around her throat.

"Aye, Fin," she managed past the ache. "'Tis the Laird of Glenscannadoo, for all that means. Can a man be a laird when he hasnae but five or six acres?"

Finlay peered at the popinjay gesturing grandly at his father's statue.

Gilbert MacDonnell had rounder cheeks than one usually saw in a man above twenty. Wispy brows disappeared into his skin. His nose was short, a perfect match for his stature. And his speech hinted at a lisp. She'd say he wore a clan chief's costume if clan chiefs strutted about like wee tartan peacocks. Most had more sense.

"No laird."

Three words in one day! "Not a real one, that's for certain," she murmured, trying not to draw undue attention. "He's dressed like that ridiculous statue." The cap, the kilt, the sporran. Even the brogues and stockings. The only difference was the tartan. Scarlet didn't translate into stone.

By contrast, the popinjay's golden-haired companion wore a sensible hunting coat and fine-fitted riding breeches. She admired the gentleman's backside for a moment before wondering who he might be.

Fine breeches, indeed.

Fin's hand squeezed hers. She glanced down to see him mouth, "Must go."

"In a wee moment, laddie." Nudging her hat higher upon her head, she squinted across the rain-spattered square to get a better look. The man was passably tall—at least ten inches taller than the laird. Of course, the laird was even shorter than Annie, so that was no great measure. The Englishman would top the well-dressed stranger by several inches. Still, she admired the lean elegance of his shoulders, the fine cut of his coat. The firmness of his seat.

Nearby, two MacDonnell women exited the dressmaker's shop. "Ye see there, Flora? Didnae I tell ye the laird had guests from Edinburgh?"

"Edinburgh!"

"Lowlanders. *Titled* ones."

Annie sidled to her left, tugging Finlay toward home. Only when she angled past the post did she spy the third figure in the trio. A woman—no, a *lady*—huddled close to the golden-haired man. Her gaze was patient boredom. Her neck resembled a swan's. Her gown was silk.

Silk. In the pissing rain of Glenscannadoo.

And not just any silk, but quite the finest blue satin Annie had ever seen. It glistened like the loch on a summer afternoon. The golden-haired man held an umbrella above her head, his shoulders canted in a posture that suggested she was delicate. Important.

Annie's stomach panged oddly. He seemed to care for her, whoever she was. Whoever *he* was, for that matter. Annie still didn't know.

"Didnae ye say he's a sir of some sort or other?" muttered Flora MacDonnell to her sister.

"A Lord of Parliament. The Lord ... now what was it? Scott? Seton?" Flora's sister clicked her tongue. "Och, all those Lowland names sound alike."

"Lockhart," grumbled Flora's husband as he exited the shop behind them. "The Lord Lockhart. Are you two done bletherin', or am I to stand here whilst you inspect the man's teeth?"

Curious, Annie wandered beyond the eave, circling to get a better look at the golden-haired man. The *Lord* Lockhart. She'd never met a lord before. Even the Laird of Glenscannadoo hadn't more than a feudal baron's courtesy title. Certainly, he was no peer.

Rain pattered her hat's brim, dripping and obscuring her view. She should get Finlay home. This was no time for ogling strangers. Her laddie's grip was loosening. She tightened her fist.

Flora and her sister edged away from Annie as she passed. Idly, she wondered if Lord Lockhart's face was as handsome as his backside. Perhaps he was married. Perhaps his wife was the lady beside him, shivering in the Scottish rain.

None of it mattered, of course. He'd never look twice at Mad Annie Tulloch, nor would she want such a thing.

Certainly not.

But newcomers to Glenscannadoo were rare. The last one had been John Huxley, and he was English. These two were Scottish ... of a sort.

Crossing the square toward the road home, she drifted closer to the golden pair. Ignoring Flora's whispers about madwomen who wore trews instead of skirts, she craned her neck to catch a glimpse of Lord Lockhart's profile.

Aye, he was handsome. Lean nose, leaf-green eyes, and a curved mouth. His lips were a bit full for her liking—similar to overripe fruit. But all in all, a braw face, splendid backside, and, now that she was close enough to hear it, a pleasing voice, despite the Lowland accent.

Wind came up, burrowing beneath her plaid until even her bones went cold.

Bloody disagreeable Scottish weather.

Moments later, something knocked into her from behind, sending her stumbling.

Her hat flew. Her boots tangled with mud. Something yanked her plaid, tearing loose her makeshift pocket.

"Ronnie!" she heard Cleghorn shout. "Come back here, ye wee dafty!"

Awkwardly, she caught herself then reached behind her to brace the boy who gripped her waist with all his might. The noises he made resembled words, but they were malformed. One, however, she recognized.

"In-ee," Ronnie whimpered. "In-ee."

Only then did she realize what was missing.

The wee, cold hand that always held hers … was gone.

Frantic, she twisted, dragging Ronnie around in circles while she looked for another laddie—*her* laddie.

"Finlay." The word was nothing but air. All she saw was mud and cobbles and emptiness. She was choking. Staggering.

Because she couldn't see him. Couldn't *feel* him.

Cleghorn stomped out into the rain to retrieve his son, who wept and clung to her.

"In-ee! In-ee gunn."

Cleghorn lifted his son into his arms, hauling him back to the shop while admonishing him for running off. Ronnie gazed at her over his father's shoulder. Tears streaked his freckled cheeks. "In-ee gunn."

Light and sound swirled while rain drenched her hair and slid icy fingers along her nape.

In-ee gunn.

Finlay gone.

Oh, dear God. Finlay *was* gone. She felt it. His absence. Their connection simply … missing.

She swayed. Wiped a rivulet from her forehead. Another snaked down to the corner of her eye, blurring her vision.

Finlay gone.

Her laddie. Her friend. Gone.

A handsome face appeared in her vision. Golden-haired. Green-eyed. Full-lipped. He frowned at her over the shoulder of a woman.

The lady held Annie's hat. "… yours, miss?"

Annie took it. Nodded. Couldn't speak.

"… should depart soon," said the man briskly, giving Annie the same look Annie might give a rat in her larder.

"… appears a bit dazed." The lady took the umbrella from him. Extended it forward to cover Annie's head, too. She had the same leafy eyes and golden hair as the man behind her. Yet different, somehow. She wore kindness like silk—as though she'd been born to it. "May we offer assistance? My brother and I have a coach. Perhaps we could give you a ride home on our way to Edinburgh?"

Grief thickened her throat. No sound could escape past the burning ache.

Finlay gone.

After more than a year, it had finally happened. He was gone.

And no one knew. Because no one else saw him, apart from a simple lad and an old, daft woman.

"… not have time for this … think we should leave her be, sister," said the handsome man, drawing the golden woman away. Lockhart. He was a lord.

Annie couldn't bring herself to curtsy.

A coach rumbled into the square. The two golden-haired Lowlanders murmured with Gilbert MacDonnell before climbing inside.

Rain fell. Wind blew. The square emptied of all but her.

Another shadow merged with hers, taller by a foot and doubly wide. Long, masculine fingers plucked her hat from her limp hand and set it upon her head. Broad shoulders stooped to retrieve her thread from the mud.

"Here, now, Miss Tulloch," the shadow said in crisp, English tones. "Don't forget this. I've heard it's the last of the lot."

Something in his voice made her seek out his eyes. Hazel—brown and green and gold, all at once. Too beautiful for a man, made more so by dense, dark lashes.

And, oddly enough, they were not kind. Not chary like the golden-haired lord's or gentle like his golden-haired sister's.

These eyes were simply calm, as though they'd seen too many storms to think one was any worse than another.

"H-he's gone," she whispered, unsure why she bothered telling the Englishman.

A crease formed between dark brows. "Who?"

She shook her head. Deep and jagged, the wound that had been gouged minutes earlier widened inside her ribs—that place where Finlay had been tethered.

Gone. Finlay gone.

It hurt so badly, she nearly doubled over.

She must find a way to bring him back. She must. But how? She'd failed to save him. Failed to halt his decline. Failed to hold him tightly enough.

The Englishman continued frowning, but he didn't keep after her. Instead, he glanced around the empty square, eyed her dripping hat, pocketed her muddy thread, and sighed.

"My cart is this way," he said, taking her elbow and turning her toward the corner.

"Unnecessary, English." Her voice sounded faint. Choked. She swallowed and breathed, took enough steps to keep pace with him. "I can walk the same way I came."

He didn't slow, didn't release her. "The cart is faster." Calm hazel slanted down at her then forged ahead. "Perhaps your stepfather will be more amiable after I drop his daughter at his door."

CHAPTER TWO

Everyone called her Mad Annie. Until now, John Huxley hadn't understood why. True, she occasionally talked to herself. But she'd always appeared sane enough to him—fiery and foul-mouthed, impertinent and utterly unconcerned with convention.

But sane.

Now, the redheaded virago had gone dead silent. She sat beside him on the cart's bench, soaked and gray, rocking subtly like a graveside mourner.

It was bloody disturbing.

He'd conversed with her a handful of times while meeting with Angus MacPherson. For all her fire, she was a little thing; the top of her head wouldn't even scrape his chin. But her size was misleading.

Angus MacPherson and his four sons were the real power in this wild, isolated Highland backwater. Hard, ruthless men with the all the charm of dyspeptic badgers, the MacPhersons were, nevertheless, wily negotiators.

And formidable opponents.

None them stood a hair shorter than six-and-a-half feet. None of them weighed a pebble less than sixteen stone. None of them was married, though Angus had been widowed twice. Obsessed with expanding their backwater empire, they'd spent the past twenty years accruing MacDonnell land around Glenscannadoo and the neighboring valley, Glendasheen. The area's residents—including the supposed clan chieftain, Gilbert MacDonnell—seemed happy to live under MacPherson rule.

Yet, after a single visit to MacPherson House, John quickly realized who ruled the MacPherson men. And she wasn't even a MacPherson. According to his solicitor, Anne Tulloch had been brought into Angus's household with her mother around the age of five. A year later, her mother had died, widowing Angus and leaving Annie to be raised by five rough Scotsmen.

She was quite the oddest female he'd ever encountered—and he'd encountered more than his share. Even so, John had grown accustomed to Annie Tulloch's eccentric ways. Often, she was bizarrely attired in buff breeches, tall boots, white tunic, and a plaid that shrouded her in blue-and-green wool until the only way to know she was a woman was from the belt at her waist.

He'd grown accustomed to the shocking brightness of her hair, raggedly shorn around her face and plaited down her back. Sometimes she covered it with a great, floppy hat, and sometimes she left it uncovered to flash like red fire.

He'd grown accustomed to her lack of proper skirts, her unnervingly brilliant eyes, her sharp-tongued taunts about his manhood.

Dinnae luik so gloomy, English. Angus is a crabbit auld man, be ye bonnie as a fresh-dewed lass or no.

Did ye steal those boots from a Scot, English? They seem a mite big for yer wee, dainty feet.

Next time, try flutterin' those girlish lashes at him, English. Mayhap he'll offer to let ye pour his tea.

Most women thought him handsome, but only Annie Tulloch managed to turn it into an insult. And God, how she relished the insults.

Brazen, mouthy woman.

She ordered her brothers about like a tyrannical sea captain. She cursed her towering stepfather to his face before patting his cheek and asking if he needed more liniment.

She dressed like a boy or, more precisely, an unkempt Highland ruffian who cut his hair with a dull knife. She was fearless. Fiery. Crackling with defiance and ignorant of basic manners.

Three years ago, he would have liked her. Hell, five years ago, he might have seduced her for the sport of it.

Now? He didn't know what to do with her.

Which might explain the disquiet in his gut after witnessing her come apart over nothing much at all.

"Ye needn't have troubled yerself, English." The tremulousness of her voice made his hands tighten on the reins. He almost wished for another insult.

"No trouble. Your house is on the way to mine." Nodding to the rutted cart path that forked into Glendasheen, he eyed the heavy clouds above, the dark hills to either side of them, and the fingerling mists caressing yellow birch and green pine. "Jacqueline may not win any races, but she'll save your boots some wear."

"Jacqueline?"

"The horse."

She fell silent, rocking with the motion of the cart.

He glanced at her hands, which flattened protectively along the right side of her waist as though covering a wound. "Did the boy hurt you?"

Eyes the color of cornflowers flew up to his. "B-boy?"

"Cleghorn's son. When he accosted you back in the square. Did he injure you?"

Destitution shadowed her eyes before they fell away. "No. Ronnie is a good lad."

Perhaps she was mad, after all.

Certainly, he'd known men who appeared normal for days or weeks at a time, only to fall into a state of sudden, confused agitation. War could produce such a plague upon the mind. So could grave losses.

He'd once befriended a tribesman in the Cape Colony of Africa. The man had spoken English, so John had hired him as a translator and guide. They'd gotten on famously until the night he'd mistaken John for a ghost from his past and tried to gut him with the spit from their campfire.

John later learned the man's two brothers, wife, and five children had been slaughtered by a rival tribe years earlier. Madness. Grief. Torment. A decade after the tribesman had buried his family, memories had risen up like an ancestral spell to sow chaos in his mind.

Now, John wondered if Mad Annie Tulloch suffered something similar. Normal behavior most of the time—well, normal for *her*—then a sudden break.

"I'm not mad." Those unnervingly blue eyes met his again. "I ken ye think so. But I'm not. So, stop yer gawpin'."

As usual, her mouthy ways struck him like an itch. He wanted to laugh and, at the same time, to shut her up. Instead, he focused on the road ahead and held his tongue. At least she'd regained some color.

"What are ye haulin' back to that decrepit auld pile of stone ye live in, English?" She glanced back at the cart's towering load, covered in canvas. "More than a bit of linen for yer drawers, I reckon."

"Materials for repairs."

A snort. "Repairing Glendasheen Castle will take more than this lot. Ye'll need a bluidy miracle."

He frowned. "I'd make swifter progress if your fellow Scots would agree to work for me."

"Better chance of Christ himself ridin' his unicorn down here for a dram and a biscuit."

"Hmm. I could use a good carpenter."

Another snort. "Amusin', English." She removed her hat and shook the rain from the wide brim before plopping it back into place. "'Tis cursed, ye ken."

"So I'm told."

"Angus didnae lie about that. Somethin' bad happened there. The castle willnae let ye get too far in yer improvements before knockin' ye back on yer arse."

"Thus far, the castle's proven more amenable than the MacPhersons. Perhaps it prefers the hands of an Englishman."

"An Englishman's hands are soft as a bairn's wee backside, right enough."

He slanted her a glance. "Examined a great many English hands, have you?"

"Nah. Just yours."

This time, he couldn't stifle the itch. He handed her the reins, ignoring her startled frown, then removed his gloves. Holding out his palms for her inspection, he tilted his head to catch her cornflower gaze. "Obviously not, Miss Tulloch."

She eyed the calluses on his palms and fingertips before raising a brow. "Well, now, a man with only himself for company will test his grip a wee bit more than average. Careful ye dinnae go blind, English."

Bloody hell. Mad or not, she never missed an opportunity to insult him in the vulgarest of terms. He tugged his gloves back on and snatched the reins from her. "Careful *you* don't invite more than you intend."

"Invite?"

"Hmm. You're fortunate I'm a gentleman."

"Is that what ye are? I have wondered a time or two."

"Another man might mistake your insults for deliberate provocation."

She snorted. "No mistake, English. When that muscle in yer jaw flickers, I feel a wee little glow inside."

"Why the devil would that be?"

Brilliant blue eyes wandered his face. "Dinnae ken." She shrugged. "My brothers say I'm contrary."

"How perceptive. Do they also say the loch is a mite chilly for swimming in winter?"

"No. But, then, they're nae so dainty as you."

The itch intensified and began to burn. Despite her admission that she provoked him intentionally, he found himself clenching his jaw.

She nudged his elbow with hers. "Dinnae be sore. Ye're a fine diversion. That's all."

"Diversion from what?" He glanced down at her, but she'd turned away, staring into the passing underbrush. Though her hat hid her expression, he could still see her lips. Ordinarily, they were quirked into an amused half-grin. Now, they were downturned. Trembling at the corners. He watched her swallow. Saw her shoulders curl inward, her hands cradling her right side.

It might be the cold. It might be madness.

But it looked like sadness.

He didn't know what was wrong with her. And even if he did, she wasn't any of his business.

No, his business was to renovate his castle, sell his land, and get the bloody hell out of Scotland. The only use he had for Mad Annie Tulloch was as a tool for softening Angus MacPherson's black heart.

As the cart rolled through a drift of yellow leaves and past a rail fence, they came within sight of MacPherson House. The old stone farmhouse was large for a cottage, small for a manor, and surprisingly welcoming. He pulled Jacqueline to a halt a few feet from the front door.

Annie remained still, her breathing shallow.

Frowning, John climbed down from the cart and rounded to her side. From this angle, he could see her face. The cold, hard pressure in his chest that he'd wanted to blame on the weather intensified.

Normally creamy-white, her skin now hued closer to gray. Her stare was vacant. She wore fingerless gloves, and he watched her form claws against her ribs, pressing and pressing.

"Miss Tulloch," he prompted quietly. "You are home, now."

She blinked. Looked at him. Her eyes were dull and mournful. They began to gloss with tears.

He held out his hand. "Come. Let me help you down."

She tightened her jaw. Raised her chin. Blinked until the gloss disappeared. "I will get him back," she whispered.

"Who?"

"Doesnae matter. I shall do it. I willnae stop until I find a way."

He nodded as though she made perfect sense. Interrupting a woman's mad ramblings with rationality was a fatal error. As the only brother to five sisters, he'd learned that lesson early and learned it well. "Right, then. Let's get you inside, shall we?"

She grasped his hand tightly and leaned forward until the brim of her hat dripped on his chin. Her other hand landed on his shoulder. Her face was inches away, her breath mingling with his.

He was relieved to see the spark return to those blue eyes, but she was too close. What was she doing?

"Ye'll come inside with me, English. I'll not be sendin' ye up to yer rubbish castle without some sustenance."

Frowning, he tried to keep a proper distance between them, but she wasn't having it. She circled his neck with one arm, tucked their clasped hands together at her waist, and climbed down from the cart by sliding her body awkwardly against his.

Bloody hell.

His heart kicked at the feel of her. What the devil was she hiding beneath all that wool? Soft, cushiony, voluptuously curved. Automatically, his free arm circled her waist, small compared with what lay above it.

Their brims bumped. Her thigh slid between his. He lowered her to the ground with a plunk, disconcerted by his body's reaction.

Clearly, he'd been too long without a woman.

He released her quickly, but she hung on, steadying herself against him.

Finally, she patted his shoulder. Then his jaw. "Thank ye, English. Ye've some ways to go before a lass could call ye graceful, but yer help is appreciated."

"Has a man ever assisted you down from a cart before?"

"Aye, of course. My brothers haul me down when they're quick enough. Otherwise, they complain I didnae wait for them."

"Haul you down."

"Aye." She frowned up at him. "Like a bag of tatties."

"They haul you down like a bag of potatoes."

"Am I speakin' Gaelic, of a sudden? Aye. Have done since I was a wee lassie." She eyed his shoulders and patted his upper arm again. "Och, I didnae mean to bruise yer tender feelings, English. We cannae all be as strong and braw as a MacPherson. Ye did fine." Turning on her heel, she crossed to the massive oak door and shoved it open, waving him forward. "Come inside, now," she ordered, removing her hat and brushing the rain from her plaid.

The brisk sweep of her hands over those mysterious curves drew his eyes.

Bloody disturbing.

"I should be on my way," he said.

"Nah. Ye should do as I tell ye. Else, ye'll have nothin' to show for your trouble, apart from soggy trousers and a hungry horse." She turned and shouted orders to a lad, who scurried outside to take care of Jacqueline.

His stomach chose that moment to grumble its emptiness. He sighed. Perhaps she had a point. All he'd eaten for the past month was fish from the loch. The thought of facing his shambles of a kitchen followed by his shambles of a bedchamber had him trailing her inside.

Warmth hit him like whisky.

Angus MacPherson's house was nothing like the man himself. It was welcoming. Clean. Cheerful, even. The walls were white plaster and wood paneling, the floors polished planks, the ceilings beamed and unusually high. All the doorways were similarly oversized. But then, so were the MacPhersons.

"Annie!" The deep, rumbling bellow traveled through the open door to his left. "Where in bluidy hell have ye been? That venison willnae cook itself!"

She took John's hat from his fingers and rolled her eyes. "Have ye tried settin' fire to it, auld man?" she shouted. "Or are ye just going to sit on yer arse and yawp about yer empty belly?"

Heavy footfalls sounded before Angus MacPherson appeared in the doorway—all six-and-a-half feet of Scottish crags and obstinance. The man had a full head of iron-gray hair and shoulders that, despite his age, nearly matched the door's width. His eyes were sharp, his nose blunt, his brow heavy. He was more than twice Annie's size.

And the moment he set eyes upon her, his glower turned ferocious. "What's wrong?"

Annie moved to deposit her hat and John's on hooks near the door. "Nothin' apart from the weather."

Angus stomped toward her, looming protectively. "Nah. Ye're off yer color. Did Huxley proposition ye?"

"Good God, MacPherson," John snapped. "Of course not."

"I wasnae talkin' to you."

Annie planted her hands on her hips and calmly met her stepfather's suspicious glare. "He brought me home when it was pissin' rain. He didnae have to. I'd take those fine English manners over a pair of muddy boots gladly. And so would you, were ye not so bluidy crabbit."

"He's just tryin' to get under yer skirts, lass."

"I dinnae wear skirts."

Angus grunted his displeasure.

"Go offer him whisky, auld man. He'll be stayin' for dinner."

John's "No, I shan't" overlapped with Angus's denial.

Their rare agreement seemed to amuse Annie. "Dinner will be ready in an hour. More than enough time for another land haggle over a wee dram, eh?"

With that, she disappeared through a second doorway, presumably headed toward the kitchen.

Angus released a bullish snort and turned his glare on John. "Lay a finger on my daughter, Huxley, and I'll turn ye into a woman, right and proper."

Recalling his earlier reaction to discovering she was, in fact, entirely female, he shrugged off a prickle of unease. "Don't be a fool, MacPherson. I require your cooperation to sell my land. Importuning your daughter is the last thing I would—"

"Aye, ye need to sell yer land. For that, ye need me to roll over like hound wantin' its belly scratched, eh? Mayhap ye believe she'll be seduced by bonnie words and a comely face. Mayhap ye think she'll take yer side, and I'll give ye what ye're really after—which isnae her. But she'll nae realize yer trick until ye've left her with naught but yer bairn in her belly."

Everything inside John went hot then cold. He glared at the towering Scot and lowered his voice until it resounded in the empty hall. "As a gentleman, I take your presumptions as a grave insult."

"No trouble with yer hearin', then."

"I also have five sisters and a mother, you bloody-minded Scot."

"Aye. And ye're male."

John glanced down at himself. "Fancy that. So I am."

"Ye're nae one of those peculiar fellows, are ye?"

"What the devil does that mean?"

"Annie luiks like her mother."

John frowned, baffled by the man's certainty that Annie was an irresistible beauty rather than a hoyden garbed in shapeless wool and worn breeches. He shook his head. How to explain without giving offense? "All I want," he gritted, "is to sell my land and leave this place. I've no designs upon Miss Tulloch's virtue, I assure you."

Angus's grunt suggested disbelief. "I need whisky," he muttered before turning on his heel and disappearing into the room he'd earlier vacated. He didn't slam the door in John's face, which John took as an invitation. It was the best he was likely to receive.

Angus filled a glass from a dark bottle and plunked it down on the outer edge of his desk. He filled another and downed it in a single swallow before filling it again and sinking into his leather chair.

The study was plain and weighty. A fire burned in the stone hearth. A lamp burned on the desk. A clock ticked from between shelved books.

John dragged a chair from beneath the window and sat across from Angus. He lifted the glass from the desk and tilted it toward the light. Then, he took a drink.

Oak, honey, and peat fire slid its seduction across his tongue.

By God, the MacPhersons might be Highland barbarians, but they made the finest whisky he'd ever tasted.

"Sell yer land to me, Huxley. 'Tis the only way ye'll rid yerself of it."

John took another sip. "I cannot."

Angus cursed. "Bluidy Ewan Wylie spites me from the grave."

"That he does." And John would not break his word to the salty old Scotsman who'd saved his life not once but thrice. Just picturing that scarred, weathered face sent a hollow pang through his chest. "You should take my last offer. I've told you I'll ensure the owner will be Scottish. A Highlander, even."

"But the land would never be mine."

"No."

"Nor would it belong to my sons."

"I cannot sell to them, either."

Angus fell silent for a time. Then, he leaned forward, bracing his elbows on the desk and fingering his glass while he peered at John through glinting eyes. "What were ye doin' with my daughter, Huxley?"

John drank again, gathering his patience. "We happened upon each other at Cleghorn's shop."

"Did that fat sod speak cruelly to her? I warned him—"

"Not that I heard." John kept his voice neutral. Careful. "Something odd did occur after she left the shop, however."

"Odd how?"

"Cleghorn's son ran out into the square. He seemed distraught. Clung to Miss Tulloch's waist, wailing nonsense." He took another drink, remembering the boy's panic, remembering how Annie had turned gray, how vivid her hair had looked against her skin when she'd lost her hat. The fiery red had dampened, darkened in the rain. She'd spun in circles, her right hand grasping, reaching for something—or someone— she'd lost. Even after Gilbert MacDonnell's well-dressed guests had approached her, she'd stood unnaturally silent, weaving as though she'd been stabbed through the heart and all she could do was bleed.

"She appeared quite ... distressed by the incident," he finished. "I thought it best to see her home safely."

Angus's fist tightened on his glass. "I kenned somethin' was wrong. Lass could scald the devil with her tongue. Isnae like her to go gentle on me."

"Gentle?" The woman had bellowed like a fishwife.

"Aye. Now, with ye, she's polite."

John barely managed not to choke on his whisky.

"Ye're English. She doesnae wish to offend."

He didn't want to laugh. For years, the urge had been absent. Now, it plagued him like an itch every time Anne Tulloch tossed an insult his way. Sighing away the absurdity, he glared at Angus and turned the conversation in a more productive direction. "The rights to the loch must be settled. The original terms of sale state—"

"The original sale was concocted by an eejit."

John swiped a hand over his beard. "We agree on that much."

Gilbert MacDonnell's father, the one whose statue towered over Cross Street, had been breathtakingly daft. But, like his son, he'd also been infatuated with his Highland heritage. So, when the MacDonnells' debts had demanded the chieftain sell off his ancestral lands, he'd rejected the path most other Highland lairds had taken. Rather than selling the whole lot to a wealthy Englishman or titled Lowlander, he'd broken MacDonnell lands into smaller parcels and sold them to Highland Scots—and not the lofty sorts, but men like Ewan Wylie, who'd earned his money on the decks of ships. Men like Angus MacPherson, who'd carved a backwater empire from sweat, dirt, cattle, and malted barley.

MacDonnell had included preposterous terms in the deeds: Each man must live upon the land for two full years; if he left for longer than a week, he forfeited his claim and his funds. For parcels with contested offers, ownership was decided at the Glenscannadoo Highland Games, a summer clan gathering in which men performed feats of strength, speed, stamina, and musicianship.

Nearly three decades past, Angus MacPherson had won his first parcel of MacDonnell land by flinging a hammer farther than any other competitor. He'd won his second by tossing a tree with astonishing precision, and his third by swimming the width of Loch Carrich in record time.

Ewan Wylie had won the land around Glendasheen Castle by being a proficient bagpiper.

With their past rivalry over Angus's first wife, relations between the two neighbors had been rife with bitterness and mutual theft. Unfortunately for John, their long feud meant he was trapped here in Scotland, unable to leave for longer than a few days, lest his claim be challenged by MacPherson's rapacious solicitors. The legal battles were ongoing. His negotiations with the surly old Scot were pure frustration. And his castle was a cold, damp shambles only slightly more welcoming than the Highlanders themselves.

He should be sailing to Antigua. He should be haggling over the price of carpets in a Constantinople market. He should be finding sweet release inside a Spanish courtesan or a French mistress—even a London mistress would do.

For John Huxley, this sort of deprivation was unnatural. And he couldn't even blame Scotland. In truth, his drive to seek out new horizons had begun withering years before he'd arrived in the glen. Ewan's death had worsened the strange void inside him, and a year of bad weather and isolation hadn't improved matters. But the place wasn't the problem. He was.

"Annie's cookery will give ye notions," Angus muttered. "But dinnae go lustin' after a second helping. We'll dine. Then ye'll leave. Ye ken?"

The mention of Annie in the same breath with lust made John blink. He squelched the unwanted sensation snaking from his belly to his groin and lifted his glass in a mocking salute. "Duly noted."

An hour later, he understood Angus's warning. Annie Tulloch's venison was tender, simmered in a seasoned onion gravy, and better than anything he'd eaten in Paris or Tuscany. Each bite made his toes curl inside his boots.

Her bread was even better. Soft. Warm. Yeasty and light. He wanted to bloody weep.

She smirked at him across the heavy, scarred dining table and poured herself a cup of cider. "Slow down, English. Cannae be certain yer delicate constitution will tolerate proper Scottish food."

She had a dot of flour on her chin, a stained apron tied over her plaid, and a scarf tied over her hair. She looked shapeless. A mess.

And he couldn't stop stealing glances. Every third bite, he surreptitiously examined the ragged, fiery fringe brushing her forehead. The elfin nose. The rounded cheekbones and cream-flushed skin. She wasn't ugly. Nor plain—her coloring was far too vivid. In truth, her features were rather pleasing if one ignored her brazen, inflammatory mouth. Overall, her face bore the fullness of a robust appetite and vigorous health. The rest of her was similarly fulsome. In fact, he'd guess her figure edged toward plumpness. A guess, merely. The woman might as well be wearing draperies.

Another bite of venison, and he dared a glance at her bosom, disguised beneath layers and folds. He hadn't forgotten the proportions. The abundance.

God, he was losing his bloody mind. Time for a trip to Glasgow. The widow he occasionally visited there would stop these asinine musings.

"Ye'll nae get what ye're after, Huxley," grumbled Angus from his left. The glowering Scot cut into his meat, his knife scraping the plate. "'Tis only a matter of time before that cursed castle breaks ye. Best ye sell the land to me and be done with it."

Before answering, John used his bread to soak up the last of his onion gravy, both mourning and savoring the bite. "As I've explained, I cannot."

"A man of yer word, eh?" Angus waved his knife in John's direction. "Aye, well, another winter will loosen that cork a bit, I'll wager."

"Perhaps the two of ye *should* wager," Annie said. "Whoever wins, at least it would bring yer daft male nonsense to an end." She drank her cider then raised a sarcastic brow at each of them. "Have a tug-o-war. Rope's in the stable."

"Och, I've no wish to humiliate the lad."

Ignoring the dig, John wiped his mouth with the dingy cloth next to his plate—the MacPherson version of a napkin, he supposed. "Whilst I appreciate the suggestion, Miss Tulloch, my terms must remain steadfast."

Amusement pursed her lips. He noted the upper was thinner than the lower. Neither was plump. But they were forever quirked or moving. Now, she licked a drop of cider from the corner of her mouth and jabbed, "And in January, when yer drawers freeze to yer arse 'til yer tender bits are all numb and frosty, surely those fine, gentlemanly principles will keep yer cockles warm, aye?"

Why was he staring at Annie Tulloch's mouth? God, he needed to visit Glasgow. He needed to leave Scotland. Her madness was catching. "Your concern is sufficiently warming, I daresay."

She frowned at his dry tone. "Somebody should be concerned about ye, English. Never seen a man so bluidy weary of his own existence that he'd run at Angus's temper like he was beggin' to be put out of his misery. Have ye no kin to speak sense to ye?"

The lad from earlier ran in to clear his plate, but John lifted it above the boy's head before rising and helping himself to another serving of venison, bread, and cider from the dishes at the center of the table. If the MacPhersons weren't going to bother with manners, he saw little point in controlling his appetite.

"Yes," he answered, after devouring his next three bites. "Rather an abundance of kin, as it happens."

"Five sisters," Angus interjected, his suspicious gaze ricocheting between Annie and John. "Married, are they?"

"Four are, at last report. The youngest hasn't yet settled on a husband."

"Nor ye on a wife," Angus said. "Yer mother cannae be happy about that."

"Everyone would be better pleased if I were free to leave Scotland. You and your fellow Scots. My family. Me." He shot Angus a dry glare. "Perhaps I'd be at liberty to secure a wife were I not yoked to a property I've little desire to keep."

It was both true and a lie. Everyone would be happier if he returned to England—except him. And on certain days, when his loch reflected blue instead of gray, he considered keeping Ewan Wylie's wild, beautiful land. But a wife? He'd no more desire to marry now than when his father had recommended it ten years ago, or when his mother had demanded it five years ago.

Annie glanced at Angus before crossing her arms over her bosom. "Make him an offer, auld man. Even the Laird of Daftness gave ye a sportin' chance to bargain for this place, foolish though his conditions were."

Releasing a disgusted snort, Angus shoved back from the table. "Ye've gone soft, lass. Coddlin' Huxley like yer favorite wee lamb."

"He's put up with yer rubbish long enough. And I've listened to the same argument too many times." With a scrape of her chair, Annie stood, took a long drink of her cider, tipping the cup back until John saw her pale throat ripple. Then she slammed the cup down on the table. "Finish it."

Angus went silent, staring at his daughter with a worried glower. "This isnae like ye—"

"I'm losin' my patience." She was also losing her color again, her mouth losing its quirk. "He paid me a kindness today. He deserves somethin' in return."

"He's had a fine meal—"

"Make an offer. Or ye can bluidy well make your own gravy from now on."

"Christ on the cross, lassie, dinnae say such foul—"

"Go on." Her chin jutted a challenge as she met Angus's ferocious glare with her own.

Angus slid his wrath in John's direction. "Fine. Here's a wager for yer bonnie lamb. I'll agree to divide the commonty rights as Huxley last proposed." Slowly, Angus grinned. It was not a pleasant sight. "Provided he meets the terms of the original deed. Two years' residence." He paused, appearing to savor the moment. "And he must win the event of my choosin' at the Glenscannadoo Games, else forfeit the land to me."

When Annie sighed and came around the table to pat John's shoulder in sympathy, he knew he was in trouble. "Well, we tried. I reckon England's winter will be kinder to yer frilly petticoats than Scotland's. Ye can be thankful for that much."

Slowly, John set his fork beside his plate. The china was chipped in two places. The fork was tarnished and bent.

His gut began burning. Hardening. The itch grew unbearable. "Perhaps I would be. But I do not intend to leave Scotland before winter."

Hands on hips, she bent forward and caught his eye. "No? Ye watched the games last summer, aye?"

"Yes."

"And ye saw the MacPhersons trounce every last man the way I stew onions for my gravy—'til they're all soft and puny."

He had, indeed. Angus's sons had trouble finding competitors, as few men wished to suffer such humiliation. They dominated every event, from the foot race to the bagpiping.

But John Huxley had been issued a challenge. True, it had been a long time since he'd felt the adventuring fire. And perhaps this fire was momentary, a flash of irritated pride at MacPherson's grin and Annie's remark about petticoats. But it was there.

After a long, cold, dry spell, the fire was there.

"We have a wager, MacPherson," he said, plucking up his knife to butter his bread. "May the best man win."

CHAPTER THREE

Yellow leaves crunched beneath Annie's boots. Last night, it had iced rather than rained, making the cart path through the narrow glen a test of boots and balance. Blowing out a breath that fogged white in the cold, she climbed over a fallen log and glanced ahead toward the loch.

It sparkled blue amidst frost-dusted pines. Bare white birch danced in its reflection. This loch was smaller than Loch Carrich, though still long and deep, a watery gouge at the center of a curving valley filled with all manner of wonders.

Two of them crossed the path ten yards in front of her. A stag and a doe.

She halted. Waited. They were cautious, making their way down to the loch for a morning drink, likely. After a pause to blink in her direction, they continued on. Just then, a fawn left the brush where he'd been hiding and followed his mother.

"Would ye look at that, Fin?" she breathed. "A family." Without thinking, she reached for Finlay's hand. Her fingers curled in upon themselves. Empty.

God. Nearly a month without him, now. She swallowed and forced herself to continue on. To move.

Hurting helped no one, least of all Fin.

Today was about helping him find his way back to her. She slipped on a patch of ice. Slammed an elbow into a birch trunk. Shoved herself forward. Cursed everything and everyone who had been so bloody useless.

Mrs. MacBean. Angus. Herself most of all.

She'd gone over and over Mrs. MacBean's books. Most of them were pure nonsense. She'd discovered a decent salve for her stepbrother Broderick's shaving rash, but apart from that, useless.

Two days ago, she'd stormed out of Mrs. MacBean's cottage when the old woman couldn't remember whether the book she'd dug out of her flower bed addressed ghosts or faeries. Turned out it was a guide to Glaswegian breweries and public houses. Apparently, there was some fine beer to be had near the rope manufactory if one didn't mind the stench.

Yesterday, Annie had stormed back into Mrs. MacBean's cottage with five fresh loaves of bread and a demand: "Dinnae tell me what ye've read," she'd snapped, dropping her basket on the table. "Tell me what ye ken."

Mrs. MacBean's good eye had looked her up and down. "About ghosties? Not as much as ye'd suppose."

She snorted. "Nae doubt of that. Just tell me what ye ken. Apart from where to have a pint in Glasgow."

"They're slippery. Waitin' til dark to appear. Never stayin' long enough for conversation. Unsociable pranksters, the lot of 'em."

"Finlay isnae like that."

"Aye, lass. He's not."

"He enjoys a good jest now and then." She'd remembered his Fin Grin. His laughter when he was giving some unsuspecting MacDonnell the chills. She'd swallowed a lump. Blinked until the watery haze passed. "But he's a braw laddie."

"Right ye are." The old woman's bony, spotted fingers had drummed on the arms of her chair. "Mayhap he's nae like other ghosties." The old woman's gaze fell to where Annie's hand reflexively covered her ribs. "What do ye ken of the lad?"

"He's been with me since I was wee."

"Since yer mam died, aye?"

Annie nodded. "His mam died, too, before he did. He stayed behind to … find her, I suppose. Then he couldnae find his way out."

"Likely he felt a kinship, ye bein' so close to his age. Losin' yer mother. Must be why he attached to ye."

And he'd been connected to her ever since. Until last year, when she'd begun to lose him, their tether deteriorating and Finlay struggling mightily to keep it intact. Losing his color. Losing his hold. Fading away.

Gone.

"I'm sorry, lass. I was certain the thistle amulet would work."

"They werenae meant to be worn, ye daft auld woman. I had to use Angus's liniment to clear up the chafing."

"Many a Highland clan wears them proudly."

"On their *banners*. Because a prickish weed that injures ye when ye step on it is a fitting emblem for this place. They dinnae wear the nasty things round their necks."

Confusion had clouded the woman's brow. "Mayhap a carvin' of a thistle would have sufficed." She'd shrugged. "These are deep mysteries we seek to plumb, lass. Dark forces and hidden realms. Answers willnae come easily."

"Or, in yer case, at all."

"Now, if ye kenned where he was buried, that would be somethin'."

Annie had glared hard at the old woman. "I told ye where he was buried a year ago, the first time ye asked."

Mrs. MacBean had blinked, her milky eye beginning to wander. She'd scratched her head. "Ye did?"

"The auld churchyard, up near the castle."

"Oh. Well, why didnae ye say so?"

Now, the morning after her conversation with the half-mad, all-befuddled Mrs. MacBean, Annie ventured from MacPherson land onto John Huxley's land on a daft mission. The castle sat at the northern end of the loch, isolated deep in the valley, a half-hour's walk from MacPherson House.

What would she say to Huxley when she arrived? She didn't know. She hadn't seen him since he'd devoured her venison with jealous zeal, then accepted Angus's ridiculous wager. Afterward, he'd donned his hat, handed her the three skeins of thread she'd dropped in the square, and driven away in the pouring rain, uttering only a terse, "Good evening, Miss Tulloch."

He was odd, the Englishman. Stubborn. Reserved, though she would have bet her best boots that reticence went against his true nature. She teased him about being so handsome he near blinded a lass, but in truth, his demeanor dulled the shine. If the man ever let loose with a genuine grin, God help every female with working parts.

As she rounded a stand of birch, the castle came into view. Craggy gray stone jutted upward between the loch's shore and a backdrop of dark pines. Mist rose from the water like clutching fingers. Light danced through varying shades of white and green.

From this vantage, Glendasheen Castle looked fair enchanted.

The house wasn't a true castle, of course, but a hunting lodge built by one of the MacDonnell ancestors. The roof, newly repaired with black slate, was a series of steep gables, including a hexagonal tower on one corner. The windows were all narrow, but there were a goodly number, and they glinted with new glass. The garden around the house's ground floor had been cleared of brambles and castoff fieldstone. Instead, it now had a shorn lawn, low hedges, and several old pines.

She wondered if Huxley had made similarly impressive progress on the interior. Smoke rose from one of the chimneys, so the place hadn't killed him yet.

Good. She liked the man, though he was addled to accept Angus's wager. Stay in the glen through a Highland winter, only to be humiliated in front of the entire village before losing his land entirely? He must enjoy suffering.

By the time she arrived at the castle's heavy oak door, her nose was numb and her teeth were grinding against a chatter. She lifted the iron knocker and pounded it seven times.

No answer.

Seven more times. "Huxley!" she bellowed, glaring up at three stories of gray stone and fanciful pointed arches. "Ye've a visitor!"

Nothing.

Damn the man, she would have liked to warm herself by the fire before mucking about amidst the dead. "Dawdling Englishman," she muttered, making her way toward the pine woods beyond the garden, where the old churchyard lay. "Cannae even drag yer arse out of bed to answer the bluidy door."

Past the main stand of trees flanking the castle, a weed-choked clearing dotted with decrepit stone markers and birch saplings surrounded the skeleton of the old church. Two high walls still stood, but everything else was rubble. Every spring, the ruins filled up with ferns and moss. Birds nested in the crannies and took flight whenever someone drew near. She'd always felt the place had a bit of magic in it. But as autumn wore into winter, it just felt frozen.

Shaking off a shiver, she hugged herself tighter and trudged over MacDonnell gravestones toward the oldest part of the churchyard. Behind an ancient fence, near the base of one of the walls, a rusted iron gate lay propped awkwardly where it had fallen when the hinges failed.

This was where Finlay had been buried. Near the gate. On the northwest corner of the ruined church. No marker. No signs that his bones lay beneath the soil. She only knew because he'd shown her the spot years ago when she'd asked where he'd been laid to rest. Finlay hadn't liked to visit here. He preferred not to dwell on his past.

Frozen grass rustled as she crouched beside the gate. Rusted iron groaned and stung her hands as she wrenched it away from the ground. Heaving it aside until it flopped flat, she cursed again. "Blasted, sodding thing," she muttered, yanking at the weeds that covered Fin's grave. Once the ground was cleared, she withdrew the small wooden carving from inside her plaid. It was supposed to be a thistle. It looked like a mushroom.

Sighing, she withdrew the note Mrs. MacBean had given her. She skimmed it silently before rolling her eyes. "Daft rubbish," she muttered.

But this was for Finlay. So, she ignored all good sense and read the words aloud. *"Spirit who lieth in hollow ground ..."* She frowned. "Hallowed ground, not hollow ground, ye daft auld woman."

She started again. *"Spirit who lieth in hallowed ground, come forth to the ring where my offering may be found."* She squinted at the paper. Glanced around. "Ye didnae mention any ring, ye daft auld woman," she grumbled. Losing patience, she rose to gather a few stones, then arranged them in a circle. Kneeling, she tried again.

"Spirit who lieth in hallowed ground, come forth to the ring where my offering may be found. For, as the seed I plant doth grow ..." She examined the carving in her hand. "Now, I suppose ye want me to bury the thing, ye daft auld woman."

Her fingers stung as she clawed the frozen dirt. Finally, she dropped the mushroom- thistle into the shallow hole, scraped the dirt back into place, and read

Mrs. MacBean's rhyming blather. *"Spirit who lieth in hallowed ground, come forth to the ring where my offering may be found. For, as the seed I plant doth grow, a bridge betwixt realms I do sow."*

She waited. Held her breath in a moment of foolish hope. But nothing happened.

Not a breeze. Not a tickle of her palm or a wee spark between her ribs.

Her fingers hurt from weeding and wrenching and digging. Her knees were wet and numb from kneeling. She'd likely have stains to scrub from her trews.

She rocked forward, her palm flattening the little mound of dirt where she'd buried the thistle charm. "I'm sorry, Fin," she whispered, barely a breath. "I'll find a way. I promise." She patted the soil. Hung her head and let herself ache. Then, she gritted her teeth and shoved to her feet.

Making her way back toward the castle, she battled despair by scrambling for new solutions. Perhaps she would accompany the MacPherson men next time they took a shipment of whisky to Edinburgh. Surely there were more knowledgeable sources than Mrs. MacBean in a city of that size. Not that she went there often. Or ever, really.

Fifty feet from the castle, she stumbled to a halt as something extraordinary caught her eye. A hammer. Soaring through the air.

Her eyes widened as the thing arced above her head. It hit a pine tree behind her and tumbled to the ground amidst a flurry of evergreen.

She scowled at the thing before turning back to retrieve it. Longer and heavier than a normal hammer, it resembled the type used to pound fence posts. She hefted it onto her shoulder and muttered, "I hope ye dinnae have another of these, English. I like my head where it is."

Then, she approached the castle, keeping a watchful eye for more flying tools. "Huxley!" she called as she drew near the main door. "Where in blazes are ye?"

When he appeared, he was in his shirtsleeves—sweat-stained linen sleeves rolled up to expose forearms dusted with brown hair.

Her eyes caught on those bare arms. The shocking thickness of the muscles. The strength they implied.

"Miss Tulloch?"

She blinked. Realized she was staring like a moony lamb. He'd rounded the corner of the stable twenty yards away, crossing the space between them in long, sure strides. His hair and beard shone brown with hints of gold.

Bare arms. Fancy that—the Englishman wearing only a shirt. The rest of him was decently covered, she supposed. Tan breeches that had seen better days. Boots he obviously wore for work rather than visiting. But he hadn't any of his usual finery.

A coat should make him handsomer. A hat should make him more polished.

So, why was her heart pounding? Because she could see his muscles? How daft.

She started forward again, tapping a finger against the hammer's handle. "Your distance is a mite short, English, but at least yer aim is shite."

He scowled and stalked closer. "What are you doing here?"

She shrugged. "Came to see if ye'd cracked your skull with a hammer yet. Appears I arrived just in time."

He plucked the hammer from her hand with enviable ease. "I was repairing the stable. It slipped."

"Right." She crossed her arms and eyed the width of his shoulders. Impressive, she had to admit. Not MacPherson proportions, but not bad. "Have ye made progress on the castle, then?"

"A bit."

"Chimney appears to function."

"I had a mason here from Inverness. He's one of the few willing to travel this far." His voice laced with sarcasm. "If only I were permitted to hire locally."

"Aye. 'Tis a bother."

He rubbed a hand over his beard and shot her a hostile glare. "Why are you here, Miss Tulloch?"

Slowly, she grinned. "Well, I thought ye'd never ask. Let's discuss it by the fire, eh?"

"I cannot invite you inside."

"Why?"

"I've no servants. We are alone here."

"And?"

He sighed. Tossed the hammer thirty feet behind him with the flick of his arm. It landed with a thudding clatter inside a bucket near the stable door.

Impressive.

"MacPherson and I made a wager. If he wishes to change the terms, he can come here himself."

She chuckled. "Angus plans to win, English. He thinks the terms are grand."

"Then, why send his daughter to be compromised?"

Compromised? As in … good God. It was a rare day when Annie was struck speechless. But just now, she couldn't move her mouth, let alone speak.

"Did you suppose I wouldn't understand the game?" His eyes flashed gold in the morning light. "You come here alone, invite yourself inside. Angus or one of your brothers comes to fetch you, finds us together. *Et voilà.* We're forced to wed, and the MacPhersons have a claim upon my land, if only through marriage."

"Wed."

"Come now, Miss Tulloch. You cannot be ignorant of what it means to visit an unmarried man's home without a chaperone."

Her head was spinning. He'd uttered something foreign in the midst of his strange ramblings, but she'd understood the rest of it well enough. He thought her a tart. Worse, a tart aiming to trap him like a stag with a particularly large rack.

Annie had Angus and four giant MacPherson brothers to take care of, along with her wee laddie, should she ever find a way to bring him back to her. One thing she didn't need was another male around, dirtying up her house and grumbling about his empty stomach. And a husband? He'd demand far more than dinner and mending. He'd want to lie with her. Naked, most likely. He'd want her to give him bairns.

If the notion of trapping herself a husband by pretending to be compromised weren't so daft, she would be laughing.

Instead, she glanced pointedly at their surroundings and raised a brow. "Perhaps ye didnae notice, but we're nae precisely hostin' a clan gatherin' out here. 'Tis but you and me, indoors or out. The only difference is that inside the castle, I've a wee chance of feelin' all my numb parts go tingly before I head home."

He blinked. Scowled. His gaze dropped to her plaid briefly before flying back up to her face.

"Och, the cold is turnin' ye all ruddy, man." She clicked her tongue. "Ye should be wearin' a coat."

"I was working. Alone. Now, if you don't mind, I should like to resume said task."

She scoffed and headed for the castle door.

"Where do you think you're going?"

"Inside," she called over her shoulder. "Where it's warm and sensible."

"Miss Tulloch—"

"Stay out here, if ye like." She grinned and yanked open the heavy door. "Ye wouldnae want to *compromise* me, would ye, English?"

Following Annie Tulloch into his castle was a mistake. Firstly, the woman was pure frustration. She was also a risk. He'd been the target of too many matchmaking schemes from far more sophisticated players to think otherwise.

Yet, as she sauntered into the entrance hall, he found himself trailing her. Watching her. Anticipating her reaction with unwelcome intensity.

She spun in a circle in the center of the hall, gazing up at the restored beams and repaired stonework, then at the three slim windows above the door where he'd installed stained glass depictions of vistas from the glen.

He waited.

Hands on her hips, she examined the floors. He'd purchased the stone from a nearby quarry and laid it himself. She lightly ran the toe of her boot over the smooth, dark surface.

Finally, she wandered to the archway leading into the main gallery. Light through the stained glass played with her hair. She wore it plaited today, he noticed. No hat. Just fire.

"Ye used the same slate for the roof and the floor. Mr. Gillis's quarry, aye? A fine, cleaved stone," she murmured, running a hand over the wooden casing of the archway. "Costly."

He noticed she wore fingerless gloves, and her fingertips were dirty, her nails a bit torn. What had she been digging?

"Did Mr. Gillis lower his price to spite Angus?" she asked. "Or was he bewitched by those bonnie eyes of yours?"

"As you know, your father has made obtaining materials and hiring laborers difficult."

"Stepfather."

"Mr. Gillis agreed to sell me the stone, despite MacPherson's intimidation."

"Gillis sells slate to Lowlanders for their grand, gaudy houses." She grinned over her shoulder. "He's nae so concerned with pleasin' the locals." She ambled beyond the arch.

He followed, wanting more from her. An acknowledgment. Something. "I had to lay the stone myself. Repair the roof myself. Replace many of the windows myself." The frustration of the past year surged as he trailed her through his half-completed house. "Had it not been for MacPherson's interference, I would have finished months ago."

"Aye," she said, wandering through another arch into the drawing room, where he'd begun paneling the walls but hadn't yet restored the fireplace. "Ye've some work left to do, that much is certain."

He wanted to growl. The guttural reaction crouched inside his chest, unfamiliar and disconcerting. What the devil was wrong with him?

"I'd have considerably less to do if—"

"Where did ye learn such skills, English?" She hovered near one of the windows then turned to face him, a tiny frown puckering her brow. "Ye seem a bit *gentlemanly* for layin' stone and hammerin' posts."

"You know nothing about me, Miss Tulloch."

Her mouth quirked. "I know ye speak like ye've been fed knives and vinegar."

"Knives and vinegar?"

"Aye. Every word is sliced clean. Polished bright."

"Is that what offends you about me? My diction?"

She snorted. "Dinnae be daft." Crossing her arms over her bosom, she looked him up and down. "Makes me wonder. That's all."

"Wonder what?"

"Who ye are."

He paused, keeping his expression flat. "Hardly a mystery. You know my name."

"Hmm. John Huxley," she murmured.

He inclined his head.

"A gentleman."

"Yes."

Her fingertips idly traced his unfinished paneling. As morning light caressed her cheek and the fiery wisps brushing her jaw, she drew her thumb over a corner molding. "And a craftsman, by the looks of it."

He couldn't account for the heat that ran through him in that moment. The way she touched wood he had fashioned. The way her blue gaze lingered on his forearms. Her slightly open lips with their slightly tempting quirk.

Her admiration was such a subtle thing—a mere taste of what fed this damnable craving. But he wanted more.

Did she know?

Was Annie Tulloch seducing him deliberately? This would be among the more bizarre methods he'd encountered. But effective. Too damned effective.

God, this was madness. To seek her approval. To lust after *her*, of all people. He'd spent too much time alone in this place. Not even the widow in Glasgow had cured it.

"You never did answer my question," he said, hardening his tone, even as he examined her hands. Dirty hands. Small. "What are you doing here?"

"Answer me first, English. How did ye learn to work with wood and stone, eh?"

He hesitated, knowing that the more information he gave her, the more he gave MacPherson. And the more MacPherson knew, the harder John's task would be.

"Here, now," she said, her smile teasing, her eyes glowing blue. "If ye tell me a wee bit, I'll tell ye why ye cannae get the window in the tower to settle without crackin'."

Bloody hell. That window frame had already damaged three panes of glass. The present one, installed only a week ago, resembled a spider's web.

"What do you know about it?" he demanded.

She breezed past him and wandered back toward the gallery. "Tell me about you. That's my price."

He followed her, shamefully intrigued by the oddest details of her form: her shapely calves, which he could see because the woman wore breeches and boots rather than skirts. Her small, dirty hands, which surreptitiously wiped on a corner of her plaid. The stains on her knees. Her hair, which flashed like copper rope and brushed the base of her spine.

Her thighs weren't visible because they were draped in tartan. So were her breasts. He'd like to see her without her plaid. He'd like to see her without her tunic. Without anything at all.

"Go on. Tell me," she said over her shoulder as they wandered from the dining room into the small corridor that led to the kitchen. "I promise I willnae laugh."

He ducked past the temporary bracing he'd added to the passage and grasped her arm. "Be careful. I'm still reconstructing this part of the house."

Though faintly lit from both the dining room and the kitchen windows, the corridor was dim and tight. Something soft and cushiony brushed his ribs as she turned.

"Aye." She patted his hand where he held her. "Dinnae fash. The fire is leadin' me straight and true. Already my backside is tinglin'." Her hoarse chuckle seized parts of his body it shouldn't even interest.

The lust was both unwelcome and exasperating, much like Annie herself.

Abruptly, he drew back, only to hit his head on the bracing. "Blast," he hissed.

"Och, ye're a clumsy one, John Huxley." She tugged him forward. "Let's warm ourselves and trade tales for a wee bit, eh?"

He didn't want to trade tales. He didn't want her here at all. Especially in his kitchen. The room was still in shambles, although he'd cleared away the debris, built a new work table, and repaired the hearth. It was functional. Barely.

She stood with her hands propped on her hips, examining the place with a stern expression. "Have ye a larder?"

"It collapsed."

"Where are ye storing yer food?"

"In the cellar. There's a door to the garden that makes it convenient."

She nodded. Held her hands out toward the hearth. Turned to warm her back. Wiggled her hips in an unconscious, highly arousing way.

"Tell me a bit about ye." She tilted her head as though this were not an attempt at seduction. "Where are ye from?"

He swallowed and tried to ignore how much her eyes reminded him of cornflowers dancing in a summer field. "Nottinghamshire."

"I've never been. Is it pleasant?"

"Lovely."

"Better weather, eh?"

"Less cantankerous. But the hills are scarcely hills at all." Without thinking, his eyes fell to her bosom. "I prefer this landscape, actually."

"Where did ye learn how to do all this, English?"

"I built ships. Sailed them. Traveled to all sorts of places. Traded with all sorts of people. Did all manner of things."

Red brows arched. "*All* manner? Sounds adventurous."

"One might say so."

"Yet ye always look *forfochen*, English."

He frowned his puzzlement.

"Weary," she clarified. "Did all that adventurin' land ye here?"

"In a sense. It's how I met Ewan Wylie. He knew ships better than most."

"So, you and auld Wylie built ships together."

"Yes. I sold the operation after he died."

"Must have filled yer pockets right and proper. Is that how ye can afford so much slate from Mr. Gillis? Or Cleghorn's finest linen for yer drawers?"

His gut hardened. He'd suspected MacPherson had sent her here, either for information or more devious purposes. Now he knew it.

"My drawers are none of your concern, Miss Tulloch," he warned softly as he rounded the table and joined her beside the hearth. The heat made his beard prickle. "Neither are my pockets."

She shrugged, but her grin faded into wariness. "I've more interest in yer kitchen than yer money, English. This place isnae fit for aught but burnin' water. How are ye not starvin'?"

"Explain about the window." With a glare, he edged closer.

She blinked up at him. Retreated a step before her cheeks went fiery, her chin defiant.

"I gave you what you asked, Miss Tulloch. Or, more precisely, what MacPherson sent you here to gather. Now, you will explain why the tower window keeps cracking. Then, you will leave."

"Angus didnae send me. If he knew I'd come, he'd be—"

"Yes, yes. Denials noted. The window, if you please."

She glowered. "'Tis cursed."

With a gusty sigh, he bit down on a foul epithet. "I thought you knew something useful."

"Such as?"

"Damp weather compromises the frame. Or the stones must be reset. Or the glass must be thicker." He tilted his head, holding her gaze. "Anything but this superstitious nonsense."

"A family was murdered in this house. An entire branch of the MacDonnells—"

"Delve into any plot of land in Britain, and you'll discover death forms the soil beneath our feet. If this place is cursed, we are all cursed."

She shook her head. "Nae like this. Do ye ken why they call this place Glendasheen?"

"I don't have time for this."

"It comes from the Gaelic, *Gleann Taibhsean*. Pronunciation changed a bit over time, I grant ye."

"Try your bizarre seduction on some other chap."

"Valley of ghosts. *Ghosts.* That's what it means." She paused. Blinked. Her eyes rounded beneath a frown. "*Wheesht.* Did ye say 'seduction'?"

"I'm afraid I've work to do."

"Bluidy hell, English." She laughed. "First compromisin' then seduction. Are ye still believin' I'm here to trap ye into marriage?"

"In my experience, a woman only asks about a man's wealth when she seeks to marry it. And a *lady* never asks."

She held her arms out to her sides and looked down at herself. "Well, now, I havenae the sort of acquaintance with fine ladies and proper gentlemen as ye, English. And I must admit ye're bonnie as a wee daisy clutched betwixt the teeth of a wee faery floatin' over a wee waterfall made of sunbeams." She grinned up at him. "But if this is seduction, I'm dyin' a spinster."

He refused to join in her amusement, despite the deep, agonizing itch she sparked throughout his body. "Play the cheeky Scotswoman if you wish," he gritted. "I know seduction when I see it."

"Evidently not." She shook her head in a pitying way. "Ye're alone too much. Up here in yer castle, nobody to talk to apart from ghosties and yer own sad self."

"It would be best if you left now," he snapped. "Before the weather turns."

She crowded him, reaching up to lay a hand on his shoulder. The position put her body too close to his. "Ye should find a woman to tup ye once in a while, English. Clear yer head."

The outrageous statement, combined with her outrageous nearness, scattered all thoughts but one—the one he shouldn't have.

With a fond pat, she sidled past him on her way to the scullery door. "I'm afraid it cannae be me, temptin' though I am with my many, many charms."

Her taunt struck him like a stag that hadn't been watchful enough.

"Oh, and English," she said, pausing in the doorway as morning light set her hair aflame. "When ye practice the hammer throw, loosen yer hips." She demonstrated by moving her own hips in a circle.

His mouth went dry. Everything else went hard.

"Then counter the weight of the hammer and extend yer reach." Again, she demonstrated, stretching her right arm opposite her jutted left hip. "Long strokes. Just at that fine edge betwixt a tight grip and losin' control. That's the secret." She demonstrated the winding motion and the release.

It was the most erotic thing he'd ever seen.

"Keep trainin', John Huxley." She tossed a grin over her shoulder. "If ye hope to win against Highlanders, ye'll need all the practice ye can get."

Chapter Four

Being hoisted seven feet in the air then hauled like a bag of tatties wasn't Annie's favorite method of disembarking from the MacPherson Distillery wagon. But it did seem to please her brothers, so she allowed it.

Presently, she steadied herself by clasping Campbell's thick neck while he lifted her down. Her eldest stepbrother was also the tallest at eight inches above six feet, so it felt a bit like being on horseback. Except horses didn't have Campbell MacPherson's grim glower.

She patted his powerful jaw as he lowered her gently to the ground in front of MacPherson House. "It wasnae yer fault."

He grunted. "Whose, then?"

Three of her brothers had returned safely from a delivery to Edinburgh. The fourth, Broderick, was in a fair spot of trouble. Shooting an exciseman was no wee matter to be resolved with a bit of coin. Broderick had been detained pending trial, even after the MacPhersons had applied maximum pressure to their contacts within the government.

"Skene," growled Alexander, hauling a cider barrel on his massive shoulder. "Bluidy putrid pile of shite. I'd lay odds that's who set him up."

Rannoch carried a second barrel inside. His usual wicked grin was gone, replaced with a deadly glint. "We'll see how certain the evidence is when Skene's ballocks are lyin' betwixt his boots."

"Damage is done," said Campbell. "Isnae Skene we're fightin' now, but the bugger who laid his fist on the scale."

Annie followed her brothers through the door and busied herself removing her hat and donning an apron. It was best to remain distracted, else she might curl into a wee knot of dread and pain.

First Finlay, now Broderick. Losing one was unbearable. Losing both would kill her.

The third of four brothers, Broderick was the best of them all—generous, charming, easy-tempered for a MacPherson. When Campbell went too quiet, Broderick played his fiddle fit to make stone weep. When Alexander descended into one of his black moods, Broderick found him a task that didn't involve killing. When Rannoch tupped the wrong man's lass, Broderick made peace.

And when Annie spoke in passing about needing a new kettle, Broderick returned with a shiny new copper one.

Och, brother, ye shouldnae spend yer money on me.

Ye always take good care of us, Annie. If I cannae spoil ye from time to time, then what's the point of havin' money at all?

He was the face of the MacPherson Distillery, the presentable one. And a rival band of smugglers, of which Skene was the leader, had arranged for an exciseman to pay an unexpected visit during the MacPhersons' recent delivery. Broderick had handled the man in his usual fashion with a discreet payment. But as he left the warehouse, someone had fired upon the exciseman—someone other than Broderick.

Campbell, Alexander, and Rannoch were convinced it was David Skene, who despised all MacPhersons, and Broderick in particular. He'd been a rival for years, causing mischief for the distillery through territorial scuffles and thievery. Every now and then, the MacPhersons swatted him like a bothersome midge. Skene's smuggling operation always reemerged and the mischief resumed.

But none of Skene's attacks had been this severe. Unless the MacPhersons found a way free him, Broderick could hang.

Angus had gone to Edinburgh to meet with solicitors and ram a few heads together, hoping to discover the identity of Skene's influential partner. The "putrid pile of shite" obviously had one. Skene was clever and vicious, but Broderick's troubles seemed too well orchestrated.

Skene had someone powerful in his pocket. And that man was pressuring the courts to charge Broderick with murder, even though the exciseman had not yet died from his wound. Campbell had assigned guards to the exciseman and paid a surgeon to keep him alive. Only God knew whether he would recover.

She'd kept busy since her brothers' return a few days past. She'd washed and mended their trews and plaids, stirred up a bit of salve for their aches and scrapes, fed them enough lamb pies and hare stew for ten MacPhersons, and forced each of them to vent their frustrations by adding to the wood pile rather than draining the whisky supply.

Busy was better. It shoved helplessness down beneath the surface.

As she followed her brothers into the kitchen, she ordered two hired lads to tend the horses. Then she fetched flour from the larder and began making bread.

While Rannoch and Alexander carried the cider down to the cellar, Campbell sat at the kitchen table, his massive arms folded over his chest. "I should return to Edinburgh."

She added salt to her bowl. "Nah. Ye should stay here and manage the new shipment, as Broderick asked ye. We'll need the funds to fight this."

As usual, Campbell bore his burdens with as few words as possible. But she knew that jaw. The tension there spelled violence. He and Alexander had once been soldiers—among the deadliest of their Highland regiment. Campbell could kill Skene five times before dinner and scarcely mind the mess. So could Alexander, albeit with less mercy and more mess. Unfortunately, Skene's death would create more problems than it solved.

"Give Angus a chance to do what Angus does," she advised, stretching to reach another bowl from the shelf above the sideboard. Campbell stood and retrieved it for her, plopping it on the table before resuming his seat.

His silence was his reply.

She let him stew a bit while mixing her eggs, butter, and milk. "Mind the shipment first," she cautioned. "Whilst the solicitors work to free Broderick, we'll deny Skene what he was after."

Campbell's eyes narrowed. "Shutting down the distillery."

"Aye." She retrieved her bottle of ale-yeast and poured her wet ingredients into the flour before working the mixture with her hand. "Once this delivery is made, ye can send Alexander to do some persuadin'."

"Why delay? I'll go tonight," came Alexander's reply as he and Rannoch returned from the cellar. Each of them carried a bottle of whisky.

"Och, now," she chided. "Nae before dinner."

Rannoch was the first to protest. "Annie, 'tis Halloween—"

"Put the bottles down," she barked, wiping her sticky hands on a towel before laying damp linen over her dough. "Come sotted to my table, and ye'll eat elsewhere."

Alexander scowled, looking every inch the ruthless, black-hearted MacPherson that he was. "Ye wouldnae dare."

She rounded the table to poke him in his black-hearted chest. "Ye ken I would, Alexander MacPherson. Now, go wash. Ye reek of horse and peat smoke."

Rannoch smirked in his brother's direction.

"What are ye grinnin' about?" she said. "Ye smell worse."

Her youngest brother sniffed his plaid and grinned wider, his handsomeness a wicked thing. "Yet, the lasses cannae resist, eh?" He swooped forward and lifted her off her feet before she could escape. Then, he heaved her up onto his shoulder as he had when they were wee. "If we cannae have whisky, then ye must make gravy," he growled playfully. "One way or another, I mean to be sotted ere midnight."

Rannoch was only an inch shorter than Campbell, so her perch on his shoulder was dizzying. She chuckled and swatted the back of his head. "Put me down, ye dafty."

He'd always been good with distractions, and his antics lightened her heart for a moment. "Ah, there's a smile, sister," he said as he stooped to set her down. "I've missed it since we arrived home."

After shooing the two younger men out to wash, she resumed preparing dinner.

"He's right," said Campbell. "Ye have been melancholy."

She gathered onions from the basket and began chopping. "The news about Broderick wasnae exactly glad tidings."

"Da said ye havenae mentioned yer laddie in weeks."

The MacPhersons knew about Finlay, and they accepted she had a friend they could not see. She'd never been certain whether they, like the villagers, thought she simply imagined the boy, or whether they believed she really did have a ghostie attached to her. But they gave her no trouble about it, and she didn't press the issue by insisting they believe her.

"What's wrong, Annie?"

She continued chopping, her knife thudding into wood. "'Tis the onions. They make me weep."

"Nah. Ye were sad before the onions. Before we told ye about Broderick."

Her knife halted on a downward slice. Tears spilled onto her cheeks, and she swiped them away with her wrist. "He's gone," she whispered.

"Yer laddie?"

She nodded.

Silence. "Have ye asked Mrs. MacBean about it?"

Campbell and Broderick had helped rebuild the woman's cottage, so they were familiar with Mrs. MacBean's "expertise" in otherworldly matters.

She nodded again and resumed chopping in angry slices. "Daft auld woman's no help at all. A few days ago, she had me burying charms and chanting spells in the churchyard up by the castle. I dinnae ken who's the greater fool, her or me."

Campbell's expression darkened. "Ye went there alone?"

"Aye."

A pause. "Did ye see Huxley?"

She avoided answering, instead scooping the onions into a pot and starting on the potatoes. The MacPhersons were a mite protective. Better for Huxley's health if they never got any wrongheaded notions about her and the Englishman. "I did everything Mrs. MacBean instructed, with naught to show for it."

"Perhaps her remedy takes a while."

"How many bride charms has she given ye?"

"A dozen or so."

"And have ye a bride?"

His response was a grunt.

Campbell was a strong, braw male in his prime. Like all the MacPherson brothers, he had heavy muscles, a full head of dark hair, stone-chiseled features, and a jaw fit to power a mill. He was five-and-thirty. He should be married by now, charms or no.

She quartered the potatoes and tossed them into the pot. "According to Mrs. MacBean, Halloween is Finlay's best chance to return. She told me that's when the realms are easiest to bridge."

"Tonight, then."

She nodded, her stomach cramping. What if he didn't return, tonight or any other night? What if she never saw the Fin Grin or held his wee hand again?

"Would that I could retrieve him for ye, Annie."

Her heart squeezed so hard, she had to set down her knife and lean against the table. She raised her head to meet Campbell's gaze, which remained solemn and steady. She nearly crumbled. Her hands curled upon the table's surface. Her eyes swam. By sheer will, she managed to blink the tears away before they spilled.

"Would that I could thank ye for it, brother."

Late that night, after her brothers had gone into the village to enjoy the bonfires, whisky, and likely a willing lass or two, Annie curled up beside the hearth in her bedchamber and struggled to stay awake. The day had been long and, with all the fashing about Broderick, her eyes were heavy. But she didn't want to miss Finlay.

She watched midnight come and go before her laddie finally found his way back to her. He appeared near the edge of the wood beyond Glendasheen Castle. She'd been riding a stag near the loch.

Dreaming, of course. Stags didn't let you ride them, much less decorate their antlers with daisies. But this one carried her to Finlay, who emerged from behind a tree holding something in his fist. She slid from her perch, sobbing and aching at the sight of him.

He raced toward her, his blue eyes lighting with joy. "Annie!"

"Oh, thank God," she panted, tears streaming now. "Thank God, thank God." She fell to her knees upon yellow leaves and opened her arms to catch him.

He was warm. Finlay was never warm, but here, somehow, he was.

She clutched him so tightly, he wriggled. "I'm sorry." She kissed his cheeks over and over. Cupped his dear, sweet face between her hands. Ran a hand over his hair. "Finlay. Are ye all right? God, how I've missed ye, laddie."

His wee hand stroked her brow, her cheek. His smile was wide and a little crooked. The Fin Grin. "Nae more than I've missed ye, Annie."

As always, his voice sounded young, but his eyes spoke of centuries.

She could scarcely keep herself together. Seeing him again—the boy who'd been with her always—was a reminder of all she'd lost when he'd disappeared. Her friend. Her wise companion. Her confidant. He'd seen everything that had happened since her mother's death.

Grisel MacDonnell's spiteful attacks.

The vicious gossip amongst the lasses of the village.

The loneliness. God, the loneliness.

Dinnae touch Mad Annie, or ye'll go mad, too!

Finlay had witnessed it all, holding her hand and lending her courage. Without him, she was truly alone.

His hand stroked her cheek again, small and warm. "There isnae much time," he said gently. "I must tell ye …"

"No, Finlay. Dinnae leave again." She squeezed him harder. "Please."

He shook his head. "I want to stay. But I …" He grew breathless, as though he'd been running uphill. "Too weak. Cannae remain with ye the same way as before. Crossin' betwixt one world and the other … takes great power. Even here in Glendasheen."

She stroked his beloved cheek, which had begun to pale. "What must I do?"

He held her gaze. Brushed away the tears she couldn't stop. "I stayed with ye, Annie. Long as I could."

"Stay longer," she gritted. "What must I do to keep ye with me? I'll build a thousand bluidy circles. I'll recite silly rhymes 'til my voice runs raw. I'll—"

"Ye must marry."

The odd floaty feeling she usually experienced in dreams whipped away, replaced by the distinct sensation of being kicked in the stomach. "M-marry? I dinnae want a husband. I've a houseful of MacPhersons to take care of. Besides, a husband will want to … do things. Perhaps pleasant. Perhaps not. But he'll nae like … well, ye wouldnae understand, wee laddie that ye are. Trust me. In the eyes of most men, I'm—"

"Must marry a lord."

Another kick. Another moment to catch her breath. "Wha … Fin. What the devil are ye …? Nah. That's pure rubbish. The only laird I know is Gilbert MacDonnell. He already has a wife. A bit puny for birthin', aye, but they're wed, right enough. Besides, his title is naught but ceremonial. No land to speak of. He'll be lucky to have a lad to muck out the stables after his debts are paid."

"Annie."

"I cannae marry a short, daft laird who isnae a laird at all but a wee tartan peacock."

"A lord, not a laird. Not … MacDonnell."

"Lords marry *ladies*, Fin. The silk-wearin' sort. Not madwomen from the arse crease of Scotland."

"Must marry a lord. Must bear a son. Destiny."

Her breath left her chest in rapid pants. "A son. Are ye … are ye sayin' …" She swallowed, her mind reeling. "Ye were meant to be laird, aye? Ye were killed before ye'd completed yer destiny. Is that what ye mean?"

He closed his eyes and leaned his forehead against her shoulder. "Wish I could be with ye, Annie."

Even within the dream, she felt her heart pounding. "Ah, God, Fin. Ye wish to be reborn to—to *me?*"

He didn't move. Didn't speak. Didn't correct her.

"Finlay." She drew back to look into his sweet eyes. Heavens, he was pale. "Ye need me to marry a lord so ye can be reborn and take yer rightful place. Is that what ye're sayin', laddie?"

It had to be. Why else would he make such a bizarre demand? Why else would he speak about destiny?

He closed his eyes again. "Cannae wait long, Annie. Will sleep now. Gather strength."

"No. Please—"

"I leave because I must."

She sensed him fading, and her heart howled its desperation as she tried to gather him close. Her hands moved through air.

"Marry a lord, Annie." His voice had faded to a whisper, yet it thrummed with odd power. "Destiny waiting."

Her Fin had fought to stay with her, and the effort to remain tethered these many years had worn him out. Now, it was her turn to fight for him.

And she was a quivering coward. In her past battles, she'd known how to fight because her best weapons had been the ones used against her. When the battles went badly, she'd had the MacPhersons at her back and Fin by her side.

This was something else altogether.

In the dream, she couldn't hold him any longer, for he'd faded into light and mist. She felt only a bit of coolness against her cheek. And inside her hand, where he'd always offered her comfort, she felt his absence.

But this time, he left her a gift. A reminder.

When she awakened to darkness, her face wet and her chest aching, she opened her palm. And saw a wooden thistle.

CHAPTER FIVE

S tanding on a scaffold three stories high while raising a pane of glass from the ground with a rope and pulley, John couldn't afford distractions. Yet that was precisely what the bright flash of scarlet approaching along the castle road constituted—a dangerous distraction.

He lost focus long enough for his grip to slacken. The rope burned his palm. The glass he'd been hoisting swung into the scaffolding's lower brace with a crack.

Damn Annie Tulloch and Angus MacPherson and every Scot ever born.

John lowered the now-useless glass to the ground, glanced at the tower window he'd intended to repair for the fourth time. Then, he cursed. Aloud. For long minutes.

"Is that you foulin' the air with yer vulgar tongue, English?"

"This is *my* castle. Who else would it be?" he grated, leaning a hand against said castle and eyeing the web of cracks in the last pane of glass he'd installed.

"Och, I can fair see up yer skirts from here." Indeed, her chuckle now floated up to him from the base of the ladder.

He hadn't bothered to look down, as he feared what he might do if he glimpsed her smirk again. "We agreed you shouldn't come here alone, Miss Tulloch."

"Nah. You agreed. I let ye think ye were right. Sometimes a man needs a wee victory amidst all the losin'."

"What do you want?"

"Now, there's a ripe question. Come down and let's discuss it."

"No."

"Someplace warm would be grand. 'Tis colder than Grisel MacDonnell in ten feet of snow. I'm breathin' frost and pissin' icicles out here."

"Then, turn round and head back to—"

"Yer kitchen is a disgrace to kitchens—"

"—MacPherson land where you belong. I've no time to deal with you today."

"—but the hearth is goodly sized. That's where I'll be when ye come down and stop yer fussin'."

"No one invited you. Go home, Miss Tulloch."

"I've a proposition for ye, English," she said, her voice traveling toward the entrance. "And some bread, if ye find that more temptin'."

He closed his eyes. Gritted his teeth. Gathered his control.

In the end, he wasn't certain which promise made him follow her—the bread or the "proposition." He wanted it to be the former. It *should* be the former. She made the best bread he'd eaten since he'd left France.

But he suspected it wasn't the bread that drew him.

Upon entering the kitchen, his body reacted to the scarlet-haired tyrant with a hunger that had nothing at all to do with his stomach.

She bent forward, poking at the low fire. As usual, her plaid swaddled her from shoulders to knees. Today, she'd added a blue knitted scarf, lowering it off her hair. Fiery strands flew outward in a messy dither.

He frowned. The plaid was thick wool, so it would provide some warmth, but she should have a cloak. A hooded one lined in fur, preferably. And she should be wearing a gown with layers of fine wool and soft linen, along with stockings to insulate her legs and feet.

Furthermore, she shouldn't be jaunting up to his castle in the middle of November without a chaperone.

She shouldn't be taunting a man like him.

And she certainly shouldn't be bending over in front of him. It gave a man indecent notions.

He shook his head and forced his gaze away from her hips. She had, indeed, brought bread, he noted. At least ten loaves overflowed the basket on the table.

"Och, ye're quick, English. I reckoned ye'd sulk a wee bit longer. Hungry, eh?"

She'd turned and now grinned at him with a teasing blue glint.

His hands clenched before he forced himself to relax. The itch would go away when she did, he assured himself. The sooner he heard what she had to say, the sooner she'd leave.

"The bread is appreciated, Miss Tulloch," he said. "However, I find your continued visits intrusive and vexing."

"Do ye? Aye, I suppose ye would." She searched his kitchen before snatching a knife he'd left on a shelf nearby. Then, she began slicing one of the loaves. "Look, English. You and I arenae so different."

She'd removed her gloves, he noticed. Her hands were bare around the knife. Small yet strong. Her knuckles were almost … pretty.

"Ye've made a poor bargain with Angus. If ye hope to win, ye'll need help."

"Are you offering?"

"I'm comin' to that."

"Get there quickly, Miss Tulloch. I've tolerated a great deal, but my patience is at its limit."

Cornflower eyes lifted to his. The knife paused. "As I said. Nae so different." With swift efficiency, she retrieved a pan, a plate, and a jar of butter before continuing, "Now, Angus said ye must win one event, so that's in yer favor. But which one? The hammer? The stone put? The caber? Nah. The one *he* chooses." She clicked her tongue. "Bad bargain, English. He'll make it nigh impossible to guess, which means ye must be skilled enough in all of them to defeat a MacPherson." She buttered the slices and placed them in the pan then held the pan over the fire until he heard sizzling. "Impossible. Ye've nothin' but *heaps* of impossible waitin' for ye, followed by cartloads of defeat. Humiliation, too. Dinnae forget that." She flipped the bread with a flick of her wrist then shot him a smile over her shoulder. "Unless ye have a secret weapon."

"You," he said dryly. "Why am I not surprised?"

"My generosity is a bit overwhelmin', I ken."

"I won't marry you, Miss Tulloch."

She'd turned away from the hearth while they were talking, so he had the pleasure of watching her jaw drop. As she was in the midst of sliding the bread from pan to plate, one slice skidded onto the table. She didn't notice, too busy glaring at him. "I dinnae recall askin'."

He leaned forward and snagged the plate of toasted bread. "Then, what do you want from me?"

"Ye claim to be a gentleman, aye?"

"A fact we've established." He bit into her bread and nearly groaned. Buttery. Warm. A hint of crunch over a cloud of softness. It was worth every second of vexation.

"Have we, now?"

"You're not in my bed, despite repeated attempts to land yourself there." He took another bite. "I'd say that establishes my gentlemanly credentials rather well."

Her frown suggested confusion. But she couldn't be confused. Coming here was a provocation. Feeding him was flirtation. Talk of "propositions" and grinning with that secret, shared humor was outright seduction. Not to mention all the references to his "bonnie eyes" and his "tender bits."

No, Annie Tulloch knew what she was about. It was as blatant as her hair.

"Better women have tried such tactics with me," he continued. "Women who knew their craft as well as you seem to know breadmaking." He saluted her with his toast. "Delicious, by the by."

Blue eyes narrowed to a glint. The pan thudded onto the table.

"They failed." He kept his voice hard. Better to be clear. "*You* will fail. Stop trying."

"I want to marry ye—"

He smirked around a new mouthful. "I knew it."

"—like I'd want a disease involvin' pustules in unmentionable places."

Swallowing nearly choked him.

"Given how many 'better women' have tossed their skirts to the skies for the honor of landin' in yer bed, I'm guessin' I cannae have one without the other." She leaned forward, glaring across the table. "I'll take neither. Guid luck to ye, Mr. Huxley." With a nod, she bent to retrieve her gloves from the corner where she'd tossed them, giving him another spectacular view of her backside.

Then, she raised her scarf over her hair and left his kitchen.

Left *him*. Alone.

She'd called him Mr. Huxley. He'd grown accustomed to "English." On her lips, those two syllables lilted with amusement. The sound was almost … affectionate.

Inexplicably, he wanted to hear it again.

Glancing down at his toast, then at the basket of bread she'd made for him, then at the pan she'd used to cook for him, he discovered his appetite had vanished with her.

Bloody hell.

"Miss Tulloch!" he called, abandoning his plate. No answer. He started after her, lengthening his strides to cover more ground at a faster pace. She was small. Surely she couldn't have gone far.

Outside, wind sent a cold, stinging blast through his heaviest coat. "Miss Tulloch!" He scanned the lawn before loping toward the castle road. Beyond the second clump of birch, he saw her tugging her scarf around her cheeks as she charged away from him.

He sprinted to catch up with her. "Stop," he panted. "Stop, woman. Good God, you move fast when you're angry."

"Ye wanted me gone. No point dawdlin' about it."

"I don't want you gone."

"It's what ye said."

He clasped her elbow, pulling her to a halt. "You mentioned a proposition."

Her lips were tight, he noticed, tight and pale. She refused to look at him, instead gazing out across the loch. "I've changed my mind."

"Nonsense. You didn't walk all this way in the frigid damp to abandon your purpose."

She snorted. "My proposition requires that ye be a gentleman with some knowledge of proper manners. 'Twas my mistake."

Rarely had John been accused of poor manners, but the uncomfortable prickle of heat rising from his neck suggested Annie's charge had merit. He had been rude. A natural reaction to her hoydenish ways, perhaps. Still, he didn't like the paleness of her lips, the bruised quality to her glare.

"Perhaps I was … too plain in my speech," he conceded.

"Perhaps ye were an arse."

He found his lips twitching. "Perhaps I was."

She sighed then glanced down to where he still held her elbow. For some reason, he'd been absently stroking her with his thumb.

"My bones are pure ice, John Huxley. Invite me to warm myself by yer hearth, and I'll consider forgivin' ye."

He released her, bent into a deep bow, and gestured toward the castle. "My dear Miss Tulloch, won't you join me by the fire?"

Her chin rose along with the corners of her mouth. "Very well, English. If ye insist."

By the time they arrived back in the kitchen, he'd begun to question the wisdom of his invitation. Whether Annie meant to tempt him or not, he found her bizarrely arousing. The way her lips pursed around simple words—*aboot* and *luik* and *looosin'*. Or the way she touched him as casually as she might stroke a pet. Or that amused chuckle after she'd lobbed an effective insult.

God, maybe he should go for a swim. The loch was frigid this time of year.

"… is why ye need me, English. The caber toss is more about aim than distance. I ken ye think 'tis merely the liftin' ye must master, but that's only the beginning."

He blinked, realizing he'd been staring at her the way a cat might watch a tasty, unsuspecting bird. Meanwhile, she pottered about his kitchen, rearranging his pans and crockery while lecturing him on how Scots prefer to heave logs.

He cleared his throat. "So, you're offering to teach me the proper techniques for each event."

"Aye."

"Forgive me, but aren't the games a male domain?"

"Aye." She grinned over her shoulder. "And a splendid spectacle they are."

Why her comment should make him want to grind his teeth, he couldn't say. He rubbed a hand over his beard and shrugged off the odd resentment.

"But what ye're really askin' is how I ken enough to train ye. Simple. I've watched the MacPhersons train—and win—for nigh on twenty years."

He nodded. Having applied her advice on hammer throwing, he'd noticed improvement in both control and distance. She knew her subject well. "And the favor you would ask in return?"

She didn't answer. Instead, she wandered into the larder he'd recently cleared and called out her displeasure. "Ye need more shelves in here. Explains why ye're so dainty. Scarcely enough storage to keep the rats satisfied."

"Miss Tulloch."

She emerged shaking her head and dusting her hands. "I'll speak to Angus. Ye should be permitted to hire a lad or two. Mayhap a maid or cook."

"The second half of your proposition?"

At first, she avoided his gaze. But eventually she came to stand before him. Her cheeks were flushed. The heat from the fire, perhaps. "I would have ye instruct me," she declared.

He frowned. "In what?"

"How to be a lady."

For a moment, he simply glared. It was one thing to continually call him "bonnie" or "dainty"—which, at six feet tall and a stone shy of two hundred pounds, he decidedly was not—or complain about his "soft Englishman's hands." But implying he wasn't a man at all was going too far.

"Enough," he uttered. Before she could smirk, he moved into her, forcing her to stumble backward. Then, he braced her lower back and turned their positions until he could bracket her against the table.

Her eyes flared as he loomed. Leaned in. Brought their mouths within inches and let her feel the difference in their sizes.

"English? Wh—what are ye—"

"I must seem rather civilized to you, Miss Tulloch." He kept his voice low and calm, though even he could hear the darkness threaded inside.

Bewilderment crinkled her brow. "Aye," she said cautiously.

"Civilization is useful." Slowly, he let himself smile. "Until it no longer serves a man's purpose."

"Have ye been eatin' many queer-lookin' mushrooms of late, English?"

He couldn't help himself. Crowding closer until the folds of her plaid pressed flat against his coat, he lowered his head and watched pink bloom bright in her cheeks. "I am a man," he murmured in her ear.

"A-aye."

"Say it."

"Why?"

He nuzzled the fiery wisps along her jaw. "Just say it."

"Well, I can feel yer whiskers, right enough. Most women cannae grow a beard. Except Grisel MacDonnell's mother. I've long hoped Grisel might inherit the ability. She's most deservin'."

Annie's scarf was bundled around her neck, and the rest of her was swaddled in wool. But he wanted to kiss her … absolutely everywhere. Her throat, her breasts, her thighs. Between her thighs. He wanted to strip her bare right here in his shambles of a kitchen then carry her upstairs to his shambles of a bedchamber. He wanted to prove he was a man and she was a woman and this agony of desire was natural. Not shocking or inappropriate or indecent.

"Admit I am a man, Miss Tulloch. A simple request."

"A daft request."

His hands curled into fists upon the table. God, she was infuriating. And God, he was hard as stone feeling those lush, soft breasts brushing his chest. "Do me the courtesy of answering, if you please."

Her exasperated sigh washed warm over his lips and jaw. "And they call *me* mad." The hoarseness in her voice, along with the way she arched against him, contradicted her words. "Very well, English. Ye're a man. Happy?"

Yes and … no. If she'd held out much longer, he'd have an excuse for satisfying his craving. A mistake, of course. Annie Tulloch was the last woman he should want, much less bed.

But want her he did.

He must extract himself. Distance himself.

She cupped his jaw, her touch light. Tentative. Then, her hand slid down the side of his neck and flattened on his chest.

The unexpected caress nearly buckled his knees.

"Ye ken I only meant to tease ye a wee bit, English. 'Tis plain ye're not a woman, though ye're bonnie enough to make one envious."

He stood rigid for a long minute, breathing her clean, sweet scent and willing his body to obey him.

She slid her hand down his ribs and gave his belly a pat. "A fit man, indeed. We'll have a goodly start on yer trainin'. There, now. Feel better?"

His control was shredded, so he couldn't stop the laugh from escaping. It emerged as a rusty cough while he braced himself against the table. "You manage men quite well, Miss Tulloch."

"I've had a lot of practice."

"So, what do you really want from me in exchange for helping me win my wager?"

She stiffened. "I told ye."

"I thought you were insulting me again."

"Dinnae be daft. I need someone to teach me to be a lady. Ye're a gentleman." She paused. "Most of the time. And ye have five sisters. Surely ye ken what's necessary."

Slowly, he forced himself to back away from her. To look her in the eye. To assess her seriousness. "Why me? Why not the laird's wife or some other female?"

Annie's eyes hardened. "No females."

"It's true I know a great deal about … ladies. But a genteel woman will have knowledge I cannot possibly—"

"I dinnae get on with other women." Her chin tilted to that familiar, defiant angle. "'Tis you or nobody, English. Ye've fine manners when ye're not out of temper. I only need ye to teach me the important bits."

"To what purpose?"

"Doesnae matter."

"It does." He frowned at her, frustrated now for a different reason. She made no sense. "Do you intend to travel to London? Edinburgh? Attend a soiree? Be presented at court? Each of these will require different skills—"

"I intend to marry a lord."

He'd been stomped by a horse once. The ill-tempered Arabian had taken exception to the heat, thrown him off its back and broken two of his ribs for good measure. Annie's declaration had a similar, lung-flattening effect. Which explained his taut, painful silence before he could inquire, "Anyone in particular?"

"Nah. I dinnae ken many titled men." She crossed her arms and leaned back against the table, nibbling her lower lip. "Only Gilbert MacDonnell, really. His title is naught but a jest. And he's married. And daft." Her nose scrunched. "His friend, perhaps. The Lord Lockhart. We spoke that day in the square. I wasnae at my best, but mayhap he willnae remember."

The prickling fire in John's chest should have died the moment she mentioned Lockhart. He should be glad she wanted his help with pursuing another man. A *Scottish* lord.

Yes, relief would be the proper response. She'd told the truth; she didn't want to marry John. And he had no intention of marrying her. So, they were in agreement. No reason to feel … whatever this was.

"I should think you'd prefer a Highlander," he murmured.

"Oh, aye. But beggars cannae be choosers. Too few Highland lairds have kept their titles, and those that have behave more like Londoners, with their hired men removin' their clansmen so they can fill their lands with sheep."

"Yet, you intend to marry for a title."

She sighed. "Aye. I must."

"Why?"

"Now, that'd be my business."

Frustrating woman. "And you want me to train you to be a lady so you may lure one of these men to the altar."

Her temper caught fire, resulting in a hard shove to his chest. "I'm nae aimin' to nab his purse, English, so ye can stow yer suspicions up yer—"

"Calm yourself. I made no mention of—"

Her chin tilted defiantly. "I'll be a good wife."

They all thought that. "Of course."

"I'll feed him proper." She nodded to the basket of bread on the opposite end of the table. "I'll let him do all the touchin' and ruttin' he wants."

A second flood of prickling fire chased the first, stronger this time. He blinked. Couldn't speak. Didn't know what to say or why he suddenly wanted to beat a man he'd never met until nothing remained but a pair of boots.

"Whoever I wed will be pleased as a cow rootin' in the oats bin, ye can be sure of that."

John couldn't look at her any longer. He stalked to the hearth and began stabbing the coals with the iron. Sparks flared upward.

"A lord will wish to marry a lady." Annie fell quiet for a heartbeat. Two. "I'm many things, English, but that isnae among them."

Something twisted hard inside his chest. He thought of his sisters, particularly shy Jane and rebellious Eugenia, who had struggled with being accepted. They'd found husbands, to be sure, and married well. But before their matches, they'd suffered for being different. And unlike Annie, they'd been trained in gentility from the cradle.

Returning the iron to its holder, he pivoted to examine her—the red hair, ragged and banner-bright. Eyes so direct, they stripped a man of his will. A mouth that scalded without mercy. And her clothing. Good God, she needed a modiste. Did she even wear a corset?

He tore his gaze away from her bosom. Best not to think about that.

"This won't be easy, you know," he warned. "You'll have to change …" He shook his head and swiped a hand over his beard. "… everything. The way you speak. The way you dress. The way you walk and sit."

"Aye."

"Titled men are a hunted breed." He should know. "They're cautious. Discriminating. Proper decorum is merely the start—every young lady manages that much. To win a lord, you'll need to be charming. Flattery, not insults. You understand?"

She swallowed. "I ken."

He came around the table to examine her more closely. The woman wore breeches, for God's sake. Breeches. Her boots were worn and muddy, her belt plain, her gloves cracked. All easily remedied by a dressmaker, of course. But her figure was plumper than the current fashion. Her walk was more striding than elegant. And while her voice was melodic, her brogue was thick. She'd have to soften it.

"Enjoyin' the view, English?"

When he raised his gaze, he kept it direct and hard. "You're going to hate this. It will suffocate you." For some reason, the thought stung. "Are you certain it's what you want?"

Before she answered, he noticed her right hand curling then stroking the side of her waist. "Aye," she said, chin rising. "Make me a lady and I'll make ye a Highlander. That's my offer."

His first instinct was to decline. But John had always despised losing. Whether it was a cricket match or a horse race or a negotiation over shipping costs, he played to win.

Over the past few weeks of throwing hammers and lifting logs and heaving thirty-pound stones, one thing had become clear: Without help, he would lose MacPherson's wager. Badly.

The cost of Annie's help would be high. Could he spend hours every day for months alone with her? Yes. Could he do so without giving in to his bizarre, Annie-fueled lust? Less certain.

She moved closer, gazing up at him with eyes the color of cornflowers. Then, she swallowed hard. A tiny, vulnerable crinkle appeared between her brows. "Will ye help me, English?"

His decision clicked into place against his will. "Very well, Miss Tulloch." Damn, he was going to regret this. He knew it, sensed it, like a storm rolling toward his ship. "When should we begin?"

CHAPTER SIX

"What a wee caber ye have there, English. I ken ye're a dainty sort, but surely ye can do better."

John gritted his teeth and let the one-hundred-fifty-pound log he was holding topple into the grass. It landed with a resounding thud. "How big would you like it, Miss Tulloch?"

"Och, the bigger the better. A man isnae a Highlander until he kens how to handle *sizable* wood."

He chanced a glance behind him at the mouthy woman who thought she was terribly amusing. She wore her usual garb, her usual smirk. And she was staring at his backside.

"Are you here to train me or hurl insults?" He raised his voice to be heard over the waterfall.

Sparkling blue eyes shifted up to his face. Her tongue darted out to wet her lips. "A bit of both, I suppose." Grinning, she sauntered deeper into the clearing where he'd been practicing his tossing. Her boots rustled amidst frozen grass. Her breath plumed white amidst the frigid air. Her hair was copper fire amidst a background of dark pines, crystalline river, gray rock, and white cascade. "This is a grand spot, English." She sighed and spun in a circle. "I've only ever been here in summer."

The waterfall tumbled off a heavily wooded slope, landing in a deep, rocky pool after a twenty-foot drop. The small brook snaked through his land, tumbling down the valley until it branched into the river that fed the loch.

"So peaceful in winter. Just wind and water. 'Tis magical," Annie murmured, turning to face him. Her eyes were intensely blue and bright this morning. Her cheeks were pink, as was the tip of her nose.

John had been working for an hour already. Even without his coat, the chill didn't bother him. But she was much smaller and wearing only a plaid for warmth. Striding to where he'd laid his coat on a large boulder, he offered it to her.

Red brows arched in surprise. "If ye want that cleaned, hire a maid."

Hissing an exasperated breath, he draped it around her shoulders. "You should have a cloak. A plaid is insufficient in this weather."

Oddly, she didn't reply, but her breathing quickened with little white puffs.

As he adjusted his coat's buttons, he wondered what smelled so good. He'd noticed it before when she was near. Had she been cooking something before she came? She smelled … sweet. Clean. He frowned. Was it apples? Honey? He leaned closer, breathing deep. Sugar? No, richer than sugar. More floral and golden. Caramel, perhaps?

Whatever it was, it made him hungry. Ravenous, even. His hands tightened on the wool until they formed fists. He swallowed then saw she was staring at his mouth.

Immediately, he released her and stepped back. Turning before she noticed how her scent affected his body, he lifted the caber and propped it against his shoulder. "Come show me the proper way to toss this thing, Miss Tulloch."

For the following hour, she instructed him with methodical patience and seriousness.

If only his mind were so disciplined.

"Lace yer fingers, English. That's it. Sliiide them down to the base. Now, when ye're ready, use yer thighs the way I told ye. 'Tis more a lift than a lunge. Ye dinnae want to lose control of yer caber, or this will be over before it starts. Good. Steady. Steeeaaady. Aye, ye have it. Deep breath, English. Deeeep."

"God Almighty," he muttered, wondering why everything she said had erotic overtones once it entered his ears. Perhaps he was deranged. Frustrated, certainly, but he'd never had this particular problem before.

"Focus, now," she advised, positioning herself ten feet to his right and pointing toward the west end of the meadow. "Start runnin'. But remember, it isnae speed ye're after so much as a proper angle. Ye need *thrust*, English. Good, strong *thrust.*"

Bloody hell. His hands were sweating. Slipping. He wished he could blame the weight of the caber or the fatigue of his muscles. But it wasn't that. It was her.

He started forward. The caber tilted. Began to overset.

"Now, English! Toss it now!"

Planting his feet and heaving the thing with all his might, he watched as it tumbled end-over-end before landing with a teetering thud.

At the three-o'clock position. It was supposed to land at twelve.

"Well, now, ye did fine, English. Just fine." She huffed as she trotted over to stand beside him, her hands on her hips. Then, she patted his shoulder in a comforting fashion. "If distance were the aim, ye'd be a champion tosser."

"Distance is not the aim."

"No, indeed."

Flexing his sore hands, he cursed. "It is harder than it looks."

"Aye. Most things are."

"What did I do wrong?"

She stroked his arm—short, soothing caresses of her fingers. "Nothin' a thousand Scotsmen havenae done a thousand times. Dinnae fash."

He frowned. He didn't want to make the same mistakes other men made. He wanted to be better. Do better. Win. "Explain," he demanded. "If you please."

Sighing, she reached for his hand.

Her constant touching was a problem he didn't know how to solve. He craved the pleasurable sensations she caused. Yet, he must maintain a proper distance if he wanted to keep his lust under control. Balancing the two urges was harder than landing a caber at twelve o'clock.

"When ye fight the weight of the wood," she said, "all ye'll do is lose. Instead, ye must use it to build the momentum ye need. It starts with yer grip." She opened his fingers and demonstrated by clasping his hand. Then she tapped her knuckles against his midsection.

"Dinnae hold the caber too high on yer body. No higher than yer navel, ye ken? Work *with* the weight, nae against it." She tapped his shoulder next. "Position it here. Find which spot gives ye the most control. Betwixt these two muscles, perhaps, or against this bone." Finally, she laid her hand on top of his shoulder blade, which, by necessity, meant her left breast brushed his ribs. "Ye're grippin' too tight at the beginnin', which causes the caber to rise too high, which makes it a bit wobbly from the outset. When ye start yer run, ye're wantin' everything to go perfectly, but it doesnae, which means ye panic a bit and run too long. By the time ye toss the bugger, it's tiltin' every which way. So, ye add too much thrust at the wrong time, hopin' to make up the difference. That's why ye have no trouble with turnin' it over but cannae control how it lands."

She'd said much that was useful and helpful and wise. He knew that. But his head felt three feet thick.

"Are these errors solvable?" he asked.

"Aye. Mostly, ye must practice. That's what everybody must do, even the MacPhersons. Practice until it feels like ye were born with a caber in yer wee fist."

God, she smelled good. And she was so damned soft. And he loved the sound of her voice, with the trilling Rs and the long, rounded Os. He wanted to plant his shoulder in her belly, pick her up, and carry her off somewhere warm.

Perhaps he'd been in the Highlands too long. He was a civilized man, for God's sake, not a barbarian.

"Och, ye're hot as can be, English." She squeezed his upper arm and patted him again, her fingers testing the hardness. "Get some rest. We'll practice more tomorrow."

Blast. She was right, but he didn't want her to leave.

She pivoted and headed toward the boulder. "I left some stew for ye at the castle," she tossed over her shoulder. "I noticed ye ate the bread already. I brought more loaves, but ye should hire a cook."

Her voice might as well be the sound of the waterfall for all that he heard of it. His attention had riveted to her hips. The way they swayed with a captivating twitch. His blood pounded hot until he could feel it pulsing his skin.

She stripped off his coat and laid it across the rock. Her fingers traced the folds as though reluctant to leave it behind. "Perhaps I should have a cloak, eh?" Her grin weakened his knees.

"You'll need a dressmaker," he called, his voice embarrassingly rough.

"Nah." Her chin went up. "Nothin' a dressmaker can do that I cannae do cheaper."

A small smile tugged at his lips. "If cheap were the aim, Miss Tulloch, I'm certain you'd be champion."

She laughed. Not a chuckle or a giggle, but a full, rich laugh that rang in harmony with the water. "Ah, ye're amusin', English."

He strode toward her, plucking up his coat along the way. "What if it rains tomorrow? Or snows?"

"Then, we'll begin my lessons." She cast him a sidelong glance as they started down the castle trail. "Ladies are indoor creatures, aren't they?"

His mood darkened at the reminder. Annie Tulloch changing herself into a watercolor miss indistinguishable from any other woman felt wrong.

Her reasons for doing so felt worse, like destroying a vivid Goya painting to sell a common gilt frame.

They passed the churchyard as the trail curved south. Annie slowed. "Do ye intend to restore this as well, English?"

He frowned at the tangled, crumbling mess of weeds and gravestones, old arches and toppled gates. "Not much to restore, really."

"Aye, I suppose that's true." She sniffed and stepped over a root. But her gaze, he noticed, remained on the old church. "'Tis haunted, anyhow. Ye wouldnae wish to disturb the spirits."

He sighed.

"I've told ye already, English. This glen is hummin' with ghosties."

"Right."

"Didnae Wylie ever tell ye about the bats?"

"Yes. He told me."

"Aye, well, they were real. And the damage was considerable. Gives me the shivers."

"You know, bats do occasionally take up residence in old structures. No spirits required."

She shot him a sharp, blue glare. "Ye're mockin' things ye dinnae understand."

He shrugged on his coat and offered his hand to assist her over a fallen log.

She ignored him and managed on her own.

"Miss Tulloch, I've been to many places."

A snort.

"Everywhere I went, people believed with great certainty in things no one can see but which must be real. Realms beyond my imagination exist, they told me. Places where creatures of myth and magic dwell. Ghosts and ancestors. Angels and demons. Shapeshifting mule women and impish sprites who will clean your laundry if you leave them a bowl of fruit."

"Well, that sounds daft. 'Tis milk that pleases them most."

"When you've heard a thousand of these stories without seeing a single impish laundress or, for that matter, your spectral grandfather returning from the grave to reveal where he stashed the good cognac, one does begin to question whether it's all a lot of rubbish."

She went quiet.

He watched her hips and noted how her neck had stiffened. "I meant no insult."

"Nah, of course not."

"I'm merely saying every culture I've encountered has similar tales. And none contain the slightest jot of proof or rationality."

Spinning to face him, she raised her chin and countered, "Have ye ever asked yerself why ye hear the same tales over and over, John Huxley? Hmm?"

He frowned. "People need stories to explain things they don't understand. Why a flood happens, for example. Or why a crop fails and a village starves. They want misfortune to make sense. But it doesn't. It just … happens."

She huffed and shook her head. "So, ye ken everythin', and all these people ye've met in all these places ken nothin'. Is that it?"

"No. That's not what I—"

"Aye, we rustic sorts are no cleverer than the dirt we muck about in." She kicked a clump of said dirt. Half-frozen leaves flew.

"I never said—"

She stomped toward him, poking his chest with an angry finger. "Or perhaps we're all mad," she hissed. "And *ye're* the only sane one."

He captured her hand. "If I asked you to believe in some outlandish thing you'd never seen, for which there was no proof apart from superstition, would you do it? Would you leap from the top of the waterfall if I promised wings would sprout from your shoulders?"

She blinked. Slowly, her eyes lost their fire. "Unlikely."

"Indeed," he murmured, stroking the back of her hand. She really should have a cloak. Her fingers were like ice. "That would not make you right or wrong. Merely sensible."

Her eyes lowered until he couldn't see the blue any longer, only gingery lashes against creamy skin. "Fair enough, English."

He frowned, noting how she'd gone from defiant to muted in seconds. He didn't like it. Worse, he didn't like being the cause.

Gently, she tugged her hand away and started down the trail, pausing a moment to gaze at the churchyard. Then, she ran a hand over her ribs and disappeared amidst the pines.

John followed slowly, examining the churchyard he often ignored, trying to see what Annie saw. There was nothing. Nothing but arches for windows that had long since shattered into dust. Nothing but weeds and crumbled stones and rust. The decay of an abandoned faith.

Annie saw magic amidst the ruins. John only saw emptiness.

Shaking his head, he quickened his pace. But at the last bend in the trail, just before the churchyard disappeared behind thick saplings and heavy pines, he heard an odd, mournful caw. He stopped. Retraced his steps. Peered through an opening in the brush.

There, atop the tallest arch, perched a raven. Or, at least, it had the shape of one. But its feathers weren't black. They were white. Its beak was pink. And its eyes were pale—perhaps even blue. He drifted closer, curious about the bird. He'd never seen one like it before, though he'd heard tales of such oddities from a naturalist chum at Oxford.

A white raven. How rare. How extraordinary.

The bird called again, scratchy and swooping, like a widow weeping for her lost man. Several more times: *caw, caw, caw*. The white bird turned its head this way and that. Then, it looked down upon him. Blue eyes flashed. Were they blue? Yes, he thought so.

Rain struck John's cheek. He reached up to wipe away the drop. Felt a sudden, frigid gust. And when he looked again at the peak of the tallest arch, the bird was gone.

CHAPTER SEVEN

Halfway through their fourth round of Lady Lessons, Annie concluded their bargain had been a bad idea. Granted, she was exhausted from staying up the previous night. Angus had arrived home with wretched news about Broderick, and she hadn't been able to sleep.

But Huxley's mood was even blacker than hers. It seemed the more time they spent together, the worse it got.

"Again, Miss Tulloch," he ordered from his dark, imperious corner of the drawing room. "This time, do refrain from stomping as though the floor were infested with spiders."

She gritted her teeth and crossed to the fireplace before "gliding" back to the lone chair at the other end of the room.

He sighed. "We've discussed this. When you prepare to take your seat, it is a gentle pivot upon your toes, not a flat-footed visit to the privy. Where are the slippers I asked you to bring?"

"I told ye—"

"Told *you*. Not ye. You."

"I told *you* I havenae any slippers."

"Haven't any."

"Aye. That's what I said."

He rubbed a hand over his beard—a sure sign of frustration—before bracing his hands on his hips. "All ladies wear slippers, particularly indoors. Half-boots are acceptable for walking dress or riding. Tall boots are not acceptable in the slightest."

By God, if he weren't the only man for a hundred miles who knew the difference between a teacup and a tankard, she'd use her unacceptable boots to stomp his infuriating—

"Again," he snapped.

She started forward, her throat burning.

"Chin level with the floor. Lower your gaze. Modesty at all times, Miss Tulloch."

She raised her chin, lowered her eyes, and tried her best to *glide* the way he'd shown her—like she was floating. Or balancing a full chamber pot on her head.

"Do not swing your arms."

She stopped mid-glide. Pivoted on her toes. Glared at the man who'd become her nightmare. "If I dinnae move my arms, I'll look like an eejit."

"Nonsense." He closed the distance between them in two strides and reached for her wrists. His grip was warm and firm when he bent her arms and folded her hands at her waist. His fingers lingered upon hers for long seconds to show her precisely the position he wanted.

John Huxley, she'd discovered, was a thorough man.

"There. Pretend you're carrying a small bird. Step lightly, now."

His nearness sent disturbing waves of heat over her skin. The sensation was worst wherever he touched her. Almost tingly. She'd noticed it more and more since that day in the square. At times, such as now, her mind filled with wool and she couldn't think of a single word to say. At other times, such as the day he'd backed her against his kitchen table and trapped her between those powerful arms, she wondered if she was mad, after all.

Only a madwoman grew hot and dizzy from the scents of autumn air and fresh-cut pine and a man's sweat. Only a lunatic thought touching him was worth any risk—and kissing him might be worth more.

She blinked away the wooliness as he moved back to his corner.

"Proceed."

She nodded, starting forward. "A wee bird," she whispered. "And a chamber pot on my head."

"Shoulders back."

"Aye, shoulders—" Her knee bumped the chair, scraping it noisily across the floor.

"Blast. If you wore proper skirts, this wouldn't happen."

"If you'd let me look where I was goin' instead of starin' at the floor like a pure dafty—"

"My instructions were clear, Miss Tulloch. You shouldn't be staring at the floor, but rather keeping your eyes modestly averted—"

She grabbed the chair and plopped down on the seat, hooking her elbow over the back. "Why would skirts make any difference?"

"Skirts give you warning. They get there first."

"They catch fire."

Now, his hand scraped down his entire face, not merely his beard.

She grinned. "Do ye ken how many good women have died wearin' proper skirts round a busy kitchen, English?"

"God, you are the most vexing—"

"Too many. I'll nae be among their number, I assure ye of that."

"Your plaid could catch fire."

"Aye. But it willnae."

Bonnie hazel eyes flared bright gold with increasing temper. "And why is that?"

She debated whether to tell him the truth. But, in the end, his opinion of her could hardly get worse. Honesty it was. "'Tis magic."

"Magic."

"From the nether realms. I've a friend who dwells there. He blessed this plaid ages ago. Said it would protect me."

Another swipe of a lean hand across a handsome, exasperated face. "Must you attempt an outrageous distraction every time you fail a lesson? I don't have a bloody eternity to waste."

"Och, English. Your vulgarity fair singes my wee, virgin ears."

"I suspect no part of you matches that description."

At first, his snarled jab stung. Then, it made her angry. Then, she noticed he was staring at her bosoms. He did quite often, actually.

Did he suppose large bosoms meant she'd lie with anybody? Even if she'd wanted to—and she'd seen enough of men's faults to know better—the MacPhersons would geld every man in the glen first.

Then there was Fin. No chaperone could be better than an ever-present ghost who looked like a sweet, innocent laddie.

God, she missed him.

Which was why she needed to swallow her anger and resume her Lady Lessons.

She must remember why she was doing this. For Finlay.

Still, Huxley needed to be set straight. "Is this how ye speak to yer sisters, John Huxley?"

Hazel eyes dragged up to her face. "No."

"Well, now, perhaps it isnae me who needs the lesson in proper manners, eh?"

A ruddy flush climbed past his beard onto his handsome cheekbones. "My sisters have better sense than to provoke such behavior. They are not hoydens."

"And I'm not a tart," she retorted. "Manners or no, I dinnae deserve to be called one."

His shoulders stiffened. After a long, hard silence, he nodded. "Quite right. I apologize, Miss Tulloch. My comment was thoughtless."

Thoughtless. Not *wrong,* she noted. Merely a slip of the tongue.

Distantly, she heard knocking.

Huxley frowned and glanced through the drawing room doors toward the entrance hall.

"Expecting company?" she asked.

He shook his head and went to answer the front door. She followed closely, curious if her efforts on his behalf had yielded fruit.

It appeared they had.

"Mr. Huxley?" inquired the short, brown-haired crofter holding his cap. "My name is Dougal MacDonnell. I've heard ye might have a bit of work for me."

"Aye, he does," she replied, ducking beneath Huxley's arm. "The kitchen floor is a disgrace. And the larder needs shelves."

A hard hand gripped her arm, tugging her backward, but not before Dougal gaped and exclaimed, "Mad Annie. Is that ye?"

"Do *not* call her by that name again," Huxley's command whipped over her head as he pulled her back against his body.

"Och, aye." Dougal lowered his head. "Sorry, Annie. Just surprised to see ye here."

She started to answer, but Huxley pulled her farther from the door and tucked her behind him. Then, he snapped, "She is Miss Tulloch."

"Easy, English." She patted his arm, noting how hard the muscles were—unusually so. "I've kenned Dougal since we were wee."

"Why is he here?"

"He needs work. You need workers."

"Your father—"

"Angus has agreed ye should be allowed to hire whoever ye like."

Until now, Huxley's glare had been boring a hole in Dougal's forehead. Suddenly, it turned on her. "What changed his mind?"

She shrugged. "I might have mentioned 'twould be to his benefit if ye restore the castle so he doesnae have to." She smiled. "Assumin' he wins the wager, of course."

His gaze lingered upon her, assessing and a bit puzzled. Then, it hardened. "Return to the drawing room," he murmured, nudging her in that direction.

"Dougal has two brothers and several cousins with bairns to feed—"

Huxley's stiff posture and flickering jaw signaled his anger, though she found it baffling. She'd done him a favor.

"Miss Tulloch. The drawing room. If you please."

She sniffed. "Fine. Just dinnae let Dougal talk ye into hirin' his sons for yer stable. Laziest laddies I ever did see."

In the drawing room, she practiced her "glide" from one corner of the room to the other. After seven or eight circuits, she discovered exaggerating her movements made them easier, though no less foolish. "Wee bird and chamber pot," she whispered over and over, her neck lengthened in a swan-like fashion. Then, when she felt perfectly ridiculous, she glided to the chair. "Pivot on toes, float onto seat." She spun and sank down. Because of how she'd positioned her hands, they landed neatly in her lap.

Her eyes widened. She'd done it. By heaven, she'd mastered sitting. She laughed aloud.

"You'll need skirts and slippers." The deep, masculine murmur came from the doorway.

She popped up and spun, sending the chair screeching across the floor again.

His arms were crossed, his expression dark and unreadable. "Have you ever had a proper fitting before?"

She swallowed, her heart pounding harder than it should have from gliding and sitting. "For boots."

He eyed her feet and shook his head. "We must find you a dressmaker."

"I can sew my own—"

"A milliner, too. Inverness may offer someone acceptable. Edinburgh would be better."

Annie hated this feeling—as though she'd been shipwrecked in a foreign land where nothing was familiar, but she was expected to speak the language. "I dinnae see why I cannae make my own—"

"Because you would be mocked. Leave the gowns to those who understand current fashions."

"I hate shoppin'. It's too costly."

He frowned. "The MacPhersons are far from poor. Doesn't your father give you an allowance?"

Her chin went up. "Stepfather. Angus pays the bills I have sent to him."

"Then, he'll pay this one."

An embarrassed flush heated her face. "I dinnae want him to."

"Why? He knows about your intention to pursue a lord, yes?"

She looked down at her boots.

"Miss Tulloch."

Then, she looked at the Englishman's boots. They were superior to hers, she noted. Probably made in London.

"Miss Tulloch." His voice was lower now. Closer. His boots moved within a few inches of hers. "You haven't told him, have you?"

"No."

"Why not?"

Because he might take it as a rejection of everything he'd given her. And she couldn't bear to hurt that beloved old man.

Huxley's sigh ruffled the hair along her forehead. "It's understandable you'd wish to minimize expenses for your family's sake, but you haven't chosen a meager endeavor. You'll need his support. I'm certain if he knew you intended to marry, he would be pleased to—"

"Do ye ken what Angus said when I first met him?"

A pause. "Tell me."

"The day before they married, my mother explained we were leavin' Inverness to live with a new family. She said I'd have a father and four brothers." She'd been nervous, her mother. Her fingers had fluttered oddly, tucking her red hair behind her ears and fussing with the collar on Annie's cape. "I kenned why. She was a widow. We'd run out of peat more than once."

She remembered her mother making a game out of the cold, swaddling Annie in several blankets and pretending they were on an expedition through a frozen wilderness. *Och, Annie. Do ye see the bear? Perhaps he'll be a friendly sort. Perhaps he'll have a wee cub ye can cuddle.* While Annie laughed and played, her mother had frantically tried to finish her sewing before the light disappeared. In winter, without candles or wood or peat, Lillias Tulloch's hours to earn a living were short. She hadn't had the luxury of remaining unmarried.

"She met Angus when he came to town for supplies. He threatened a shopkeeper who was fussin' over a bill she hadnae paid. Then he paid it. Then he offered her a position as a governess for his sons." Annie smiled. "When she explained she had a daughter, he offered to marry her. All within an hour of first settin' eyes upon her. He'd never admit it—to this day, he claims he only married her because his sons needed civilizin'—but I think Angus was smitten from the first."

"And your mother?"

"She needed a husband."

"Hmm. What did you think of him?"

"I didnae meet him until the day of their wedding, outside the kirk doors. Angus and his sons came walkin' up the road wearin' their kilts and lookin' like a band of black-haired giants from a storybook." She chuckled at the memory. "I was so frightened, I started greetin'."

"Greeting?"

"It means weepin'. I was wee." She shrugged. "I'd never seen a man his size before. But Angus wouldnae have it. He went to his knee right there in the dirt. He showed me his wrists and said, 'Have ye ever seen such a big set of bones as these, lassie?' Of course, I hadnae. But it stopped me cryin'. Then, he says, 'Feel it. Go on, feel it.' My hands were so tiny, even two of 'em didnae cover half of his wrist. Then, he says, 'From now on, yer mam and ye are a part of me as much as these bones. And ye need never fear again, for I'll stand betwixt ye and all the dangers of the world.'"

Her throat tightened, and she fought the tears that always came when she let these memories surface. "After my mother died, he didnae say much for a long while. When he finally did, he told me, 'I married yer mother. But my first promise was to ye, Annie. And I mean to keep it.'"

Warm knuckles brushed her cheek. Her eyes flew up and collided with his. Brown and green and gold—mostly gold. Too beautiful for a man.

"Why haven't you told him you're seeking a husband?" he asked.

"He owed me nothin', English. He and my mother were married naught but a year. Yet he gave me a home. A family. Permanent as can be. Should I thank him by leavin'?"

"He loves you." Somehow, his fingers were still stroking her cheek. Somehow, their mouths were a whisper apart.

"Aye. And I love him."

A frown tugged at his brow. "Why do you insist on calling him your stepfather?"

"What do ye mean?"

"You often correct me. He calls you his daughter, but you go out of your way to call him your stepfather."

She dropped her gaze to his beard, then focused on his lips. They were perfect. Defined at the edges, more thin than full. The upper curve seemed made for smiling, though he rarely did.

"Two reasons," she answered. "First, I want all the daft villagers who believe me mad to remember that Angus and I dinnae share a bloodline. That way, should my brothers ever sort themselves out enough to find wives and sire bairns, there willnae be any question."

"And the second reason?"

"To remind myself that he didnae have to love me. He chose to."

Another stroke of a knuckle over her cheek. Another warm sigh across her lips. "I'd wager it was less of a choice than you suppose," he murmured.

Loud, distant banging, like stone being struck with a hammer, rang throughout the castle. She blinked, realizing they'd been standing much too close to one another. Huxley seemed to realize it, too, given how swiftly he dropped his hand and backed away from her.

It felt like having her blankets torn away on a cold morning.

Gathering her composure, she nodded toward the door. "Dougal, I presume?"

He cleared his throat. "I've asked him to start straight away."

"The kitchen?"

"The bedchamber."

"Nah. Ye should put him to work on the kitchen first."

Huxley frowned. "I'll be hiring enough men to address all the necessary repairs. Household staff, as well." He paused. "This brings me to the topic I intended to discuss with you."

"Good. The kitchen floor is a disgrace. Anybody could stumble on the loose stones and land in the fire."

"You mustn't come here alone again."

"The larder, too. Ye need shelves, English. Once they're built, we can fill them up. It willnae be long before yer fine figure is big enough for tossin' a caber."

"Miss Tulloch. Are you listening to me?"

"Enough to ken ye make no sense."

He scraped a hand over his beard. "Already, Dougal MacDonnell has seen you here. Word will spread quickly."

"Dinnae be daft, English."

"You asked me to teach you how to be a lady, did you not?"

"Aye."

"Well, here is the first rule: No lady allows herself to be compromised."

"Ye said yourself I havenae landed in yer bed."

His eyes flared oddly. Hands on hips, he paced to the doorway then returned, his jaw flickering. "Being alone with me is sufficient to sully you. The more people who know, the worse it will be."

"What rubbish. Everybody in Glenscannadoo thinks me a madwoman. I'm already as sullied as Mr. Cleghorn's pig after he's had his way with Flora MacDonnell's sow. The pig, I mean. I dinnae think Mr. Cleghorn has a fondness for sows."

"Good God, you are the most vexing—"

"Besides, ye havenae so much as kissed me, English. What sort of sullying can there be without kissin'? None at all, I'd say."

He froze. Pinned her with a hazel gaze that burned gold. He mouthed a foul epithet then shook his head. "I won't kiss you," he breathed.

"I wasnae askin'." Only a small lie, really. She wouldn't mind knowing how those perfect lips felt against hers.

"The next time you come here, bring a chaperone." His command, spoken in that precise, clipped English voice, sparked her temper.

She crossed the few feet between them and glared, her chin jutting. "Or what?"

"Or I'll refuse to instruct you further."

"Hmmph. Do ye ken what I think, English?"

"It doesn't matter what you think. You'll obey me or this agreement ends."

The fire in her belly intensified. "I think ye're afraid of what would happen if ye did kiss me."

His jaw flexed until she thought his teeth might crack.

Slowly, she grinned. "Poor, dainty Englishman. Frightened of wee Annie and her not-so-wee bosoms."

"Stop." The word was nothing but gravel. She liked the sound, raw and a bit slurred. She wanted more.

"Dinnae fash, English." She flicked his coat's lapel. "I'll be gentle."

With a swift motion, he trapped her wrist in his grip, dragging her close before encircling her waist and flattening her against him. "You think this is amusing."

Amusing? Far from it. The sensation of being pulled tight against him shocked her senses. Stole her breath. Made her vision blur. She'd never imagined feeling her breasts pressured by his hard chest would both ease and enflame her. She hadn't predicted how powerful he would seem when all that control began to unravel.

The fingers of his free hand traced the top of her ear, sending shivers rippling across her skin. "You think you can ignore my warnings, laugh away the risk, and suffer no consequences." He lowered his head until she felt hot, damp breath against her neck. "I understand why," he whispered.

"Y-ye do?" She barely managed to breathe the words. Everything inside her tingled. Her skin and scalp. Her breasts and lips. Her thighs—even her knees. Heavens, what was he doing to her?

"Yes." He nuzzled the loose hair between her ear and cheek. "A gentleman seems so very harmless."

"English," she whispered against his bearded jaw. It was all she could say, for every other thought had fled. Her body sizzled from shoulders to thighs. Every heated breath he released against her skin stoked the heat in her middle. She ached. Ached for *him*.

"Let this be your next lesson, Miss Tulloch." Teeth nibbled her earlobe. Lips stroked her jaw. "Heed it well." His voice was pure rasp.

Somehow, she'd wadded his lapels in her fists. Now, she used her grip to drag him closer. Tighter. "Aye?"

"When you're alone with a man, nothing apart from his honor prevents him from taking what he desires." His hand slid up from her waist to her breast. "Be it a touch."

She moaned and arched into the caress. Her eyes squeezed shut so she could digest the sensation. His palm. Her nipple. Wee pulses of zinging pleasure and the swelling ache of need.

"Or a kiss." He brushed his perfect lips across hers.

Her tongue darted out to capture the tingles he left behind. The tickle of his beard against her skin disappeared as he carefully withdrew. She followed him blindly, clutching his neck, focused on returning his lips to hers.

But he resisted with ease. "Or an intimacy only your husband should enjoy."

Suddenly, he grasped her thigh and raised it alongside his. Then, with a practiced motion, he ground his hips into hers, the hard ridge beneath his trousers taking the liberties he spoke of.

Heat and pleasure surged where his hardness intruded upon her soft folds. Separated only by layers of cloth, his body pressured hers, driving upward along ripe, tender nerves. She gasped with the pleasure of it. Heat weakened her until she could only cling to him, burying her nose in his cravat and panting.

Panting.

Panting for more.

Was there more? Her head spun and her middle ached. She wanted him to … she didn't know. Kiss her, probably. Remove the barriers between them, certainly. Then, what?

"English?" she panted, uncertain what she was asking him to do. She raised her mouth to his jaw, seeking his kiss again.

And he resisted again.

Slowly, she opened her eyes to find him staring down at her. She wasn't certain what she'd expected to see. Lust, obviously. Perhaps a measure of the same dizzying heat she felt.

But not this. This was calculation. He was *assessing* her. Watching her react to his touch the way a man training a horse watched the animal react to the bit.

Cold rushed in to replace heat—all except her face. That went hot with humiliation. She tried to yank away from him, but he held her fast, his hand gripping her thigh. "Leave go," she gritted, shoving at his chest.

His head tilted. "I will. Because I am a gentleman. But now you understand how swiftly you can lose everything." His eyes fell to her mouth. "A single moment of carelessness, and the only role you'll play for a lord is his mistress."

She shoved again, this time digging the heel of her hand into his shoulder. "Ye've made yer point. Now, leave go."

"Have I?" he muttered. "I wonder."

His arms slid away, and she immediately backed up several paces.

The look in his eyes was foreign. Always before, he'd seemed weary or frustrated or flat. Now, his expression glowed darkly, focused and watchful. It confused her.

Made her retreat another step before she stopped herself.

"Next time, bring a chaperone," he said, calmly straightening his lapels. "A woman would be best."

How could he be so cool while she still felt like her bones had melted? "I dinnae ken any women who will—"

"Find one."

She glowered. "It's nae so easy as that."

"I never claimed this would be easy, Miss Tulloch."

"Aye." Needing to look away from him, she glanced around the room. He'd finished the paneling, but the fireplace still wanted repair. "Impossible things never are."

Silence was her answer.

She swallowed and risked another glance in his direction. A lock of brown hair had fallen over his brow. It was the only thing about him that hadn't been perfectly contained.

Raising her chin, she challenged, "Just wait until ye must learn to throw a weight over the bar without brainin' yerself, English. Then, ye'll see what impossible really means."

The faintest quirk—nearly a smile—curled one corner of his mouth. "I await your expert instruction, Miss Tulloch." Then, he bent at the waist and gave her a mocking bow. "With great anticipation."

CHAPTER EIGHT

A week later, Annie led her new chaperone along
the road to Glendasheen Castle. The old woman's
nonsense had come in a steady stream the entire
journey from MacPherson House.

"Ye'd be pleased, lass. I planted another rowan
outside yer brother's house. He'll have a fine hedge
when he returns from prison. Good protection, that."

Annie tugged Bill the Donkey along the shore of the
loch and released an impatient breath. "Broderick needs
protection *now*, Mrs. MacBean. After he returns will be
a mite late."

The old woman frowned. Then dug about inside the
leather pouch she often carried. "Mayhap I could curse
the man who put him there."

Patting Bill's neck as they rounded a stand of birch,
Annie swallowed her worry and focused on the lapping
water. "If we kenned who that was, a curse wouldnae
be necessary. The MacPhersons would see to the
matter."

"Och, a curse works just as well as killin'. I'll need four looking glasses—"

"Dinnae bother, auld woman. I told ye—"

"—and ashes from an ancient yew tree."

"—we dinnae ken who's behind Broderick's troubles."

"Oh, and a new whisky cask struck by lightnin'. No need to remove the whisky. I'll drain it myself."

Despite her aggravation, Annie snorted. "I've little doubt of that."

"Lightnin' adds a fine smoky flavor."

Annie spoke to Bill, who seemed the more lucid of the two creatures behind her. "Do ye suppose a curse is stronger if ye shove a thistle up yer arse?"

Bill's long ears twitched. Mrs. MacBean appeared not to have heard. Instead, she dug inside her leather pouch then held up a worn scrap of tartan. "Which clan did ye say yer man is from?"

"I told ye, he's nae my man."

"Aye, aye. But ye aim to marry him. I'll make ye a charm he cannae resist."

"I dinnae aim to marry him, ye daft auld crone." Even if his kiss did turn a woman's bones to hot gravy. Where had he learned to do such things?

"No, of course not. Now, which clan was it? The Brodies?"

"Oh, for God's sake. I already told ye, his name is John Huxley. He hasnae a clan. And he's nae my man. He's teachin' me to be a lady."

"Ye were a lady in yer mother's womb, lass."

"Well, I'm female, right enough." She shot a wry glance down at her bosoms. "But I must marry a *lord*. Remember? This is about Finlay."

"Oh. Aye, now I recall. Are ye certain the laddie kens what he's about? I've never heard of a ghost bein' reborn, let alone demandin' a title."

No, Annie wasn't certain of anything. She'd worked herself into exhaustion these past weeks hoping for another visit from Finlay, but all she had left of him was the thistle charm. Now, she felt for it in her pocket, the sole sign that her dream hadn't been merely wishful thinking. "I must believe he spoke true, Mrs. MacBean." She swallowed, letting the sound of lapping waves soothe her. "'Tis all the hope I have."

The old woman fell silent for a time. Then, Annie felt a pat upon her shoulder. Mrs. MacBean leaned down from atop Bill's back, her good eye shining with sympathy. "I'll make ye a grand charm. Dinnae fash. This Huxley fellow willnae be able to tell up from down, he'll be so smitten." Another pat, and she returned to digging in her pouch. She withdrew another scrap of tartan. "So, the Huxleys are a Lowland clan, then?"

Annie sighed. "He's English. And a far sight more proper than ye usually find in Glenscannadoo." She eyed the woman's wiry shrub of hair and ragged clothing. "While ye're actin' as my chaperone, best keep talk of curses and charms to yerself."

The old woman nodded sagely. "Right ye are. Englishmen arenae like Scotsmen."

No, they weren't. A Scot wouldn't dismiss curses and ghosts as pure rubbish. A Scot wouldn't suppose the only eyes capable of seeing were his.

And another thing—if a Scot fancied a lass, he wouldn't kiss her as some sort of *lesson* then act as though she'd scuffed his boots. Only Englishmen did that. Pompous, superior, infuriating Englishmen.

The castle came into view. "Just promise ye'll pretend to be sane," Annie said. "We dinnae want to frighten him too badly."

"A bit weak-kneed, is he?"

"Nah," Annie replied after lengthy consideration. "Nothin' about John Huxley is weak."

Her point was proven when they arrived outside the castle. Annie pulled Bill to a halt and stared while Mrs. MacBean murmured, "I see what ye mean, lass."

John Huxley was in his shirtsleeves again. This time, he was helping lift a massive table out of a long cart. Two MacDonnell cousins held one end. Huxley held the other on his own. His arms and shoulders rippled with the effort.

"Into the dining room, gentlemen." His voice was calm. Authoritative. "Off we go."

She'd seen brute strength before, of course. The MacPhersons regularly hauled three-hundred-pound barrels of cider on their shoulders. But they were built for it. Huxley was leaner. A gentleman. Yet, he was scarcely winded by the weight of the table, which had to be fifteen feet long.

As the men carried it through the castle doors, Huxley's profile became visible—and heat bloomed outward from her belly to her fingertips.

Good heavens. He'd shaved his beard.

"My word, lass. Yer man's a braw sight to behold."

Annie swallowed. "He's not … not my man. I told ye …" She watched him until he disappeared inside the castle. Only then could she breathe properly. What was wrong with her? She'd seen him without his whiskers before.

Gathering her composure, she helped Mrs. MacBean down from Bill's back before taking the donkey to the stable. She noted the new timbers and freshly built stalls, the tidy tack room and clean floors. Giving Bill's neck a pat, she glanced around at what had once been open-air piles of old stone and rotting wood.

Even before Huxley had hired men, he'd worked wonders with Glendasheen Castle. She shook her head at the transformation. It was more than admirable. It was very near a miracle, considering the castle's curse.

Somehow, he'd avoided the unnatural calamities of the castle's previous owners. One MacDonnell chieftain had rebuilt the tower seven times before conceding defeat. Another had lost the use of his leg when a section of roof collapsed without warning or cause. A third gave up when the castle caught fire for the fourth time. Ewan Wylie's misfortune had been less violent, perhaps, but his setbacks were no less effective—an invasion of bats, hearths that refused to stay lit, a tree falling upon the stable. Eventually, the expense and discomfort had forced Wylie to abandon the glen for employment elsewhere.

John Huxley, by contrast, had made startling progress in just over a year.

"Appears the spirits favor yer man," Mrs. MacBean commented from the entrance. "The castle hasnae slowed him down, that's for certain."

Annie nodded. "Aye." She'd given up on correcting the old woman's assumption that Huxley was hers. "I've noticed the same thing." She ran a hand over the nearest stall's gate. "Why do ye suppose that is?"

"Cannae say. Spirits have naught but time and whim to weigh upon them." The old woman brushed a piece of straw from her sleeve. "Mayhap they enjoy lookin' upon his face. Dinnae blame them for that."

A fair point. Annie recalled those handsome, refined features. The sculpted jaw. The aristocratic nose. The captivating eyes.

When they exited into the stable yard, his handsome face was wearing a scowl. He came toward them carrying a basket of apples. "When did you arrive?"

"A few minutes ago." Annie grinned to disguise her fascination with his naked jaw and perfect lips. "Ye appear a mite pained, English. Strained a muscle, eh? Perhaps ye should leave the heavy liftin' to proper Scotsmen."

He ignored her to set his apples beside the stable entrance. Then, he returned to address Mrs. MacBean. "Madam," he said quietly, giving her a respectful nod. "I don't believe I've had the pleasure. I am John Huxley."

The old woman ran a hand over her wild shrub of hair. "Mary MacBean, maker of potions and cures for ailments of every sort." Her eyebrows bobbed. "And the pleasure is mine, lad. All mine."

Huxley's eyes crinkled at the corners, though he didn't smile. He inclined his head before shifting his gaze to Annie. "Your chaperone, I take it."

Annie raised her chin, daring him to complain. "Aye."

"I'm afraid our lessons must wait, Miss Tulloch. Today, I'm traveling to Inverness for supplies. Perhaps next week—"

"Nah. Ye should stay here and keep yer end of the bargain."

He propped his hands on his hips. "Next week will be soon enough—"

Her temper flared. If he thought to avoid her after their kiss, he could think again. They'd made an agreement. He'd given her his word.

"I didnae drag Bill and Mrs. MacBean all this way to turn round and—"

"Bill?" He tensed. "Who is Bill?"

"More of a gentleman than you, I tell ye that much."

"Does he work for your father?"

"Stepfather. And aye, in a manner of speakin'."

Hazel eyes raked her from boots to shoulders and back again. "I don't have time for this," he muttered, perhaps to himself.

"Och, Bill is a fine, muckle fellow," Mrs. MacBean interjected. "Ears are a wee bit longer than may be regarded as attractive, and I've never encountered such a gassy creature. But all considered, he gave me a most pleasurable ride."

Huxley blinked at the old woman. Paused a moment. Then his brow cleared. "Bill is a horse."

"Donkey," Annie corrected. "Now, do ye intend to keep yer word or not?"

Immediately, his scowl returned. "I always do."

"Good. We'll have our lesson today, then."

"I must fetch supplies, Miss Tulloch."

"What supplies?"

"None that need concern you—"

"Fetch them another day. Next week, perhaps."

He scraped a hand over his mouth and jaw as though missing his beard. "By God, you are the most vexing woman."

"Mrs. MacBean is auld, English. Half of her doesnae work right, and the rest doesnae work at all."

Mrs. MacBean, having watched their conversation with interest, nodded her agreement. "'Tis true."

"I'll not ask her to come all the way to Glendasheen Castle on a *dreich* day like today without a bluidy good reason. Ye demanded I have a chaperone." Annie gestured to the old woman in question. "She's here. Now, do yer part."

His jaw flexed in familiar fashion. Like a dram of whisky, it sent a shot of heat blooming through her.

"Very well. We'll have our lesson." His low voice sounded more threatening than conciliatory. Still, she'd take the victory.

She slid her arm through Mrs. MacBean's and tugged her toward the castle.

"Where are you going?" he inquired as they passed.

She stopped. "The drawing room."

He drew up beside her and lowered his head. "Oh, but our lesson won't take place inside the castle."

Uneasy about his triumphant tone, she slanted him a sideways glance. "Where, then?"

A small smile curled one corner of his mouth. He smiled so infrequently, she had to blink to be sure.

But, aye. There it was. Like a wink from star.

"We're going shopping," he said, that wee smile growing as he observed her reaction.

Which, naturally, involved dread and nausea. "No," she breathed.

"Oh, yes. Today, you will learn what all ladies must." He actually licked his lips—licked them like a cat that had a mouse right where he wanted her. "How to properly spend a gentleman's money."

At long last, John had the maddening Annie Tulloch right where he wanted her. Well, perhaps not *right* where he wanted. His bed was back at the castle.

But from a battle-of-wills standpoint, he'd won. And that was even more satisfying.

Well, perhaps not *more* satisfying.

"Dreadfully quiet back there, Miss Tulloch," he commented, glancing over his shoulder at the hoyden fuming in the bed of his long cart. "Are you certain you don't wish to postpone our lesson? Next week, perhaps."

God, it felt good to be the one doing the taunting. He shouldn't relish it. But he did.

She hugged her knees to her chest and leveled him with a venomous glare.

He grinned. He couldn't help himself. "If you'd prefer, I could take you home instead. It would be no trouble, I assure you." They'd just entered the village. He'd expected her to cry off as they passed MacPherson House, but she was stubborn. They'd stopped only long enough to return her donkey to the MacPherson stable and leave a note for Angus.

"'Tis most solicitous of ye, Mr. Huxley," said Mrs. MacBean. "Which clan did ye say ye were from?"

The half-blind old woman sat beside him on the cart's driving bench. Annie had insisted. For all her griping about the woman being daft, he'd noticed how much care she gave her "chaperone."

"The Huxleys are my family," he replied gently. It was the fifth time she'd asked. "We're from Nottinghamshire."

"Have ye a tartan, then?"

"I'm afraid not."

"Well, why didnae ye say so?" She resumed digging inside the leather pack she carried in her lap. "I've nothin' appropriate in here. Now, if ye were a Brodie, that would be somethin'."

He started to answer when Annie interrupted with, "Just smile and nod, English. Correcting her will do ye no good at all."

By the time he pulled the horses to a halt outside Cleghorn's Haberdashery, Mrs. MacBean was calling him Mr. Brodie and reminiscing about his "braw" uncle, with whom she'd apparently had a liaison.

"Ah, he had a silver tongue, that John Brodie. Separated me from my virtue more than once, I can tell ye that."

How a woman could surrender her virtue more than once, he didn't know—and didn't want to.

"'Twas when he brought out the butter *and* the honey jar, I said, 'Och, no, ye scoundrel. The sixteenth time will be the last, by heaven.'"

Ignoring Mrs. MacBean's alarming recollections, he climbed down from the bench and secured the horses before assisting the old woman down from her perch. He moved to help Annie, but the stubborn female had already helped herself. She leaned against the side of the cart, arms crossed.

"I hate shoppin', English. I already told ye."

He grinned. "Is that so?"

"Ye ken it is."

"But you require gowns, Miss Tulloch." He allowed himself a lingering sweep of her lush form before continuing. "Desperately."

"I'm a fair hand with a needle. All I need is—"

"A dressmaker. We'll start here in Glenscannadoo. If the local woman won't suffice, you'll accompany me to Inverness."

Looking slightly ill, Annie shoved away from the cart. "Fine," she spat. "Let's have done with it."

He nodded toward the shop two doors down from Cleghorn's. "I'll meet you there. I've a few errands to attend first."

She glowered suspiciously but retrieved Mrs. MacBean and tugged the old woman toward the shop.

He hurried through his errands, eager to see Annie's reaction. Would she allow herself to be measured? She'd have to remove her plaid. Would she refuse to cooperate and scurry home? She'd have to admit he'd won the argument.

Either way, anticipation quickened his stride as he retrieved his post—another stack of letters from his family—before making a few purchases to ease the journey to Inverness.

He was almost certain Annie would cry off before leaving Glenscannadoo. *Almost.* But it was best to be prepared. The woman was far from predictable.

Upon entering the dressmaker's shop, he paused. The shop was narrow and dark, so it took a moment to find her. And when he did, his heart kicked so hard, it bruised his stomach.

She was surrounded by women—four of them, to be precise. He recognized one as the dressmaker, Flora MacDonnell, a blonde with a sharp nose and dull mind.

Another was Flora's sister. The third might be the saddler's wife. The fourth was an ash-haired, moon-faced MacDonnell named Grisel.

The four women were laughing.

And Annie was not. Rather, her expression had tightened to stone.

Little wonder. The women appeared to be pointing and plucking and laughing—at *her*.

"Do ye suppose she'll even ken what to do with skirts?" sneered Grisel. "Might as well expect yer sow to play the fiddle."

"She's more lad than lass, true enough." Flora's pitying glance was its own form of ridicule. She spoke slowly and loudly, as though Annie were simpleminded. Or mad. "Ye really must have a corset first. I cannae fit ye properly with ye bein' so ..." The woman fluttered her fingers at Annie's bosom. "Indecent."

The second woman snorted her agreement. The third woman giggled. Grisel added, "Best ye wear gloves if ye're forced to be near her, Flora. Mad Annie's been known to bite."

As they all laughed, a storm gathered in his chest.

"Miss Tulloch."

Annie's eyes flew to his.

They gutted him. She looked hunted. Tormented.

He didn't know why she hadn't already lashed the women with her sharp, defiant tongue. He didn't know why she was pale and holding herself protectively. All he knew was that he must remove her from this place. Now.

He beckoned her with a wave of his hand. "We are leaving," he said, using every ounce of authority he'd learned from his father.

She gave a jerky nod and started toward him. Grisel grasped her arm and whispered something to her as she passed. Annie flinched and yanked her arm free.

John's fury was ordinarily the slow-burning sort. But not now. Fire flooded his veins until his vision tinged red. He charged forward and clasped Annie's hand in his. She seemed startled but didn't pull away. In fact, she hesitated only a moment before squeezing his hand in return.

"Come along," he said, directing his most superior tone to the women who'd insulted her. "No sense purchasing gowns from a dressmaker who will very shortly be out of business."

Flora MacDonnell blinked, her mouth agape and her face red. The others slunk backwards. Perhaps they understood their error. Perhaps not. But they soon would. He would make certain of it.

"M-Mr. Huxley," Flora stuttered. "I think there's been a misunderstanding—"

"I think a proprietress who'd like to keep her shop should treat her customers with better courtesy." He lowered his voice. "I'd wager the MacPhersons agree."

"Oh, no. I—I mean, aye." Flora darted glances at the other women, but they all looked away. "I was only tryin' to be … helpful."

Annie's fingers squeezed his again. "We should go," she murmured.

He tucked her behind him then gave the women one last, hard look. This was not the first time they'd tormented Annie, that much was clear. Every one of them would need to be dealt with. He must speak with Angus. How had the MacPhersons allowed this to go on?

Another tug on his hand. A gentle touch on his back. "English."

The whispered plea worked. He ushered her out of the shop and toward the cart. "Where is Mrs. MacBean?" he asked, struggling to keep his anger from boiling over.

"The haberdashery. She's lookin' for tartan and seashells. Oh, and an ivory button." Annie's small, amused snort eased the pressure in his chest a bit.

He pulled her to a halt beside the cart's wheel. "Tell me what happened."

"Who can guess what sort of oddity she has in mind? Daft auld woman."

"Not with Mrs. MacBean. In the dressmaker's shop. Why were they—"

Her eyes skated away from his. "I told ye, English. I hate shoppin'."

"That's not shopping. They were ... blast, they surrounded you like a pack of feral hounds."

"Worse." A tiny grin curled one side of her mouth. "Bitches."

Another small part of him eased. Her spirit wasn't gone, merely hiding. "How long has this been happening?"

She didn't answer.

His gut hardened. "A long time, then."

"Dinnae fash yerself. It's only bad when they're all together. Most days, I'm able to avoid them."

Except today, when he'd forced her to enter her tormentor's shop and request the woman's services. Never again. He'd make sure nothing like this ever happened again. "I intend to speak to your father about this," he gritted.

She laid a hand on his chest. True, he was wearing his heaviest coat and another layer of wool beneath. But still. He felt her touch.

"Stepfather," she murmured, her smile warming. "I'm fine. No need to involve the MacPhersons."

"They should have ended this long ago."

"They dinnae ken anything about it."

"Why in blazes not?"

She shrugged. "I never told them."

He started to answer, but Ronnie Cleghorn came running around the cart. The russet-haired boy collided with Annie's hip and clutched her waist.

"Nannee!"

Immediately, Annie's face lit up. She stroked the boy's hair then crouched down to hug him tightly. "Ah, ye're a breath of summer on this *dreich* day, laddie. Did yer da let ye keep that pup ye found?"

The boy nodded emphatically. "Stahbee."

"Ye named him Strawberry?"

Another nod.

"Well, now, since that's yer favorite fruit, he must be a grand pup, indeed."

Mrs. MacBean joined them, informing Robbie his father was searching for him. Smiling, the boy patted Annie's cheeks. "Ah miss Innee," he said quietly.

Annie's eyes glossed and her lower lip firmed as though struggling against grief. "Me, too, laddie," she whispered. Then, she kissed his forehead and sent him back to his father.

John didn't know what the last part of their conversation had been about, but when she stood, her expression was wistful. It changed quickly when she met his gaze.

"Spare me yer pity, English," she snapped, snatching her hat from the bed of the cart and tugging it low over her forehead. "I dinnae want it."

What he felt wasn't pity. It was hotter and deeper and more tender. But delving too far into what it was would only invite more complications. His connection with Annie Tulloch was complicated enough. "I can take you home, if you like," he offered. "It's fully three hours to Inverness."

"I already said no. What's the matter, English? Frightened I'll start weepin' and stain yer cravat with my womanly tears?"

He examined the defiant tilt of her chin, the stubborn glint in her eye. "The topic of our lesson hasn't changed. We will be shopping. Are you prepared for that?"

"Help Mrs. MacBean onto her seat. A gentleman doesnae keep a lady waiting." Turning on her heel, she marched to the back of the cart before climbing on with surprising dexterity.

With each moment that passed, his smile grew. "Very well." He tugged his own hat tighter and offered his hand to Mrs. MacBean, who'd been watching with keen interest. "The shops of Inverness had best gird their loins."

"And why's that?" Annie's tone was as sullen as the low, gray clouds above.

He lifted the old woman into the cart and came around to take his own seat before answering. "I suspect they've never had a customer as extraordinary as you."

CHAPTER NINE

"Opera dress?" Annie's query rang sharply off the shop's fancy walls. She couldn't help it. They'd officially entered the realm of the ridiculous.

She'd stood by silently while Huxley and the dressmaker, Mrs. Baird, discussed cloaks lined in "ermine"—a fancy word for weasel. She'd held her tongue while they discussed walking gowns—as though she couldn't walk unless she was dressed a particular way. She'd even stayed quiet while they debated whether fichus had run their course. What on earth was a fichu? A kerchief women wore to cover their bosoms, evidently. Why couldn't the gown's bodice do its job properly? She didn't know. No one did. Instead, dressmakers shaped bodices indecently low, requiring women to stuff spare fabric into their necklines to prevent exposure.

Fichu. It sounded like a sneeze. The word was French, according to Huxley. Annie thought French women must be fond of displaying their bosoms, and French men rather clever for encouraging such fashions.

Still, she hadn't uttered a single protest during the fichu debate or the ermine discussion or the walking gown nonsense. But *opera* dress? This was too much.

Huxley turned, blinking as though he'd forgotten he'd anchored her by his side to "observe."

"I've never been to an opera, English. And I dinnae intend to go. Why should I pay for a gown made especially for doin' somethin' I'd never do?"

"Ladies in London—"

"I'm nae goin' to London."

"Edinburgh, then. Regardless, London sets the fashions."

She crossed her arms and glowered up at the man who knew far too much about ladies' clothing. "I thought that was Paris."

His sigh was pure exasperation.

"Isnae that where yer *mistress* was from?"

Ruddy color stained his cheekbones. "Former mistress. You asked how I knew so much about—"

"The modest one, aye?" She snorted. "Doesnae sound so modest to me."

"*Modiste*, Miss Tulloch. She was a modiste."

"I dinnae need an opera dress."

The yellow-haired dressmaker, who'd been gaping throughout their exchange, decided to add her nonsense to the conversation. "You may call the ensemble an evening gown, if you prefer, Miss Tulloch. One needn't wear it solely to the theatre." Mrs. Baird was pleasant for a shop owner. She had a bonnie face that made it difficult to tell her age. And she spoke with the light

Scottish inflection Huxley had been encouraging Annie to adopt.

Annie hated her. Which made no sense, since the woman had been perfectly polite since they'd entered the Inverness shop an hour earlier. She hadn't sneered at Annie's hair or mocked Annie's trews or implied Annie was mad even once. Rather, she'd welcomed them into her shop with a warm smile. Mrs. Baird had remarkably lovely teeth.

Another reason to hate her.

The shop was a pleasant place, large and airy with white draperies everywhere and clean windows looking out on High Street. It was the kind of place where her mother might have worked, had she not had Annie to care for.

Annie imagined it was the kind of shop Huxley's not-so-modest mistress might have run in Paris.

Her stomach burned. She narrowed her eyes upon Mrs. Baird before replying, "Mornin' dress. Evenin' dress. Dinner dress. Walkin' dress. What a load of shite."

The woman's yellow eyebrows arched. Huxley ran a hand over his jaw.

"I'll nae be changin' my gown every time I visit the privy. I'd never get anythin' done."

Huxley's jaw flickered. "Please excuse us, Mrs. Baird." He grasped Annie's elbow. "We'll only be a moment."

The yellow-haired, bonnie-faced, white-toothed woman smiled. "Of course."

Annie's stomach burned hotter as Huxley tugged her to the opposite corner of the shop, near the windows and the small sofa where Mrs. MacBean appeared to be dozing. "Well, now, ye appear to be developin' quite the affection betwixt ye, English. Ye've a taste for dressmakers, I see. Mayhap ye should make *her* yer mistress."

He spun her to face him. "What the devil is wrong with you?"

"Nothin' at all."

"Do you want to be a lady or not?"

Her chin went up. "Aye."

"Then, you must dress like one."

"A gown or two will do fine."

"No. It won't." He released her arm to prop his hands on his hips. Then, his gaze flickered to the window as though he was having trouble looking at her without throttling her. "You clearly don't understand the task you've taken on."

"Are ye callin' me daft?"

Bright hazel eyes came back to fix upon her. "I'm saying you will fail. Is that what you want?"

She snorted. "Now, who's daft?"

"Bloody hell, woman." His glower darkened into a storm. "Listen carefully. *Ladies* do not concern themselves with their skirts catching fire in the kitchen. Do you know why?"

She didn't bother answering. It was usually best not to interrupt when a man was having a wee fit of temper.

"They do not cook. Rather, they order their *cook* to cook. They do not clean. That is what maids are for. Neither do they concern themselves overmuch with 'getting things done.' Because most of their tasks have no particular timetable. They manage their household. They plan entertainments. They embroider. When the weather is fine, they ride or take a pleasant walk."

"Fascinatin'."

"They wear morning gowns whilst they drink tea and write gossipy letters to their cousins. They wear walking gowns whilst they visit shops and spend their husbands' money. They wear evening gowns for dinner, ball gowns for dancing, and opera dresses for attending the theatre. Ladies strive to be pleasing, modest, and inoffensive. They do *not* speak of visiting the privy or use the word 'shite.'"

The burning in her stomach hardened into stone. He'd told her this endeavor would suffocate her. Suddenly, she could feel it doing precisely that.

His eyes lit. "Ah, understanding at last."

"So, I'm to be useless." She flicked the white curtain on one side of the window. "Bland and decorative. Like draperies."

"Precisely." He didn't appear pleased about it. If she didn't know better, she'd think he wanted her to abandon her goal. But that would mean he preferred her as she was, which made no sense at all.

She crossed her arms. "Well, I dinnae ken if I can be bland, English."

This time, he was the one who snorted.

"But decorative. Perhaps that I can do."

That straight, refined nose flared. Hazel eyes ran from her forehead to her feet. For some reason, she felt his gaze like a stroke. "I agree. First, you'll need to be … fitted."

She frowned. Why was he speaking to her bosom? "Aye. But I cannae afford all those gowns. Angus will have a bluidy apoplexy."

"Do not concern yourself with the expense."

She chuckled. "Ah, ye're amusin', English. I havenae married a lord just yet. I'm afraid we rustic, non-decorative sorts must earn our livin' before we spend it."

"I will take care of it."

He spoke the absurdity so calmly, she needed a moment to recover. Another moment. Or three.

"Dinnae be daft."

"Husband hunting season begins in spring. Gowns take weeks or months to make. You haven't time to—"

"You are *not* payin' for my clothing, English."

"Oh, but I am. This is part of your training." Slowly, he smiled. "As your instructor, I insist."

"That's ridiculous."

The blend of arrogance and satisfaction in his gaze confounded her. He appeared to believe he'd won a victory. "When you marry, your husband will pay for all your gowns. He'll consider it a routine expense." He leaned closer and flicked the same curtain she had earlier. "Like buying new draperies." His grin sent a swooping pang through her belly. Daft, charming Englishman.

She squinted at him, shaking her head. "Just how wealthy are you, English?"

"Wealthy enough."

"Well, it's driven ye mad."

"Only you could accomplish that, Miss Tulloch. Only you."

An hour later, Annie awakened Mrs. MacBean from her nap, and they headed out of the dressmaker's shop and into the draper's shop next door.

Huxley's behavior continued to baffle her. She cast a glance at the odd Englishman, who'd worn that same triumphant expression ever since she'd tacitly agreed to let him spend ridiculous sums on her gowns. What did he think he'd won?

Watching him discuss rich, plum silk with the gentleman behind the counter, she shook her head again, unable to untangle the answer. It wasn't only his claim on her dressmaker bills, either. When Mrs. Baird had started to take Annie back into a curtained area for measuring, he'd tried to follow them.

His triumphant gleam had dimmed briefly when Mrs. Baird halted him with a starchy glare and a firmly closed curtain. Before that, his eyes burned a hole in Annie's plaid. What did he suppose she hid beneath it— gold bullion?

Perhaps that was why he was so eager to pay for her gowns. He thought she kept treasure stitched into her trews. In truth, all she had beneath her clothes were drawers and serviceable linen stays. The corset had no boning, no real structure. She'd crafted it to lace in front, so it was easy to manage on her own and supported her bosoms enough for comfort. But Mrs. Baird's dubious, careful glances had told her she'd best order new undergarments if she didn't wish to be embarrassed.

She wondered if Huxley intended to pay for her corset. Perhaps her petticoats and stockings, too. The thought made her chuckle.

"Och, lass. Are ye findin' that yellow tartan amusin'?" Mrs. MacBean asked. "'Tis a pitiful choice of color, I'll grant ye. Reminds me of milk gone sour."

She examined the old woman, who'd been both patient and generous to accompany Annie all the way to Inverness. "Which one do ye favor, Mrs. MacBean?"

she asked, waving to the long wall lined with wool ranging from deepest blue to boldest red.

Mrs. MacBean gave the bolts a long, considering perusal. Then, she pointed to two, both tartans in shades of brown and green. "These are bonnie. Mayhap ye could make yerself one of those fancy walkin' gowns out of 'em."

Annie raised a brow. Apparently, Mrs. MacBean wasn't as sound a sleeper as she let on. "A grand idea," she murmured, watching the old woman drift toward a display of linen.

Glancing back to ensure Huxley was still huddled in conversation with the bespectacled draper, she continued along the wall until she reached the tartans at the end. There, in the shadows, she found the one she wanted.

It was a simple pattern woven of midnight blue and pine green. Similar to her plaid, but perhaps even richer, the wool was soft and fine. She rubbed it between her fingers. It would pleat beautifully.

Annie waited until Huxley was distracted by more of Mrs. MacBean's bawdy tales about his "uncle," then completed her purchases. She tucked the paper-wrapped bundle beneath her arm just as Huxley approached.

"Night falls early this time of year," he murmured. "We'd best depart soon."

She nodded, ignoring his curiosity about her purchase, and led the way to his cart. She'd already clambered up into the cart's bed when Mrs. MacBean called up to her.

"Och, lassie. Might I persuade ye to trade places with me? I'm fair weary after our long travels."

Annie frowned. She didn't look weary. She'd spent two hours in the dressmaker's shop napping. But old people tired easily, and it was no bother to comply, so Annie made up a pallet of blankets and straw for the woman then climbed onto the bench. Huxley handed her another blanket as he took his seat and started the horses forward.

Odd how large he seemed beside her. Their thighs were different sizes—his were thick, indeed. Thick and muscular. The length between his hip and knee was nearly twice hers. Then there were his shoulders. Were they wider than when she'd first met him? Possibly. He'd been working like a bloody draft horse to restore his castle. Additionally, he'd been heaving cabers and stones every day, as she'd instructed. That would add muscle to any man. She blinked as she realized she was staring at his jaw. The one that flickered when she vexed him. The one that made her glow.

She sighed. It was daft to moon over the Englishman. The man's sole aim was to sell his land and leave. Her sole aim was to marry someone else. Besides which, he seemed a mite cynical toward women—especially *ladies*. Which was strange, considering he was so knowledgeable about them.

Still, he was the bonniest man she'd ever seen. His lashes were a pure luxury. His eyes, with their gold-glowing, changeable hues made her think of a woodland sunset. And his lips—good God, they were—

"Do you intend to use that blanket? Or merely clutch it like your favorite doll?"

She frowned. "Why did ye insist on payin' for my gowns, English?"

He cast her a sideways glance. "Perhaps I like the thought of you being beholden to me. Perhaps I'm betting it will ensure you keep your end of our bargain."

She snorted. "Ye wasted yer coins, then. Ye dinnae need such a debt. I've given ye my word."

"Hmm. I prefer more tangible bindings."

Why was he staring at her hands that way? She couldn't make sense of it.

"Well, whatever the dressmaker charges ye—"

"The draper, too." His mouth quirked. Again, that hint of triumph entered his expression. "Don't forget him."

Odd, exasperating Englishman. "I'll be payin' ye back for everything ye spend."

"No, you won't."

"Aye, I will."

He didn't reply, but his answer was clear. He wouldn't accept repayment.

"Look, English. As matters stand, you payin' for my clothing makes it appear I'm yer ..."

His jaw hardened. His thighs flexed. He stared straight ahead. "My what?"

Mistress. His mistress. But she couldn't say that. There was too much between them, too much that tempted her to brush the lock of hair from his forehead or soothe that hard jaw with her hand.

"Kin," she finished. "Mayhap a sixth sister."

Those bonnie eyes lit and burned. "Nobody would mistake you for my sister, Miss Tulloch." He licked his lips, stared at hers, then tore his gaze away. "Nobody would be that blind."

She swallowed and let silence fall between them as they crossed the bridge and left Inverness behind. Wind came up, damp and icy. She shivered and unfolded the blanket he'd handed her earlier. A bundle of letters tied with twine tumbled onto her lap.

"What's this?" She plucked them up to examine them.

"My correspondence, obviously." He frowned and reached for the bundle. But, seeing his eagerness to remove them, she held them away.

"Are these from yer family, English? This top one appears written by a woman. A *lady*, perhaps." She grinned as he frowned deeper. "I've heard ladies enjoy writin' letters with their mornin' tea."

"It's from my mother."

She plucked through the corners of the stack. "And this one?"

"My father."

The last four were from three of his sisters and his boyhood friend, Robert.

She examined the bundle carefully. "Fine paper, these. Every single one." She wrapped the bundle in a second blanket and tucked it into the corner of the cart beside Mrs. MacBean. "Yer sisters married well, then."

His tension eased once the letters were out of sight. "You might say that." A small smile curved his lips. "The oldest, Annabelle, married my best friend."

"Robert?"

His smile widened as he nodded. "They live near my parents in Nottinghamshire. Their youngest son is named for me."

"They called him 'English,' then?" she teased.

He laughed. It was the first time she'd seen him do so with such ease. "Only you are permitted to use my special Highland moniker, Miss Tulloch."

His broad grin struck her speechless.

She swallowed, tilting dizzily at the sight. Dear God, did he realize the effect he had merely by smiling? She hoped not. It was dangerous—a bit like being blinded by the sun.

"They called him John," he said proudly, his smile lingering as he turned to watch the road. "Last I saw of him, he could fit in my pocket."

Annie spent the next two hours querying him about his family. Apart from the occasional odd hesitation and careful dodge, he seemed eager to tell her about them. First, he shared stories about his childhood in Nottinghamshire: fishing with his hands in a rock-strewn river, sledging with his sisters when they had a good snow, playing soldiers with Robert until well past dark, and crashing his neighbor's phaeton into a hedgerow.

"To be fair, I was twelve," he explained. "I'd never so much as ridden in a phaeton, let alone driven one."

Then, he described his parents. His mother was fond of long hugs, strategic meal planning, and cats, which made his father sneeze. His father, according to Huxley, had a decidedly tolerant disposition.

"My family was always a bit unusual in that regard. Mama and Papa preferred to allow their children to grow in their own directions." Huxley chuckled. "It made for a number of eccentricities."

"How so?"

"All sorts of ways, really. Kate is the youngest. She quotes Shakespeare in casual conversation and attempts to sing far too frequently. My second-youngest sister, Eugenia, is obsessed with hats. So much so that she worked as a milliner until she married last spring."

Despite the chill of the evening air, his affection for his family warmed her. She wanted to hear more. "What is she like?"

"Eugenia? Charming. Opinionated—about feathers in particular. Never minces words. You and she would get on famously, I expect."

Annie doubted it. She'd never gotten along with other females.

"Let's see. My third-youngest sister, Maureen, enjoys cookery even more than you do. Every Christmas, she makes these little cakes." Sadness clouded his smile.

Christmas was only a week away. Annie imagined he would miss spending it with them. Perhaps she'd invite him to dine with her and the MacPhersons. They weren't his family, but at least he wouldn't be alone. Yes. That was the solution. She'd insist he join them for Christmas dinner. And Hogmanay, too. And Twelfth Night. Did he bother celebrating Twelfth Night?

Before she could ask, he continued, "Jane is the second-oldest. She and her husband live in Yorkshire with their vast brood of offspring. Jane would collect every book in the kingdom if she could. Despite having two libraries, she insists her husband's definition of enough is never quite enough."

Annie raised a brow. "*Two* libraries? I'm beginnin' to understand why a bill from an Inverness dressmaker doesnae so much as flutter those bonnie eyelashes of yours."

His smile faded. His jaw flexed. It was a long while before he answered coldly, "Whatever wealth I own has been earned, I assure you. Every farthing."

She frowned. Obviously, she'd touched a sore tooth. "I didnae assume otherwise. Now, who drowned yer drawers in starch all of a sudden?"

"When you've seen as much of the world as I have, you realize a man's birth tells you very little about his true substance." His voice snapped like icy sails.

Confusing man.

Annie glanced behind her to where Mrs. MacBean slept soundly. She drew the old woman's blanket higher to protect her from the cold. Her fussing gave her time to formulate an answer. "If ye mean to imply I'm a wee bit curious about how rich ye are, then I must admit, ye have me."

"Naturally." A faint sneer curled the corner of his mouth. "Most women want to know what you can give them, be it fortune or title."

Ah, they were back to that, were they? She let a moment pass so he could hear himself. "So, yer mother—the one who loves cats and begs her son to come home for a visit—she's a mercenary sort, eh?"

He frowned. "No."

"Perhaps it's yer sisters. Let me guess. Annabelle married yer best friend for his title."

The frown deepened. He rolled his shoulders. "Of course not. She's been in love with Robert since they were children. He had no title."

"Not yer sisters, then. Hmm. Perhaps it was the modest mistress from Paris who soured ye."

"For the last time, she was a modiste. I should never have told you about her."

"Why did ye?"

"You asked how I learned about women's fashions. That is how."

"Right." She snorted. "And all the women's *fashions* ye've removed in yer time had naught to do with it, eh?"

"God, you are the most vexing—"

"Who was it that tried to trap ye like a prize stag, John Huxley?"

His breathing seemed to halt. His eyes flashed to her then away. He didn't answer.

Despite his stiffness, she nudged his shoulder with hers. "'Tis why ye havenae married, aye? Why ye've lingered here in the arse crease of Scotland, rebuilding a castle ye've no intention of keepin', makin' rubbish wagers with a crabbit auld man, wastin' yer time teachin' a hoyden to be a lady."

"You are not a waste of time."

She patted his knee. "I'd wager a mother like yers has a bride or two picked out for ye. A bit like preparin' a feast to welcome ye home—except that *ye're* the poor beastie on the platter. That's why ye dinnae answer her prayers and return to Nottinghamshire, where ye belong."

"Ewan Wylie helped me build the wealth you're so curious about. I owe him a great deal, not least my life. I've remained in Scotland to honor his wishes."

"That's pure shite."

He scraped a hand over his jaw. "Bloody hell, woman."

"Ye could have kept yer piece of Glendasheen without ever settin' foot upon Scottish soil. With Angus's nonsense, ye're better off keepin' the land than sellin' it, anyhow." She snorted. "Not like ye need the funds. Payin' dressmaker bills for lasses ye're not even tuppin' tells me that much."

"I had to settle matters with your father—"

"Nah. Ye had to hide somewhere. Glenscannadoo may not be the most hospitable place, but it's a long, miserable ride from Nottinghamshire. No obligatory visits to fash about. No schemin' *ladies* conspirin' to birth yer bairns and spend yer money."

Stony and scowling, he refused to look at her.

Aye, she had him. Bonnie as he was, her Englishman had probably been pursued since the day he'd donned trousers. And, given his descriptions of his childhood, she'd guess his family had been both wealthy and well connected. Phaetons weren't much use in farm fields and quarries, after all.

"So, who was the sly vixen that tried to steal yer purse and claim yer manly bits for trophies, eh? A London lass? A Nottinghamshire neighbor?"

His glare didn't budge from the road. While they'd been talking, darkness had begun to fall. It cast strange shadows over his eyes.

When he finally spoke, his voice was crisp. Quiet. Precise. "You're a fine one to ask such questions, Miss Tulloch, given you seek to marry a title." His eyes shifted to her. They were colder than a Highland winter. "Any lord will do, hmm?"

"I notice ye didnae answer my question."

"Why should I? You've avoided mine since our bargain was struck."

She frowned. He had a point. "It's not so much that I *want* to marry a lord. It's that I must."

"Why?" The word was low. Seething.

"To save a friend."

"What friend?"

"Ye dinnae ken him."

His jaw flickered.

"It's complicated," she insisted, fingering the edge of her blanket.

"Then explain." He gestured to the empty, darkening road and the half-treed hills around them. "We have time."

She sighed. "Ye willnae believe me. And ye'll think me mad. Everyone else does."

"Explain anyway." He used his commanding tone—the one that both frustrated and weirdly excited her.

She examined his hands, the way he held the reins loosely, never letting his tension affect the horses. His posture was straight and yet comfortable, his movements controlled. Despite her provocations, he hadn't bellowed threats or lobbed insults. He was a gentleman in the truest sense. More than that, he loved his family, eccentricities and all. Perhaps he would understand. Or, at least, listen.

"Very well, English," she said softly. "His name is Finlay."

As the last of the daylight weakened into gloom, she told John Huxley everything about her laddie. How he'd been with her since she was wee. How he'd comforted her when spiteful Grisel had convinced all the other girls to spit upon her as they passed, claiming it was the only way to protect themselves from her madness. How he'd blessed her plaid and promised it would keep her safe—which it had. How his wee little face had started turning gray, and his wee little voice had thinned, and how she'd panicked at the thought of losing him.

How she'd mourned him every day since he'd gone away.

Then, she explained about his visit. About his plea that she marry a lord so that, as her son, he could claim his rightful destiny.

And all the while, John Huxley listened. Silent. Calm. Unreadable.

"There ye have it, English," she finished. Her hands strangled the edge of the blanket. "Now ye ken why they call me Mad Annie. And why I must marry a lord."

A tiny frown formed between his brows. He nodded. But he didn't speak.

She twisted the blanket harder.

Silence thickened as he guided the horses around a bend. "Wanting to marry a title is hardly unique," he said finally. "There's no need to invent outlandish stories to justify your aim."

This time, she was the one who fell silent. Her stomach burned. Her jaw locked tight.

Of *course* the Englishman didn't believe her. Why should she expect him to be different? Even the Scots she'd known since childhood—who had all grown up believing tales about ghostly glens and cursed castles— thought she was mad.

This wasn't how ghosties behaved, they'd said. Mad Annie had simply invented a "friend" because she hadn't any real ones. That was why she talked to herself and dressed in such a peculiar fashion.

Nobody considered that she might be telling the truth. They were too eager to toss her in the rubbish pile.

After a while, Huxley ventured, "Dougal mentioned the trouble with your brother."

She watched the moon slip behind a cloud.

"Calton Hill Bridewell is an unpleasant place," he continued. "Broderick has been imprisoned there for, what, two months? I understand his trial has been deliberately delayed in hopes of charging him with murder rather than assault."

The wind picked up. She adjusted her blanket a bit higher and tucked her plaid a bit tighter around her neck.

"Someone powerful must be working against him," he murmured. "Assault might earn him transportation. Murder will mean hanging."

One of the horses snuffled. She thought it might be Jacqueline. She wondered if the horse had been named for Huxley's modest French mistress. The animal did have an unusually broad backside.

"If you are seeking a connection with sufficient influence to help your brother, marrying a lord is a rather permanent way to go about it."

She snorted. Shook her head. The Englishman was desperate to fit her into a frame he understood. Well, she didn't fit. And he could stow his suppositions up his—

"Miss Tulloch."

She rubbed her arms and blew into her hands. Full dark brought on a deeper cold. They had at least another five miles before reaching Glenscannadoo. She busied herself lighting the lantern.

"Annie."

Hearing her name on those perfect lips twisted her up tighter than rope. She steeled herself to remember who he was. Remember what he thought of her. "Aye, English?"

"Perhaps there's another way. Perhaps I—"

"This isnae about Broderick."

"It's understandable you'd want to help him. If a member of my family were imprisoned for shooting—"

"Broderick didnae shoot anybody." She secured the lantern and kept her gaze upon Jacqueline's backside. Looking at Huxley's perfect features only made her weak. "The craven bastards who conspired against him have no bluidy idea of the hell they've brought down upon themselves." Absently, she rubbed her ribs, wishing Finlay were with her now. Every time she thought about Broderick, her chest ached. "The MacPhersons protect their own."

"Does that include you?"

"Aye."

"Have you told them your intentions?"

Annie could feel the Englishman's eyes upon her. Studying her. Thinking he understood. He didn't.

"Obviously not. Look, marrying a title is ..." He sighed. "It's an ambitious prospect for anyone, Annie. Even daughters from prominent families, those who prepare their entire lives for an advantageous marriage, have little certainty of landing a lord. Most fail. Or require multiple seasons. Or both."

"Are ye backin' out of our bargain?" she snapped.

A long pause. "No."

"Then *haud yer wheesht*. Ye dinnae ken what ye're talkin' about."

"The marriage mart?" His chuckle sounded cynical. "I know it all too well, I'm afraid."

Wind surged again, this time gusting through the thickening trees. Jacqueline nickered and shook her head. The lantern glowed bronze amidst the vast blue dark, but it didn't penetrate more than a few feet.

Annie checked on Mrs. MacBean, who appeared to be enjoying her snug bed. Then she glanced at the

Englishman. Evidently, he was done smiling for the evening, his mouth now flat and his eyes weary.

An odd jangle sounded ahead of them. A series of clicks. The creaking whine of an old wheel. Annie straightened. Squinted. Blast. She couldn't see a bloody thing with the steep hills and dense trees blocking the moonlight. "Did ye hear that, Engl—"

Three figures emerged from the thick underbrush to stand in front of their cart. Two had pistols.

One was David Skene.

Chapter Ten

"Tell me, English," Annie said loudly as John drew the horses to a stop. "What are the chances of findin' three men who could pass for rodents on the same stretch of road?"

John quickly sorted through all the ways he could shut her up. Her comment was reckless, though not far wrong. The three men were all wiry, filthy, and wearing hats that had seen better centuries. But each one shared verminous features. Perhaps it was the eyes. Beady as all hell.

"Mad Annie Tulloch," said the one in the center—the rat, obviously, with his conical nose and long teeth. He was the only one without a pistol. John judged him the greatest threat. The other two—a mole and a vole, respectively—were holding their pistols all wrong. Were the weapons even loaded? It was too dark to be certain.

John elected to keep his posture relaxed. He pretended to shift positions while transferring the reins into his left hand. "Did you gentlemen lose your way in the dark?"

"Nah," Annie replied before John could shush her. "They're out here runnin' their shite whisky where they shouldnae be." That foolish, defiant chin thrust forward. "Isnae that so, Skene? Either that or ye're lookin' for a fist to flatten that unfortunate nose."

"Ye offerin', lassie?" The rat leered at her. "I fancy a scrapper."

John's blood heated until the urge to do far more than flatten the man's nose beat a pounding rhythm in his ears. But he needed to stay calm. Reasonable. He needed to get them out of this with minimal bloodshed.

Annie saw no such necessity. "Only tuppin' ye're likely to experience is with the mud ye land in after the sheep rejects yer advances."

The rodent on the right snorted. The rat swatted his fellow's head, knocking his cap to the ground.

"Why did you stop us?" John kept his voice low and calm. If he'd been alone, these men would have already been dispatched. But Annie was with him.

For John, Annie changed every calculation.

The rat ambled closer and patted Jacqueline's neck. The horse snorted. She'd always been a discerning sort.

"Thought to pass a message is all." Those beady eyes focused on John. "Ye're English."

John didn't bother to affirm the observation.

Annie, on the other hand, couldn't resist. "Brilliant, as always." She sat forward, drawing the blackguard's eyes back to her. "Wee bit of advice, Skene. When ye're operatin' with half the wits of everybody else, best ye apply them to useful matters. Like pissin' with yer back to the wind. Or keepin' yer smugglin' routes clear of MacPherson territory."

Skene's lips slid back to reveal his prominent front teeth. "Since we're tradin' advice, lass, here's mine: Ye've naught but a fancy Englishman by yer side. I reckon he'd make ye a fine cup of tea, but he's nae MacPherson." His grin faded as he tilted his head toward the men with pistols. "Best *ye* mind yer shrewish tongue."

Annie started to answer, but John had had enough. "What is your message?" he demanded.

Skene's gaze slid to him then back to Annie. "My mates at the Bridewell tell me things are a wee bit rough for yer brother there."

John felt Annie's stillness.

"Bad as they are," Skene continued, "they can always be worse." The rat grinned. "I could ask my mates to look after him, provided the MacPhersons dinnae trouble me too much. Be a pity if somethin' happened before his trial, eh?"

"Ye disgustin' piece of—"

John grasped her arm, squeezing to shut her up and keep her in place. "We'll convey the message," he said. "Now, I fear we must be on our way."

"Bluidy hell, English. Ye're just going to let him—"

He gave her a small shake then tipped his hat. "Gentlemen." The men didn't move, but he did, snapping the reins. The horses started forward, but Skene grasped Jacqueline's bridle and slunk near Annie. Then, the blackguard made his greatest mistake of the evening.

He put a hand on Annie's knee and gripped.

In an instant, John withdrew his own pistol from inside his coat, leveled it upon Skene's forehead, and cocked the weapon. "Remove your hand," he ordered softly.

Shock froze the rat's features. Round, beady eyes crossed as they took in the barrel. Skene swallowed. Lifted his hand. Backed away.

John held his aim. "Remote roads are dangerous at night, gentlemen. Years ago, I traveled a similar route in the mountains of Spain. The brigands who waylaid me then would likely warn you of the risks—were they breathing. Alas, they were buried right there by the roadside." He smiled. "What remained of them, at any rate." He handed Annie the reins and withdrew his second pistol, pointing it at Skene's fellow rodents. "We'll be on our way, now. It's been a pleasure."

Annie took his hint and started the horses forward again. The men lowered their pistols and parted.

For the next quarter-hour, John let her drive while he kept watch. Finally, they rounded a bend and began the long descent into the glen. The loch glistened in the moonlight. Trees sighed in the softening wind. The faint glow of the village flickered in the distance.

Annie held her silence while he tucked his pistols back inside his coat. When he reached for the reins, however, she asked hoarsely, "Why didnae ye say ye carried weapons with ye?"

"On remote roads after dark, any fool would." He frowned at her. "Why would you assume I'd do otherwise?"

Her long pause was unflattering.

"I've survived a lot of places more dangerous than 'the arse crease of Scotland,' you know." He watched her expression, trying to discern whether she'd been rattled by the encounter with Skene. The stiff set of her shoulders indicated she had. Perhaps a distraction was in order. "In Africa, an unwary man makes a fine feast."

"Feast? Ye mean … lions?" She stared at him, round-eyed, as though she'd never met him before.

"Mmm. Or leopards. Or rhinoceros." He gave a theatrical shudder. "Bloody heavy when they sit on you."

Her frown signaled the first hint of skepticism, though curiosity shone in those wide blue eyes.

"Oddly, predators weren't the creatures I found most unsettling."

"What, then?"

He leaned closer. "Giraffes."

"Are they dangerous?"

"Oh, no. Not unless you're a treetop. Leaf-eaters, the lot of them."

"Then, what's unsettlin'?"

"Too gangly. Dreadfully long necks. It's simply unnatural."

She glanced around. Narrowed her gaze upon him. Then swatted his arm. "Cheeky Englishman. There's no need to invent *outlandish stories*. I'm certain the giraffes trembled at the sight of yer wee pistols."

He chuckled, glad to see his distraction had worked. Keeping his tone light, he remarked, "Skene seems a rather unpleasant fellow. I take it he and the MacPhersons share a mutual dislike."

"Skene is a smuggler. A few years past, he offered to transport MacPherson whisky up to Inverness and down to Glasgow. Broderick declined. Skene hates him. Until now, he's been naught more than a pest."

"So, you suspect he's behind Broderick's arrest."

"Aye."

John frowned. "Has he a partner?"

She snorted. "Yer thought is the same as mine. That rat-faced bugger is certainly hateful enough to do this to Broderick. But is he smart enough?" She shook her head. "Not likely."

"The courts are surprisingly difficult to manipulate. If it were easily done, I'd have settled my land dispute with Angus months ago."

She didn't reply.

"Annie," he murmured. "Whoever is helping Skene must hold a good deal of sway with the justiciary."

"I ken." She sniffed and straightened her blanket.

"He's either blackmailing someone or wielding significant coercion. The kind of coercion only a peer can manage."

"Aye."

"Do not put yourself between these men."

"Broderick is my brother, English. I'll do what I must."

Like bloody hell she would. John would speak to her father. The MacPhersons should be warned. They should protect her from men like Skene. And the harpies in the village. And her own infernal recklessness.

Behind them, blankets and straw rustled as Mrs. MacBean stirred from her long doze. "Are we nearly there, Mr. Brodie?"

He'd given up on correcting her in favor of keeping their conversations brief. As it was, he'd never look at butter or root vegetables the same way again.

"Not long now, Mrs. MacBean. Fortunately, you slept through the more tedious parts of our journey."

"Hmmph. That's just what yer uncle used to say."

"Dear God," groaned Annie. "Not this again."

The old woman patted his shoulder fondly. "Did I ever tell ye about the size of John Brodie's caber, laddie? Now, that was a sight to behold."

From the moment John delivered Annie to MacPherson House until the moment he walked out the door, he doubted he'd survive the night. On one hand, it was gratifying to know he wasn't the only one Annie brought to the point of bellowing madness. On the other hand, while she casually dug her own grave, she also dug his.

Minutes after she led him into the small parlor, three towering MacPherson brothers flanked the door with their arms folded, glowering menacingly in John's direction while Angus questioned Annie.

"I left ye a note, auld man. Is it my fault ye dinnae bother with readin'?"

"Yer note said ye'd gone to the dressmaker." Angus's rumbling voice reached a roar. "Ye didnae say in bluidy *Inverness!*"

"I didnae say it was here, either."

"And ye went with *him!*"

"We had a chaperone."

"She's half blind!"

"She sees well enough to make yer liniment." Annie shrugged. "Most days."

Angus began to redden with rage.

Annie, of course, could not resist making it worse. "Ye're just vexed because I'm helpin' him win yer wager."

"I'm vexed because now ye'll have to marry the sodding—"

"Rubbish."

"—Englishman, which means I'll never be rid of him."

John cleared his throat, preparing to object—or at least correct Angus's assumptions.

Annie answered first. "I'll not be marryin' Huxley, ye crabbit auld man."

Angus crowded his daughter until half of her stood in his shadow.

She merely raised a brow.

"Ye'll marry him if I say ye will."

Her chin rose. "That would be daft."

"If he's touched ye, lass—"

"He hasnae. For God's sake, he's nae courtin' me. He's *teachin'* me."

"To do what?" Angus roared.

"Land myself a lord!" Silence fell, thick with the tension between father and daughter. "I want to marry a lord."

From Angus's sudden stillness, John surmised it was the first she'd told him of her endeavor. Internally, John winced. Angus might be wealthy for a Highlander, but his origins were humble. He had little use for titles and less regard for their unearned power. Hearing that his daughter pursued a husband from the peerage must have felt like a rejection.

When he finally turned his furious black gaze upon John, the man's eyes were nearly bulging. Yes, indeed.

Rejection and rage. And, because Angus would sooner die than vent that rage at Annie, John became the sole, unfortunate target.

He attempted reason first. "Calm yourself, MacPherson. There's no need for violence." John retreated toward the windows, giving himself room while he braced for attack. Could a man prepare for four sets of MacPherson fists doing maximum damage? Probably not. "I was the one who insisted she obtain a chaperone."

Breathing like a bull, Angus shot a questioning glance toward Annie, who nodded.

"Miss Tulloch seeks to marry a peer," John continued. "I've some ... connection to that world. She asked if I might serve as a tutor in matters of decorum." Unbidden, his eyes returned to Annie, whose hair was damp from the misty night and whose plaid could use a proper washing. Her gaze narrowed as though anticipating harsh judgments of her appearance. If she knew what he really thought—what he really wanted— she wouldn't be glaring. She'd be blushing.

Her father was more perceptive. "Huxley, I've warned ye already," Angus growled. "Ye keep those bluidy English hands off my daughter, or it willnae matter whether yer *connections* include that fat king of yers." The man stalked toward John, leaning close and quietly growling, "Or an earl's whelp."

John froze. He *knew?*

John glanced behind him at the three towering brothers. Rannoch seemed amused. Alexander seemed murderous. Campbell seemed forbidding. Nothing unusual there. Did they know, too?

Did Annie? She was frowning at her father, arms crossed, head shaking. Annoyed, perhaps. But no. John didn't think she knew.

Angus continued his threats at a volume only John could hear. "Unless ye mean to put yer ring upon her finger, lad, ye'd best keep yer distance. No matter who a man is, gelded is gelded, I reckon."

His ring? Cold flooded his body. No. He didn't want a wife. He especially didn't want one as frustrating and fiery and foul-mouthed as …

Annie. There she stood, chin tilted and cornflower eyes flashing.

"Och, ye're waddin' up yer drawers fer nothin', auld man," she scoffed. "Huxley is too bluidy *proper* to luik in my direction." She came forward and tugged Angus's arm, trying to pull him away from John and soothe him at once. "Dinnae fash."

Angus didn't budge. "He wants ye. I can see it."

"Nah. 'Tis likely he'll marry some milk-faced lass his mother serves up at a Nottinghamshire supper." Those cornflower eyes caught him unawares. They should be teasing. Amused. They were not. Rather, they seemed melancholy as the moon. "Isnae that so, English?"

Something foreign moved through him. He couldn't name it. Couldn't describe it. All he knew was that the wistful note in her voice made him want to howl. And lift her off her feet onto his shoulder. And haul her out of her father's house back to his castle. Then, he wanted to …

His breath halted. His hands clenched into fists.

He wanted to … God, he wanted to …

Claim her.

Yes, that was it. The knowledge surged. Thrummed. It took everything he had to hold still.

What the devil was wrong with him? He didn't know, but something obviously was. She was bent on marrying a title—any title—regardless of the man who came with it. He'd spent his life avoiding women like her.

Apart from which, her father had just threatened to remove what Annie called his "manly bits." And he heard at least two of her brothers making growling noises near the door. And her hair was a ragged, damp mess. And she couldn't get through a sentence without cursing. And, despite his best efforts, he suspected she'd never be comfortable dining at his mother's table.

And the way she'd spoken to a simple, freckled boy about his new pup had stirred something inside him he didn't understand. Something needful. Near painful.

"I should go," he rasped.

He didn't belong here. Annie didn't belong to him. Or with him. Or beneath him, moaning his name. Yet, he'd spent the day buying her gowns, envisioning her in each one. Fantasizing about how azure silk would look with that fiery hair. Contemplating what a proper corset might do for her lush bosom. Had he lost his bloody mind? Probably.

"English?" Her brow puckered with concern. "Ye've gone a bit peely."

"I should go," he repeated, pivoting toward the door.

"Angus didnae mean it. He's just fashed I'll marry ye and he'll have to pay someone to cook his dinner." She followed him to the door where her brothers waited like ominous sentries.

From inside the room, Angus spoke. His voice was remarkably quiet and threaded with steel. "Ye're not to see her again, Huxley. No more teachin'. No more visits."

Annie spun to face her father. "Dinnae be ridicu—"

"*Haud yer wheesht* and listen, lass," he barked. "Ye seek him out again, and I'll make that bonnie face of his far less bonnie. That's a promise. Ye ken?"

"But I—"

"Dinnae try me, Annie." His voice was harsh. Unyielding. "If ye want to keep yer place in my house, do as I tell ye!"

Shock widened her eyes and rounded her lips. Watching her expression, John knew Angus had never before made such a threat.

"Da," she whispered as though it was the only word she had left.

John hated the hurt on her face. He wanted to gather her in and hold her tight until it disappeared. He'd felt the same after the women in the dress shop had ridiculed her.

But she wasn't his. He must remember that. He might have fooled himself for a while, savoring their game more than was wise. She might make him feel alive after a long stretch in the grave.

But she bloody well wasn't his. And he was damaging her by pretending differently.

Using her distraction as an opportunity, he nodded his understanding to Angus, who looked devastated to have wounded his daughter but determined not to show it. Then, John slipped between the tallest two brothers and made for the entrance hall.

Just as he exited the front door, Campbell caught up with him. "I need to speak with ye."

Silent and unsmiling, Campbell MacPherson was intimidating on a good day. Now, in the frost-coated dark, the man seemed more monster than man.

"Your father made himself clear." John tugged on his hat. "I'll keep my distance. Nothing more to say."

"Annie mentioned ye ran into David Skene on yer return from Inverness." Amusement entered the other man's voice. "She said ye handled yerself in a right entertainin' fashion. Two pistols. A wild tale about Spanish brigands." He paused. "Ye kept her safe. I'm grateful to ye."

"There was never any question," John replied softly. "And the *wild tale* was true."

This time, the pause was longer. "Da believes ye'll use Annie to gain an advantage then cast her aside when ye return to England."

"I'm aware."

"A man bent on such a scheme would have no use for a chaperone. He'd take what he wanted because he could."

"Indeed."

A nod was followed by another deep, considering silence. "Skene's attacks have been bolder than I anticipated."

John scowled at the memory of Skene's hand reaching for Annie. "You'd do well to dispatch that problem sooner rather than later."

"Aye. We plan to."

John hesitated, willing his next warning to remain where it belonged—in his head. But out it came, dark and true. "If he comes near her again, I will do it myself."

Campbell stilled then edged closer. In the faint light from the windows, John could just make out his expression. The heavy brow was furrowed and the jaw was hard, but he wasn't threatening. At least, not toward John. "Do ye ken which lord Annie aims to wed?"

"No." Another surge of resentment made him grind his teeth. He'd felt it before. It was stronger now. "My impression is that she seeks the title, not a specific man."

"'Tis likely Skene has a backer. We dinnae ken who, but he's almost certainly titled."

"I concluded the same."

"Broderick is in danger." A wince around the man's eyes spoke of anguish carefully disguised. "Skene's gang runs a portion of the Bridewell. We must find a way to free him. Soon."

John glanced at his cart then at the windows of MacPherson House. Then, he eyed the man before him and sighed. "Miss Tulloch's title hunt may succeed, but it's unlikely to bear fruit before summer." He hesitated before making his offer. God, he was an idiot. "When you've run out of options for freeing your brother, come see me. I have connections which may be of use."

Campbell nodded.

John climbed onto his cart and took up the reins. Then, he paused. "MacPherson."

"Aye?"

He hesitated. Bloody hell, he shouldn't be doing this.

She wasn't his. Only an idiot would intervene where no one wanted him.

An idiot. That's what he was.

"The first dressmaker your sister visited today was here in Glenscannadoo. The women in the shop made things extremely unpleasant for her. I gather this was far from the first time such abuse has occurred."

Campbell didn't speak, but the look in his eyes mirrored John's fury. Good. She should have told her family long ago.

John named the women involved before continuing, "I plan to speak to the man who owns the shop's building. Such poor business practices shouldn't be tolerated in a fine place like this, wouldn't you agree?"

"Aye," came the low growl. "I do."

For the first time since arriving at MacPherson House, John felt satisfaction curving the corners of his mouth. "Splendid." He touched the brim of his hat. "Do give my best to your brothers."

"And my sister?" Campbell's question was weighted with meaning.

His smile faded. His chest tightened.

She wasn't his.

The truth was she never would be. So, he snapped the reins, drove into the dark, and let silence be his answer.

CHAPTER ELEVEN

When a man hired a cook, he hoped—no, *expected*—to recognize the dishes on his table as food. John had been many places and eaten many unusual things. But the bowl of grayish, mealy soup before him was a mystery.

He set his youngest sister's letter on his desk and peered at the tray his new cook had laid before him. Proudly, no less.

"What is it?" he inquired.

Marjorie MacDonnell, Dougal's mother, grinned until her angular cheeks rounded. She used her apron to wipe her hands. "Skink, sir. Cooked as ye'd find it round Moray."

Just how badly did these Scots hate him? Enough for poison?

He eyed the steaming bowl of *whatever*, which smelled like old fish and cold ashes. His stomach winced. "My thanks, Mrs. MacDonnell." He slid the tray to the other side of his desk.

"Ye dinnae favor finnan haddie?"

If he knew what that was, perhaps he could say one way or the other. But the evening had grown late, and he was tired. "I haven't much appetite, I'm afraid."

She frowned like the mother she was. Then, she laid a roughened hand upon his forehead. "Nae fever," she diagnosed, clicking her tongue. "Yer appetite's been poorly for nigh on two months now. Man yer age should be eatin' twice what ye do." She patted his shoulder. "I ken what ye need."

He doubted it.

"Somethin' a bit sweeter, eh? My shortbread would tempt a dead man to rise for breakfast."

Given that her regular bread was dry crust all the way through, he suspected the only thing that would prompt a man to rise was being pummeled by the weighty loaves.

The woman tapped her chin. "A wee bit late to start on it tonight. We'll plan for tomorrow instead." She patted his shoulder again before moving to the study door. "Had ye hired me ere Hogmanay, I'd have made ye my clootie dumplin'. Now, there's a rare treat."

Clootie dumpling did sound closer to what he was craving than gray skink, but he didn't think Mrs. MacDonnell had any solutions to offer him.

Only one woman did. And God, he missed her more than he should. Crusts of hard, dark bread mocked him from the tray near his elbow.

Annie's bread was a thing of splendor.

He wished it was all he missed. He wished he'd kissed her properly when he'd had the chance.

Running a hand over his face, he shoved up from his chair and wandered to the hearth. Before he could stop them, thoughts of her invaded his mind like mist over the loch.

How was she faring? He wanted to know. Was she practicing her glide? Had she managed to curb her vulgarities? Did she still go silent now and then, thinking of Broderick's suffering?

He had no way of knowing. They'd both kept their distance. The few times he'd glimpsed her crossing the village square or riding beside her brothers in the MacPherson wagon, she'd appeared the same. Thinner, perhaps. Whiter. That banner-bright hair was more neatly trimmed around her cheeks, he'd noticed.

Winter had been hard. Twice, snow had come in great loads, lingered a week or two then melted and refrozen. The glen's third blizzard presently gusted outside, a final blast before spring.

John was accustomed to being alone. He'd often been so during long weeks at sea or crossing mountain ranges from one country to the next. He'd never minded, really. Never pined for companionship. Rather, the lands themselves had fed him—an orange sun sinking behind umbrella-shaped trees, a dolphin leaping from impossibly blue water, a heated rainstorm scented with plumeria.

He missed that feeling—the wonder of a sight no one else had seen. The real problem, of course, was that he'd stopped feeling it long before he'd come to Scotland. Long before he'd stopped seeking it.

By the end of his life, Ewan Wylie had begged him to go home before he got himself killed. Now, John wanted to laugh. Because being dead sounded better than this bloody emptiness.

He rubbed his returning beard. It made his face itch, but he couldn't be bothered to shave. She'd liked him better without it, he recalled.

The thought made him smile. Lately, she was the only thought that did.

The last day they'd spent together, admiration had lit her up every time she'd looked at him. He pictured her now, standing inside an Inverness dressmaker's shop, licking those pert lips and maddening him with her arguments.

Well, I dinnae ken if I can be bland, English. But decorative. Perhaps that I can do.

Indeed, she was anything but bland. He missed her. *Craved* her the way some men craved strong drink or poppy smoke.

At night, the craving had transformed into dreams so erotic, he'd become desperate to have them end—and equally desperate to have them return. In the past, finding a willing woman to manage his needs had been simple. Women liked him. Always had. A playful grin, a bit of flattery. Easy.

Now, nothing made him grin but her.

Nothing made him hard but her.

Nothing made him want but her.

How incomprehensibly mad. It was the worst thing to happen to him since the emptiness had begun seven years earlier. Back then, he'd distracted himself with wayfaring in Africa and building ships in Sunderland and making runs to the West Indies with a half-sotted Ewan Wylie bellowing at the mast.

Then, Ewan drank himself to death. And the emptiness caught up with John. Now, here he was in the arse crease of Scotland longing for a scarlet-haired hoyden to walk through his door and call him English.

Just that. Her voice. A sweet lilt of amusement. A wry taste of taunt.

He rubbed his jaw, watching the fire dance. It looked like her hair. Cursing, he returned to his desk. Perhaps whisky would improve this cursed mood. At least it might let him sleep.

Minutes later, a knock sounded at the study door. "Come," he called hoarsely.

"I'm headed home, sir." It was Dougal, looking weary from the day's labors.

They'd nearly finished the castle's interior. With Dougal, his two brothers, three sisters, and his mother all working at Glendasheen Castle, the place was coming alive, transforming into a proper house with a proper staff and real furniture.

When spring arrived, John would put Dougal and his brothers to work improving the gardens and the road along the loch. They'd need better roads if the MacDonnells were to travel safely to and from the village. Visitors, too. He didn't want visitors coming to the castle until that road was repaired.

A brief vision of a red-haired hoyden struggling to pull a reluctant donkey through a muddy mess flashed through his mind. He shook his head. No. He couldn't have that. What if she hurt herself? What if she fell?

"Er, Mam said ye werenae keen on her skink." Dougal again. He was eyeing John's untouched tray and wringing his cap between two hands. "I hope ye're not set on dismissin' her, Mr. Huxley. She does burn the potatoes from time to time, but it's not for lack of tryin'."

John frowned. "Is that why the soup is gray?"

Nodding sheepishly, Dougal explained, "It's usually white. A fine dish, well prepared. If ye fancy smoked haddock, that is." He paused. "She makes a grand shortbread, sir. I promise if ye keep her on, she'll do better."

Clearly, the man had oversold his mother's talents. But John didn't know how much longer he'd be in Scotland, so there was little point in seeking out a replacement. Dougal's family needed the employment. They were all hard workers, respectful and reliable.

"Not to worry," John replied. "Your mother's position is safe."

"Thank ye, sir." Dougal dropped his gaze to his hands. "We cannae thank ye enough for all ye've done."

"Thank me with shortbread, hmm?"

The other man smiled gratefully and turned to leave.

"Dougal."

"Aye, sir?"

John hesitated. "Have you heard anything about the MacPhersons?"

Dougal turned solemn. "Nothin' good. Broderick MacPherson's bein' charged with murder. His kin are fightin' the High Court, but it doesnae bode well."

As he left, cold settled into John's gut. All winter, he'd waited for Campbell to ask for his help. None of the MacPhersons had contacted him. He imagined Annie's pain as she waited for her brother's fate to be decided. The urge to see her, to comfort her was a deep, agonizing itch with no relief in sight.

He shouldn't feel this. She shouldn't matter this much.

To distract himself, John picked up Kate's letter, thinking he should finish reading it. His mother insisted his youngest sister needed "brotherly guidance"—whatever that meant. He'd just started on the second page when another knock sounded.

"Come," he said absently, wondering what on earth Kate meant by quoting a lengthy passage from a Walter Scott novel, followed by a brief scene from *Macbeth*. She appeared to be asking about tartans and clans, but with Kate, conversation often ran in nonsensical circles.

Dougal cleared his throat. "Beg yer pardon, sir."

"Did you forget something, Dougal?"

"As I was leavin', I discovered a gentleman outside. I fear the cold has him a wee bit addled. He asked for *Lord* Huxley."

John's head jerked up. The man entering behind Dougal was roughly John's height but had broader shoulders and nearly black hair. That hair dripped across a scowling face. Leaning upon his cane, the man moved stiffly into the lantern light.

"Con?" John blinked to be sure. But yes, it was Robert Conrad. Here. In his castle. In bloody *Scotland*. John bounded to his feet and embraced his sodden, weary best friend. "Good God, man. What are you doing here?"

"Presently? Freezing to death."

They pounded each other's backs before John asked Dougal to have his mother prepare tea then invited Robert to sit by the fire. "Annabelle sent you, I take it," John said. He handed Robert a glass of whisky and took a sip of his own. "Her last letter sounded motherly."

Sighing, Robert relaxed into his chair, propped his cane beside his knee. "She is a mother many times over. But no, she didn't send me." Brooding blue eyes grew solemn. "I came on my own accord. Your letters have been more bleak than usual the past several months."

John stared into his glass. "It's winter." He took a drink then pointed to the window. "As you can see, bleak is something of a theme."

"There's more to it than the weather, man." Robert shrugged out of his coat and resettled himself before saying quietly, "I'm here to tell you it's time."

"Time for what?"

Robert took a drink and ran a hand through his thick, damp hair. "For you to stop running."

John's gut hardened. He tilted his glass to indicate their surroundings. "Odd sort of running. I've been here two years."

"You know what I mean."

He knew. But he didn't have to like it. "My father is in excellent health. Chances are he'll outlive us all."

"Producing an heir is important, but that's not what I'm talking about, Hux." Robert stared down into his glass, swirling the golden liquid. "Do you think we don't see? You've been miserable for years."

Cold settled deep. John tossed back the last of his whisky and hoped the burn would help. It didn't. "Miserable is a strong word."

"Is it?" Robert shook his head and sighed. "Don't forget, I spent seven years in a similar state."

"That was different."

Robert raised a questioning brow.

"You knew what was missing."

A smile touched Robert's lips. "Annabelle. Yes. But knowing did not lessen the pain of it." The smile faded. "I do understand, Hux. The need to prove your mettle. The need for distraction. To fill the emptiness with something—anything." He swirled his glass thoughtfully. "It works sometimes. So, you keep doing it. But more often, it doesn't work at all. Even when it does, you're left with less than you had before. Somehow, the things you do to distract yourself corrode the hollow places, leaving nothing but a cavernous hunger that will never be satisfied."

Yes. That was it precisely. John wished hearing Robert describe his problem helped. It didn't. If anything, he felt colder. Older. Tired. He refilled his glass and Robert's then sat back with a sigh. "Let us drink, old friend." He raised his glass. "To Annabelle. Thank heaven she is more forgiving than you deserve."

Robert chuckled. "I'll drink to that."

Mrs. MacDonnell entered with tea and informed John she'd readied a bedchamber for his guest. When they were alone again, Robert eyed him with a speculative light. "You could be happy, too, you know. Perhaps the solution is the same for you as it was for me."

"A wife?" He snorted. "For the thousandth time, I don't want a—"

"Was she so very special, then?"

His chest tightened. He took another drink. "Who?"

"You know who."

He rubbed his jaw. Then his eyes. They burned. God, he was tired. "Special? No. That's the problem. She was entirely commonplace."

She was Jacqueline Marchand, a half-French diamond-of-the-first-water who, as it turned out, had muddied her waters rather thoroughly before entering her first London season. He'd met the stunning beauty at Almack's seven years earlier.

John was seven-and-twenty by the time he decided to return from his extended grand tour to partake in the season. Naturally, his mother and father were over the moon.

"About time, son," his father had cheered, hazel eyes twinkling. "A wife is just the thing to settle a man's restlessness. No need to seek splendors abroad when you've a fine woman at home."

Mama had cooed and fussed, insisting he hire a tailor and a valet. "Oh, you're the image of your father, dearest," she'd wept, patting his lapel. "My sweet, handsome boy. A husband. And soon, a father, too?" She'd waved her hands and clutched her handkerchief, squeezing him so tightly, he'd thought she might crack a rib.

For a while, he'd let their excitement infect his thinking.

He'd entered Almack's one cool April evening with an odd shiver of anticipation. Perhaps he'd find a woman to love the way Robert loved Annabelle, he'd thought, or the way Papa loved Mama. He'd scanned the crowd of watercolor misses with their shy glances from behind fluttering fans. Could the one in the pink dress be her? Would the one with the yellow sash make him long for home more than the next shore?

He didn't know. But the adventure of it all had turned his head.

Then, *she* had walked into the room. Her hair wasn't an extraordinary color, merely a dark shade of blonde, looped in fetching curls along her cheeks and adorned with a sparkling tiara. But her face. Her face had been exquisite. Full lips that trembled just so. A petite nose and long lashes. She'd been slender. Remote. Graceful. A moonlit nymph glistening among gauche pretenders.

He'd wanted her with all the vigor and blindness of a man in thrall. He'd persuaded an acquaintance to perform an introduction. Like a trout after juicy bait, he'd trailed her the rest of the evening, ignoring all the other young ladies who angled for his favor. Who would notice mere mortals when *Jacqueline* was near?

After that night, her hook was truly set. Every event she was rumored to attend, he'd wheedled an invitation. Every waltz a hostess promised, he'd positioned himself to claim. Within a few short weeks, he was planning their wedding. St. George's, of course. His sister, Jane, had married there. The breakfast would be at his family's townhouse on Grosvenor Street. He'd wear his midnight superfine tailcoat, the one Eugenia and Kate both agreed fitted him best.

He still remembered Jacqueline's voice, like gossamer satin. Her skin, glowing with a blush that seemed almost otherworldly. He remembered kissing her in her uncle's parlor, the taste of marmalade still on her lips, sweet with a hint of bitter. He remembered her sigh as she insisted they must wait. Wait until marriage. He wouldn't wish to disgrace her, would he?

God, his blindness had been stupefying.

He'd been on his way to beg her uncle for her hand, stupidly imagining how their babes might look with his eyes and her nose, when he'd discovered her naked and moaning beneath another man.

The father of the babe she carried, as it turned out.

Romping inside a stall of her uncle's stable, the pair hadn't heard him enter. But he'd heard everything. Jacqueline giggling as she never did for him. Panting and grunting as she never would for him. Declaring the man between her thighs her "amour" as she never had with him.

And afterward, he'd punished himself by hiding. Lingering. Listening. He'd heard the man chuckle at the idea of being kept like a mistress.

Where will you keep me when you are Lady Huxley, my love?

Nearby. A cottage, perhaps. Oh, Gerard, I must have you close, for I cannot bear the thought of our babe being too far from his father.

What of you? Surely you will suffer with only Huxley to satisfy this greedy little body.

A moan. A gasp. *That is why I must keep you near,* mon amour. *I can bear his touch only by clinging to thoughts of you.*

A masculine laugh. *And thoughts of his fortune,* n'est-ce pas?

John's discovery of Jacqueline's true nature had been a brutal lesson, but it had also been a boon. No longer had he been blinded by the rare good fortune of men like Robert or Papa, who'd found loyal, loving wives to drive them mad.

Women—most of them, at any rate—sought marriage for practical reasons. He couldn't even blame them, really. A woman without a husband had few options. Some might rely on family or find steady employment. Some might sell themselves to men in a more direct fashion. But the rest were left to languish and age until death arrived to claim them—women like Mrs. MacBean, for example, scraping together a meager existence from forage and MacPherson charity.

Marriage for love was the exception. The rule was trade—a title or fortune in exchange for access to a soft body and a fertile womb. Jacqueline might have wounded his pride, but he'd escaped her trap before any real harm had been done.

The lesson had been invaluable. Thereafter, he'd been watchful for signs of a woman's avarice—her focus upon material possessions and social connections, her excitement at the anticipation of victory in the marriage hunt—and he'd never been disappointed.

It was all a game. By the end of the season, he'd had enough.

Since then, he'd seen very little to change his mind. Even Annie wanted to marry a title.

A damned, worthless title.

Would she accept a doddering, toothless man? A cruel, witless fool? He'd seen women marry worse to become a countess or baroness or marchioness. Who would Annie allow to touch her? Who would she let rut between her thighs, grunting and huffing and sweating as he planted an heir in her belly? Who would she make fat on her bread and gravy? Who would she—

"Careful, Hux," murmured Robert. "You're going to shatter that glass. Then you'll be bleeding all over. Your housekeeper has gone to bed, and I'm too deuced tired to clean up after you."

John blinked. Indeed, his hand was white with tension.

"I didn't think the Frenchwoman still mattered enough to vex you."

He blinked again. Frowned. "Who?"

Robert took a sip and raised a brow.

John shook his head, hoping to clear it. "She wasn't who I was thinking about."

"Hmm. Intriguing. Go on."

John blew out a breath. Eyeing Robert carefully, he wondered if his old friend might offer some advice. God knew, when it came to Annie, he needed it. And Robert had always been sensible. "There is ... a woman."

"Naturally."

"She is unlike any female I've ever encountered."

Robert's heavy brows arched. "Unusual."

"Yes, she is that."

"No, I meant it's unusual for you to discover a specimen you've never seen before." His friend's mouth quirked. "As I recall, you sampled every variety available—and they were *all* available to you."

John smiled faintly. "Youthful sport, merely. No, Annie is ... different. I cannot explain it." He sat forward and set his glass on the floor, leaning toward Robert to make his point. "She says whatever she's thinking, be it vulgar or insulting or brazen. No matter. Out it comes."

"Hmm. How old did you say she was?"

"Four-and-twenty. Roughly. I'm not certain when her birthday is. I shall ask Dougal tomorrow. They've known each other since childhood. Or, as she likes to say, 'since we were wee.'"

"Wee. So, she is Scottish, then."

John rubbed his lower lip between his thumb and finger. "She makes the best bread I've ever eaten, Con. I've no idea how she does it. Like clouds. Warm, crusty clouds. And her gravy." He closed his eyes and groaned. "Good God, she could tempt armies to fall at her feet for one blessed taste."

"Or a smitten Englishman, it seems."

Vaguely, John knew Robert had said something aggravating. But he was preoccupied with finding the proper way to explain her. How did one describe the indescribable? "I took her to Inverness," he murmured. "We went shopping. She hates shopping. Understandable. The women in her village have treated her abominably." He waved a hand. "Not to worry. I took care of it."

"You did."

"Oh, yes. Flora MacDonnell's work as a seamstress has dried up. A new dressmaker moved into her former shop. The rental income is meager, but I was able to purchase the building for quite a reasonable sum."

"You purchased a building so that you could evict its tenant."

"Hmm. And Grisel MacDonnell has been finding Glenscannadoo a hostile place, indeed, since her husband took the children and left for Canada. Seems all he needed was a bit of funding for his passage. According to Dougal, Grisel has talked of relocating to Dingwall." He sighed. "As punishments go, it is insufficient, I admit. But I cannot call them out. They are females, after all."

"Indeed. But you felt it necessary to intervene on behalf of … Annie, was it?"

"I had to. They'd tormented her for years."

Robert cleared his throat. "Has she family?"

John nodded. "A stepfather and four brothers. Good men. Large. A bit rough. One of them is in a spot of trouble. I'm considering stepping in. They haven't asked yet, so I'm still thinking about it."

"Right. And her mother?"

"Dead." John ran a hand through his hair. "Little wonder Annie's run a bit wild. Raised by rough men. No mother."

Silence thickened in the room until the only sound was the crackling fire. "Hux."

John looked up.

"Is she married?"

His gut tightened. "Not yet."

"Then why isn't she here instead of me?"

"Don't be absurd. I don't want to *marry* her."

"No, of course not."

"Damned right, of course not." John glowered while Robert sipped his whisky. "Now, where was I? Oh, yes. I took her shopping."

"What were you two shopping for?"

"There were three of us. She had a chaperone. I insisted."

"*You* did."

"We were buying her gowns. The woman wears breeches, for God's sake."

Robert smiled, his eyes sparking with amusement. "Is that so?"

"Breeches and boots and a plaid. I had to do something."

"By 'do something,' you mean …"

"Buy her new clothing. What she wears is a disgrace. She's apt to catch her death every time she walks from MacPherson House to the castle. She needs proper gowns and a cloak."

"So, *you* paid for her gowns."

"Thirty-five dresses?" He snorted. "She would hardly have bought them otherwise. No, if it were up to her, she'd have sewn a gown or two for herself and left it at that. I doubt she'd have even bothered with the silk stockings or petticoats, let alone the slippers."

"Hmm. I see the dilemma."

John frowned. "You do?"

Robert nodded, pressing the rim of his glass against his lips and lowering his brows thoughtfully. "She is an unusual woman, as you say."

"Yes. Extraordinary, really." He blew out a breath, wondering why his chest hurt. "I want to … every time I see her, I want to … and when she's gone, I cannot … but it's been months since we've spoken." He ran a hand over his face and muttered, "Feels like bloody years."

"Why the separation?"

"Her father threatened to geld me and toss her out if she comes near me again."

"A bit harsh."

"He's concerned for her, as he should be. The woman has no idea what she's doing." As his chest tightened more, his voice grew louder. "Do you know she's planning to marry a lord?" Unable to stay still, John shoved up from his chair and threw his arms wide to make his point. "Any lord! No one specific. Oh, no. Not for Annie Tulloch. Just a title will do, thank you very much. Old. Young. Fit. Fat. No matter!" He slammed the heel of his hand into the mantel. The thud was loud and satisfying. "Give her a title and she'll become your wife. Easy as that."

A log popped in the fireplace. Wind howled outside. He wanted to howl, too.

"*You* have a title, Hux." Robert made his point quietly, but it felt like a stab to the gut.

He reeled back. "No."

"She could be *your* wife."

"I said no. I'll not marry a woman who only wants me for my pedigree."

"Does she? Only want you for your pedigree, I mean."

"She doesn't know about it. I haven't used my title in years. I prefer to be measured by more than a name."

"So, you've become … close with a woman you find extraordinary, despite her knowing nothing of your father or—"

"We made a bargain." He rubbed his forehead, feeling a headache start behind his eyes. Briefly, he explained about the wager with Angus and Annie's offer to teach him Highland tossing techniques in exchange for Lady Lessons. "We are at an impasse, I'm afraid. Perhaps she'll persuade Angus to relent. Perhaps she doesn't care to bother."

A gust whistled outside, where swirling white gathered in little drifts on the windowpanes. Robert's sigh blended into the sounds of a Highland winter. John glanced at his friend, whose eyes were sharp and speculative, despite his weariness.

"You think I should pursue her, don't you?"

"I think if there were not something holding you here, you would have left Scotland long before now. It's what you do, Hux. Leave. So, why haven't you?"

John stared at his friend wishing he had the answer.

Robert drained the last of his whisky and set the empty glass on a low table. He rubbed his bad leg and released another sigh. "Do you remember when I told you that one day you'd find a woman who makes madness a pleasure?"

John frowned. "I am not in love with Annie Tulloch, Con."

Robert chuckled. "No. Of course not." He plucked up his cane and levered himself to his feet. "Certainly, you'll be cheering as she waltzes away in the arms of some other chap, wearing the gowns you bought for her."

Images flashed. Annie wearing plum silk as she vowed to love another man. Annie's hand flashing with the ring of another man. Annie's smile offering seductive fire to another man. Fury billowed upward like smoke, filling his chest and throat. It wouldn't let him speak. It burned until he wanted to roar. Cheering? He wanted to slam his fist into his new mantel. He wanted to ride out in this dark blizzard, find her and demand she abandon her foolish scheme. The mere thought of her with anyone else drove him …

… mad.

Distantly, he sensed Robert beside him. Solid. Patient. Robert's shadow blended with his own as the truth began to unfurl.

She mattered. He wanted her. Not for an hour. Not for a week.

Forever.

He wanted her in his kitchen. He wanted to watch those pretty hands making bread. He wanted her here in his study, teasing him about his fine manners and finer tea. He wanted to hear her pleasured cries echoing off the new paneling in his bedchamber. Feel her hair brushing his skin. Watch her cornflower eyes go soft then glow like blue fire.

He wanted his child in her belly.

His heart pounded, pulsing in his skin. Oh, God. Yes, that was it.

Annie swollen with his child. His ring upon her pretty finger. His claim fully made.

She'd be his wife.

Bloody hell. She could be *his*.

"It's damned disorienting, I know," Robert said quietly. "The first time you realize what's happened, it changes who you are." He patted John's shoulder, and even that small nudge set him off balance. Perhaps it was the whisky.

John had to swallow twice before he could speak. When he finally did, his voice was thin and hoarse. "If—if I do pursue her, I must be certain she wants me." He caught his friend's sympathetic gaze. "Me, Con. Not my name. Not my fortune. Me."

Robert nodded. He knew everything, of course. They'd been friends since John had dragged him home for Christmas pudding at age six. Robert knew about Jacqueline. And before Jacqueline, the governess.

They never talked about the governess. But Robert obviously remembered. The understanding was there in his eyes.

John could not marry a woman who only wanted the name he could give her.

Which left one solution: He must make Annie fall in love with him without telling her about his title.

As though reading his thoughts, Robert squeezed his shoulder and gave a half-smile. "Perhaps I should warn Miss Tulloch. Seems only fair."

John raised a questioning brow.

"Whatever your other talents, Hux—and there are many—wooing females into abandoning all good sense is your particular specialty."

True enough. Slowly, John's grin grew. He hadn't applied himself to the task in a long while, but he'd always excelled at it. And with Annie? Anticipation surged, heady as Highland whisky.

Robert chuckled. "Poor woman. She has little notion of what's coming her way."

CHAPTER TWELVE

"*Ooph!*" Annie glared over her shoulder at Mrs. Baird, who was hoisting Annie's bosoms by crushing her ribs. "This isnae a corset. *Ergh.* It's—*unh*—a bluidy vise."

"Nearly done," Mrs. Baird huffed, giving the laces a firm yank. "There." The yanking stopped. The dressmaker breathed a sigh of relief.

Annie would do the same if she could gather more than a teaspoon of air. She glanced down. What the devil had this contraption done to her bosoms? They were enormous. Hiked up from beneath, they resembled great mounds of rising dough.

Cupping herself incredulously, she felt the boning along her waist and intricate stitching flaring over her hips. "I look like a stuffed pigeon. What have ye done?"

Mrs. Baird chuckled, grasped her shoulders and turned her to face the full-length mirror in the corner of Annie's bedchamber.

Annie gasped.

"What *we've* done, aye?" The dressmaker grinned, her lovely teeth gleaming in the light from the window.

"Wh—why do I … That's not …" Swallowing, Annie wandered closer. She moved her hands along the center, where a wide busk separated her bosoms and drew a flat line down past her belly. The corset was exquisite—satiny-soft white cotton with flared rows of quilted stitching. She traced the delicate crisscross pattern over her hip.

"The quilting is *trapunto*. I used silk thread for strength." Mrs. Baird turned away to sort through the gowns she'd brought with her. "Ye'll find the corset does soften over time, but the stitching and boning will ensure it keeps its structure. Now, where did I put my pins? Ah! There."

Slowly, Annie shook her head. Somehow, watching her own movements in the looking glass startled her. This woman with the small waist and swollen breasts and fine linen petticoat could not be her.

"Let's begin with the morning gowns."

Annie's head spun. "I dinnae want to."

Holding pins in one hand and a pile of flounced white in the other, the dressmaker tilted her head and gave a gentle smile. "Remember what we discussed? These are your garments. Fitting them properly does not mean ye must wear them. But I must finish my work."

God, Annie wished she could hate this woman. But from the moment Mrs. Baird had arrived at MacPherson House—after fully twelve letters begging Annie to come to Inverness for her final fittings—the dressmaker had been nothing but kind. Firm to the point of motherliness, but kind.

And she was quite the most talented seamstress Annie had ever met. Once again, Annie traced the curvaceous stitching along her belly. It even extended onto the gussets covering her breasts, a wee panel of crisscrosses. *"Trapunto,"* she whispered.

Mrs. Baird hummed lightly. "Arms up." White flounces descended over Annie's arms and head, cascading down over her figure. The dressmaker clicked her tongue and patted Annie's waist. "Ye're a wee bit smaller here than before. Have ye lost yer appetite?"

She had, but she didn't wish to discuss it. "If I wear this gown in the kitchen, I'll be singed inside a week." She plucked at the sleeves. "Lace and ruffles. Hmmph. Might as well add beeswax and a wick. Are ye tryin' to kill me?"

The woman arched a yellow brow. "With so much cookery, I'd have predicted ye'd be bigger, not smaller."

Annie tightened her lips and held her tongue.

"How does Mr. Huxley fare?"

Silence. That was the best defense.

"When he sent his last payment, he seemed unaware that ye hadn't yet taken delivery of the gowns." The dressmaker plucked and fussed and pinned. When she paused, Annie dared to meet her eyes in the mirror.

Heavens, they were a pair. The well-groomed Mrs. Baird with her pretty face and perfect hair. Annie with her unruly crop of fire pinned in a lopsided knot. Mrs. Baird's motions were graceful, like a doe crossing a stream. Annie's movements might charitably be called efficient. Mrs. Baird's language was crisp and proper. Annie's was coarse and blunt.

Annie was a hoyden, just as John Huxley claimed. She was not a lady. Certainly not enough of one for him.

"Surprisin' that he mentioned me at all," she muttered, dropping her gaze to her hands. "I havenae heard from him in some time."

Again, Mrs. Baird hummed. "'Tis hard not to miss such a handsome face, aye?"

Annie swallowed a lump while Mrs. Baird tied a lavender silk sash around her waist. Yes, it was hard not to miss him. Annie had tried. She was still trying. But when she closed her eyes, there he was, a maddening, tempting, bonnie Englishman with a smile she had to work for. Some nights, she awakened soaked from half-remembered dreams of his hands and lips and crisp, deep voice.

She was a fool for wanting him. He wasn't a lord. And he obviously didn't miss her. Otherwise, he would have approached her any of the half-dozen times she'd seen him in the village over the past three months. She drew a shuddering breath. Time to change the subject.

Squinting at herself in the mirror, Annie asked, "How do I make my hair look like yours?"

Mrs. Baird's smile warmed above her shoulder. "Cooperate whilst I finish pinning the rest of the gowns, and I'll show you."

Annie examined the morning gown she wore, how it finally fell properly across her bosom and hips, how the sash made her waist look small. Or perhaps that was the corset. Her eyes lifted to the dressmaker's. "Agreed. Just dinnae make me look daft."

Two hours and thirty-four gowns later, Mrs. Baird tucked the final pin into Annie's hair. The simple arrangement involved coiling the length at the back of her head then fussing with the shorter bits around her face until they looked purposeful. The wisps fringed lightly across her forehead and framed her cheeks becomingly.

Why hadn't she done this sooner? No long plait to catch fire when she turned to fetch a pot. And for once, her frizzing curls were smooth.

Mrs. Baird's humming had turned musical while she worked. At first, Annie had thought it might grow irritating, but she liked it. She liked the dressmaker's gentle hands and cheerful smile. She liked Mrs. Baird.

She also liked Mrs. Baird's work. Glancing down at the silver-green wool of her simple, long-sleeved day dress, she traced a finger over the delicate embroidery on the scooped bodice. Leaves of silver, gold, and russet swirled as though they'd just fallen from their branches. Such a lively addition would not have occurred to Annie. But Mrs. Baird knew how it would play against the vividness of her hair and the whiteness of her bosom.

"Ye'll need a maid to assist ye with the gowns and corset, likely," the dressmaker murmured. "A proficient one will ken more ways to dress this lovely red hair."

Annie was about to argue that she didn't want a maid when one of her hired lads came to inform her of visitors at the door. Frowning, Annie left Mrs. Baird to work on the gowns that needed alteration and followed him downstairs. As she descended, the pair of dark-clad gentlemen came into view. Both stood with their backs turned, holding their hats politely in hand. One leaned upon a cane.

The other sent excitement surging from her aching middle out across her skin in sparkling rivulets.

Reeling, she stalled on the bottom step. Steadied herself against the banister. Tried to catch her breath.

He was here.

What was he doing here?

"Mr. Huxley," she managed, albeit faintly.

The two men turned. Ah, God. Bare jaw. Perfect lips. Leaner and paler than before, but still heartbreakingly handsome. Vaguely, she noted the darker-haired man had very wide shoulders and a heavy brow. He was also handsome, she supposed. But not as bonnie as John Huxley.

Nothing compared with those enchanting hazel eyes, the ones that now flared wide and raked her from head to toe before settling on her bosom. Lingering. And lingering. And stroking. And lingering. His chest heaved on a breath. His cravat moved as he swallowed.

Taking a deep breath of her own, she ordered her pounding heart to calm down and reminded herself of how they'd last parted. How he'd left her without a proper goodbye.

"After ye scurried off into the dark at the first wee bit of trouble, I didnae suppose ye'd dare provoke Angus again." She raised her chin. "Appears dainty Englishmen require a few months to locate their ballocks, eh? I'll ken better next time."

He didn't respond. Just kept staring at her as though he'd never seen her before.

His companion cleared his throat and nudged Huxley with an elbow.

Huxley continued staring, his eyes gold and green and glowing hot.

Annie clicked her tongue and strode forward to take the other man's hat. "I'm Annie Tulloch. My stepfather's at the distillery this mornin', else I'd introduce ye. Seems

I'd have to, seein' as Mr. Dafty here cannae be bothered to speak."

A small smile quirked the man's lips. His deep-set eyes were a different shade of blue than hers. Darker, more solemn.

"A pleasure, Miss Tulloch. I am Robert Conrad, an old friend of Mr. Dafty."

Startled and delighted, she immediately grinned. "Robert? Ye're *the* Robert?"

"Er, I don't know about *the* Robert, but yes. That is my name."

She swatted him with his own hat. "Och, why didnae ye say so? After all of Huxley's tales about the two of ye chasin' trouble together, I'd have thought ye'd visit him sooner."

"Indeed, I should have done." Robert glanced cautiously at his friend. "I wasn't certain how long he would remain in Scotland. But his lands are splendid and the people charming. Understandable that he would lengthen his stay."

"Well, come into the parlor and sit, for God's sake." She placed his hat on the hook and led the men into the adjacent room. Shooing one of her cleaning lads off to fetch bread and cider, she tutted, "Ye havenae come all the way from Nottinghamshire to stand about bletherin' in my doorway. Has he fed ye properly yet?" She gestured toward one of the sofas. "I heard he hired Marjorie MacDonnell to be his cook." Clicking her tongue, she called toward the doorway where Huxley had halted—still hovering, still staring like a pure eejit. "I warned ye Dougal would try to saddle ye with his entire clan, English. I hope ye didnae hire his worthless sons to clean yer chimneys. Whole castle'll burn down before those laddies do aught that's useful."

He wandered deeper into the room. Flexed his hands. Swallowed again. "Her bread is dreadful," he uttered.

At the sound of his voice—crisp and deep—her heart drummed faster.

He stopped about a foot away. "It's nothing like yours."

God, his eyes were burning her alive. Her chest ached. Her fingertips tingled with the need to touch him. "Ye've gone too thin."

"I've been starving."

"It—it's yer own fault, stayin' away from … my kitchen so long. This willnae do if ye intend to win yer wager."

"No. It won't do."

"I'll give ye loaves to take with ye."

His breathing quickened. "Is that all?"

"Mayhap I've some venison left over from last night."

He groaned. "Yes."

Slowly, she smiled. Warmth glowed in her middle. "Ye like that, English?"

"I do."

"Perhaps I could offer ye more."

"I want everything. Everything you can give me."

Heavens, she was hot. Her skin was pulsing. Her breasts felt swollen. Maybe it was the wool gown or the corset. Maybe her lads had built the parlor fire too large.

"You look … different," he whispered, licking his lips.

"'Tis the gown."

"Mmm."

"Also the hair." She touched the smooth strands above her ear. "And Mrs. Baird made me proper stays."

Another groan. He closed his eyes briefly, moving his lips in a silent chant she couldn't decipher.

"She's still upstairs workin' on the alterations. Ye bought far too many gowns, English."

"I wanted you to have them." He lowered his head and his voice. "Remember our bargain?"

She blinked. "Is that why ye've come? For a lesson?"

"Angus and I settled upon an … understanding. I spoke to him early this morning at the distillery."

Alarm streaked through her. Immediately, she reached for him, patting his shoulders and inspecting his arms and ribs and hands. Finally, she drew his head down and ran her fingers over his scalp.

"Annie," came his hoarse, amused response. "What exactly are you doing?"

"Did he hurt ye?" She hadn't felt any lumps or swellings, but head wounds could be deceptive. "Is that why ye're actin' daft?"

He clasped her wrists and drew her hands down against his chest. "I'm fine," he said gently. "Campbell was there. He kept the peace while your father and I discussed a few matters. Angus has no objection to our continuing our lessons."

She turned to Robert, who stood quietly beside the fire looking bemused. "He didnae shoot Angus, did he?" She looked at Huxley. "Tell me ye didnae shoot him with yer wee pistols."

"Of course not."

"No 'of course' about it, English. The last time I mentioned yer name, Angus threatened to carve out yer heart and feed it to Bill the Donkey with a side of oats and gravy."

"It's been three months. His temper has had time to cool."

"This was yesterday." She crossed her arms and glowered up at the Englishman, who wore familiar triumph on his bonnie face. "What did ye say to Da that he's so *agreeable*, now?"

"I simply talked to the man."

"Angus doesnae talk."

"I employed reason."

"Angus doesnae reason."

"Well, in this instance, he was persuaded. So long as our sessions are chaperoned, you and I may continue as we did before."

She *hmmphed* and glared her suspicions at Robert. "Is that the truth, then?"

Robert examined his own boots while his lips fought a smile. Then he glanced up. "Your father did agree to allow it."

Why did she have the feeling both men were dancing around the important bits? She *hmmphed* again. Her lad entered carrying a tray full of bread, cheese, thin-sliced lamb, and cups of cider. He deposited it on the center table, and Annie encouraged the men to sit.

Both moved to the sofa but continued standing. Huxley stared longingly at the food.

Annie frowned. "Well, dinnae be bashful. If ye've been dinin' on Marjorie MacDonnell's handiwork, ye're probably famished."

Robert leaned into his cane and cleared his throat. Huxley gestured toward the opposite sofa. "You must be seated first," he said gently.

She blinked. Was that one of the rules? They hadn't reached that particular subject in her Lady Lessons. Heat prickled in her neck and cheeks. "Oh." She strode to the sofa, remembering too late that she was supposed to glide. Blast. Striving to salvage the situation, she turned upon her toes, folded her hands as though carrying a wee bird, and sank down.

Only to leap up an instant later at the piercing pain in her right buttock. "Arrgh! Bluidy pins can go to bluidy hell!"

In a flash, Huxley was beside her, running his hands over her hips and legs. "Where are you injured?" he demanded.

Annie swatted at his wandering hands. "Even I ken ye shouldnae be puttin' yer fingers there, English." She managed to dislodge the pin from her flesh. "Devil's ballocks, that's bluidy painful."

Robert suddenly broke into a fit of coughing. Huxley glared at his friend.

"Oh, dear," said Mrs. Baird from the doorway. "I should have warned ye about the pins." The lovely woman glided into the room. "My deepest apologies, Miss Tulloch." She smiled at Huxley and Robert. "Gentlemen, I hope ye'll forgive my intrusion."

"Of course." Huxley straightened and bowed before introducing her to Robert.

Annie noticed he didn't have any trouble speaking now. No, indeed, he was all polite polish. The perfect gentleman.

She glared up at him while he carried on pleasantries, explaining to Robert what a *lovely* shop Mrs. Baird had established in Inverness, and how remarkably *knowledgeable* Mrs. Baird was, and how *appreciative* he'd been to find such a resource without having to travel to Edinburgh.

By the time he finished his lengthy praise and they all took their seats—very carefully, in Annie's case—Annie decided once again that she hated Mrs. Baird. Perhaps even more than before.

Mrs. Baird glided without effort. Mrs. Baird's speech was soft and lilting, not wound up like a corkscrew. Mrs. Baird's kindly smile put everyone at ease. Even Annie. Her manners were impeccable. Her conversation made Huxley and Robert chuckle and nod thoughtfully by turns. Her hair was yellow rather than an absurd shade of orange.

And John Huxley did not stare at Mrs. Baird as though she were some mad, wild, confounding problem he must solve. He did not go silent gaping at Mrs. Baird. He appeared perfectly charming, perfectly at ease.

Annie watched him while the trio chatted and ate her food. His eyes were livelier than she remembered, almost gleaming with excitement. Within minutes, he devoured four slices of bread piled with lamb and topped with cheese. Remarkably, he did so neatly and politely without dropping a crumb on his black riding breeches. He readily conversed between bites, charming everyone with his wit. Especially Mrs. Baird.

Were smooth hair, white teeth, and a pleasant manner all it took to gain his admiration? Apparently so.

God, she hated that woman.

"… late husband's mother was from Nottinghamshire." Mrs. Baird hummed her approval as she delicately sipped Annie's cider. "Where do ye make yer home there, Mr. Conrad?"

"North of Nottingham. A lovely spot of woodlands and countryside along the River Tisenby."

"Ah, it is splendid there. Mr. Baird and I passed through that very spot several years before he died. Have ye any relation to the Conrads of Rivermore Abbey?"

Robert paused. "Some connection, yes."

"Then perhaps ye were acquainted with the Marquis of Mortlock. Such a noble gentleman. When Mr. Baird's horse went lame, he lent us one from his stable."

Again, Robert paused before speaking. "Lord Mortlock passed away some years ago, I'm afraid."

"Aye, of course. I was sad to hear of it. Our last visit to England was fully twelve years ago. How quickly time passes." As Mrs. Baird leaned forward to refill her cup, Annie noticed her hair wasn't entirely yellow. It was threaded with white. "I only mention it because he showed us such kindness." Ms. Baird took another sip of her cider and eyed Robert above the rim. "So did his grandson, as I recall."

The conversation struck Annie as odd, but she had no chance to delve further. Huxley chose that moment to spring to his feet and declare that he and Robert must leave. "Robert's already been in Scotland a month. He is anxious to return to his wife and children."

Annie frowned, wondering why Huxley didn't mention that Robert's wife was his sister. Strange.

Before she could ask about it, Huxley pivoted to address her. "Miss Tulloch, thank you for the refreshments. Divine, as always."

Both Robert and Mrs. Baird murmured similar sentiments, but Huxley rushed to finish, "I must be away for a short while. When I return, we'll resume our lessons."

She blinked. "Away?" No! She'd already been without him too long.

Oh, heavens. Where had that thought come from?

"I'm afraid so." He took her hands in his, drawing her to her feet while sending tingles up her arms. "I shall return as swiftly as I can. Count upon it."

His eyes seemed to promise something, but frustratingly, she hadn't the faintest idea what it was. Once again, before she could ask or even bid him farewell, he and Robert departed.

Moments later, she stood in her parlor, her backside smarting, her chest aching fiercely, and wondered where she'd gone so wrong.

This hurt. Badly. And she couldn't explain why.

A gentle, competent hand clasped hers.

Startled, Annie met the gaze of the woman by her side.

The dressmaker squeezed. "A gentleman always keeps his word, ye ken. I'd wager yer Mr. Huxley will race to return to yer side."

"H-he's not mine."

Mrs. Baird hummed noncommittally.

"He's not."

"These gowns are quite a change for ye, I gather. Are they intended for a new life? With a husband, perhaps?"

Annie blinked. "I … they're …" She swallowed. "Aye. I do aim to marry."

The dressmaker nodded and offered a sympathetic smile. "Becoming a wife can be a joy, but also daunting. Establishing a new household, endearing yerself to yer husband's family." She paused. "Learning new skills so ye make yer husband proud as ye go about in society."

Annie's heart sank. Even Mrs. Baird had noticed how inept she was at being a lady.

"If ye should need advice from a woman with some experience of marriage, I'd be glad to share what I ken." She gave Annie's hand another squeeze.

Now that she stood closer, faint lines around Mrs. Baird's eyes, whitish patches at her temples, and a small crease along her forehead were visible.

Annie frowned. "How old are ye, Mrs. Baird?"

Yellow eyebrows arched. "Why do ye ask?"

"Ye must have been widowed young." Annie hesitated before explaining, "My mother lost my father when I was a wee bairn. I think of that sometimes. How she was younger than I am now when she was left to care for her child alone."

Mrs. Baird nodded, her eyes going a bit sad. "My James left me with two lovely daughters, though they were nearly grown by the time he died. They are both married now with wee ones of their own."

"Nah. Ye cannae be old enough to …"

"I am six-and-forty." The dressmaker's smile turned wry. "But your disbelief is fair turnin' my head."

For the first time since John Huxley had walked out her door, Annie laughed. "I cannae credit it. I took ye for thirty at most."

Mrs. Baird spoke of her daughters and two grandchildren, who all lived near Edinburgh, where Mrs. Baird was from. When Annie asked if she'd considered moving there to be near them, she said, "Oh, aye. But Inverness is where I settled with Mr. Baird. It is where I have my shop. Every time I think of leavin', my heart refuses. Besides," she continued with a fond glance at Annie's gown, "I've too many friends and customers I would miss dreadfully."

Once again, Annie found herself liking Mrs. Baird. She offered to help with the alterations if the dressmaker would show her what must be done. Perhaps she could ask for advice on becoming a lady while they sewed together. After all, if the goal was to behave more like Mrs. Baird, Annie could think of no better instructor than Mrs. Baird.

They were headed toward the staircase when the front door swung open with a gust and slammed closed with equal force behind a thunderous Angus MacPherson.

Annie's father wore a black coat and a blacker expression. He turned to hang his hat on the hook. "Annie!" he bellowed before bothering to glance in her direction. "Where the devil are ye?"

"If ye'd bother lookin' instead of shoutin', ye crabbit auld man, ye'd see I'm right here."

He spun. Then blinked. Then turned a bit ruddy. "What in bluidy hell are ye wearin'?"

She had the feeling he would have shouted the words if he hadn't been so shocked. Planting her hands on her hips, she glanced down at herself and back up at him. "Well, I might be mistaken, but I believe it's called a dress."

"What in bluidy hell have ye done to yer hair?"

"Now, that's called brushin'. It's a new thing. I thought I'd give it a try."

He stomped toward her, looming as he often did. "What in bluidy hell are ye doin' to yerself?"

She snorted. "Far less than ye're doin' to my floors, auld man. Now, before ye take another step, ye'd best go wipe yer boots. I've no patience for mud or yer crabbit ways."

He ignored her warning, glaring hard and looking fearsome.

Despite her irritation with his bluster, she saw strain around his eyes and mouth that worried her. She drew closer, intending to ask what had caused it, when a delicate *"ahem"* sounded behind her.

Angus's black gaze shifted to Mrs. Baird, narrowed and glittering.

"Och, I'm a pure dafty," Annie said, hoping to defuse the sudden tension. "Da, this is my dressmaker, Mrs. Baird. Mrs. Baird, this cantankerous giant is my stepfather, Angus MacPherson."

Neither one spoke a word. Annie glanced between them, dismayed by the nervousness on Mrs. Baird's face and the black fury on Angus's.

"She's here to finish my gowns," Annie prompted, hoping one of them would say something. "She traveled all the way from Inverness."

Angus waved a finger at Annie's skirt. "This shite is yer work, then?"

Annie glowered. That was rude, even for him.

A suddenly pale Mrs. Baird laced her fingers tightly at her waist. "Th—this *gown* is my work, aye."

"Ye turned my lass into a bluidy tart."

"Da!" Annie protested. Why was he aiming his wrath at a kindly dressmaker?

Mrs. Baird seemed terrified yet continued to hold Angus's gaze. "Yer lass is a fine young woman," she replied quietly. "I should think ye'd be glad to see her looking so lovely."

Oddly, this seemed to anger him more. "My daughter was always bonnie," he growled. "She doesnae need yer obscene frocks revealin'—"

"That's more than enough, auld man!" Annie charged forward and braced a hand on the center of Angus's chest. "Mrs. Baird, I beg yer forgiveness for this great beastie that plainly hasnae been trained to do aught but soil the furniture."

"Now, listen here, lass—"

She held up a finger to silence him then spoke to the dressmaker. "I'll join ye upstairs in a wee bit. Just let me have a moment with Angus."

A long pause came from behind her while Angus fumed. "If ye're certain, Miss Tulloch."

"I am. Dinnae fash. I've dealt with this beastie many times. He's more smoke than teeth."

As Mrs. Baird moved up the staircase, Annie glared at her father, who watched the dressmaker's retreat with something approaching hatred. "What on earth is the matter with ye?" she demanded.

He blew out a long breath and shrugged out of his coat.

Annie moved to help him. He nodded his thanks.

"Too much is changin', lass. I dinnae like it. First that bluidy Englishman interrupts my work to bargain with me—"

She crossed her arms. "Aye. And what made ye change yer mind about him, eh?"

He scoffed. "Lad made an offer."

"What sort of offer?"

"Nothin' ye need fash yerself about. Train him all ye like. He'll never win against yer brothers anyway."

Annie eyed her surly, beloved father for signs of senility. Dark eyes flashed; a hard jaw remained stubborn; thick brows drew down low. No, he was weary and frustrated but sound. "Somethin' happened." Her stomach panged oddly. "What is it, Da?"

His gaze shifted away then came back.

When she saw anguish in eyes that never despaired, her chest collapsed beneath a crushing weight. She reached for his hands. Immediately, his big paws clasped and held her. He always did that. Always lent her his strength.

"Please," she whispered. "Tell me."

"Rannoch sent word. Broderick is …" He swallowed hard. "He is near death, lass. We've tried to protect him. Paid guards inside the prison. Every time we do, those men are dismissed and new ones hired. Skene's men have done great damage. 'Tis a miracle he's lasted this long."

Annie's head spun. Over the past three months, the case against Broderick had gone from bad to worse. The MacPhersons had assigned physicians to keep the exciseman alive. At one point, the man had even regained consciousness long enough to give a statement to the MacPherson solicitors. He'd declared Broderick could not have been the one to shoot him because the shot had come from the opposite end of the warehouse. They'd all hoped this would be enough to exonerate Broderick, and her brothers had traveled to Edinburgh to press for his release.

But before they'd arrived, someone had persuaded the exciseman to recant his original statement, claiming it was the product of MacPherson pressure. Then, inexplicably, he'd signed a second statement charging that Broderick had, indeed, attempted to murder him.

None of it had made sense until the exciseman, despite being on the mend, had mysteriously died. That was when Alexander had discovered a large cache of coins beneath the bed of the exciseman's widow.

Someone wanted Broderick to suffer. Someone wanted Broderick to die. And, whoever "someone" was, he was very close to getting his wish.

The reality of losing her brother sent her heart into a panic. "No. No, no, no. We must go there, Da. We must get him out—"

"Aye. We will. There's a new plan. If it works, he'll be released within a fortnight. Be ready to journey to Edinburgh. Pack everything he'll need. Bandages. Clothing. Food. Prepare yerself, too. He's not ... not the man he was." At her fretful reaction, he drew her into his arms and held her tight against his massive chest. Kissing her head, he whispered, "We will bring him home, Annie. And when we do, he'll need us more than ever."

She breathed her father's scent: wool and peat and wild Highland air. She clutched her father's waistcoat and felt seven years old again. Missing her mother. Wondering about her place. Aching and aching and aching for a life she would never have again. Her throat closed painfully.

"Bad enough ye aim to leave for some soddin' lord." His voice was graveled. Tight. Fierce. "I cannae lose two of my bairns, lass. I cannae bear it."

Holding her breath against a sob, Annie gathered her strength to give him what he'd always given her—reassurance. "Ye'll never be rid of me, Da." She held him tighter, prayed silently for Broderick, and made her vow. "Whatever else happens, I'll always, *always* be yer daughter."

CHAPTER THIRTEEN

Annie squelched the urge to snap at her new lady's maid. For the love of God, what had she been thinking? Mad Annie Tulloch shouldn't have a lady's maid. She might as well tie pink ribbons to the horns of a hairy cow. Ridiculous. But Mrs. Baird had assured her she would need one, so Annie had employed the only female in the village more scorned—and, thus, more desperate—than she was.

Dougal MacDonnell's freckle-faced, brown-haired wife might be a shy mouse who rarely raised her eyes above anyone's navel, and yes, she was a former prostitute from Glasgow. But like the rest of Dougal's family, she needed employment. Besides, her gowns were always plain but clean, and her hair was always neatly trimmed, so she knew more about such things than Annie.

Now, however, Annie stood before the three gowns laid out on her bed, reminding herself that she could not shout at Betty MacDonnell because Betty hadn't done anything wrong. She hadn't spoken more than two words, in fact. Granted, those two words had been, "Aye, miss," whispered to the floor. But shouting at her would be like kicking a kitten.

Annie gritted her teeth. "What do ye think of the lavender one, Betty?"

No answer.

She chanced a glance at the maid, whose eyes widened and darted away.

It was the final straw. "Ye've seen me in the altogether every day for the last seven," Annie snapped. "Nobody here is any better than anybody else. Stop actin' like ye're embarrassed to be breathin'."

The other woman flinched and cowered.

Bloody hell. With an effort, Annie softened her tone. "All I mean is that ye needn't be nervous to speak yer mind. I hired ye because ye've a bit of talent for"—she gestured to the gowns then swirled a hand around her own head—"this sort of thing."

"I'm sorry," Betty whispered.

"Dinnae apologize, for the love of …" Annie bit down on the remainder then patted the woman's spindly shoulder. "Let's try the lavender one, eh?"

Betty nodded. Then hesitated. Then moved to the grass-green walking dress. "Th-this one is a bonnie shade fer spring."

Despite her own melancholy, Annie gave Betty an encouraging nod. "Right ye are. A much better choice."

Betty smiled then helped her dress. A short time later, while Annie's new maid removed wee wraps from the curls along Annie's temples, one of her lads ran into the bedchamber to deliver a note from Angus.

As she read his blunt, blockish scrawl, Annie's stomach tightened and swooped and panged. Then, her chest expanded until she felt it might burst. She covered her lips with trembling fingers. Could it be?

Betty whispered, "Is the news dreadful, then?"

Annie shook her head in wonderment, struggling to contain herself. "No," she choked. "Ah, God bless us all. The charges against Broderick will be dismissed. The Lord Commissioner has accepted the exciseman's original statement, and Broderick's sure to be released." Without thinking, she stood and embraced Betty, who gave a startled jerk at the gesture.

"Och, I'm a pure disaster." Annie drew back, sniffing and swiping at damp cheeks. "I'll need yer help with packin'. Angus will want to leave for Edinburgh straight away. Ye must stay here."

Betty hesitated, blinking and moving her mouth as though she wished to speak.

Annie explained, "Broderick's health is quite poor, and he'll need a lot of care when we bring him home. I'd like ye to prepare his old bedchamber on the ground floor. He has a fine house of his own, 'tis true. But for a time, he must stay where we can care for him properly." Annie patted Betty's shoulder, swallowing the lump in her throat. "I'll want yer help with that, too."

"Of course." Betty's eyes went soft with sympathy. "We'll have him feelin' braw in no time."

Two hours later, Annie and the MacPherson men left the glen and headed south. While she remained dry inside the enormous travel coach her father had hired, Campbell and Alexander rode their horses alongside, their postures intimidating and vigilant. Angus rode outside with the coach driver, his favorite hunting rifle braced across his knees.

David Skene had not yet been found, after all.

For the following three days, they set a rapid pace over muddy March roads. The few times Annie had traveled such a distance, she'd sat between her brothers in a rough wagon. She'd worn her trews and plaid and tucked her hair up beneath her hat. Now, she was dressed like a lady in a proper gown with a proper straw bonnet. She sat upon cushioned seats and slept against a tufted coach wall. She watched out the window while the starkly beautiful mountains and steep, green glens of the Highlands gradually softened into hills, swells, and finally, rolling pastures.

And she hated every moment. Idleness drove her mad. She spent the first couple of days working on her sewing projects. Those were coming along splendidly, but the motion of the carriage and uncertain light made for slow work. Without anyone to talk to, she slept when she was able. And she practiced speaking the way Mrs. Baird did, with softer R's and gentler O's. Mostly, she tortured herself with thoughts of everything she might lose.

Her brother.

Her laddie.

Her … whatever John Huxley was.

From time to time, despair overwhelmed her, and she reached for the thistle charm in her wee purse—or reticule, as Mrs. Baird called it. The little carving had been discolored and smoothed by her hand over the past few months.

She rubbed her thumb across its contours now as the coach rolled into the heart of Edinburgh. "Are ye seein' this, Fin?" she whispered when the tall, crowded buildings of Lawnmarket gave way to the tall, crowded buildings of High Street. They passed Parliament

Square, where Broderick's fate had been weighed and decided. "This is the place where all the *important* men gather."

Important men. She'd come to despise the thought of marrying one. To imprison Broderick MacPherson for five months without a conviction, a man had to have significant power. More than anyone should, in her estimation. And to gain such power by accident of birth? The injustice made her seethe.

A thousand lords could not equal a single Broderick MacPherson. Or a single John Huxley, for that matter. The Englishman had built ships. He'd explored lands where giraffes nibbled the treetops. He'd turned a crumbling castle into a proper home. He'd earned Angus MacPherson's respect. These were no accidental achievements but the results of raw effort, a strong heart, and a sharp mind.

John Huxley was no *lord* given privilege and power with his christening gown. He was a *man.* Very well, an Englishman. But a man worthy of admiration, nonetheless.

As the coach drew to a halt outside a High Street inn, she squeezed the thistle charm one last time and deposited it in her reticule.

She wished he were here. Huxley would know what to say to quell her queasiness. He'd tell her a daft story about a lazy rhinoceros or the sorts of fish that let you tickle their bellies. He'd make her laugh.

But he wasn't here. So, she smoothed the sleeves of her dark-blue carriage dress and gathered her courage. First, inside the inn, they must meet with the solicitors. Then, they must travel to Calton Hill to retrieve Broderick from the Bridewell. She examined the interior of the coach, hoping it would be big enough to carry him.

Campbell opened the coach door. Beneath the brim of his hat, his eyes were red and weary. He held out his hand. Annie took it and stepped down from the carriage like a lady. They'd been practicing on this journey, and although Campbell was not precisely pleased by the change, he'd been accommodating.

She hugged his arm as they crossed the inn's courtyard. "We'll have to fashion a litter for him inside the coach," she murmured. "I've enough blankets, but we'll need canvas and wood. I dinnae want him to be folded in half."

Campbell grunted. "Perhaps the wagon would have been better, after all."

She didn't bother answering. She'd told him as much before they'd left home, but the MacPhersons had all insisted the coach was more appropriate for a lady and better protection for Broderick.

Angus and Alexander opened the inn's door and urged her forward. Inside, two short, bespectacled men and one thin, long-nosed man rose from their table.

She sighed. Solicitors were such an aggravation. "I'll find the innkeeper and arrange for proper food," she said. "We'll need a goodly quantity for the journey home."

Midstride, Alexander turned and scowled. "Dinnae wander round this place alone, Annie. That's trouble from the start."

Raising a brow, she replied, "Ye'd ken a lot about trouble, right enough." She patted his arm. "I'll be quick as a lass's lashes when she's flirtin' with Rannoch."

"Speakin' of Rannoch, he's supposed to arrive—ah, there he is." Alexander reversed course when he spied their brother entering behind them.

Annie used the distraction to escape and made her way toward the small, walled-off section of the main dining room, adjacent to the bar. She entered the quieter space, noting that its inhabitants were better dressed and better fed than the riffraff beyond the partition.

She'd just spotted a man she thought might be the innkeeper when a flash of red caught her eye. Peering across the dim interior, she blinked twice to be certain. But yes, it was a wee tartan peacock. Gilbert MacDonnell stood near the bar in his brilliant red kilt and pom-topped cap, laughing uproariously at a jest from one of his companions. Another of his companions rolled his eyes. A third glanced away and drank his beer.

A fourth had a very fine backside.

Annie blinked again. Golden hair and a fine backside. It must be Lockhart. She couldn't see his face, but he lived in Edinburgh, and this inn was a frequent haunt of those who had business in Parliament Square. Lords often did. It still begged the question of what Gilbert MacDonnell was doing there, but perhaps Lockhart's presence was a stroke of luck.

If she had to marry a lord, he seemed less repulsive than most. Of course, she didn't know him at all. And he'd only seen her once on the worst day of her life. Perhaps she should leave him be. Or perhaps she should approach, hoping he didn't recognize her.

Blast. Pursuing a lord was harder than it sounded. Ladies had to be modest and coy. They had to plan their attack carefully so as to capture a man's interest without appearing too aggressive.

She wished John Huxley were here. He would know what to do. Then again, whenever he was near, she only wanted to tease him until his eyes turned gold and that wee muscle in his jaw flickered. He was a pure distraction, her Englishman.

A quiet, feminine *ahem* came from behind her. "I do beg your pardon."

Annie spun. Golden hair. Green eyes. Swanlike neck. Lockhart's sister smiled tightly. "May I pass?"

"Oh!" Annie moved aside. "So sorry."

A single, regal nod was her answer. Then, with swanlike grace, the woman glided toward the wee tartan peacock's gaggle of companions. She looped her swanlike arm through Lockhart's and said something close to his ear. He turned his head to listen then frowned at her. Then argued. Then seemed to grow angry.

Annie watched the exchange with interest, wondering why she'd assumed being a lady meant you never had disagreements with your brother. But Lady Swan was clearly vexed. Her cheeks and nape reddened until they matched Gilbert MacDonnell's kilt. Her shoulders went stone-stiff beneath pink silk. She withdrew her arm from her brother's—or tried to.

He held onto her with a firmness Annie didn't like. Lady Swan muttered something that resembled, "Let me go." She tugged against her brother's grasp. He twisted, causing a faint wince of pain around Lady Swan's mouth.

In all her life, Annie had argued with her brothers countless times. They'd shouted and bellowed and cursed. They'd lifted her off her feet and tickled her without mercy. But the moment she wanted free, they released her. Always. Not once had they used their strength to hurt her. Not once had she feared they might do so.

Lord Lockhart apparently had no such qualms.

Muttering, "Bluidy hell," beneath her breath, Annie sighed and started forward. Lady Swan had been kind to her once. Annie believed in paying her debts.

"Well, now," she said at a cheerful volume that drew the golden pair's attention. "Miss Lockhart, it's been an age." She ignored Lockhart's annoyed expression and instead caught Lady Swan's gaze. "Last time we saw one another, ye wore yer blue silk gown. Do ye recall?"

Flustered, Lady Swan blinked several times then seemed to realize what Annie was doing. Slowly, she nodded.

"Aye, a masterpiece, it was. Gold trim. Wee little tucks on the sleeves." Annie tilted her head in a chiding fashion. "Now, ye did promise when we met again, ye'd confess the name of yer dressmaker." Annie extended an open hand. "Come. Ye can tell me all about her while I search for the innkeeper. He disappeared when I was distracted by Laird Glenscannadoo's *brilliant* tartan."

A small smile touched Lady Swan's lips. Her brother was less amused. His lips—which, Annie noted, were revoltingly fleshy—tightened into a disapproving pout. Nevertheless, the other woman slid her hand into Annie's. For a moment, Annie feared she and Lockhart might engage in a tug-o-war.

But he released his sister after a long hesitation. "Do not go far," he ordered.

As Annie drew Lady Swan toward the entrance, the taller woman lowered her head and murmured, "I don't even ken your name."

"Anne Tulloch. Ye may call me Annie."

"I am Sabella Lockhart. Forgive me, but you seem ... familiar."

"We met in Glenscannadoo. Ye retrieved my hat."

Green eyes rounded. "Oh!" She examined Annie's blue wool carriage dress. "My apologies. I ... didn't recognize you."

Annie waved away any slight. "I've acquired new gowns since then. My dressmaker is Mrs. Baird of Inverness. She's quite skilled."

Lady Swan kept pace until they exited into the courtyard. Then, she tugged Annie into the shadows of a nearby close and pulled them to a halt. "I am grateful to you, Miss Tulloch."

"No need for that. Ye offered me kindness when I sorely needed it. I'm simply returnin' the favor."

A bit of injured pride caused Lady Swan—or, rather, Miss Lockhart—to stiffen. "My brother ... he is not usually so ..."

"Aye?"

"He's suffered some disappointments recently. Now and then, his temper gets the better of him. I do hope you will not judge him too harshly."

Annie glanced around the courtyard, watching gentlemen come and go. Some still wore their courtroom wigs; some were road-weary travelers of middling means; and some hurriedly examined watches only wealth could purchase. One portly fellow in a shabby gray coat helped his elderly mother down from a travel coach. The mother kissed her son's cheek, and he kissed her hand with an affectionate smile.

Did she judge Lord Lockhart harshly? Annie thought she'd judged him quite well. "Ye shouldnae let him hurt ye," she warned. "If he does it again, remind him who pours the tea in yer house."

Miss Lockhart's eyes went round again.

Annie patted the gloved hand that still clasped hers. "Then, when he begins to ken ye're serious, remind him who ensures the rats in the larder arenae a bother."

"M-Miss Tulloch, I couldn't threaten—"

"Oh, 'tis no threat. Ye must mean every word, ye ken?" Annie held the other woman's green gaze, thinking how young she seemed. How very young and, despite her lofty position as a lord's sister, easily damaged. "It only works if ye mean it."

"I think you frighten me, Miss Tulloch."

Annie chuckled. "I've been told I have that effect."

Miss Lockhart withdrew her hand and dropped her gaze. "I must return. He'll be anxious by now. I shouldn't like to worry him."

Suddenly, Annie wished she could help the young woman more. But there wasn't any way. Until she married, Sabella Lockhart would be entirely controlled by her brother. Annie examined the young woman's slender, graceful neck and narrow nose. She noted how pale the lass's lips were, how pinched and delicate she seemed.

Blast. Annie had too many troubles of her own to go about solving someone else's.

Miss Lockhart took a shuddering breath and cast another fretful look at the inn's door.

Annie's heart twisted. "If ye're ever in need, take the mail coach to Glenscannadoo and ask for me." The offer leapt from her lips before good sense could lock the gates. "I've a spare bed or two. And I serve fine venison with onion gravy."

The lass inclined her head and gave Annie a trembling smile. "You are far too kind."

"Nah. I wouldnae mind the company." She shook her own skirts and sniffed. "And yer advice on how to keep mud from stainin' my new silk hems. It's a fair bother, I tell ye."

Miss Lockhart flashed a pretty grin then thanked her and reluctantly returned inside.

Annie pitied the lass. When he'd twisted her arm, a hint of satisfaction had been visible on Lockhart's face. She knew that look. She'd seen it on Grisel MacDonnell too many times. Fortunately, Grisel had no real power over Annie the way Lockhart did over his sister. If Annie's brothers had been similarly cruel … but they weren't. They were good men. The best, really. Especially Broderick.

Needing a moment alone, Annie lingered in the narrow, shadowy close between the inn and a hat shop. She patted the thistle inside her reticule, shut her eyes for a moment, and remembered her brother as he'd been the last time she'd seen him.

Broderick's grin always made her lighter. The day he'd left for Edinburgh, he'd teased her about her hair.

"Perhaps I'll bring home some proper scissors for ye, Annie." He'd wrapped a long, muscular arm around her shoulders and fluffed the strands along her forehead. "I've sheared sheep with better precision."

"I'll care about my hair when ye trim that overgrown shrubbery on yer face."

Laughing in his deep, infectious way, Broderick had rubbed his beard thoughtfully. "The midges dinnae seem to mind."

She'd swatted his fingers away and grasped his chin playfully. "Ye've too fine a face to cover it."

His answer had been to kiss her cheek and draw her in for a tight squeeze. Broderick had always been affectionate. His eyes, dark as a Scottish storm, danced and creased at the corners when he laughed. His hands, while massively strong, cradled rather than crushed.

That was simply Broderick.

He teased rather than blustered. He calmed rather than roared. And in her lowest moments, he sang until her heart sang in tandem.

How easy he was to love. How agonizing to think of him …

Broken.

Her throat tightened. She covered her mouth with a gloved hand. Held her breath. Daylight swirled as she leaned against the stone wall and reminded herself that he was still alive.

He'd be different, yes. Damaged. But so long as he was alive, there was hope.

She dug inside her reticule for a kerchief to wipe her stupid tears. When she looked up, she saw a figure at the opposite end of the close.

Drifting deeper into the dark, narrow space, she wandered toward him, thinking she must be imagining things. Perhaps she needed him so badly, she'd begun having visions. Oh, God. Was she going mad?

No. He was there, at the other end of the close where daylight streamed down onto lean, strong shoulders and a bonnie, masculine face. Beneath his hat was hair of sun-streaked brown. By his side was a man with a cane.

And gathered around him were two men in wigs and another two men dressed in even finer garb. One had blond hair and the other dark hair with gray wings at his temples. Both were her Englishman's height, give or take an inch or two. Both were handsome in the patrician way of aristocracy.

Who were they? And why was John Huxley in Edinburgh, near Parliament Square, talking to two men who looked like Lord Commissioners of the Justiciary and two more men who looked like they should be wearing crowns?

Her pace quickened. What the devil was Huxley up to? Why hadn't Robert left Scotland already? Did this have something to do with Broderick?

Was this part of the bargain he'd made with—

Her toe caught on a rough plank hidden inside a rubbish pile. "Bluidy hell," she cursed, hopping on the opposite foot while waves of agony pulsed from her abused toes.

Masculine voices halted. She braced her hand on the stone wall and glanced up.

Oh, God. He'd spotted her. Hazel eyes flashed with recognition beneath his hat's brim. He said something to Robert and started forward at a stalking pace.

She stumbled back, trying to avoid the pile and regain her footing. "For the love of … blast."

"Annie? What are you doing there?"

"Avoiding the damnable solicitors. And breakin' my foot." She frowned up at him as he bore down upon her. "Did I ever tell ye why I prefer tall boots to worthless slippers?" She gestured to said slippers. "Well, now ye ken."

His perfect lips quirked. "Very sensible."

"What business have ye here, of all places, English?" Her eyes narrowed. "'Tis a mighty odd coincidence."

He glanced over his shoulder before herding her backward and tucking them both into a doorway. The sudden change of position—and his sudden nearness— sent her head spinning. She grasped his arms as he effortlessly hauled her up a step and deeper into the crevice.

Heavens, he was strong. And bonnie. And warm.

Crowding close, he braced her against cold stone. Then, he lowered his head until those splendid, glowing eyes leveled with hers. "I missed you," he whispered.

Ah, God. He'd just echoed the wailing cry of her heart. Breathless and hot, she rested a fluttering hand upon his chest. If she weren't wearing a bonnet, she'd lay her cheek against him and beg him to hold her. Instead, she could only sigh, "English."

"Your carriage dress looks even better than I imagined."

"Ye cannae even see me in this darkness."

"I can. I feel you, too."

She grunted a protest. "Dinnae use yer sweet words on me, John Huxley. I've questions for ye."

With a sensual smile, he traced a line from her earlobe to her throat. "You smell good."

She snorted. "Now I ken ye're lyin'. Whatever's in that rubbish pile, it isnae perfume."

His hands moved to her waist, squeezing as he nuzzled her jaw. "The only scent I perceive is your skin. You always smell clean to me. Clean and golden and sweet, like caramel or ..." Nuzzle. Tickle. "... honey." Were those his lips?

Her hands fisted his coat. Her bones liquified into caramel and honey. "I must smell like distraction."

"You do."

"Fitting. Because that's all this bonnie talk is, I reckon." Perhaps her point would have more impact if she didn't purr it against his jaw and rub her bosom against his chest. On the other hand, it felt heavenly to be in his arms.

Focus! She must focus. "Who were ye meetin', English?"

"Friends."

"What friends?"

Suddenly, he clasped her nape with lean, strong fingers and cinched her tightly against his hard body with an arm around her back. "I'm going to kiss you. Properly."

A dozen responses flashed through her mind, starting with "About time," and finishing with "Which parts?" But his voice and his breath and her full-body flush annihilated her wits.

"That sounds ... fine," was the best she could do.

"Afterwards, I'm going to walk away, and you're going back into the inn with your family."

"How did ye—"

Perfect lips brushed hers. Tingling sparks flickered to life. "After you return to Glenscannadoo, we are going to do more than kiss."

"W—we—"

"Much more."

"Y—ye—"

"But for now, I'll have this, Annie. A taste to tide me over."

Suddenly, his mouth fused to hers. And his tongue, sleek and hot, slid inside. And Annie's world turned inside out. Because no man—Englishman or Scot— should be able to steal a woman's soul the way John Huxley stole hers with a single kiss.

John used every trick he knew. Nearness. Flattery. Touching. The right sort of honesty at the right time. Then, the promise. And, finally, the kiss.

God, the kiss.

For the first few seconds, he kept his head. A bit of nibbling pressure. A confident slide of tongue.

Then, she moaned. Hummed against his lips. And her honey scent spiraled him into intoxication.

His mouth wanted more of her. His heart hammered against his chest. He tightened his muscles, resisting the urge to drive her higher against the wall.

Shouldn't.

Needed to keep control. This was about distraction. She was the one who must forget herself. Not him. John Huxley did not lose control. Not with women. Not ever.

Her arms slid around his neck. Her mouth tilted. Opened. Begged him for more.

Better for everyone if he maintained command of himself. How hard could it be? He'd always managed it before. With other women. Other kisses.

She shifted so her thigh moved between his. Brushed and pressed. Shot him into the sky. Her softness against his hardness. Lush, round breasts pressing flat until he could feel her hard nipples. Delicious lips opening like a flower. Need for her spun him in spirals of heat.

He clasped her harder. Gripped her neck and pulled her mouth tighter. Ate at her like a starving animal. And it still wasn't enough.

Soft, sweet lips. Not merely willing but eager. She whimpered and pulsed her hips against him. Circling. Grinding. Demanding.

Somebody growled, deep and primal. He thought it might be him.

How long had he lived without this? Without her? How hungry had he been? So hungry he hadn't understood its vastness.

Until now.

Blind and hot and hard enough to take her ten times without stopping, he drove her body upward against the wall. Grasped her skirts. Raised them higher. Gave up her mouth to take her throat. God, her scent drove him mad. He hadn't lied to her about that. She was sunrise over the loch. She was dew upon heather. She was honey and sugar and hot whisky sliding over his tongue. The wanting was like nothing he'd ever known—an inferno. His lungs couldn't get enough air.

But he would die happy. Gladly. For one. More. Taste.

"Ah, dear God, English," came her husky plea. "Ye're burnin' me alive."

Yes. He felt his hat tumble away. Felt her fingers clawing at his hair. Felt her legs parting and his fingers sliding and the sleek, hot wetness of ripe, honeyed folds.

Whimpering as she kissed his jaw, his ear, and his brow, she panted harshly and finally threw her head back with a low moan.

Her skin tasted like her bread, soft and sweet and salty and complex. Like clouds formed of lust. Automatically, his fingers worked on stroking the ripe petals between her thighs. If he could, he would bare her breasts. Suckle them while he drove her to ecstasy. But he was busy. Obsessed. With her skin and her wet, swollen—

"What are ye doin' to me? I'm going to … ah, English. Please. With yer hand. Faster. Dear God. Aye. That's it."

His cock shot so hard and tight, he was sure he would come. Right there in her arms, with his fingers strumming and sliding, with her fingers fisting his hair, with her pleasured cries in his ear.

Tightening every muscle—his buttocks and shoulders and thighs and arms—he willed himself not to release. It took everything he had. To let her come for him. To feel her body dance and writhe against his. To feel her delicate nub swell and throb against his fingertips as she cried her euphoria against his neck.

Heaving gasps undulated her body, arching her against him in rhythmic shudders. His arm swept beneath her backside and lifted her, wanting more. More of this victory. For, victory it was. Like nothing he'd ever felt.

Her pleasure. Because of him.

The mere idea of it stretched his skin tight over muscle and bone. He took her lips again while she cradled his jaw and kissed him back, lush and languid. She mewled while her soaked thighs quivered, a little uncertain, a little unsteady in the wake of pleasure.

His sanity returned gradually. First, she stroked his face with tender motions and kissed his jaw softly as she might a man with a fever. The touches soothed him in ways he hadn't realized he needed. So long he'd gone without her. So long he'd hungered for something he couldn't find.

But her skin and her breath, her lips and her whispers led him back from the brink.

"English," she sighed, stroking his brows with her thumbs. She kissed his lips. Softly. Chastely. Then, she caught his gaze and smiled, her eyes as blue as cornflowers dancing in a summer field. "I missed ye more."

And just like that, his heart broke open. He didn't know what to say.

He'd wanted her so badly. In time, he'd decided to claim her. Make her his wife. It was sensible. She'd be a good mother. She'd guard their children ferociously and feed him bread regularly and order him about with that fiery mouth. He'd known marrying her was the right choice.

But until now, he hadn't known he loved her. *Loved* her. The way his father loved his mother and Robert loved Annabelle. The way that made madness a pleasure.

He eased her down, unable to speak. With great reluctance, he withdrew his hand from between her thighs. He'd been cupping her there, holding her as long as possible so he could feel every sweet pulse. As he lowered her skirts, sound returned—carriages and horses and distant voices of pedestrians at both ends of the long, narrow close.

God, what had he been thinking? The close remained empty, and the doorway was deep in shadow, so he had no fear anyone had seen them. But he'd only meant to kiss her. A distraction. That was all.

He'd put his hand up her skirts, for God's sake. He'd made her come. He'd nearly come, himself. In truth, he'd lost his bloody mind. And his cock still ached like a wound, demanding he finish what he'd started.

"Dinnae fash," she whispered. Her cheeks flushed scarlet as she began to tidy his cravat and coat. "Yer hat didnae go far."

"Annie." His voice was shredded.

"Hmm?"

"I'm sorry I kissed you here." He chuckled dryly. "Next to a rubbish pile."

"Aye. A nasty one. My toe is still smartin'."

"But I'm not sorry I kissed you."

She arched a brow. "Well, now, that makes two of us."

"When we return to the glen, perhaps we'll test a few locations. See what suits."

She chuckled and smoothed his lapel. "I'm glad ye were here, English. Even if ye willnae tell me why." When she raised her eyes, they glistened. "Today, we fetch Broderick from the Bridewell. Seein' him promises to tear my heart from my body."

He started to speak, but she pressed her fingers to his lips. "It will. I ken the pain is comin'. But all the way to Edinburgh, I kept thinkin' how ye'd make it just a bit better. Seein' that bonnie face. Hearin' that braw voice, crisp as a Highland mornin'." She smiled, her eyes shimmering with tears. They spilled over. "And ye did make it better, English. Ye did."

She pulled him down for a kiss, and he gathered her tight in his arms. Held her close enough to make them one body. Wished with everything inside him that he could do more. When they separated for a breath, he offered, "I'll come with you. Let me come with you."

"No. This is MacPherson business." She cupped his cheek. "But if ye were at home next time I visited the castle, if ye were to invite me inside to warm myself by yer hearth, I wouldnae say no." Kissing him one last time, she slipped away, heading toward the inn.

John braced himself against the wall and breathed to ease the ache in his chest. For some reason, it took longer to dissipate than the ache in his groin. In fact, by the time he retrieved his hat and found Robert and the others at the tavern where he'd suggested they meet, he began to wonder if the vise tightening around his heart would only wrench harder until the moment he could hold Annie Tulloch in his arms again.

He sat down at the scarred table where his companions waited.

"Everything all right?" Robert asked.

John nodded. "It will be." He met the eyes of the other men at his table. "As soon as I discover who targeted my future wife's family and make him pay a very dear price."

CHAPTER FOURTEEN

There was something perverse about a prison built to resemble a palace. As far as Annie was concerned, the Bridewell should be an eyesore. Instead, it was a four-story castle with symmetrical gabled wings topped by gleaming crosses. To the rear was a third wing, semicircular in shape. The whole was surrounded by high walls and iron fencing, to be sure, but the main gate was a turreted masterpiece.

Annie gaped as their coach passed through into the inner courtyard.

How she wished she'd taken Huxley up on his offer. Her hand reflexively gripped the wee thistle charm, but it wasn't the same as holding her Englishman's strong hand.

She leaned her cheek against the coach wall to get a better view out the window. Campbell and the taller solicitor handed a gaoler the papers ordering Broderick's release. The gaoler was dark and small, his clothing neat. He nodded at something the solicitor said and waved to another set of gaolers.

"How bluidy many of ye does it take to read an order?" she muttered. The thistle dug into her palm. Her other hand hovered on the door handle. Angus and her brothers had warned her not to leave the coach. But, by God, if these damnable wretches didn't bring her brother to her right this moment, she would walk into that prison palace and fetch him herself.

The second and third gaolers nodded their understanding, and they waved Campbell and Alexander through a second set of gates.

The coach door opened.

Angus gave a disgusted grunt and climbed inside, hunching as he took the bench opposite Annie. He looked haggard and old. "Not long now, lassie."

She eyed the makeshift litter they'd installed diagonally across the benches. Made of a canvas sling lined with blankets and straw, it should prove comfortable for a normal man. But she didn't know the extent of Broderick's injuries. When she'd asked, Rannoch had gone deathly grim. "It's bad, Annie." Her youngest brother had run a hand over his eyes. "Very bad."

Now, she saw her own dread reflected in Angus's face. "Da."

He glanced up.

"We have him back. He's free. They cannae charge him again, can they?"

Her father didn't answer straight away. Instead, he leaned forward with his elbows on his knees and patted the bedding she'd assembled. "This is fine work ye've done."

"Da—"

"Ye'll give him proper care, Annie; I've no doubt of it."

"Of course I—"

Dark eyes met hers. "The truth is, we dinnae ken who hates him enough to do this."

"What of Skene?"

Angus shook his head. "Merely the hand that pulled the trigger. He's gone to ground. Even Alexander couldnae track him."

Her heart sank. If they couldn't locate Skene, they couldn't find the man behind Skene. The one with the real power. She reached for Angus's hand. "We'll discover who did this, Da. We must."

He squeezed her fingers and opened the coach door. "Aye, lassie. We must."

Long minutes passed. Sullen rain began to fall.

She watched Rannoch and Angus pacing in the courtyard, glimpsed gaolers passing by on rounds, saw women and men beyond the inner gates working, chatting, and peering out at them.

Prisoners. They milled about as if nothing were amiss. Women carried baskets and men pushed wheelbarrows. Even children dashed by as though this were a normal castle inhabited by busy servants.

It seemed an absurdity to Annie. She closed her eyes and tried to think of something more pleasant. The scent of her kitchen when dinner was almost ready. The waterfall just north of Glendasheen Castle.

John Huxley's kiss. Oh, heavens.

She sighed and sank back, remembering his lips. His hands. His fingers and the wondrous things he'd made her feel. And her chest ached. Because, as pleasurable as their kiss had been, what she most longed for were the moments afterward, when his eyes had blazed down at her with rapturous fixation. Seeing John Huxley as ensnared as she was had been glorious. Knowing how much he wanted her, how willing he'd been to forgo his own pleasure for hers, and how she'd calmed him with her touch—these were the reasons she'd lost her soul to him.

How utterly daft. And utterly true.

She chuckled softly at the thought, picturing him flushed and handsome, his hair thoroughly mussed, his perfect lips a bit swollen. Hugging herself now, she tried to hold on to the memory. To let it warm her while rain pattered then poured.

Slowly, the cold intruded. So did sound. She wanted to block it out. Squeezing her eyes tighter, she prayed the agonized growling she heard amidst the rainfall wasn't a father's rageful anguish.

She opened her eyes.

It was.

Oh, God.

Oh, sweet Christ.

He was a corpse. Two of her brothers carried a third between them. Long arms stretched across their shoulders.

Nothing but long bones covered by grayish skin. His face. Unrecognizable.

One of his eyes was …

Annie's throat closed. She was going to vomit. Bloody hell, she must. Not. Vomit.

No! Her head disconnected from her body, floating toward the coach's ceiling. But her hands knew what to do. They flung the door open. Her feet climbed down and raced toward her brother.

Her mouth sobbed a denial. Her heart screamed that she would kill whoever had done this. She would kill them and serve them their own hearts for supper.

Apparently, she screamed these things in her head, because nobody heard. Rather, she was stumbling toward Broderick when Rannoch grabbed hold of her. He held her firmly with an arm across the front of her shoulders. "He'll heal, Annie," he rasped. "We'll help him. Dinnae cry, sister."

She clung to him, her knees collapsing. "Ah, God, Rannoch."

"I ken. I ken."

Campbell and Alexander carried their brother past her, and she could finally see what the Bridewell had done.

Every gruesome detail. That strong, square MacPherson jaw lacerated and swollen. The bones of his cheeks distorted as though they'd been broken again and again. The nose that she'd always teased him must have come from his mother, for Angus's nose could never be so handsome—that nose was weirdly angled and flattened. And his eyes—those dark-storm eyes fair broke her in half. The one that remained intact was flat and distant. It didn't flicker with recognition. It didn't glance her way. His other eye was … not an eye any longer.

She wanted to touch him. Tried to touch him.

Rannoch held her fast. "Wait, Annie," he murmured. "He's injured everywhere. Ye must take care, ye ken?"

Breathing fast, she clung to Rannoch and forced herself to listen.

"Aye, ye ken." Rannoch hugged her, drawing her closer and rocking her a wee bit. "Let us load him into the coach. Then, we'll take him home."

She nodded. Rannoch moved away to help from the opposite side.

She swayed in place as she watched Campbell and Alexander carry Broderick as carefully as a bairn. Watched as Angus, hovering at the rear wheel, staggered and caught himself.

"Da," she sobbed.

He turned to her, his eyes burning with a father's grief. Then, he opened his arms.

And she ran into them. Not to be comforted, though his strength often did that.

But to comfort the man who had chosen to be her father.

And had just lost his son.

Two months passed before they could even consider leaving Edinburgh. In the townhouse Rannoch had rented, Annie took charge and prepared a chamber for Broderick. Cooked a fortifying broth for Broderick. Hired four lads to clean and fetch water and wash linens for Broderick. She scarcely slept. When the physicians weren't stitching or dosing or murmuring their doubts, she tended a vacant, feverish man's wounds and sat beside his bed, keeping vigil.

She had no time to mourn. Every second was needed to hold what was left of her brother together.

The other MacPhersons did everything else. They interrogated gaolers at the prison. They bribed and coerced those who worked in the infirmary. They met with men they refused to name in parts of the city she hadn't known existed. They stayed gone until the wee hours, and when they finally trudged through the door at day's end, they looked as exhausted and helpless as she felt. Sometimes, they returned with bloodied knuckles.

She knew because she was awake. Someone must keep watch, she reasoned, in case Broderick decided to leave them.

After several more weeks of care, Broderick made his decision. His breathing steadied. His fever receded. His eye began to follow her around his chamber as she tidied and chatted and read to him. The physicians pronounced him "on the mend."

Throughout their stay in Edinburgh, they had visits from John Huxley. Annie's focus upon Broderick lifted like a thick fog in a bracing wind each time she heard his crisp, English voice at the door. She'd wander downstairs, dazed and worn and a pure mess. He'd open his arms for her. She'd let him enfold her with his strength and heat, feeling such relief she couldn't speak. Neither of them spoke, really. She didn't ask why he was there, why he kept visiting every few days. She only thanked God for those few precious minutes until Angus sent him on his way so she could sleep—which she rarely did.

Eventually, the physicians decided Broderick could tolerate travel, so she arranged for the house to be cleaned and packed up, prepared a new litter for the coach, and waited for John Huxley's next visit. Instead,

Angus informed her Huxley had headed back to the glen. Her heart plummeted, though she understood. She still didn't know why he'd stayed so long in Edinburgh.

Now, five days later, she stepped from the coach, watching Rannoch and Alexander carry Broderick into MacPherson House. The long journey home had been an arduous one. Early summer rainstorms had turned the roads muddy, and the motion of the carriage disturbed Broderick. He didn't speak, of course. He made no sound at all. But Annie had come to recognize every tiny twitch of his face.

When she could, she comforted him with piles of blankets, the laudanum from the physicians, and the soup he loved best, the one with leeks and potatoes. Because her voice seemed to help him rest easier, she'd read aloud from newspapers and blethered on about things that had happened while he'd been away.

She'd told him about Flora MacDonnell losing her dress shop. About Grisel MacDonnell moving to Dingwall. About hiring Betty MacDonnell to be her lady's maid.

Mostly, she'd told him about John Huxley—more than she should have, perhaps, but Broderick was a good listener.

Now, standing in the drive outside her house, Annie watched her lads rush out to unload the coach and care for the horses. In her mind, she was listing everything she must do—rally her kitchen lads to get water boiling, start preparing dinner, ensure Broderick's chamber had been properly aired and a fire properly built—when the muscles in her abdomen and thighs began to quiver. Her blinking fell out-of-rhythm.

Then, light began to dim.

She frowned. The afternoon was bright for a change, no clouds in sight. Why was it darkening? Her next blink went on too long. Birds chirped in the leafy birches, but the sound washed in and out like waves on a shoreline. The stones of her house blurred strangely. The doorway wavered. Shaking her head, she felt herself tilting. Or was that the ground?

"Annie?"

Weak. She was so bloody weak.

Her legs turned to water. Folded.

"Och, my sweet lass."

Wool and peat and Highland air. Strong arms that had never failed her. Lifting. Carrying.

"Ye've fair worn yerself to the bone, daughter. 'Tis time ye slept."

A kiss upon her forehead. Then, the light was gone.

Sound sifted into Annie's consciousness through a thick, gray fog. Her eyelids weighed a ton. Try as she might, she couldn't force them open.

"… cannae let ye press her into such a decision until she's improved."

"I've waited months already, Angus. Bloody months."

"Aye."

"… continue my search … after Annie … my wife … refuse to be separated from her … belongs with me …"

To her great frustration, his voice kept fading in and out. But she recognized her Englishman. She wanted him closer.

"… appreciate all ye've done, lad."

"Then, let me—God, just let me—"

"Ye're nae thinkin' straight. She's done in. Give her a day or two."

Annie wanted to protest. She'd never be too tired to reach for him. Gathering every ounce of her stubbornness, she forced her eyelids up. The light was a bit blurry, a bit gray. It was her bedchamber window, she supposed. She recognized the blue checked curtains she'd sewn herself. With another great, heaving effort, she drew a breath and mumbled, "English." Her pillow half-smothered the word.

But he heard.

The next sight to appear was his face. Ah, God, that bonnie face. Golden-hazel was surrounded by weary creases and streaks of red.

She blinked. Tried to move her arm. It weighed more than her eyelids.

Her Englishman knelt beside her. Then, the mattress moved, and he lay on his side next to her, his face inches from hers, his arms scooping her body into his.

"Huxley," Angus warned from the doorway across the room. "Mind yerself."

She ignored her father's growl to sigh and smile. "English."

Perfect lips touched her cheek. A bristly jaw chafed her mouth. "Good morning, love."

Suddenly, she wanted to cry. Her eyes didn't want to stay open. She felt like she was folding in upon herself. "English," she whimpered.

He gathered her tighter, his arms binding her body to his. "Shhh, Annie. Rest, now. You've exhausted yourself, and you need sleep."

Her breath stuttered. "B-Broderick?"

"He's settled in. Betty is tending him, along with the surgeon from Inverness. Marjorie MacDonnell has been helping manage things here whilst you recover. Everything is fine."

The world darkened to gray again. She didn't know how long she drifted, but when she opened her eyes, he was still there. A warm, lean hand caressed her back. Gentle fingers played with her hair.

"H-how long … since we returned home?"

"A few days."

"How many?"

"Three."

She fought to lift her hand from where it nestled on his chest. She only just managed to trace his jaw before her strength gave out. "Ye've … stayed with me, English?"

"Yes."

"Here?"

"Yes." Warm lips caressed her eyelids, which had a great deal of trouble remaining open. "Angus is none too happy about it. But he can go hang. Wherever you are, that is where I belong."

She wanted to thank him. She wanted to tell him how deeply she'd longed for him every day. Every hour. Every second he wasn't beside her. But the sleep she'd missed over the past weeks robbed her strength.

With the scraps that remained, she whispered to her Englishman, "Dinnae let Marjorie MacDonnell near my kitchen."

A deep, surprised chuckle sounded from his chest, moving through her ear and cheek. "No, love. I wouldn't dare."

And this time, she fell asleep with a smile.

CHAPTER FIFTEEN

Annie tugged Bill the Donkey along the newly graveled road, thinking how lovely it would be if every day could be this grand. The water of the loch shimmered in a soft summer breeze. All around, light danced and leaves laughed and birds sang a merry tune.

John Huxley had stayed with her for four days and four nights before she'd ordered him to go home, change his shirt, and have a shave.

That had been yesterday. Today, she would see him again. She shimmered like the water, danced like the light, laughed like the leaves, and sang like the birds.

She glowed bright as the bonnie sun. Because of him.

"Careful ye dinnae float away, lass," said Mrs. MacBean with wry affection.

Annie grinned over her shoulder. The old woman looked rather handsome in her new tartan gown. When Annie had presented her latest gift to Mrs. MacBean earlier that morning, she'd insisted on helping with the woman's wild hair, as well. Apart from a milky eye and a vaguely puzzled expression, Mrs. MacBean now looked like a proper chaperone.

Except for the apron. A worn, not-quite-white apron did not belong on such lovely wool.

"I'd be happier if ye didnae cover that fine gown I made ye with ugly auld canvas."

"I'll nae go soilin' such a bonnie dress."

Annie rolled her eyes.

"'Tis a protective cover," Mrs. MacBean insisted. "Akin to the ones on books." A pause. "Mayhap I should have a *leather* apron."

Annie laughed. Then sighed. Then petted Bill's nose. Then kissed Bill's nose. He snorted as if to say she was mad.

Perhaps she was. Utterly mad for a certain Englishman.

"Now, *yer* gown, that one is made for seein'."

Annie glanced down at her own dress, a simple sweep of satiny blue silk. She ran a hand over her hip and felt her skin warming at the thought of her Englishman's face. How his eyes would glow. How his jaw would flicker. She lifted her hem. How much better it would be if she didn't stain the silk with mud before he ever saw her.

Fortunately, the road to Glendasheen castle was much improved from the last time she'd made this journey. Dougal and his brothers had done fine work, widening the lane to better accommodate a cart or carriage and reinforcing the banks with larger rocks.

Huxley had truly turned a cursed castle into a blessed one.

They arrived in the courtyard to find Dougal directing his sons to return to the stables, as they hadn't finished their tasks. Annie rolled her eyes. "Dougal, ye'd best stop spoilin' those laddies," she called. "Else, ye'll be feedin' them 'til they're fifty."

Dougal's grin broadened. He tipped his hat and repositioned it on his head. "Miss Tulloch, ye look bonnie as a summer day."

"How do lasses go about in these dresses without fashin' about every splatter of rain? It's beyond my ken."

He chuckled. "No fashin' necessary. My Betty will take good care of ye."

"Aye, that she has." Annie looked around the courtyard as Dougal helped Mrs. MacBean down from Bill's back and took the donkey's reins. "Where is Mr. Huxley?" She tried to sound casual as she retrieved Huxley's gift from the saddlebag.

Dougal directed them to the waterfall. "I think he meant to do a bit of anglin'."

Annie nodded her thanks then linked arms with Mrs. MacBean and started toward the northern trail. She drew a shuddering breath scented with warm pines and damp grass.

Mrs. MacBean patted her hand fondly. "Dinnae be nervous," she soothed. "If the lad has anythin' betwixt those handsome ears, he'll love it."

Annie's smile trembled. "I hope so."

As they passed the old church, Annie slowed. Her heart squeezed. A chilling breeze passed through her, and she slid a hand over her ribs.

"Did ye see somethin', lass?"

"No."

"Then why did yer light suddenly go out?"

Annie's throat closed around an ache. She looked down at the package in her hand. Then, she looked again at the rusted gate and the empty arches. The gravestones that were being worn away by time.

She'd forgotten. True, there'd been numerous distractions—the Lady Lessons and the new gowns and the trouble with Broderick. But she'd *forgotten* him. How could she have done that?

"Och, dinnae let these auld, dead spirits darken yer day," Mrs. MacBean admonished. She lightly shook Annie's arm, drawing Annie's gaze back to her half-sighted, age-crinkled countenance. "Ye've a braw, handsome man waitin' for ye. And if his uncle is anythin' to go by, ye're a very fortunate lass."

She attempted a smile, but it shook until it fell. "Aye. Ye're right."

They started forward again. By the time they approached the clearing, Mrs. MacBean was pulling ferns from her hair and complaining about the heat.

"I told ye, auld woman, ye shouldnae be wearin' that heavy apron over a wool walkin' dress. For God's sake, it's summer."

"Aye, and the midges are swarmin'." Mrs. MacBean slapped her neck. Then slapped Annie's.

Annie swatted her hand away and tugged aside a long bramble branch that had grown into the path. Ducking past it and raising her voice to be heard above the fall, she said, "There's no use killin' the wee beasties. They'll just …"

She stumbled as the waterfall came into view. All her air and every thought left her body. Then fire rushed in.

"Sweet Christ and all his unicorns, lass. Is that …?"

Annie tried to swallow, but her throat was too dry. Everything else was wet.

Especially … him.

He stood in the pool at the base of the waterfall, hands raking through his hair as water cascaded over his chest. His naked chest. The one with hard, defined muscles and a bit of brown hair in all the right places. Mostly on the muscles.

"I've some herbs and such to collect from the riverbank," said Mrs. MacBean. "And other places. Bog myrtle for the midges. Also, mushrooms. Och, so many things to find. I'll be gone an hour. Mayhap two." She patted Annie's shoulder before whispering, "Enjoy, lass."

Annie's chaperone disappeared, and she barely noticed. Who gave a bloody damn about anybody but the mostly-naked John Huxley?

Certainly not her.

She wandered closer, uncaring about the grasses brushing her skirts or the midges stinging her arms. Wee little thrills traveled her skin. Her pounding heart pulsed and swelled against her bones.

She crossed the field slowly, savoring the sight of him. The waterline splashed around the rippling muscles of his abdomen. Was he fully naked? She'd like to see. Purely out of curiosity, mind.

"English." God, her voice was ragged. And no wonder. Her blood was hot, her nipples peaked, her belly aching. *Everything* was aching. "English," she said louder.

His head turned. They locked eyes. He blinked then fixed upon her. Brilliant hazel began to glow. "Annie?"

She nodded.

Slowly, he came toward her, swimming through deeper water with strong strokes then standing. And rising. And—oh, dear heaven—all he wore were drawers. Probably Cleghorn's finest linen. The kind one could see through when it was wet. Which it was. Very wet.

She tried to breathe. Then tried to look away. Then decided that was foolish, as he was not bothering to hide anything. So, she looked. And gasped. And wondered whether a caber that size made riding more difficult.

"Enjoying the view, are you?"

Aye, that she was. When she finally forced her gaze up to his face, he was grinning. No modesty, no shyness, no hesitation. He behaved as if he stood mostly-naked before lasses every day of his life.

Arrogant, seductive Englishman.

"I—I brought ye somethin'."

He glanced down at himself as he retrieved his trousers and shirt from a pile on the bank. "Likewise."

Heat flooded her cheeks. Her entire face prickled like it had been stung by midges. "A gift, ye devil. I brought ye a gift."

His grin was a wicked taunt. "Your gifts are most welcome." He eyed her breasts and ran a hand through his hair before shrugging on his shirt. When he pulled on his trousers, a wee little part of her mourned.

"I'm nae talkin' about my bosoms."

"Pity."

"I made ye somethin'."

"Bread?"

"No."

He strode closer, taking his time, looking at her like *she* was his favorite meal. "Butter?"

She blushed harder. "No."

He stopped a breath away, both hot and watery-cool. "Honey?"

"God, English."

"I missed you."

"Ye saw me yesterday."

His smile was the most riveting, sensual thing she'd ever seen. "Too long," he rasped. "Where's your chaperone, love?"

"She's wanderin' about collectin' herbs and such."

"Have I ever mentioned how much I like Mrs. MacBean?"

Annie snorted. "Well, she likes ye back, that's for certain."

He cast a glance around them before crowding close and lowering his head. "How long do I have?"

She swallowed. "An hour or so." Heavens, his mouth was close. And so, so tempting. "But I must ... I must give ye yer gift."

He sighed and stroked a knuckle gently down the side of her neck. Shivers shook her. "Very well," he said, nose flaring. "What did you bring?"

She closed her eyes and rested her free hand on his chest. He felt damp and hot and hard. Gathering her strength, she stepped back and held out her package.

He quirked a puzzled smile before unwrapping the brown canvas she'd used for covering. Inside, the blue-and-green tartan lay folded neatly beneath a handsome belt she'd asked Rannoch to purchase for her in Edinburgh. He had an eye for fine leather goods. Angus had helped choose the sporran, of course, which was black with silver trim and white fur tassels. It was embossed with a proud stag's head that resembled the one from Glendasheen Castle's new windows. Campbell had selected a dirk with a similar design etched on the blade, and Alexander had fashioned a *sgian-dubh* with a stag's antler handle.

The kilt itself was entirely Annie's creation. She'd agonized over every stitch. She'd sized it from memory, picturing her Englishman over and over as she'd measured the wool and sewn the pleats. She only hoped it fit properly. And that he liked it. And that he would say something.

Instead, he stared at the items as though he didn't know what to do with them.

"'Tis a kilt," she said helpfully.

He blew out a breath. Nodded. Ran a hand over his jaw.

Oh, blast. Did he hate it? He must hate it.

"Ye—ye'll need one if ye still wish to compete. In the Glenscannadoo Games, I mean." Her stomach sank when he wouldn't even look at her. "It doesnae have to be this one, of course. I only thought ye might—"

His hand cupped her nape and brought her mouth up to his. The kiss was a fierce claiming rather than the gentle caresses or the sensual seduction of their past encounters. By the time he finished with her, she was reduced to little more than butter and honey and desire.

"I love it," he panted against her lips.

"Ye do?"

"It's the best gift anyone's ever given me, Annie."

She grinned like a pure dafty. "Aye? Well, let's put it on ye, then."

Explaining each piece of the ensemble as she laid them out on a flat stone, she finally shook out the kilt and offered it to him. "We'll put it over yer breeches for now, but when ye wear it to the games ye must have nothin' underneath, ye ken?"

The gleam in his eye was devilish. "I ken, love."

"Stop lookin' at me that way."

"I can't help it. You are stunning. Do you know your hair looks like fire?"

She touched the wisps around her cheeks.

"And your eyes. They are the color of cornflowers."

Her breathing quickened. "A—a lot of nonsense. That's what this is. *Ye're* the bonnie one, here."

He grinned wide, his eyes crinkling at the corners.

"Now, stop distractin' me," she said, her gaze riveted to that smile. "We must see if this kilt fits ye."

Raising his arms out to his sides, he arched a brow. "I am at your service, Miss Tulloch."

As she wrapped the wool around his waist, she tried not to breathe. Not to touch. Not to let her breasts brush against him. She failed miserably on all counts. By the time she'd fastened the buttons hidden inside the waist and correctly positioned his belt, a great deal of touching had occurred. In fact, unusually sensitive parts of her had swept across unusually hard parts of him at least eight times. On the final pass, he might have groaned.

"There," she panted, refusing to look him in the eye. "Ye're perfect. Er—yer proportions are ... a perfect fit."

"They will be."

She turned away to fuss with his sporran and the scabbard for his dirk. "No need to add all this today. When the time comes—"

"I'll need you there with me."

Oh, God. He stood directly behind her, his hot breath on her neck, his shadow mingling with hers. Then, his lips touched her skin—just the spot where her shoulder met her throat. She felt his cool, damp hair and his newly shaven jaw and the mass of tingling sensations that burned through her whenever he was near.

"I need you with me always, love."

She sank back into his body, weak and molten. How badly she needed him, too. The ache was maddening.

He began plucking pins from her hair, kissing his way across her shoulder and up her throat. His arms banded her waist and pulled her hips back into his.

Her vision grew so bright, she had to close her eyes.

"Marry me, Annie."

At first, she thought she'd imagined the husky murmur. So, she simply raised her hand to cup his cheek while he nibbled her neck and swept one of those lean, talented hands up to her breast.

She moaned as he began stroking her nipple through the silk of her dress and the cotton of her corset.

Then, he said it again. More insistent, this time. "Marry me." He nibbled her earlobe and squeezed her nipple with not-quite-enough pressure. "Be my wife."

Engulfed by heat and desire, Annie nearly answered with the word that was pounding from her heart. *Yes. Yes, yes, yes.* But just as her lips parted to speak, a tiny chill of sanity struck. She slid her hands over the tops of his. Held as tightly as she could.

And remembered why she'd thought of marrying in the first place.

Finlay. To have him in her life again, she must marry a lord.

John Huxley was a gentleman. John Huxley had stolen her heart. John Huxley might very well be the only man she would ever truly want. But he was not a lord.

So, it came to this: She must choose one or the other. Her laddie. Or her love.

Her throat closed. Realization choked her, and she dug her fingertips into her Englishman's strong hands.

He'd felt her body still, and now, his did the same. "Do you intend to answer?" Quiet. Cold. His arms fell away.

She tried to hold him, but he was distant, now—a ship casting off into the dark. Her chest went so tight, she couldn't breathe. Her ribs hurt. Everything hurt.

Finlay. She squeezed her eyes closed, taking shallow breaths and hugging herself.

Finlay.

"Perhaps no answer is answer enough, hmm?" Ice-cold, her Englishman. Withdrawing. Leaving her.

She must say something. Or at least look at him. Could she look at him? Not without falling apart. "English ..." She turned. And fell apart.

He was shaking his head, his lips a bitter twist. Whatever glow had shone in his eyes was gone. What remained was flat acceptance and the barest hint of pain. "Not to worry, Miss Tulloch. It was my mistake. A bit of wishful thinking, you might say."

Every inch of her trembled. Something was tearing out her center. She stumbled toward him. Wanted to explain. "No, English—"

But he turned away. Gathered up the items she'd brought. Raised them in the air. "My thanks for the souvenirs. When I return to England, they'll be good reminder of something I never should have forgotten."

"Please," she begged.

He strode away, ignoring her. Long strides carried him along the riverbank and into the trees then out of view.

The wind suddenly gusted, blowing her hair into her eyes. She scarcely noticed. Everything bloody hurt. So much that she bent forward, trying desperately to hold herself together. But her ribs felt battered and crushed. Her lungs wouldn't work right.

She should follow him. She should explain, even though he hadn't believed her the first time. Even though he wouldn't believe her now.

But the choice was impossible. How could she have allowed herself to fall so deeply in love with him? How could she have so carelessly let Finlay's absence make her forget?

"Lass?" Old, gnarled hands came into view. Cupped her cheeks and raised her face. "Didnae ye hear me?" The single, milky eye seemed oddly penetrating. The low, scratchy voice seemed oddly resonant. "What's ailin' ye, Annie?"

That was all it took for her to crumble. She collapsed to her knees, there in the grass. And for a long while, Mrs. MacBean held her while she rocked back and forth. Finally, she managed to whisper, "He wants to marry me."

The old woman patted her back and kept rocking. "Aye."

"I didnae answer."

"Because of yer laddie."

Annie nodded.

"Do ye wish to marry the man?"

Another nod.

"Aye, of course ye do." A deep sigh. Then, the old woman pushed to her feet and bent to help Annie do the same. "Come."

Dazed as she was, Annie didn't argue. She allowed Mrs. MacBean to lead her back along the trail toward the castle. When they reached the churchyard, the woman tugged her toward the spot where the gate had once stood.

There, being overtaken by grass and a clump of thistles, was the wee ring of stones Annie had laid for Finlay.

"I cannae bear it," she whispered, the confession torn from her heart. "I cannae bear to let him go."

Mrs. MacBean squeezed her hand. "Which 'him' are ye referrin' to, lass?"

The world turned watery. Light blurred and a tear splattered onto the soil. Another sharp gust blew through her, nearly knocking her flat. She clung to the old woman and gasped to catch a sob. "John Huxley." Angrily, she swiped at her cheeks. "I love that bluidy Englishman until I cannae see straight."

"Aye." Mrs. MacBean patted her arm. "I ken."

"But how can I abandon Finlay?"

"Mayhap it was always goin' to end here." She gestured to the unmarked grave, the little circle of stones with its tangle of weeds. "Mayhap some friends arenae meant to stay forever, but only until ye dinnae need them quite so much."

Annie covered her eyes. Pictured Finlay's sweet face. His wise voice—a lad's voice carrying centuries inside it. How could she say goodbye? She'd promised to do whatever was necessary to bring him back to her.

But she hadn't thought that would mean cutting out her own heart.

She tried to imagine feeding some other husband. Kissing some other husband. Conceiving a son with some other husband. Even if that son was Finlay, everything inside her screamed it was wrong. Annie should be *John's* wife. She should feed him and love him and make him laugh because nobody else seemed able to do it quite so well.

So, she must let Finlay go. He'd be born to someone else. The void where he'd once been tethered would never entirely heal. And she would miss him. God, how she would miss him.

Another gust rocked her, colder this time. A bird called, loud and close. Annie blinked. Lowered her hand. Raised her eyes.

And there, on the tallest arch, was a white bird. It looked like a raven. She'd never seen anything like it. "D-do ye see that?"

Mrs. MacBean didn't answer. The bird called again. Its caw was a bit scratchy and distorted. It took flight and disappeared inside the church. A moment later, it landed on the arch again, this time with something in its beak.

A scrap of fabric, she thought, though it was difficult to see.

The bird looked directly at Annie, and for a moment, she would have sworn its eyes were the same color as Fin's. Then, it flew away.

But the scrap of fabric floated down, twirling and dancing on the newly vigorous wind. It landed in the center of the stones.

Blue and green tartan. The very same she'd used to make her Englishman's kilt.

"Och, that clever bird must have snatched it from my pouch earlier when I was gatherin' bog myrtle." Mrs. MacBean bent down and retrieved the little scrap of wool. "I used this for yer marriage charm."

Annie blinked at the old woman who always seemed so daft.

Mrs. MacBean smiled and tucked the scrap into the pouch she wore on her hip. "Seems I still have a bit of magic left in this auld blood, eh?"

"W-was the bird …" Annie pointed to the now-empty arch. "Was that—"

A pat of her hand. A tug toward the trail. "These are deep mysteries we seek to plumb, lass. Dark forces and hidden realms."

"Aye. Ye've said that before. Why do I suspect ye ken a lot more than ye're sayin'?"

Ignoring the question, the old woman bent to gather a handful of moss from a nearby rock and stuffed it into her pouch. "Do ye suppose Mr. Brodie's uncle will attend yer weddin', lass?" A daft sigh. "Ah, that would be a grand surprise. I havenae enjoyed a good caber toss in far too many years."

CHAPTER SIXTEEN

Annie waited to change into her lilac gown until after Betty had gone home. She sat with Broderick until she felt him ease into sleep and waited until Angus's door had closed to don her half-boots. She waited until the house was silent but for the night insects and owls outside.

Then, she made her move, slipping out the door into the bright, silvery night. Took the road north into Glendasheen, enjoying the crunch of gravel and the scent of green and the silken summer air on her skin. Soon, she was rounding the loch and approaching the castle.

Next, she was opening the door.

Near midnight, the castle stood quiet and dark. The MacDonnells had all gone home or gone to their beds. Now, standing in John Huxley's entrance hall with moonlight pouring through his new windows, she wondered if she'd find him in his bedchamber or awake in his library or milling about his kitchen in search of food that Marjorie MacDonnell hadn't ruined.

She wondered if she'd find him alone.

God, she hoped she found him alone.

Her body shook. Her hands sweated. Her throat was dry.

There was nothing for it now. She'd come here with an aim, and she meant to have it done. Slowly, she picked her way across the slate stones her English gentleman had laid with his own hands. She journeyed down the corridor to the stairs and felt her heart pounding thrice for every step she took.

She'd begin with his bedchamber, she decided. If he was there alone, she'd have her say, and that would be that. If he wasn't alone … well, she didn't know what she'd do. Probably something unladylike—insults about copulation with farm animals followed by sudden, vicious thrashing of tender body parts, perhaps. If he was elsewhere, she'd search until she found him, for she did not intend to leave here until her Englishman had been set straight. The pain in his eyes as he'd walked away haunted her.

She paused as she reached the upper floor. His door, made of planked oak that he'd repaired and refinished himself, was the last one on the left. Her heart squeezed. She took a breath. Found the handle. And went inside.

The room would be dark if not for moonlight beaming through three arched windows on the southern wall. The planks beneath her feet creaked a bit as she padded nearer the center, where she knew she'd find his bed—the green-draped bed she'd witnessed last year being hauled from his long cart, along with a massive carpet, several tables, and two tall leather chairs. Both chairs now sat facing the hearth on the east wall. It was summer, so no fire. No lantern. No light except the moon.

She could hear her own heart, her own breath, clamoring with frantic speed.

Pushing away from the door, she moved a few paces deeper into the room. That was when she heard the clink. A glass being placed on a table.

"E-English?" she queried softly.

Leather creaked, so she knew he was in one of the chairs. But he didn't rise.

"Are ye ..." She swallowed. "Are ye alone?"

A deep, cynical chuckle floated past the empty bed. "I was." A sip and then another clink. "Until a Scottish hoyden decided she fancied another taste."

Her heart twisted. "That's not what I—"

"Why are you here?" he snapped. "Eager to be bedded, are you?"

"No, that's not—"

He stood beside the chair, a dark, ominous presence. "Perhaps you desire a good tupping before you sell yourself for a pedigree."

"I dinnae intend to—"

"A title offers no assurances, you know. Titled men take mistresses with some regularity. Titled women have their playthings, as well." He tipped back his glass before setting it on the table. "Perhaps you'd care to keep me, hmm? A bit of sport when the man you marry fails to satisfy." With long, slow strides, he stalked toward her. He gripped the hem of his shirt and yanked it loose. Then, stripping it off over his head, he tossed the wadded fabric across the room.

When his face passed through a shaft of moonlight, the wounded fury there cracked her heart in two. "English. Listen to me."

He didn't want to listen. He wanted to rage. "Perhaps you simply like the idea of bleeding your prey before you devour him."

"No. God, no, I would never—"

"But I am no easy prey, for I've survived the hunt before." He drew very near. Inches away. Then, he lowered his head until she smelled whisky and pine and her beloved Englishman. "This stag has horns, love."

"I ken ye're angry."

"I'm not angry."

"Aye. Ye are." She wanted to touch him, but she feared his reaction, so she laced her fingers together at her waist. "English, please. Just listen."

His head snapped up. "Do not call me that. My name is John Huxley."

"Very well. John."

Something about that seemed to disturb him, but he merely stood there, his face so starkly shadowed, she could only see the faint gleam of his eyes. They were not gold in this light. They were ice. "Tell me why you're here."

"Ye misunderstood me this mornin'. When ye offered ... when ye said ... what ye said."

"That I wanted you to be my wife." The statement was so flat, she winced.

"Aye."

A corner of his mouth twisted into a snarl. "Say it."

"When ye asked me to marry ye."

"And you reacted as if I'd thrust a knife in your belly."

"Ye didnae understand, and I couldnae explain."

"That, as they say here in the glen, is pure shite." He tilted his head. "I understood perfectly. You didn't seek to marry a title in order to save your brother."

She blinked. Frowned. "I told ye that wasnae the reason."

"You told me outrageous tales of devotion to a phantom."

"Aye. That was the truth."

"No. The truth has nothing to do with devotion and everything to do with greed."

"Ye're anglin' in dangerous waters, English. Best pull yer rod before it gets bitten off."

He wasn't listening. Didn't seem aware of her growing anger. Too blinded by his own, she reckoned.

"Admit it, Annie. You sought to marry a lord because, like most women, you wished to elevate your station. What better way to ensure your *bairns* never have to haul whisky or muck out stables? That you needn't—"

"Speakin' of pure shite."

"—settle for a man offering only callused hands and a decent kitchen."

"Ye bluidy arrogant English arse!"

His scowl deepened into a menacing snarl. "Think you'll enjoy having some ancient prune rutting on top of you? Provided he can manage such a feat, of course. Age does unfortunate things to a man's caber."

"I dinnae *want* to marry another man, ye daft, insultin', arrogant—"

His sneer disappeared as his voice deepened to a wounded rumble. "Then why in God's name didn't you *answer!*"

"I would have if ye'd granted me a bluidy minute to think!"

"That's where we differ." His eyes flashed. His nose flared. "Whenever I'm near you, all thinking stops. Perhaps that's the problem."

"There is no bluidy problem, ye great, arrogant, insultin' English boil on the arse of a worthless donkey!"

He stared at her for long seconds. Slowly, his lips curled again, and his tongue darted out to wet them. His breathing now matched the racing rhythm of hers. His eyes weren't flat any longer, nor cold. They gleamed with a strange fever. "Arrogant, am I?"

"Aye," she panted.

"What else?"

"All the things I mentioned. And impatient, besides."

"Is that so?"

"An impatient arse who doesnae listen when a lass tries to tell him—"

"You shouldn't have come here."

"—that she'll happily be his wife if he'll give her—"

"Because an impatient, arrogant man has no reason to swallow his hunger."

"—a bluidy minute to say how much she—"

Suddenly, she was bent in half with her belly over his shoulder. He lifted and hauled her four paces to the bed, then tossed her like a bag of tatties onto the mattress. She bounced and *oophed*.

"Marry me," he rasped.

She braced herself on her elbows and eyed his naked chest. "I've already said aye." She arched her back. Licked her lips. "Or perhaps ye're eager to convince me."

"By God, you drive me mad, Annie Tulloch." He was unfastening his fall. Staring down at her like some English conqueror and unbuttoning his damned trousers.

She could scarcely believe the turn of events. This wasn't how she'd pictured things going. Worse, she was so aroused, her skin fairly pulsed.

The muscles of his chest and belly were even more pronounced in the moonlight. The contours of his face remained shadowed, but the muscle in his jaw flexed and flickered.

Her breasts swelled their approval. Her legs slid against the coverlet, and her thighs squeezed against a drumbeat of desire. "Mad for me, are ye, English?" she taunted. "A wee, greedy Scottish lass has ye wound up tight, eh?"

Stripping away the last of his clothing, he ran a hand over his face as though the end of his rope was a frayed memory. With careless, practiced flicks, he found the hem of her skirts and tossed them above her knees. "Yes. And I mean to claim you."

That rendered her breathless. Her nipples peaked until they cast moonlit silhouettes on lilac silk. Until they ached to be stroked.

"I'm going to marry you. And you're going to sleep here in my bed. You're going to cook for me, woman."

Her voice turned low and husky. "What will I cook, hmm?"

His knee staked a claim on the mattress between her legs. As he crawled over her, she caught a glimpse of his naked cock.

Oh, heavens. Her belly gave a needful squeeze. Her heart kicked faster.

"Bread," he rasped. "You'll toast it with butter and feed me pieces with your fingers."

She licked her lips, glancing to either side of her head where long, muscular arms now braced his body above hers. He hadn't even touched her yet—not really. Yet she was slick and ready.

"When I'm satisfied with that," he continued, "I'll carry you up here and plant my babe in your belly."

Her entire body shivered with the thrill that burst through her. "Ah, but bairns dinnae simply happen, English. I do believe ruttin' is required."

"A lot of it," he growled. "You said you'd let your husband do as much rutting and touching as he wants."

"Aye."

"I bloody well *want*, Annie."

She glanced between them at the intimidating proof of his statement. "As do I."

"So, you'll marry me. And cook for me. And laugh for me. And let me touch—"

"Aye."

"—you everywhere. And you'll never *think* of letting another man near you. Title or no."

She reached up and stroked his flickering jaw. "Why would I want another man when I have my bonnie Englishman?"

His arm scooped beneath her back and raised her up into his kiss. While his tongue slid inside to play with hers, she gripped his neck and ground herself against him wherever she could—lips, breasts, hips. Nothing mattered but getting closer.

She didn't know how he managed it, but between one kiss and the next, he removed her gown. By the third kiss, she was entirely naked, sprawled half beneath and half beside his naked body. How John Huxley knew so much about removing women's garments, she'd rather not know. All she wanted was him. But giving a man everything without demanding anything in return was a certain path to misery. So, she gripped his thick hair and tugged until he looked her in the eye.

"Listen, English. Ye've said what I'm to do for you. What will ye be doin' for me?"

"I'll give you sons."

She snorted, pretending derision. "More mouths to feed."

"I'll give you a castle and a kitchen."

"A castle to keep clean and a kitchen to cook yer meals, eh?"

His eyes burned with a silvery light. They raked across her breasts and belly, down to the hungriest part of her. "I'll give you pleasure, woman. Endless, torturous pleasure."

"Hmm. A fine beginnin'. Go on."

"I'll give you more gowns to wear so I can strip them from this delectable body."

She swallowed. "I like gowns, English."

"In winter, I'll take you places you cannot even imagine, where the rain is warm instead of cold. Where you may lie naked in hot sand and gaze up at a cloudless sky."

"What if I wish to stay here, where there's nothin' but snow and darkness?"

"Then, I'll build a fire in your hearth to rival Hades."

Where had the air gone? Not in her lungs, certainly. "I suspect ye'll have no trouble in that quarter."

"When summer comes, I'll take you standing beneath the waterfall."

She groaned. "What of autumn?"

"I'll wrap your naked body in a plaid. Then I'll hold you while you tell me outrageous tales about bats and poorly framed windows."

"And spring?"

"Rutting season."

"I thought that was every season."

"It is."

She laughed husky and low. How could any lass ever resist this man?

"God, you are beautiful." His hand traced the bones at the base of her throat before sliding down over her left breast. "These are ... an unmatched wonder." He cupped and plumped and squeezed. "I must warn you, I'm a bit obsessed."

She had no response, for he'd begun dragging his palm across her nipple in a steady, entrancing rhythm.

"I'll want to suckle these rather vigorously, you see. Might make them a bit tender."

"Oh, God." Her hips arched off the bed. "Best get on with it, English. All this talkin' has me ready to—"

His mouth engulfed her right nipple at the same moment his fingers tightened on the one he'd been stroking.

Pleasure burst from her breasts and rippled in every direction. She gasped, dug her heels into the bed, and sought his cock with her thigh. He was hot and hard and so ready for her, she didn't know how he'd last.

Of course, everything she knew about this process she'd learned from overhearing men boast and rib and talk pure nonsense when they thought she wasn't listening.

Nobody had ever told her how she would feel. How badly she would need to cradle his head closer and dig her fingers into his neck and beg him both to stop and never to stop because the pleasure was like liquor and too much for her sanity.

Her nipples wanted more of his mouth, his teeth, and his tongue. They pouted when he switched, abandoning one to the solace of his fingers. They swelled and grew almost unbearably sensitive to every stroke.

She writhed. She cursed. She called him vile names and promised she'd cook him venison with gravy every blessed day if he would only finish what he'd started.

"Oh, love," he groaned with a grin in his voice. "Honey is all I crave."

His suckling grew stronger. Her gasps grew sharper. He refused to touch her between her thighs, even though that was where she most needed him. Desperately, desperately needed him. He wouldn't even allow her to grind her needy center against his legs or his cock.

"What are ye tryin' to do to me, ye bonnie devil?"

"Make you come."

"Then touch me here—"

"No. This first. I've waited so long. Dreamt of making you come with only this."

He went at her again. Mouth and nipples and fingers and—ah, God. Just his voice. Just that. Desire turned that crisp, cultured English voice raw and graveled.

The sheer pleasure he drew from her—and the thought of him fantasizing about doing this to her—coalesced low in her belly. Hot between her thighs.

Deeply pulsing inside her core. She groaned and arched into him, letting his mouth and hands carry her higher. Letting the waves of pleasure grow stronger and tighten. Letting them burst and then hold and then burst brighter. Higher. Rolling and blissful.

Then, she was floating, sifting her fingers through his hair while he kissed his way down her body.

"English?" she murmured. Her voice was in shreds. Had she been shouting?

"This will only take a moment."

She blinked, confused.

He was nibbling her belly. Then lower. Then he grasped her hips and shifted her until her thighs fell open. He pressed them wider. The air blew cool across the dampness of her inner thighs and swollen folds. He positioned himself with his shoulders between her knees and his head between her legs.

Right there. His mouth was … right there.

"Er—English?"

"You don't believe you can be aroused enough to come again, but I'll show you. Not to worry." His fingers stroked down in a long, strumming motion that made her eyes flare wide and her entire body jerk. "Shh, love. Easy. You're very swollen here." He touched her center with his fingertip.

She whimpered.

He pulsed a bit of pressure.

She arched and ground her hips against the mattress.

Something wet and sleek touched her there. Right there. Right where all the pleasure of the universe resided. It flickered and danced like light upon a rippling loch. It drove her up the same slope as before.

Faster this time, as though her body knew the way by heart.

A long finger slid inside her sheath. Then a second. Then, he stretched her. And she came apart. Flew into a thousand shimmering pieces and came back together and flew apart again.

She thought he whispered something about a wee bit of pain, but her mind was roaring like the pounding ocean. Her muscles quivered and went limp. His hand streaked along her thigh, gripping and raising and finally, hooking her legs around his waist.

Then, a blunt, hot pressure began to open her sheath. Demanded entry, which she gladly gave. The way was eased by her immense arousal, and she was glad of it, for his size was difficult to accommodate.

She supposed it was because she was untried. And he was big. And—blast, why was this stretching not finished yet? She shifted her hips and tilted them up. He gripped her hard, holding her still.

His neck muscles strained and his jaw clenched. "Bloody hell," he cursed. "Stay with me, Annie."

She tried to relax. It helped a bit. But then, he thrust and the stinging pain intensified to a peak. He thrust again and slid deeper. Again, deeper. The sharper pain faded as the pressure grew. He moved easily, or at least it seemed so. She gripped his hips with her thighs to encourage him.

The man was obviously trying to impress her with his stamina. But she had already reached her peak twice. He should take his pleasure so they could sleep.

She stroked his hair and kissed his mouth while he tried not to move. Then, she made a decision. The man needed a good tupping, and she meant to give him one.

So, she placed her mouth at his ear, nibbled a bit, then whispered, "Is that all ye've got, English?"

He uttered a foul curse. Groaned her name. Thrust deep and wickedly hard. Then hammered away at her like she was a post that needed setting.

It should have hurt. But oddly enough, the friction and the pressure and the pleasure in his groans was stimulating. Heat inducing. Heart stuttering. Her breasts slid against his chest, her sensitive nipples scraping skin and hair with each bruising thrust. The astonishing rebirth of a fire she'd thought well quenched made her wonder if John Huxley weren't some sort of magician.

Whatever the root of his powers, when he slightly altered the angle of his hips to hers, she caught fire for the final strokes. What she could see of his face looked red and mad and desperate. "Again," he growled. "Give over to me again."

She ran her thumb across his perfect lower lip. Below, where they were joined, her sheath rippled a warning while her swollen nub dragged with every long, hammering thrust of his cock.

He reached beneath her to cup her buttocks and bring her hips higher. Tighter. Then, he did the last thing she expected. He stopped. His hips halted at the top of a thrust, and rather than withdraw, he held himself still inside her, pressing the head of his cock hard against the mouth of her womb. "Again, love." His chest heaved like a bellows. Sweat slicked his skin. Yet, he held still. Then kissed her with near chasteness. "Do you feel it? How tight you are around me?"

She shook her head, not as a denial but simply because all thought had ceased. She spun inside a whirlwind.

"Yes," he insisted. "Tight because you were meant to be mine alone. Wet because your nipples need my mouth. We'll do that again tonight if you're not too sore. You want me to move?"

She nodded. Whimpered. "English."

His cock slid deeper, the pressure intensifying. "There. Better?"

Her answer was to arch her back and gasp for air. For bloody sanity.

"There it is." He sounded utterly pleased. "That's the way. Your body longs to be filled, love. Let mine be of service. That is why I was born." His eyes burned and his arms shook and his muscles hardened to stone. "*You* are why I was born."

Her pleasure broke open. Her body seized upon his with screaming force. The relentless waves milked and milked him, demanding he do precisely what he'd promised—to fill her completely. And so he did. With a hard, agonized groan, he applied himself to the task, taking her and taking her and taking her. Pounding and pounding and pounding. Heat coiled. Friction ignited. A few more ramming strokes, and she rejoiced as ecstasy consumed him in a blaze. He roared with it. He shook the bed with it. His body strained and writhed in its grip, filling her with his seed. His need. His pleasure and strength. Burying his face in her neck, he collapsed upon her, his muscles slowly easing, but his hot, damp breaths a pulsing remnant of his pleasure. In the aftermath, he eased his weight to the side but slid her thigh up over his, refusing to pull free of her.

Happily replete, she lay half beneath him, still joined, running her fingers over his remarkable arms and savoring the thought of lying like this each night. Of touching him whenever the whim took her. Of carrying his bairns inside her womb. Of watching him laugh and eat her food and become a father.

He would be a good one, she thought. Then, she tried moving a bit and grinned when he sleepily gathered her closer, refusing to let her budge an inch. John Huxley would be good at most things. Best of all, he'd be a spectacular husband.

"Marry me, Annie," he murmured against her throat, the words slurring and drowsy. "Say you will."

"Aye, English. I want nothin' more." She stroked his jaw with all the tenderness aching inside her—and regret at the pain she'd caused him. "I'm sorry it took me so long to say so."

A long breath whooshed from him as though he'd been holding it in for years. He held her tighter. Wrapped himself around her. Then, as his heavy muscles relaxed fully into sleep, he muttered, "Sorry it took me so long to find you."

CHAPTER SEVENTEEN

Why had she ever accused John Huxley of being dainty? The man weighed a ton. And he slept harder than a bloody rock.

Annie managed to lift his hand from her breast, but his other hand immediately squeezed her bottom and scooted her further beneath him. She'd be pleased to accommodate him if daylight weren't already pouring through the window. But she must return to MacPherson House before Angus sent her brothers to kill the man she loved.

"Devil's ballocks, English," she panted, cradling her future husband's head, which lay between her bosoms. He was impossible to wake. She patted his cheek. No response. "I'd reckon ye up and died on me if yer cock hadnae decided to wish me a good mornin'." She stroked the length of his braw, strong back and stretched to caress his equally braw backside. "A very good mornin', indeed."

She longed to stay. Sore though she was, she wanted to remain with him until he awakened. She wanted to watch his eyes burn gold for her in this bright dawn light. But she had to go.

With a great heave, she shoved his shoulder. It took an additional four shoves and a lot of sliding to accomplish her aim. He turned onto his back, but his grip on her lower back rolled her with him until her body plastered atop his. Their position suddenly spread her legs wide over his hips and nestled his cock in the seam between her thighs.

She dropped her forehead onto his shoulder and laughed. "Even when ye're dead asleep, ye're ready for another tuppin'." She raised up to kiss his bonnie lashes and perfect lips. "If I didnae ken better, I'd think ye were Scottish."

Heavens, he was arousing. Every hard, delicious inch of him. But she had to go.

Really.

She sighed. Really, she should ...

She kissed him once more. Caressed his jaw and traced his handsome, patrician nose with her fingertip. "Do ye have any idea how much I'll miss ye, English?" she whispered. "Even an hour feels like torture."

But she must leave. So, she braced her hands on his shoulders and sat up.

His eyelids fluttered. Then lifted. His body tensed—and not in a lustful way. Rather, he seemed startled and threatened, like hunted prey.

One moment, she sat astride the man she loved.

The next, she lay pinned to the bed with a madman above her.

"What were you doing?" he growled, his hands gripping her wrists with hard pressure. "What the devil did you think you were doing?"

All the hues of his eyes, green and brown and gold, were visible because his pupils were pinpoints. But as beautiful as they were, they didn't see her.

"English?" She kept her voice calm and low, as he was holding her much more tightly than he would have done if he were not in the grip of something ferocious. "Perhaps ye were dreamin', but ye're awake now."

He shook her. "You were on top of me."

"Aye." She winced. "I didnae mean to give ye such a start." Despite the discomfort of being pinned, she attempted to lighten the mood. "Och, ye're a hard sleeper, English. In more ways than one. I had to grow new muscles to roll yer dead weight off of me. And ye still refused to loosen yer grip on my backside. That's how we wound up playin' rider and mount. Not that I'm opposed to new positions, mind. Standin' on my head might be out of the question. But most other things, I'm available for persuadin'."

His brow crinkled. He blinked. His breathing slowed from a harsh pant to a steady rhythm. "Annie?"

"Good mornin', English," she said with a gentle smile.

He glanced to where he held her. Went a bit peely. Then instantly released her and rolled away. "God. I'm sorry. I—did I hurt you?"

"Nah. I've had worse tussles with a leg of lamb. Nearly put out an eye once." Cautiously, she sat up. Her wrists were a bit red, but they didn't hurt. "Was it a nightmare, then?"

He didn't answer. Merely ran a hand down his face then plucked up her hands to examine her wrists.

She scooted closer. "Can ye tell me what happened?"

Frowning, he shook his head and laid the gentlest kisses on the insides of each wrist. "I am a deep sleeper. Sometimes when I first awaken, I'm a bit … disoriented." More kisses. A nuzzle or two. "I am dreadfully sorry, love," he whispered.

She slid into his lap and wrapped her arms around his neck. "Seems ye thought ye were bein' attacked, hmm?"

Again, he didn't answer.

Sighing, she cupped his jaw, kissed his mouth, and stroked his cheek with her thumb. "I ken ye'd never hurt me, English."

"I would die first." Blazing gold, his eyes lifted to hers. "And I would kill anyone else who tried."

Enchanting, ferocious Englishman. She grinned. "Aye, of course. Now, I dinnae need anyone killed today, but I could use a bit of help with my gown."

"Why? You're ravishing like this." He stroked her loose hair and dragged his lips along her naked shoulder.

"I must dress so I can return to MacPherson House." She kissed him and slid off his lap. "Before Angus arrives with his huntin' rifle."

"I'm coming with you."

She climbed off the bed and began gathering up her gown and underclothes. "Nah. Ye should stay here." After tugging her shift over her head, she bent and plucked a stocking from beneath one of the leather chairs. "I'm more than a wee bit fond of yer bonnie face."

"I am coming with you. End of discussion."

Glancing at him over her shoulder, she arched a brow. "Ah, ye're amusin', English. Come help me with my corset."

An hour later, Annie sat in her lilac gown upon Jacqueline's back with her amusing Englishman's arms wrapped around her. She didn't know which of them had won the argument. Once he'd begun helping her fit her bosom into her corset, she'd completely lost track of her point.

But as MacPherson House came into view through riffling birch leaves, she began to fret about Angus's reaction.

"Best let me do the talkin'," she warned.

"Your father and I have an understanding."

Her da wasn't the understanding sort.

"Everything is fine."

She snorted. "Mayhap ye enjoy havin' yer teeth removed by another man's knuckles, but I'd prefer to feed my husband more than soft tatties."

"Hmm." His chest rumbled on a deep chuckle. "Soft tatties sound … appetizing."

"Be serious, English."

"Will there be gravy on the tatties?"

"Good God."

"How about butter?"

She swatted his arm then laced their fingers together. "We'll have to wed straight away. Angus will insist. Ye ken that, right?"

He nuzzled her ear. Tightened his hold on her belly. Then whispered, "I'm counting on it, lass."

On the rare occasions when John imagined the woman who might one day become his wife, he'd pictured someone pleasant. Agreeable. Perhaps even boring. He'd imagined a proper English rose from a good family, a gentle lady who took her tea in delicate sips and complimented his mother's new settee and embroidered handkerchiefs with subdued enthusiasm.

Perhaps that explained why he'd resisted marriage for so long. He hadn't known Annie Tulloch existed.

Because no other woman came close to matching his Scottish lass.

As he lifted her down from Jacqueline's back, he fought to contain himself. Nothing had prepared him for how he felt now, knowing she was his. The pressure expanded against his bones, demanding he take her over and over. Demanding he shout his claim to everyone in the glen. Everyone in the bloody world.

She was his. His.

This fiery, foul-mouthed, uncouth, unacceptable woman was his.

This doggedly loyal, tenderly sweet, fiercely passionate woman was his.

"What are ye starin' at, English?" She frowned up at him, smoothing the sides of her hastily pinned hair. "Do I look a proper mess?"

Doo I luik a proper meiss? Those enticing lips pursed along the rounded vowels and trilled r's while a hint of vulnerability creased between scarlet brows.

God, how he loved her. Boundlessly. Inexpressibly. And, because he loved her, he must tell her the truth.

"Annie."

Cornflower blue raised in question.

A deep bellow sounded from the doorway of MacPherson House. "Where in bluidy hell have ye been?" Angus stomped out onto the drive and held up his hand. "Dinnae answer that. I've just eaten."

Annie spun, tripping herself as she faced her father.

John steadied her and met the man's glower. "Angus, I must speak with—"

"Haud yer wheesht, lad. Annie, yer brother is up and about and complainin' about his stomach. Said somewhat about havin' eggs for a change."

Annie frowned. "Rannoch never wants eggs. He doesnae care for 'em."

"Not Rannoch. Broderick."

Grasping John's hand, she squeezed and caught his gaze with wide, hopeful eyes before turning back to her father. "B-Broderick? He's up?" Her voice thinned with emotion. "He's askin' for breakfast?"

Angus grinned so broadly, John thought his jaw might crack. "Aye, lass." The man's eyes shone with suspicious moisture. "He's askin' after ye, as well."

Tears shimmering, she brought John's fingers to her lips, kissed his knuckles, then flew into her father's arms. "Thank heaven, Da," she cried. "Ah, thank the Lord."

No sooner had Angus patted her back than she tore away and rushed into the house.

Angus's grin disappeared as soon as he caught John's eye. "Ye'll marry her today."

"Yes, I—"

"I dinnae give two shites whether ye'd planned a grand ceremony in a London church with yer entire clan there to pass judgment."

"No, I—"

"Ye'll marry my daughter today, Huxley, and we'll never speak again about where she was last night. Ye ken?"

John ran a hand over his jaw, then looked at the ground, then back at Angus. Then, he laughed. Likely a mistake, but he couldn't help it.

"What the devil's so amusin', lad?"

"You know very well I am desperate to marry her. Nobody has to force my hand."

Angus crossed his arms and angled closer, attempting intimidation with his superior height. "Well, ye've bluidy well forced mine, havenae ye?"

John shrugged. "A man does what he must."

Angus snorted. "And when do ye plan to tell her who ye are?"

"How do you know I haven't?"

"Because she still treats ye like her favorite wee lamb. Once ye've felt the raw side of Annie's temper, ye'll be fortunate if ye merely find yerself in her stew pot."

A cold sensation sank into his gut. "I was hoping she'd be pleased at the news. She did aim to marry a lord."

A boy ran from behind the house to take John's horse. Wanting privacy, Angus nodded toward the south corner of the front garden, inviting John to follow. When they both stood beneath a tall willow, Angus released a breath and shook his head. "Annie doesnae tolerate lyin'. I'm walkin' naked through a bramble thicket, myself, keepin' yer secret as I've done."

Blinking at the image, John frowned.

"There's thorns gougin' away at tender bits, ye ken?"

He stifled a grin. "Yes, I take your meaning."

"My wee lass is a mite proud."

"I hadn't noticed."

"She willnae care that she might be carryin' yer bairn. If ye prick her temper, she'll make ye pay."

John considered his options. "You think she'll refuse me, then?"

"For a time, aye. Forever? Dinnae ken." Angus scratched his chin. "When she was naught but thirteen, I fibbed to her about a calf she'd grown fond of. She'd given the beastie a name, fed it by hand, doted on it. I told her she shouldnae grow attached, as it was meant to be meat. But she's stubborn. Time came, I had to tell her I'd sold it to a man at the fair who had a farm on the Isle of Skye. A big farm with acres and acres of grazin' land and grand plans to raise the wee beastie into a bull that could breed his herds."

"What was your fib?"

"Her calf wasnae sold. It strayed from the herd and was torn apart by feral dogs. Alexander tracked the dogs and put them down. I buried the calf. Changed my shirt. Then, I went home and lied to my daughter." Angus shook his head. "Tenderhearted lass. She kenned straight away. Forced me to tell her the truth." He sighed. "Didnae speak to me for a fortnight. It isnae when she's shoutin' fit to bring the roof down upon yer head that ye must fear, lad. 'Tis when she goes quiet."

This did not bode well. "We must marry straight away, Angus. After last night …"

"Aye. I ken."

"I could wait to tell her about my title until after we're married, I suppose."

"Best option. No doubt of it."

John removed his hat and ran a hand through his hair. Turning the hat in his hands, he considered what awaited him after she found out. Perhaps she would understand once he explained his reasons. Once she realized he'd given her everything she'd claimed to want. Perhaps she'd be vexed for a short while then forgive him quickly.

"Aye, she'll hate ye pure and proper. Dinnae ken how long it will last. A year, mayhap. Two. Annie is a lass of strong sentiment." Angus braced his hand on John's shoulder. "But better she has yer name first, eh? Then, even if she kills ye, her reputation is safe."

John groaned and rubbed his jaw.

"I recommend gifts, lad. Cannae go wrong with gifts."

"Bloody disaster," John muttered.

"Aye. But take heart." The older man gave him a reassuring pat. "What ye've done for this family is no small thing. My son would be dead—*dead*—if ye hadnae intervened." Angus's dark eyes flashed first with grief then with gratitude. "I'll nae soon forget that. And neither will she. Once she kens, of course."

John nodded an acknowledgement of the man's thanks. His efforts hadn't been for Angus's sake or even Broderick's. Everything he'd done had been for Annie. "I am truly heartened at how Broderick has improved. All that remains is to discover who may be held responsible for the atrocities he suffered."

"Have ye heard aught from yer kin?"

"Not yet. Dunston has promised he will send word soon."

Angus grunted and gave John's shoulder a squeeze before shifting to gaze out at the wildflower-strewn pasture. "I'm grateful to ye, son. 'Tis a fair spot of luck ye came here. I kenned an earl's whelp would have connections. I didnae think ye'd be related to the entire bluidy aristocracy."

John chuckled. "I admit, being an earl's son does have its advantages."

Bees hummed amidst the wildflowers. In the distance, a trio of cows mooed and munched. Warm, lazy wind picked up speed. Suddenly, a sharp breeze burst forth, swirling through willow leaves. It carried the scent of … honey.

He froze.

"Earl's … s-son?"

Slowly, he turned.

"English?" Her face was cloud-white. "Tell me ye were speakin' of somebody else."

"Annie." He reached her in three strides.

She didn't try to stop him. Just begged with those wounded blue eyes as if she simply did not understand why he would hurt her.

His hat plopped in the grass as he took her limp hands. "I intended to tell you; I swear it." He stroked her knuckles, alarmed by her pallor. Her silence. "Love, nothing has changed."

"Nothin'." The word was a whisper.

"My father is an earl, yes."

"An earl."

"The Earl of Berne. But *I* am John Huxley. Merely a man. The man who loves you."

"Ye're his son."

"Yes."

"Ye've only sisters." Her voice was faint, her breathing shallow. "That makes ye his heir, English. Ye're his heir."

He nodded. "We've many years before—"

"So, ye're a lord."

He tightened his jaw. "I have a courtesy title."

"Do ye, now?"

He might as well have it all out. "Viscount Huxley. I haven't used it in some years."

Several breaths passed. *"Lord* Huxley."

"It doesn't mean anything," he gritted.

Her fingernails dug into his hands until his palms stung. "Do ye have any idea what I had to sacrifice to marry ye, John Huxley?" She ripped her hands away. Stumbled back. Tripped and stumbled again.

He reached for her, and she veered toward the house.

Then she spun and screamed, "Do ye?"

His throat tightened until he couldn't bloody breathe. Her pain was pouring out of her, and he was flattened amidst the gale of it.

"Nah!" she shouted. "Because ye never. Bluidy. *Believed* me!"

She could only be referencing her absurd tale about a ghost boy. What had been his name? Fraser? No. Finlay. That was it. He'd assumed she invented the story. But what if she hadn't?

What if the boy had been real—at least to her? Then, by agreeing to marry John, she would have believed she was abandoning a friend, cutting herself off from any hope of seeing her "laddie" again.

He went cold. Sick. "Annie."

She shook her head. Covered her eyes. Her throat rippled with the effort to stifle her gasps. But a few of them emerged as tiny whimpers.

The sounds cleaved him in two.

"Naebody believes me," she rasped finally, dropping her hand. Her face was wet, her nose the only spot of color. "I'm daft to expect it. I ken that." Grief-stricken blue eyes locked upon him. "But I thought I could trust ye to tell me who ye are. At least that."

Out of pure instinct, he moved toward her. "I am entirely the man you know. I promise you, Annie."

She flinched away as he reached her. "Dinnae touch me."

"I am sorry. Please listen. I am bloody sorry."

Her face crumpled. Her hands came up to cover it again, and he couldn't bear the distance between them.

He wrapped her in his arms. Held her while she sobbed against him. "You can have him back, love," he whispered. "We'll marry, and you'll have him back. Everything will be as you wanted."

She tore away and retreated toward the house.

"Annie!"

She didn't answer. Rather, she disappeared inside, leaving him hollow and desperate.

He whispered her name again.

"Go home, lad," said Angus from behind him. "I'll speak to her when she's calmed a wee bit."

He didn't want to leave. He wanted to chase her inside, demand that she keep her word and marry him.

He wanted to hold her until she stopped hurting.

Instead, he nodded.

Angus laid a hand on his shoulder before following his daughter into the house.

And John could only stand there and listen to the bees and the cows and the leaves and the wind. And the silence that was now his punishment.

CHAPTER EIGHTEEN

Annie had a bath. A hot one in a deep tub, which she rarely had time for. Then, she drank two cups of wine and a full dram of whisky. Then, she dressed in a clean shift, wrapped herself in her plaid, curled up in her bed, and wondered what she was going to do. Apart from weeping and carrying on like one of Grisel MacDonnell's poor bairns, that was.

He'd lied to her for months. Years, even.

She could understand hiding his parentage when he'd first arrived in Scotland. Englishmen weren't particularly well received in the Highlands. An English title would only add to his trouble.

But he hadn't told her the truth when she'd fed him dinner. He hadn't told her when she'd visited his castle or bargained for Lady Lessons or trained him to grip his caber. He hadn't told her on the long journey from Inverness, when they'd spoken about his family. His sisters. His best friend. His papa and mama, who made him smile with such affection, she'd wanted to kiss him to feel his happiness curving against her.

Instead, he'd carefully avoided any hint that his family was among the most elite in England.

The Earl of Berne. She'd heard the title before but knew little about the family. Now, she knew John was a viscount who would one day be an earl.

Even the man she'd briefly considered for marriage, Lord Lockhart, was of a lower rank. Laird Glenscannadoo was lower still.

She sniffed and sat up to pour herself another dram. The whisky burned pleasantly, warming her belly.

He'd lied to her. Seduced her with burning glances. Lain with her in this very bed. Kissed her and made love to her and insisted she become his wife. And, all the while, he'd lied and lied and lied. She hadn't asked why, but she could guess.

A woman. Perhaps the modest modiste from Paris. Perhaps someone else. Regardless, John Huxley was bitterly cynical about women. He'd misjudged her motives from the start, accusing her of all manner of seduction when she'd done naught but compliment the man's eyes once or twice. Pure nonsense. He was bonnie as the sunrise, for God's sake. Was she meant to ignore it? And his laugh sent waves of pleasure down her spine. And his love for his family fair melted her heart. And … well, John Huxley was a braw slice of heaven when he wasn't accusing her of being a greedy conniver.

Sipping her dram, she stared across the room at the lilac silk gown he'd purchased for her, draped across the back of a chair. Lovely silk from an enchanting man.

No, he'd obviously been targeted before. And he wanted a wife who wanted him without the title attached. Which was why he'd been so wounded by her indecision when he'd proposed.

She wished that made everything better. She wished understanding his reasons meant she could trust him again. But she had wounds of her own, and not being believed was the biggest one of all.

A knock sounded at the door. "I'm comin' in, lass," Angus announced in his deep rumble. "Are ye decent?"

She took another drink, leaning back against her pillows and enjoying the deep fire of MacPherson whisky.

Her door inched open. Angus's iron-gray head poked inside. "Annie?"

"This is fine stuff." She held up the glass, admiring the golden color. "Better than last year's lot."

He entered and closed the door before sitting gingerly on the foot of her bed. "Aye. Take care ye dinnae drown yerself in it."

Her head was swimming, but she thought Angus sounded quieter than usual. Hesitant. Angus was never hesitant.

"What am I to do, Da?" she whispered.

He held out his hand. She slid hers inside. That big, strong paw closed around her fingers as he looked her in the eye. "Marry the lad."

With the glass in her hand, she rubbed at the ache beneath her breastbone. It slid against her plaid, but the pain did not ease. "I cannae trust him."

"Ye think ye cannae. But he loves ye." Angus paused. "I love ye, too."

His face blurred. She dropped her gaze to their hands. "Then, why did ye keep the truth from me?"

A deep sigh. "'Twas part of the agreement. He came to see me at the distillery." In low, deep tones, Angus described how John Huxley had gone from being the curse upon her father's lips to a friend and ally worthy of Annie's hand.

Months earlier, John had approached Angus and Campbell with Robert Conrad by his side. He'd immediately assured Angus of his intentions to marry Annie, presenting Robert, his brother-in-law, as a witness to his promise. That had calmed Angus's concerns long enough for them to sit down and talk over a dram.

Huxley's offer, it seemed, had been to court Annie as befitted his future countess, to woo her gently in hopes of gaining her admiration and her agreement to become his wife. Angus had wanted assurances that Huxley would neither use coercive measures nor abandon his suit should improprieties occur. Huxley had agreed. Angus had demanded that Huxley keep possession of his Scottish lands and make his home with Annie permanently in the glen. Huxley had agreed. His only request had been that Angus avoid revealing John's title, saying he preferred to win Annie's heart without the lure of being a lord.

Then, Huxley had offered his help. He'd explained that he and his family were connected to some very powerful men.

"Which powerful men?" Annie asked.

"I'm comin' to that."

"Well, get on with it."

A tiny smile tugged at her father's mouth. "Impatient. Ye always were. Aye, then. Ye'll recall Broderick was still imprisoned at the time." He shook his head. "We were out of options, lass. We needed a bluidy miracle. Huxley offered one on a golden plate."

Her mind was a wee bit sluggish thanks to the whisky, but even half-sotted, she realized what the offer had been. Huxley had gone to Edinburgh because he'd been helping to free Broderick. He'd been speaking with judges when she'd spotted him. Then, he'd kissed her and stolen her soul there in the dark, narrow close—because he hadn't wanted her to discover what he was doing. Because then, she might ask how a simple, bonnie Englishman had managed such a thing.

"Before he approached me about ye," Angus continued, "he wrote his kin askin' for their help. By the time he came to the distillery, he'd already put his plans in motion." Angus's finger touched her chin, drawing her gaze up to his. "Huxley said whatever my decision, he planned to help yer brother. He *wanted* to help us, Annie. Because he loves ye."

She gripped his hand tighter. "And you believed him?"

"A man doesnae bring a witness to a marriage proposal unless he's in earnest, lass." Angus sighed. "Huxley brought a future marquis."

Blinking, she glowered. "Are ye speakin' of … Robert?"

"Aye. Happens his father is the Marquis of—"

"Mortlock," she said faintly, recalling the strange conversation between Robert and Mrs. Baird, who must have recognized him.

"Conrad claims his father's at death's door, and his older brother is both sterile and sickly. Shouldnae be long before the title devolves to him."

"A marquis. Good God."

Angus grunted. "That's not the half of it."

Annie blinked again, feeling like she was being pummeled. "What's the other half?"

"Remember how Huxley said his sisters made good marriages?"

"Aye."

Angus looked a wee bit uncomfortable.

"Da?"

"Ye did say ye wanted to marry a lord."

"Da!"

"One of his sisters is wife to the Duke of Blackmore."

Air left her in a whoosh. Blackmore was an enormously powerful figure within England. He also had familial ties to influential figures in Edinburgh— including two men on the High Court of Justiciary. "H-Huxley's sister is a duchess?"

"Aye. The eldest sister will be a marchioness soon, as I said. Two more are countesses." Angus sighed. "And that's just his kin. I havenae even mentioned his friends."

She was afraid to ask.

Angus answered anyway. "The Marquess of Wallingham. Their families have been friendly since before he was born."

Wallingham. Another near-mythical name whose influence stretched across Britain. Her stomach burned and gave a sick lurch. She slid her empty glass onto the table. "Da?" she breathed. "I dinnae think I can do this."

He patted her hand. "Ye'll be fine."

No, she wouldn't. John's deception had cut her to pieces precisely because she'd never thought a wound would come at his hands. Could she forgive him? Perhaps. Trust him not to hurt her again? Uncertain.

But the entire bloody question was now moot, for his family would never accept her. A brash, trews-wearing, vulgar hoyden from the arse crease of Scotland? His mother would swoon—and rightly so.

He'd even warned her that her goal of becoming a lady was nigh impossible. In the dress shop, he'd explained what real ladies were like, illustrating how different Annie was from that description. She'd reassured herself at the time by imagining some lowly, minor lord, perhaps a kindly widower in need of good meals and an orderly household. She'd told herself such a marriage would be a half-step up from being a housekeeper, and surely she could manage politeness and gown-wearing for a few months while she searched for a lord desperate enough to wed her.

What a fool she'd been. Failure had awaited her. Miserable, humiliating failure. Even if she'd found some desperate, obscure lord willing to take her on, she couldn't have gone through with it.

She'd already lost her heart to a bonnie Englishman. Marrying another man? No. Not even to have Finlay with her again. Which left her only one choice—marrying John.

Except that John Huxley's sister was the Duchess of Blackmore. His father was Lord Berne. The rest of his kin—all titled. And one day, his wife would become a countess.

A *countess.*

The very thought made the room shift around her.

Her hand slid over her belly as it twisted. "I cannae be his wife," she whispered, the realization crushing her.

"Eh? Why in blazes not?"

"Look at me, Da. Do I seem like a countess to you?"

His jaw hardened. "Ye seem like my daughter. And Huxley is damned fortunate to have captured yer fancy."

Shaking her head, she whispered, "Dinnae ken about that."

Angus plucked up one of her hands and wrapped her fingers around his wrist. "Feel these bones, lass?"

Her eyes welled until his beloved face swirled. She nodded.

"Ye're a part of me as much as they are. Have been since I first spotted yer wee, red head outside the kirk doors." He knuckled a curl from her cheek. "We're like Highland thistles, you and I. Tough and stubborn. A mite hostile when we must be. Our nature doesnae suit everybody. But we grow where we've landed. We hold our ground. And we dinnae shrink from a fight, even when we're trampled. Ye ken?"

She dashed away the tears that had spilled. Sniffed, then nodded.

"Good lass. Now, here's what's about to happen." His voice grew stern as the craggy rocks of the glen. "Ye'll go to Huxley and tell him ye're ready to marry him."

"No, I cannae—"

"Ye ken how bairns come to be, aye?"

She swallowed. Her hand tightened over her belly. "Of course, I—"

"And ye took yer chances anyway."

She felt her cheeks go fiery. "Da."

"So, ye'll marry Huxley. Punish him as long as ye please. Once he's yer husband, that will be easy to do." Heavy brows lowered over dark, forbidding eyes. "But ye *will* marry him first. Ye'll live in Glendasheen Castle. Ye'll birth his bairns and bring them here to see their grandfather. And ye'll cook yer venison and gravy for me. An auld man needs his comforts."

A smile trembled on her lips. "I suppose all this will happen just because ye say so."

His chin tilted to a familiar, obstinate angle. "I'm yer father, lass."

"Aye, Da." She squeezed his wrist, feeling the weighty Highland bones. "That ye are."

John exited Gilbert MacDonnell's small manor house with a better understanding of Annie's disdain for the man. Glenscannadoo's laird was tiny, daft, and puffed up like a peacock. He'd invited John to take tea with his sallow, drunken wife in an ornately furnished drawing room that smelled of wax and heavy perfume. After extolling the value of an Oxford education for men in positions of leadership, Laird Glenscannadoo had fed him mediocre shortbread and bragged of his family's heroism in sustaining the traditions of his clan.

The wife had nodded off in the midst of their conversation. Only then had Glenscannadoo taken John to his tiny-yet-ornate library, where a stag's head was mounted on the wall. Even that had been small. And, John had noticed, the antlers had a faint seam near the animal's skull, as though a larger set had been added. Compensation for shortcomings, no doubt.

Everything about the man irritated John, from his wheedling, nasal pomposity to his ornamental gold dirk. He wouldn't be there at all, and certainly would not have used his title to gain access. But Gilbert MacDonnell had the one thing John needed—a record of the MacDonnell ancestors.

"Finlay MacDonnell? No, I cannot say I recall such a name," he'd replied to John's query. "But you are certainly welcome to glance through our clan history." He'd pointed to the large, gold-lettered book perched on a marble stand between two bookcases. "We keep excellent records."

Proud as the man was of his heritage—or at least its trappings—John didn't doubt it. However, after a lengthy search through page after page of MacDonnells, he found no trace of the name he was seeking.

"Is it possible some names have been left out?" John had asked. "The branch that perished in the castle, perhaps?"

Glenscannadoo had stiffened, seeming offended, then flipped to a page about a third of the way into the book. "Here. The branch that *falsely* attempted to claim the lairdship. Even those who did not survive past infancy are noted." He'd pointed to the names, none of which were Finlay. "The fire spared no one, I'm afraid." He'd sipped his brandy and sniffed. "Tragic."

Now, John waited in the short drive outside Glenscannadoo Manor for one of the laird's stable lads to bring his horse. Preoccupied with thoughts of Annie, he failed to notice the donkey ambling down the lane until it turned into the drive and headed directly for him.

When he raised his head, his heart nearly stopped. Scarlet curls gleamed in the patchy sunlight. They peeked out from beneath a straw bonnet with a blue silk ribbon that matched her gown.

The same gown she'd worn the day he'd proposed to her.

His body's surging reaction was predictable, but seeing her so unexpectedly intensified it tenfold. Then he noticed her bosom. The motion of the donkey was not quite a walk, not quite a trot. And it made everything … bounce.

The lust hit him so hard, he nearly bent in half.

She should be wearing a riding habit, of course. But Annie wasn't like other women. At the moment, her brows were drawn in consternation as she attempted to ride a donkey in an evening gown.

God, how he loved her.

And despite the pain of his arousal and the sharp need she invoked in him, he smiled. His grin had turned to a chuckle by the time she reached him.

"Ye're a fine one to be laughin', John Huxley," she snapped. "I'd like to see ye try to ride wearin' a skirt."

He couldn't stop. He was so bloody happy to see her. The past three days had been agony. "I'll wear anything you like, love. Riding with you is one of my favorite diversions."

"Stop yer nonsense and help me down. Bill is a mite aggravated. We rode all the way to yer castle only to have Dougal say ye'd come here to visit the wee tartan peacock."

He looked at the long-eared donkey. The animal gave a lazy blink. "I suspect Bill is not the one who is aggravated," he observed before gripping her waist and lifting her down.

Admittedly, he held her against him for longer than necessary. And he cupped her backside more firmly than necessary. And, very well, he ogled her bosom much more than necessary.

But she was irresistible. An enchantress from his deepest fantasies.

"If ye fancy keepin' that bonnie nose unbroken, English, ye'll take yer *lordly* hands off my backside."

With great reluctance, he raised his gaze from the luminous bounty of her breasts. Her lips were pink and her cheeks flushed from the summer heat. Cornflower eyes snapped with ire. He wished her anger diminished his arousal.

It did the opposite.

"Why did you seek me out?" he asked hoarsely.

"A better question is why are ye here?" She nodded toward the manor house. "Never thought ye had much use for the wee tartan peacock."

He considered not telling her. For long moments, he weighed the likelihood that she would hate him even more. But keeping things from Annie was a mistake he didn't want to repeat. So, he told her the truth. "I came to view the MacDonnell ancestry."

She stared silently for several breaths, glanced away, then said softly, "Ye were lookin' for proof that Finlay existed." A breeze ruffled her pretty hair. "Because ye dinnae believe me."

His heart ached at the signs of hurt around her eyes. "I only wanted something tangible."

"Did ye find it?"

"No."

She nodded. Drew a deeper breath and blew it out. "Aye, then." Her eyes came back to his wounded but resolute. "I sought ye out today because we have a matter to settle between us."

Yes, they did. Whether she forgave him or not, he must persuade her to become his wife—and soon. Even now, she could be carrying his child.

Behind him, the lad arrived with his horse. John took Jacqueline's reins and waved toward the lane. "Will you walk with me?"

Annie nodded and, together, they led their mounts down the short drive and along the village road. Glenscannadoo Manor sat a quarter-mile from the market square amidst a few pleasantly landscaped acres above the loch. Surrounding the laird's groomed gardens were small farms filled with sheep. Most of the trees had been cut down for pasture. But the lane was lined with young oaks planted in tidy rows obviously intended to add grandeur to the manor's approach.

"So, what do they call ye, English? When ye're usin' yer title?" She asked the question idly, as though they were having a friendly chat.

Guilt assailed him. "Annie, I am sorry I didn't tell—"

"Lord Huxley, aye?" She didn't look his direction, merely kept her eyes forward as they walked, her bonnet shading her expression. "And yer wife would be Lady Huxley. A viscountess. Do I have that right?"

His chest ached. "Yes. You would be Lady Huxley."

She nodded, her neck tight, her lips pursed. "And one day, yer son will have a title, too."

"Our eldest son will become Lord Huxley, yes, when I become the Earl of Berne. Which will not be, as I explained previously, for some years. My father is in excellent health, barring any future cohabitation with cats. Never know when Mama will make another disastrous attempt to bring one home. But, in general, we Huxleys are reliably long-lived." He smiled wryly. "Prolific, too. But that is a subject for another day. I shouldn't like to frighten you."

Her lips tightened as though stifling a smile.

The sight made him hard. But then, everything about her made him hard. He cleared his throat and surreptitiously adjusted his coat.

"Have ye responsibilities from yer title? Parliament business or some such that requires ye to live in England?"

"No. I only visit England to see my family. My father has a seat in the House of Lords. He and my mother visit London each spring whilst Parliament is in session. By the time summer arrives, they are eager to return home to Nottinghamshire."

She drew a shuddering breath. "But yer father is healthy, ye say."

"Yes."

"And it will be some years before ye and yer wife would have to travel to London for yer lordly duties."

He frowned. "Yes."

She nodded. Whispered something to herself. Then halted in the middle of the road. Finally, she turned to face him. Her eyes blazed with odd defiance. "Ye're goin' to marry me, John Huxley."

He froze, riveted in place as lightning coursed through him. Had she just said …?

"Tomorrow," she specified. "I bribed the priest to marry us at the auld churchyard near the castle. He didnae want to do it there. But his purse is empty, and he's desperate. Gamblin's a sinful habit. Do ye suppose it's more sinful to gamble with church funds?" She clicked her tongue. "I'd say so, but perhaps God doesnae care for context."

"Annie," he breathed.

"Fornication. Now, there's a sin with context, aye? Outside marriage, sinful. Inside marriage, encouraged." She shrugged. "Either way, we'll be doin' that, too, English. A *lot* of it."

"Bloody hell," he groaned.

"No sense complainin' about it. Cannae make bairns without fornication."

"Excellent point. I shall apply myself to the task with considerable vigor," he murmured, scarcely able to form a sentence.

"This doesnae mean I forgive ye. Because I hate liars, John Huxley." Her lower lip firmed and her chin went up. "Ye cannae trust them."

"Annie, I'm so bloody sorry. I should have told you."

"Aye, ye should have. Perhaps forgiveness will come, but we cannae wait that long. I mean to have my laddie back. And ye're the one who'll make that happen."

He was startled to have her agree so readily to his precise conclusions. Annie was a sensible woman with a pragmatic approach to most things. But he'd hurt her deeply. He could see it in the way she looked at him, that beam of admiration dimmed and tainted by pain he had caused. "I will earn your forgiveness, love." He moved closer but stopped when she stiffened. "Once we marry—"

"Tomorrow."

"Yes, tomorrow."

"In the auld churchyard."

"Yes. I'll ask Dougal to clean it up a bit, shall I?"

She nodded. "Angus and my brothers will be there. Broderick, too, if he can manage. Mrs. MacBean. Mrs. Baird."

"Your dressmaker?" Didn't she hate the woman?

"Wear yer blue coat. It looks grand on ye."

Slowly, he smiled, realizing the tension beneath her defiance was nervousness. She was nervous. Because of him? This called for reassurance. "I cannot wait to make you my wife, Annie. Nothing on earth could bring me greater pleasure. Apart from fornication, of course." He'd hoped to make her smile, but she didn't.

Instead, she swallowed, staring at his mouth.

"Must we wait until tomorrow?" he asked.

"Aye. And one last thing, English."

"Anything."

"Ye cannae tell yer family. Not even Robert. Not yet."

He frowned. "Why?"

"That's my condition. Ye cannae tell them we're married until I say so."

Damn it, he *hated* her condition. He wanted to proclaim his marriage across Scotland and England and the whole bloody world. He wanted his mother to weep with joy and embrace Annie in a long, relieved hug. He wanted his father to clap his shoulder and congratulate John on making such a fine choice. He wanted Annie to meet all his sisters and all their husbands and all the nieces and nephews who would doubtless worship her as much as Ronnie Cleghorn did.

As much as *he* did.

But she wanted to wait to tell them. He'd agree to anything to have her, so he would comply with her wishes. However, if she thought to escape the marriage later through annulment or divorce, she could think again.

"Once you're mine," he grated, "you're mine. Our marriage will not be undone."

She scoffed. "Dinnae be daft. Of course not. No sense in marryin' in the first place if ye're goin' to be weak-kneed about it."

"Good."

"Fine."

"We'll marry tomorrow, then."

"Ten in the mornin'. Let's hope it doesnae rain."

"Annie?"

She blinked up at him.

"I love you."

She held his gaze for a moment then dropped hers. A breeze lifted the curls around her face. A faint, bittersweet smile curved her lips. "I love ye, too, English."

Her words were precisely what he'd hoped. He only wished she hadn't spoken them with such sadness.

CHAPTER NINETEEN

When Mrs. Baird arrived a wee bit late from Inverness, Angus was pacing the entrance hall with a scowl. "What took ye so long, woman?" he barked the moment Annie opened the door. "We've a wedding to get started."

Annie winced as the fair Mrs. Baird stared up at Angus as if he was about to leap upon her and take a bite. And no wonder. He was a foot-and-a-half taller than the dressmaker, at least twice her width, and ten times her strength. He could lift her over his head and toss her in the kitchen hearth, if he cared to. Of course, he'd sooner dive head-first into the hearth himself than hurt a woman, but Mrs. Baird didn't know that.

Annie stepped between them and practiced her manners. "Mrs. Baird, how kind of ye to make the journey. Will ye come inside and have a bit of tea while I finish dressin'?"

"Aye." Her smile was weak and trembling. Her eyes flickered cautiously to the looming giant behind Annie's shoulder. "I brought the items ye mentioned."

Angus glared outside at the one-horse gig parked in the drive. "Is that *trinket* what ye traveled here in?"

Annie sighed and rolled her eyes. "Da, we dinnae have time for yer complaints about transportation." She glanced at Mrs. Baird, who still wore an expression of cautious dismay. "I apologize for …well, him."

"It's a bluidy miracle ye didnae crack one of those spindly wheels in half, with the ruts on that road." His glower shifted to poor Mrs. Baird. "What were ye thinkin', woman? Have ye no proper vehicles in Inverness?"

Before Annie could warn her against it, Mrs. Baird cleared her throat and replied, "I prefer the gig, actually. It is light and manageable."

"It's an invitation to be robbed and left for dead."

Annie closed her eyes, breathed, and prayed for patience. "For God's sake, Da."

"First thing that happens is yer wheel strikes a wee pebble, and crack! No more wheel. Next thing that happens is ye're tossed out of yer seat into the muck. Yer skirts are over yer head, yer trinket is broken, and ye're alone in the middle of bluidy nowhere while—"

"I should think riding my horse to the nearest village would be step three, Mr. MacPherson."

"Suppose ye could do that before the thieves find ye, eh?"

Mrs. Baird was no longer pale. In fact, her cheeks had a bit of a blush to them. "I've managed quite ably to avoid such catastrophes thus far. But I do thank you for your concern."

Annie noted Mrs. Baird's speech grew primmer when she was vexed.

Angus, on the other hand, grew louder. "Well, ye didnae *manage* to arrive here on time, now did ye?"

That was it. Annie did not have the patience for this. "Stop yer bellowin', auld man! It's my weddin' day!"

Angus emitted a half-growl-half-grunt and muttered something about whisky before stalking into his study and slamming the door.

Sighing, Annie gently looped her arm through Mrs. Baird's limp one and ushered her toward the parlor. "He's fair crabbit this mornin'. Angus has never reacted well to big changes, I'm afraid."

"Aye. Evidently."

Both of them set the incident aside while Mrs. Baird showed Annie the items she'd brought: a long, lace veil; a sash of the same tartan she'd used for John's kilt; and a pair of sky-blue silk slippers to match the sky-blue of her gown. John had never seen this gown, as she'd saved it for her wedding day. The skirt had no flounces, merely an overlay of gossamer tulle. The bodice was long-sleeved and lovingly fitted, trimmed with rows of white ribbon in a V-shaped pattern to her waist. There were no spangles, nothing to glitter or flash. Rather, it resembled a Highland summer sky traced with wispy clouds.

Running her hands across her ribs, she shivered imagining her Englishman's expression. He'd focus on the deep neckline, no doubt. Her bosoms did look grand.

Mrs. MacBean and Betty MacDonnell entered the parlor a few minutes later with the necklace Annie had requested and the pouch she would wear sewn into her petticoats. The shy, freckled maid dressed Annie's hair with looser curls than usual, forming a lovely tumbled pile at the base of her head. Then, she added two wee plaits on either side, draping them and pinning them artfully in place. Delicate white flowers Mrs. MacBean had brought from her garden added a finishing touch.

Annie eyed the old woman in the small dressing mirror. "These best not give me a rash, auld woman."

"Och, no. Yarrow is harmless as a wee bairn. Now, the yellow ones, those are poisonous. Dinnae touch those."

Annie's gaze drifted to the bouquet Mrs. MacBean had assembled, which lay beside Annie's hand. Among the white roses and blue cornflowers were yellow, daisy-like blooms with darker rust centers.

Mrs. MacBean patted her shoulder. "I didnae mean *those* yellow ones. They're safe enough if ye dinnae eat them."

When Betty finished with her final pin, Mrs. Baird came forward to fasten the long, lace veil into Annie's hair. The two women worked together, and in the end, Annie thought the effect rather ethereal.

"Oh, my, Miss Tulloch," Betty breathed.

"Indeed," Mrs. Baird concurred. "Ye're a fair angel, lass."

Annie grinned at the two other women in the mirror, and for a moment, she almost believed it. She would never be beautiful, of course. John Huxley would have to resign himself to that fact. Her eyes were too oddly blue. Her lips were nothing special. Her hair was too bright and her cheekbones too wide and her chin too stubborn and her skin too pale. But today, perhaps, she could be bonnie for him.

She lifted her mother's necklace from its case. It was the same one Lillias had worn on both her wedding days. The wee silver cross was simple and plain. As Betty fastened it around her neck, Annie remembered playing with it as a child while she sat on her mam's lap and listened to her read. Today, she would have her mother with her as she became a wife.

Then, she added the tartan sash and slid her feet into the slippers.

Last, she slid the small, worn thistle charm into her petticoat pouch and gave it a pat. Finlay would be with her, too.

Finally, she thanked the three women who had become her friends, hugged each of them in turn, and asked them to meet her in the coach after she checked on Broderick. She entered his room a few minutes later with a soft knock.

"Broderick?"

The bed creaked. "Annie?" His voice was a graveled, distorted version of what it had once been. But at least he was speaking. For months, he hadn't said a word. Now, he turned from where he'd sat on his bed, staring down at his damaged hand. They'd broken it over and over until the fingers were bent at odd angles. He blinked at her. Then blinked again. His scarred cheek tightened. "Ah, ye look bonnie, sister."

Her throat tightened. She moved to his side and stroked his hair back from his forehead. "Are ye certain ye're well enough to come? I want ye there so badly, I fear I've pressed ye too hard."

He leaned his cheek into her hand for a single heartbeat before pulling away. "Aye. I'll nae miss it."

She folded her hands at her waist. "Rannoch will take ye in the cart. Alexander and Campbell are bringin' the cider and food. Da will ride with me."

He didn't reply, just stared down at his hand.

"Broderick," she whispered.

His dark, beautiful eye came up.

"I'll visit every day. Whenever ye need me. I—"

"Nah, ye willnae." Slowly, painfully, he unfolded his long body and pushed himself up until he stood before her. Somehow, she'd forgotten how tall he was. "Yer place is with yer husband."

"I cannae leave ye—"

"Annie. Ye've done yer part. The rest is mine." He reached for her hand and squeezed briefly before turning away. "Now, go. Da's waitin'."

A half-hour later, Annie climbed down from the coach and took her father's arm. Mrs. Baird, Mrs. MacBean, and Betty MacDonnell had finished fussing over her gown and handing her the bouquet, and now they led the way down the path to the old church. There, the ancient arches were decorated with vines and flowers. The yard had been cleared of weeds and debris, and a path through the stones had been laid with gravel and lined with wood planks. The gravel crunched beneath her slippers as she walked toward the steps then through the missing church doors. Inside the long, open rectangle where a church once stood, her family was gathered. Rannoch with his wicked smile. Alexander with his dark frown. Campbell with his stony strength. And Broderick, scarred and broken but standing.

Her eyes turned to the priest, scrawny and sweating. She watched her three friends find their places standing on the left side of the "aisle," a strip of mown grass down the center of the old ruin. Finally, she drew a breath and found him.

Her Englishman.

He made her heart stop then pound then swell then ache. Intermittent sunlight touched the gold streaks in his hair. Those hazel eyes flared as they raked her from flowery head to slippered feet. She felt her middle glow hot as his jaw flickered.

He'd worn his blue coat. And the kilt she'd made for him.

As she began her journey toward the handsomest man she'd ever seen, she was floating like a tuft on a breeze. There was no music, only wind rustling the trees, carrying the scent of warm pine. Then, the birds began. The sound started as a bit of chirping. Built into more. And soon, the caw and chirp of dozens of birds blended into a strange symphony. She felt rather than saw an entire flock launching into the sky from atop the arches. The flurry of fluttering white disappeared just as she came to a stop before her Englishman.

For the length of the ceremony, she felt spellbound, unable to look away from him. She saw his lips moving, making promises to her. Felt her own moving, making promises in return. Heard her da saying he gave her in marriage, joining their clans, before he pinned John's plaid. Then came a moment when Mrs. Baird took her bouquet and John took her hands and a ring slid onto her finger.

She looked down and saw a brilliant flash as the ring winked back at her. Blue. It was a sapphire the color of the flowers in her bouquet. The color of her eyes. And it was surrounded by wee, sparkly diamonds. Her eyes rounded as they came up to his.

He raised a brow and gave her an arrogant grin as if to say, "You were expecting cheap?"

Then, at long last, the sweaty priest pronounced them man and wife, and John Huxley's eyes went pure, molten gold. His nostrils flared, his jaw flickered, and his cheekbones flushed.

For a moment, she feared she might leap upon him in front of everyone. Chances were, he wore nothing under his kilt, after all. Fortunately, Angus grumbled about missing breakfast and she regained her senses. As she and John retreated down their grass aisle, she spotted a flicker of white out of the corner of her eye. The white raven gazed down at her for a split second before it launched into the sky and was gone.

In the churchyard, Dougal began playing the bagpipes and his brothers joined in with their fiddles. Annie shook off the odd moment and, alongside John, led the procession down the path toward the castle.

For several hours following the wedding, MacPhersons and MacDonnells feasted and laughed, danced and told amusing tales. Annie danced two reels with her new husband, enjoying his flush as he eyed her with simmering hunger. Together, they ate a shockingly delicious cake made by Marjorie MacDonnell and drank MacPherson whisky from their shared *quaich* until they were both a wee bit dizzy.

In time, John grew impatient, and he tugged her out into the corridor, up the stairs, and through the last door on the left. Inside his bedchamber, the music was faint and the light was soft. She leaned back against the oaken door, her head spinning after so much cider and whisky.

John immediately set to work unbuttoning his coat and tearing away his cravat. He was a wee bit more careful removing his sporran, dirks, and belt, but he made quick work of them, as well.

"Have I said how beautiful you are?" he asked.

No, he hadn't. But his eyes had been devouring her since she'd first set foot on the grassy aisle.

Breathless and burning, she licked her lips while she watched him unbutton his waistcoat. "Ye havenae said much since our vows, English," she panted.

"All my thoughts are a bit obscene, I'm afraid. Wouldn't want to embarrass you."

"Gentlemanly of ye."

"Your gown is exquisite."

She looked down at the swells of her breasts, which he hadn't torn his eyes from since entering the room. "Do ye think it flatters my shape?"

His head tilted to a predatory angle. Hazel eyes were little more than amber rings around large, dark pupils. He wetted his lips and took a sharp, shuddering breath. "Yes."

It took her a moment to reply. Another. And another. "As this marriage is purely for procreation purposes, I'm glad ye find me pleasin', husband."

"More than pleasing." He shook his head as if to wake himself and ran a hand over his jaw. Then, he tossed away his waistcoat and crowded closer. A frown tugged. "Who says our union is meant solely for procreating?"

"I say. That's what this marriage is, English. A venue for procreation. I want a bairn. Sooner the better."

His eyes burned. His hands braced on the wood to either side of her head. "Oh, love. Did you just challenge me?"

For a moment, she might have gone a wee bit faint. Her new husband was a potent blaze of seductive power. Luckily, she was able to regain her senses and put him in his place. "Nah," she replied, her voice only a little raspy. "Merely spoke the truth. Perhaps ye should try it."

His body, surrounding her in heat and hardness and pine-scented lust, went still. But he ignored her dig. "A bairn, you say?"

"Aye."

"So, pleasure is unimportant."

"Well, I wouldnae say that," she hedged, though her body wanted to scream the denial.

"But the point is to plant the seed, as it were."

"Aye." God, her throat was dry. And her knees were weak. And her nipples were so hard they ached. And her skin pulsed with every breath.

"No kissing, then." His lips brushed hers with the barest slide. "Or unnecessary touching." His knuckles stroked her breast's upper swell before moving down to swirl around her nipple. "Just my cock deep inside you as frequently as possible."

She whimpered. Melted against the door. Nuzzled his jaw like a cat in heat and arched her back, begging for more of him.

"I think you *are* challenging me," he whispered in her ear. "And here's my reply, love." With swift efficiency, he plucked at her skirts until they were bunched around her waist, leaving her naked to his touch. Then, using his wrist to keep her skirts raised, he slid a knuckle directly over the slick knot of sensation that swelled and pined for him.

Her shocked gasp turned to a faint moan.

Only then did he give her his answer. "I accept."

This woman drove him mad. Her defiant chin. Her feisty tongue. Her taunting smirk.

He wanted her until his teeth ached.

And she wanted a babe.

Far be it from him to shrink from a challenge.

"First things first," he murmured, tasting the skin of her soft, creamy throat. Between her thighs, he unfurled his finger and gently slid the length downward amidst her ripe petals. When he reached the tight opening he sought, he circled. Circled. Breached. Then sank his longest finger inside her. "Must ensure you can take me comfortably, hmm?"

Her head fell back, her inner walls squeezing his finger while her damp thighs gripped his wrist. Her only reply was a deep, throaty moan and a bit more panting. She also gripped his hair with both hands. Good signs, all.

He added a second finger. "So tight here, love. You'll need to be very wet." He nibbled her ear—she loved that—and repositioned his body so his chest teased the tips of her breasts. "My cock is significantly bigger than my fingers."

A long, feminine groan. "Ah, devil's ballocks, English."

He grinned and worked her swollen nub with his thumb. "Those are substantial, as well."

"If ye mean to say ye're the devil, I'll believe ye." She tried to draw his mouth to hers. "Kiss me. Please."

"Oh, I shouldn't like to waste my efforts"—he began thrusting his fingers in and out of her pulsing sheath—

"on meaningless pleasures." He nipped her shoulder. "We've a task to attend, after all."

Her hands tightened in his hair as she struggled to pull him in tighter. "I've changed my mind. Ye may kiss me. I'm certain ye've enough energy for all manner of pleasures. Large ballocks, and all that."

Despite feeling like his skin was too tight and his cock might burst into flames at any moment, he chuckled. "No, no, love. I'll just ensure you're wet enough to take me, shall I?" He moved his fingers in a deliberate rhythm, giving her just a bit more pressure with his thumb. "Focus, now."

Her sheath tightened like a vise. She bit her lip, groaned and worked her hips against his hand.

"That's it," he encouraged, watching the cords in her neck and wishing he could bare her breasts. Later, perhaps. Once she'd fully surrendered, he'd indulge himself for hours. "Nearly there."

Her patience ended with a growl. Small fists gripped his shirt. He thought he heard a seam tear.

"Now," she demanded with harsh, rapid breaths. "Take me, damn ye."

Her rough command struck him like a flaming arrow through a gap in his armor, straight into a spot he hadn't suspected he was vulnerable—the place that itched when she insulted him. Where his need to claim her lived.

He'd planned to draw this out. Make her come and then pretend disappointment. Pleasure her with his mouth until she admitted he was more to her than a husband to father her bairns. More than a title or a convenience.

But she smelled like heated sugar and ripe summer fruit. She welcomed his touch with lush eagerness, arching her back and spreading her legs to let him have her. She dared command him to take her.

All his thoughts burned away. His control slipped. His muscles tightened. His cock was nothing but an aching throb. "Annie," he whispered, trying to hold on amidst the dark, shocking flood of long-denied need.

She opened her eyes, midnight with her arousal. Her lips were full and lush, wet from her tongue. They should be wet from his.

And he lost command of himself. Bloody lost it.

Light streamed through the windows and painted her skin bright gold. Her hair was pure flame. She was all he saw. He traced her throat with his free hand. Cupped her neck. Withdrew his fingers from her sheath, but only to grip her thigh and yank it wide over his hip. Then he lifted his kilt. Lifted his wife high against the door.

Blue eyes flared and feminine fingertips dug into his nape as he positioned his cock at her entrance. "English?"

His first thrust was hard, driving a gasp from her throat. He should have been gentler. Likely his lust made him a bit larger than normal. And she was small. Tight.

So damned tight.

She grunted as he thrust again. Deeper. He needed to be deeper. Hot, wet, silken grip. Soft, sweet-scented woman. His fingers held her bare thighs tighter. Wider. Pulled her hips up so she could take him harder.

More. He thrust. More.

"... too bluidy massive like this," she was panting. "But I need ye. It's good. Move, English. Aye, move. Like that."

Harder and harder. The door banged with every thrust, but he didn't care. Burying his face against her throat, he finally sank as deep as he could go, feeling her soft flesh grind against the root of him. His heart pounded and pounded, drowning out everything but her voice. A sweet Scottish rasp, calling him English. Telling him how much she wanted everything he could give her.

And the pleasure he'd thought to delay coiled up his spine. Sparked and ignited. Drove his pace to a hammering frenzy.

"Annie," he groaned, thrusting and thrusting and thrusting. Needing her so much, his pleasure was pain, his madness pleasure.

She clung to him, her sheath gripping and giving and rippling a warning. Her fingers raked his hair while her hips writhed into his, riding his cock with helpless cries of pleasure. Then, she seized upon him. Cried and clung as her body was wracked with culminating ecstasy.

For him, the explosion came when she put her lips to his ear and murmured in a shaky purr, "I'll have all of ye, English. Ye're mine, do ye hear? Ye *belong* to me."

He roared as it seized him. Lifted him into the sky and broke him open until he shattered into dust. Shimmered like stars.

As his body worked to fill hers completely, he gasped against the skin of her neck, smelling sweetness, tasting salt, feeling the thrill of her hands cradling his head and kneading his shoulders. The wrenching spasms of his climax slowly eased. Her lips found his brow, his cheek, his jaw, and finally, his lips. Those she claimed with sweet passion and a determined tongue.

He answered with a sensual stroke of his own, though he was fully wrung of all his strength and the kiss turned beautifully lazy. They stayed like that, weakened by one another and leaning upon one another, until he gathered enough strength to carry her to the bed. Even as he sat with her straddling him, he refused to leave her body. Already, his was readying again.

A husky laugh sounded in his ear. "Are ye certain ye're not a wee bit Scottish, John Huxley?"

He grinned as she continued kissing his neck and jaw in tiny Annie-sized bites. "I do find the kilt has significant advantages."

"Mmm. Quick access. Do ye aim to have another go, then?"

His answer halted as she tugged his shirt up and stripped it off over his head. Blue eyes danced as her pink tongue darted out to wet her lips. She began plucking pins from her hair. Withdrew her veil and laid it gently on the bedside table. "Do ye like my backside, English?"

His hands were squeezing her firm-yet-cushiony buttocks, instinctively trapping her in place. "Yes," he said.

She grinned and glowed, a sensual, flame-haired queen. "I like yers, too." Her hands stroked down his chest, pausing here and there to sift through a bit of hair or dance over his nipples. "Are ye pleased with yer wife's bosom?"

"You know I am." His voice was shredded.

She leaned forward and rubbed her silk-encased breasts against him. When she sat back, her cheeks were fiery, her eyes now molten with new desire. Her hands traced his jaw, her finger his lips. A tiny frown appeared. "My bonnie Englishman. I'm not the lovely sort of wife ye might've had, am I?" she whispered.

"What do you mean by that?"

"I'll never be beautiful."

He frowned, utterly confused. "You are."

"Nah." Her gaze fell to his shoulders and down his chest. "Nae bonnie or fine, like you." Her gaze lifted, shining bright as a flame. "But I'll fight for ye, English." Her body squeezed his where they were joined. "I'll fight to pleasure ye 'til yer dainty toes curl and those enchantin' eyes roll back in yer head."

"God, Annie."

She leaned forward and took his mouth. Kissed him passionately, caressing his jaw then wrapping her arms around his neck. "I'll fight to make ye proud of me."

"Love, I *am*—"

She touched her forehead to his and stole his next breath by rolling her hips. "Ye'll teach me what pleases ye."

"You please me. You."

She began to take him. Stroke by stroke, she rode him.

They breathed and moaned together. Kissed and touched and sighed together.

"And another thing. Ye're goin' to tell me who hurt ye, John Huxley," she said as she clung and drove him higher with a slow, rhythmic ride. "Ye're goin' to tell me why ye lied."

He didn't want to tell her. He wanted to put her on her back and thrust harder until they both came again. He wanted to leave the past where it belonged.

He kissed her to shut her up. Kissed her because he needed her pleasure as much as his own. He threaded his hands through the silk of her hair and held her beautiful mouth still for his pleasure. Then, he pulled back to grate, "I'm going to *tup* you until you can't walk. That's what I'm going to do."

"Is that so?" She grinned breathlessly. "Suppose ye'll have to carry me, then. Careful ye dinnae strain those wee, dainty wrists."

"God, you are the most vexing woman."

"Do I spark yer temper?"

"Yes," he gritted, loosening the fastenings at the back of her bodice.

She ran the tip of her smallest finger across his lower lip as he finally spread the silk and drew it down her shoulders. Shrugging free of her bodice and sleeves, she ran her hands over the lines of her corset, cupping her own breasts from beneath. "Would ye like a taste, English?"

He'd thought it would take him longer to reach this state, the one where his skin felt scorched and overly sensitized. After his explosive climax earlier, he'd assumed he could go on a leisurely exploration.

But that was before she began taunting him. Stoking him. Provoking him.

"Take them out," he growled, gazing down at the creamy, tempting swells. When she hesitated, he tugged the laces at her back to loosen the stays. "Now."

Because he was buried inside her sweet, tight warmth, he felt how his command affected her. A rush of her arousal bathed his cock, and her sleek muscles tightened and fluttered.

"Aye, husband." She slid her fingers into the corset's cups and lifted out her breasts, letting them rest on the edges of the boned fabric.

Nipples of deep, rosy pink were flushed nearly scarlet at the tips. Those sweet buds, he knew, would darken and swell when he tended them properly. For now, they were highly aroused and diamond hard. His mouth watered. His cock thickened. Readied.

He needed her, but not like this.

Within seconds, he reversed their positions, laying her on her back, spreading her hair out upon his pillow, and wrapping her legs around his hips. Then, he settled in.

His wife thoroughly enjoyed his hands, of course, the way he plumped and stroked, pinched and plucked. But she reserved her loudest, most enthusiastic approval for his mouth.

He suckled her for long, luscious minutes while pleasuring her below with slow, deliberate strokes of his cock. With every deep pull of his mouth and stroke of his tongue, he pushed her a bit further, mindful of signs of her nearing peak. When he finally felt sharp nails scoring his shoulders, he increased his rhythm. Took her harder and harder until the ramming strokes shocked even him.

But she loved it. She clawed and growled and demanded more. Her heels dug into his backside and her mouth ate at his. "Sweet Christ and all his unicorns, English," she rasped, grunting as he thrust deeper. "Ye're a bluidy magician. Ah, I cannae … I'm about to … *Ahh!*"

She sounded so astonished when her peak came, that he nearly laughed his triumph. Then his own peak followed hard on its heels, flooding her with his seed as her body wrung his dry.

In the tender moments afterward, she held him and traced tickling patterns on his back. He lay with his ear over her heart, listening to the steady thud. His palm slid from her thigh to her waist. Then, he cupped her soft, velvety belly.

And let himself imagine how beautiful their babes would be.

CHAPTER TWENTY

Annie's husband of precisely seven days flexed his jaw and stared out the library window with visible frustration. "I did tell you about my family," he argued, tossing the letter he'd been holding on his desk. "All the important bits, at any rate."

Over the past week, she'd softened toward him. How could she not? The man was tireless. She hadn't laughed so much or floated so much or sighed like a pure dafty so much in all her life. On top of which, he'd moved heaven and earth to help Broderick.

The letter from Dunston was more proof of that.

And John did regret hurting her; that much was clear. He'd demonstrated his remorse over and over, doing everything she'd asked. He'd even promised to name their son Finlay.

He'd also explained his cynicism regarding title-hunting women.

They'd been lying in their bed a day after their wedding, exhausted from lovemaking and enjoying a breeze off the loch. At her insistence, he'd finally confessed how a half-French tart had tried to trap him years earlier.

"I had a London season where it seemed … prudent to seek a wife," he'd said. "At the time, I didn't know you existed, or I would have understood how ill-suited she was for me."

"A milk-skinned beauty, was she?"

"A beauty, yes. Lovely to look at. Her charm lay in coy flirtation. She pretended to be drawn to me against her will."

"Ah, very seductive." Annie reckoned setting the woman's hair on fire would make coy flirtation a wee bit harder. Perhaps one day, she'd have the chance to test her theory.

"This was seven years ago." He'd quirked a wry half-smile. "I was too eager to have what I'd seen in good marriages. It made me foolish. Blind."

"Nah," she'd murmured, tracing the muscular ridges of his belly with her thumb. "Just hopeful, English."

"I pursued her long enough to begin planning our nursery and imagine spending our winters in Marseille."

She'd frowned. "Marsae?"

"Marseille. In France. She was half-French."

"Frenchwomen do seem to light yer wick. Her name didnae happen to be Jacqueline, did it?"

"Perhaps."

He'd winced as her fingertips dug into his ribs. "Easy, love."

"Modest French mistress. Half-French tart with badly singed hair. A pattern's a pattern, John Huxley."

"For God's sake, Annie. I found her romping in her uncle's stable with another man. A *Frenchman*, by the by.

She'd already been impregnated. She planned to wed me for my title, pass the child off as mine, and keep her lover for sport." Frowning, he'd trapped her hand in his. "Why do you think I named a horse after her?"

Probably an insulting reminder to himself. Still, she didn't like it. They'd have to change the horse's name. "So, she cuckolded ye before ye'd married her?"

"Yes."

"Was her vision very poor, then? Too vain for spectacles, perhaps?"

A frown tugged. "No."

"Are ye certain? Because the only other explanation is her sufferin' a head wound as a wee lass. Happens from time to time. Poor weans grow up simple. Cannae make proper judgments. Like when it's appropriate to chew a bit of rope. Or keepin' yer legs shut when ye have the bonniest man ever to draw breath offerin' to make ye the luckiest lass ever to set eyes upon him."

His eyes had glowed bright as sun-struck amber. "I'm the lucky one, love."

His recollection had helped her make sense of why he'd lied, why he'd needed Annie to choose him without the title.

But some of the wounds he'd dealt her remained raw. This morning, when he'd reluctantly shared the letter from his brother-in-law, those wounds had opened again.

Now, Annie tossed aside her attempt at embroidery and shoved to her feet, coming to stand beside his chair. She crossed her arms and leaned back against the desk. "Ye told me Jane fancies readin'. Ye didnae tell me she was the Duchess of Blackmore."

"When you meet her, you'll understand why it doesn't matter."

"Neither did ye say Maureen is wed to the Earl of Dunston."

He sighed.

She tapped the letter near her hip. "Who happens to work for the bluidy Home Office."

John's right leg began twitching, a sure sign of restlessness. "That's not precisely—"

"Or that Eugenia—the milliner, mind—is actually wife to one of the richest men in England. Another earl, no less."

"Her marriage was a recent—"

"Or that Robert will soon be a marquis, givin' ye a matched set. The full assortment of titles perched in yer family tree."

He ran a hand through his hair. "I have already apologized in every way imaginable. I've begged your forgiveness, promised to restore the churchyard, bought you a coach"—he gestured to the carriage parked in the drive below—"specifically so you could visit MacPherson House in a godforsaken Scottish deluge."

She glanced out at the absolute downpour. "'Tis a wee bit damp."

"Would you have me on my knees, woman?" He sounded positively crabbit.

"Och, I would enjoy that, I must tell ye, English. Seems that's where ye do yer best work."

"God, Annie." He gave an exasperated chuckle, bracketed her hips and drew her to stand between his knees. The emotions in those enchanting hazel eyes were as complex as the colors—adoration, frustration, regret, lust. "You're vexed that I failed to inform you about my family, yet you've barred me from telling them about our marriage."

"For now."

"Why?"

She hesitated. "They'll expect ye've married a lady."

"You *are* a lady."

"Nah. I'm a hoyden, English." She brushed at her skirt. The light brown wool was very fine. But the woman wearing it? An imposter. "I'll need many more Lady Lessons before I'm fit to be kin to a duchess."

Silence. When she dared a glance at his face, the banked fury there surprised her.

Warily, she continued, "Mayhap in a year or so—"

"Absolutely not," he grated. "Whether now or later, they will love you. If more Lady Lessons will put you at ease, then by all means, resume training. But I will not wait a year. We might have a child by then, for God's sake."

Crossing her arms, she narrowed her eyes and stewed for a moment. John's family was important to him. Perhaps they could strike a bargain. "Very well. Ye may tell them before our son is born."

"I'll give you until the ball at the Glenscannadoo Gathering."

"Bluidy hell, English. That's naught but a month from now!"

"We'll attend together, and you may demonstrate your skills for the laird and his fellow landlords. Thereafter, I'll invite my family to visit. September is a lovely time here in the glen."

Anxiety gnawed away at her middle. "Fine. I'll agree to have them for a wee visit."

"Splendid."

"If ye win one of the events at the Highland Games."

His arrogant smirk was her first hint that perhaps she'd made a bad bet. John Huxley thrived on a challenge. "Done."

"Y-ye havenae asked which event."

"Unimportant." He leaned forward, drawing her close until his mouth hovered near hers. "If it means I may finally show you off to my family, I shall win." He kissed her and beamed that confident grin she found so irresistible. "Count upon it."

How was she going to master gliding in only a month? And dancing! She'd have to dance at the ball. And speak like a Lowlander. And learn how to serve a multi-course meal to a table full of countesses, earls, and the like. Oh, God. She'd need so many supplies. A proper teapot. Plates and cups and saucers and linens. She longed for John's family to love her, as he'd repeatedly insisted they would. But Annie would settle for not disgracing herself or her husband.

She glanced at the settee where she'd discarded her embroidery, a middling result at best. Real ladies embroidered much better. Real ladies had clean napkins and china cups with wee flowers on them.

"English."

"Hmm?"

"We must go to Inverness."

"I'm planning a trip next week to speak with the constable—"

"Today. I must visit Mrs. Baird. And purchase a proper teapot."

He sighed and drew her closer to nuzzle her neck. "Really? Now? When it's raining and our bed is so close?"

"Aye, now. No time to waste. We've a great deal of shoppin' to do."

"I thought you hated shopping."

"Not this sort." She cupped his face and raised his eyes to meet hers. "Are ye ready for me to spend yer money, husband?"

He sighed. Glanced out at the sheeting rain and arched a brow. "I suppose if you made several hours in a coach worth my while, I shouldn't be too out of sorts about it."

"Is that a challenge, ye cheeky Englishman?"

He gave her a grin and squeezed her backside. "Perhaps."

She leaned forward and whispered against his lips, "I accept."

Three hours later, Annie's elbow wedged in the corner between the coach seat and the tufted wall. Her right heel rested on her husband's naked backside. Her left heel rested on the floor. And her head lolled halfway off the bench.

"I'm a pure mess, English," she panted, her body still pulsing with remembered pleasure. She blew a red curl out of her eyes and laughed. "Ah, God. Ye've done me in."

The coach jostled through a rut, causing them both to groan. "I'd apologize for ravishing you, love, but I'm not sorry."

In fact, they were both a bit of a mess. She'd wrinkled her skirts by kneeling between his knees. Then, she'd wrinkled his trousers when she'd taken his hard length in her mouth, a particular treat she enjoyed when she wanted to drive him mad. But she'd scarcely had time to tease him before he'd dug his fingers into her hair, tumbling it loose from its pins. Then he'd grasped her arms and pulled her up into a kiss. Eager for him, she'd immediately straddled his hips and impaled herself upon his cock while he tore at her drawers and yanked at her bodice to force her nipple free for his mouth. Her bodice had certainly been creased. Perhaps even a wee bit torn.

As she'd ridden him, she'd clawed his cravat, which presently lay on the carriage floor. She frowned now, recalling how his mood had darkened to a near-primitive state. He'd growled through gritted teeth, his eyes maddened. Then he'd picked her up, rising to tumble her back onto the opposite seat, seemingly incensed at having her anywhere but beneath him. He'd wadded her skirts carelessly around her waist—more wrinkles, naturally. Then he'd pressed her legs wide, forcing her bent knees toward her shoulders so he could go deeper and harder. Her peak had come with such force, she'd bitten his fine wool collar to stifle her screams of ecstasy.

Now, she surveyed their surroundings—the black cushioned seats and silver velvet curtains. "This is a very fine carriage," she murmured.

He lay heavily upon her, hot breaths fanning her neck. "Glad you like it."

"I think I may have damaged your coat."

"I have other coats. You may damage them later."

She sifted her fingers through his hair. Turned her head to kiss his brow. "It seems ye dinnae like me to sit astride ye for very long, English," she whispered tenderly. "Why is that?"

He stilled. His muscles tensed. He levered up and away from her, expression shuttered. For the next few minutes, he didn't speak. Rather, he busied himself reassembling his clothing then helping her do the same.

She made an attempt to redress her hair, but her arms were limp as overcooked cabbage.

"Let me help," he rasped, gently turning her until her back was to him. Then, she felt his fingers against her scalp, lacing through her curls and stroking the length before winding it into a coil and fastening it at the back of her head. Every moment sent waves of silvery shivers washing across her skin.

She sighed and reached for him, bringing his hand to her mouth so she could kiss his palm. Then, she held his hand between her own. "Ye go a wee bit mad when ye awaken with me on top of ye. It's happened twice. And it's plain ye prefer to be the rider rather than the mount. Can ye tell me why, English?"

He withdrew. She shifted so she could see his face, but he'd turned away to stare out at the rain.

"I've told ye everythin' about my life," she said. "The parts I love, the parts I hate, even the parts I didnae think ye'd believe. How Finlay and I would play ghostie tricks on the villagers and how Broderick would sing to me in Gaelic when I fell ill. How Grisel made me want to crawl into the grave with my mam once or twice."

She watched his throat ripple and his muscles tense. He was fighting the same rage he'd shown when she'd first told him about the spitting and taunts—all the small cruelties she'd endured until she'd learned how to avoid them.

"Do ye think I willnae understand?"

"I think you'll view me differently."

"Nah. I ken who ye are, John Huxley. Even if ye did lie about bein' a lord."

Slowly, as the rain pattered on the roof and the outskirts of Inverness became the town of Inverness, his shoulders lost some of their tension. His fists loosened. His hand slid over hers.

His other hand raked through his hair. "You really wish to hear this, do you?"

"I really do."

"Fine." His lips paled with tension. "She was a governess. Came from an old but impoverished bloodline. My parents hired her to instruct my sisters when I was sixteen." His right hand, she noticed, was gripping the seat beside his leg as though to keep himself in check. "I was home from Eton. The first week, she attempted to flirt with me, but my interests lay elsewhere at the time."

"She was ugly, then."

"No, she was pretty enough. Merely less fetching than the village barmaid who'd captured my fancy."

"Did the barmaid have large bosoms?"

"I don't wish to discuss it."

"Aye, she did. This explains a great deal, English. Mayhap ye'd like me to wear a barmaid's dress, hmm?" She waggled her brows. "I could serve ye whisky, and ye could act very *lordly.*"

He didn't laugh, but the tension around his mouth and eyes eased, which had been her aim. "The governess sought me out numerous times, approaching me in empty corridors and pretending to *accidently* find me alone in the library. She hinted that she'd been meant for a higher station in life, that she'd let me do as I liked to her if she knew we would be wed. That sort of thing."

Annie sensed where this was going and had to picture serene waterfalls to keep her temper. "Bold of her. But ye werenae interested."

"No."

"And she wasnae pleased with that answer."

Several heartbeats passed while he stared down at her with a bleak expression. "No."

Annie didn't want to ask. "What did she do?"

"I was asleep. When I awakened, she was … astride me. Attempting to impregnate herself."

She swallowed hard, nausea and fury building. "Without yer bein' conscious."

He nodded. "At a minimum, she hoped I would feel obligated to support her and her child for the rest of her life. But she knew my family. Knew there was a good chance I would be forced to marry her for honor's sake. Fortunately, one of our loyal maids had learned of the governess's scheme and alerted my father. Papa and the maid entered my bedchamber before the deed was … finalized. I woke to find the governess atop me and my father shouting."

Annie told herself to breathe, though it was difficult when her chest felt so painfully tight. "She tried to take what ye wouldnae give her willingly. So that she might be elevated. By a title."

His mouth twisted. "Some would suggest a young man should find pleasure in such a scenario."

Her temper, already at the edge of combustion, went dark. "And I'd suggest those daft bastards should shut their ignorant bluidy mouths."

His brows arched in surprise.

She couldn't bear it any longer. Bracing her hand on his shoulder, she rose and pivoted then knelt beside him on the seat, wrapped her arms around his neck, and held him as tightly as she could. "She tried to trap ye while ye slept. For God's sake, ye were sixteen. Naught more than a lad." Her eyes began to fill, and she blinked faster to stop them from leaking. "How old was she?"

He stroked her back. "Six-and-twenty."

"I want to kill her. Tell me her name."

"It's not important."

She gripped his shoulders then drew back to hold his gaze and whisper fiercely, "It's damned important to me, English."

Multi-hued eyes that had been stark while telling his story slowly warmed and softened. "I've only ever spoken of this with two other people, you know. My father, who dismissed the governess that very night. And Robert." His hands roamed her waist and hips before one came up to brush her cheek, as though he needed the contact for comfort. "I always assumed my reaction was … strange. A man's body at that age is a bit ungovernable, his desires far from discriminating. But when I awakened and saw her …" He sighed and drew her closer. "I cannot explain it. My skin began crawling. I felt smothered and sick." His gaze dropped briefly while she stroked his jaw with her knuckles. "After my father tossed her out, when I realized what she'd intended, I … I vomited." He looked at her, and for a moment, she could see a boy's pain. "I didn't want her to do what she did, Annie."

"I ken," she answered, holding his face between her hands. "I ken it well."

A breath shuddered in his chest then whooshed out in a sigh. "At any rate, a number of years later, I happened upon a cousin of hers. He told me she'd died. Apparently, after being dismissed, she returned to London, where she made similar attempts to entrap an heir to a coal fortune. The heir was fifteen at the time. His father thrashed her and threw her out into the street. She became a baronet's mistress for a short time. Then she fell into prostitution and eventually perished whilst trying to rid herself of the pox by drinking arsenic."

"I hate her," Annie gritted. "I'm glad she's dead. She deserved worse."

A smile touched his lips. "Worse than pox and arsenic?"

"She killed somethin' innocent in ye. Somethin' she hadnae any right to touch. So, aye. Worse."

His smile grew. "My fierce Highland lass."

She kissed him tenderly. "If we werenae almost at Mrs. Baird's shop, I'd show ye how fierce I can be." Another kiss. "Alas, we'll have to play lord and barmaid a wee bit later."

Several hours and a great deal of shopping later, the coach pulled up to the constable's office. Her husband eyed the downpour before opening the carriage door. He advised her to wait in the coach.

"I may be a lass, John Huxley, but I'll nae be left behind whilst ye go about havin' yer manly conversations," she said sharply. "Broderick is my brother, and I ken the smugglin' routes better than most."

His smile turned wry as he retrieved an umbrella from the coach floor and opened it. "Indeed. But I thought you might like to wait until I have this open."

He tapped the handle of the umbrella he held above the door. "Or perhaps you enjoy being drenched."

She paused. Gazed at her husband. He'd always treated her like a lady, she realized. Even when she'd been a perfect hoyden wearing trews and hurling insults, he'd insisted on a chaperone and resisted improprieties that might compromise her. John Huxley treated her as though she were delicate. Precious.

But he also afforded her the respect of making her own decisions. When she'd exhausted herself caring for Broderick, he'd understood it was what she had to do. So, rather than forbidding or taking charge, he'd given her his arms as a shelter. Without her needing to ask, he'd used every connection at his disposal to help her brother, not to gain her favor but because he knew how Broderick's suffering broke her heart.

True, he hadn't believed her about Finlay. That still stung. He'd failed to listen when he should have. And he hadn't trusted her to love him for more than his title. But she understood his reasons better than before. He wasn't perfect, her Englishman, but the way he loved her was.

Even now, he offered his hand with a look of amused expectation. She took it and stepped down into the shelter he offered. Rain pattered and splashed. His shoulder was getting wet.

"I love ye, English," she said softly.

Warm, golden hazel sparked. A slow, devastatingly handsome grin appeared. "And I you." For a moment, she thought he might kiss her, but he offered his arm and gestured toward the door of the two-story stone building in front of them. "Shall we?"

She nodded, overwhelmed by the glow inside her. "When we're done here, ye're goin' to have a good night," she said casually, looping her arm through his. "*Very* good."

He chuckled, low and sensual. "Mmm. That sounds splendid, Lady Huxley. Does this mean I am forgiven?"

Arching a brow as he opened the door, she replied, "It means ye'll be glad ye married a wee Scottish hoyden."

He closed the umbrella and lightly cupped her waist before murmuring in her ear, "Too late, love. If I were any gladder, you'd never stop blushing."

Chapter Twenty-One

Constable Neil Munro was a barrel-chested man of middling height with long, gray side whiskers and a steely demeanor. His office was spartan, small, and orderly. A framed letter of commendation hung on the wall. A plain but clean hat hung on a rack in the corner. And a sketch of David Skene lay on the desk.

"I do wish I could be of help to ye, my lord," Munro said. He stood erect, his hands clasped behind his back in a military pose. "'Tis my earnest desire to dismantle Skene's operation and put the blackguard where he belongs. If only I'd the resources available to do so."

Given the zealous light in Munro's eyes, John believed him. "We have reason to think Skene remained in Scotland. You've pursued him in the past. Is there anywhere he might consider sanctuary? His kin, perhaps?"

"He has none apart from a brother who hates him. The brother helped us shut down his distilleries last summer."

John frowned and glanced at Annie. She shook her head as though this were the first she'd heard of it.

"Skene's gang doesnae depend upon his own distilleries, so it was a temporary victory," Munro explained. "Transport is his game. He has whole villages beholden to him. Allies that protect him. Makes catchin' the rat nigh impossible."

Nodding, John asked, "Do you know who his backers are?"

Again, the feverish light of a zealot entered the constable's eyes. "I've a notion."

Annie clutched John's arm harder. "Who?" she asked.

Munro's gaze slid over her dismissively before returning to address John. "Angus MacPherson."

Annie's head snapped back. "Are ye mad?"

John comforted her with a stroke of her waist. "Mr. Munro."

"*Sergeant* Munro, m'lord."

"Of course. Sergeant. I am … acquainted with Angus MacPherson, and I can assure you, he despises David Skene."

The man bristled. "The MacPhersons skirted the law with their distillery for many, many years. Over my strenuous objections, they were granted a license last month."

Indeed, John had helped facilitate it. He couldn't have Annie's family—his own family, now—at risk of being jailed for running an illegal distillery. But the MacPhersons had operated outside the excise laws for a long time, well earning the dislike of Sergeant Munro, which was why John and Annie were the ones paying him a visit. If Annie could refrain from revealing they were her family, John was likelier to get helpful answers than her father or brothers.

The officer continued, "I've no proof of their partnership, only a suspicion. But MacPherson control of Glenscannadoo is absolute. And I ken Skene's support is centered there."

"In Glenscannadoo? How do you know?"

"Last year, we intercepted his men transporting a load of French brandy between Inverness and Glasgow. One of the men carried a note from Skene to somebody in Glenscannadoo. Didnae say who. But every man, woman, and child in that village protects the MacPhersons no matter what. Excisemen come, their distillery is empty. My men and I go about askin' questions, nobody kens anythin'. The MacPhersons are the only power in the glen."

"What did the note say?"

Munro gave John a hard stare before rounding his desk and plucking a square of paper from beneath the sketch of Skene. He offered it to John.

The note contained a few sentences—no greeting and signed only with an S. As John read it, his blood went cold. "When did you obtain this?"

"September."

Annie plucked it from his fingers. Her eyes widened with horror. "Good God, English. This is—"

He clasped her wrist gently and handed the note back to Munro. "You're certain this was to be delivered *in* Glenscannadoo."

Munro frowned. "Aye. Their route forked west when it should have continued south. One of Skene's newer lads said they were meant to stop in the glen. He didnae ken where."

Annie looked pale, so John thanked Munro and guided her back to the coach. As he gave instructions to the driver and climbed in behind her, she rasped, "Somebody we ken did that to Broderick, English. Somebody I *ken.*"

"We'll discover who it was, love." He offered his hand and instantly, she laced their fingers together.

"I must speak with Da."

"Of course. We'll speak with all the family."

"That rat-faced piece of shite put his men in the Bridewell to kill my brother." A tear fell down her cheek before she swiped it away angrily. "And somebody I've spoken to, perhaps somebody I fed at my table, paid for it to be done."

The note had been chilling.

Twenty more in place at Calton Hill. Payment received. Delivery imminent. Best avoid Glenscannadoo 'til all roads clear.

The MacPhersons had long suspected Skene, of course. They'd spent the past several months tracking down every man who had taken part in the beatings Broderick had suffered. They'd made those men pay dearly. Then, they'd systematically destroyed Skene's smuggling operation. Piece by piece, route by route, town by town, they'd taken every resource he had and ground it to dust. They'd even discovered a rich cache of cognac Skene had planned to sell in Edinburgh— obviously intended to fund the rat's escape.

That was how John and the MacPhersons knew Skene was still in Scotland. He hadn't the funds to go anywhere else.

John gathered his wife gently into his arms. Immediately, she turned her face into his neck, wrapped her arms around him, and heaved a great sigh.

"We'll find out who did this," he assured her.

"Aye. Then I'll kill him."

He smiled and kissed her forehead. "Fierce Highland lass."

She snuggled closer. "I dinnae understand. Dunston's letter said the backer had to have been in Edinburgh round the time Broderick's charges were dismissed."

"True. The resistance came too swiftly for it to be otherwise."

"And to have the necessary influence with the High Court, he'd have to be highly placed."

"A peer, yes."

"There arenae any peers in Glenscannadoo."

John frowned, staring out the window as the wet streets of Inverness rolled past. "What of the laird? Not a peer, but titled. Perhaps he's grown jealous of the MacPhersons having more land and vastly more respect in the glen."

She snorted. "The laird is naught but a joke. Best thing he offers his people is the Gatherin', and that's only so he can invite all his Lowland friends to admire …" She trailed off then sat up straight. "English."

"What is it?"

"The wee tartan peacock *was* in Edinburgh."

A chill scurried down his spine. "When?"

"I saw him at the inn. The same day ye kissed me near the rubbish pile." She slid her hand inside his coat and withdrew Dunston's letter. Quickly, she scanned the first page. "Aye, here. 'Per my contact in Edinburgh, three men at varying times have argued for more severe charges and swifter prosecution. None are acquainted with MacPherson, nor have they advocated such harsh measures in past cases.'" She paused, her lips moving while her finger traced down the page. "This. This is it. 'The sole commonality I've observed between the abovementioned men—apart from their association with the High Court—is that each is rumored to have been a member of a certain clandestine club wherein acts of a scandalous nature are performed.'" Annie frowned. "Does he mean tuppin'?"

John cleared his throat. "I suspect it's a bit more than that. Dunston is far from prudish."

"What if Glenscannadoo is a member of this club? What if he's blackmailin' them?"

"It's possible, I suppose." Recalling his impressions of Gilbert MacDonnell, he struggled to make the possibility fit. "He did serve me brandy when I visited. I would have expected whisky."

She nibbled her lower lip. "And brandy was in the load that Munro intercepted."

"Yes."

Silence settled between them as they both worked at the puzzle. Finally, Annie shook her head. "Nah. Cannae be the wee tartan peacock."

His mouth quirked. "Why do you say that?"

"He's a pure dafty. Comes from dafty stock." She hissed out a scornful sigh. "The man spent a bluidy fortune to put that ridiculous statue in the middle of the village. He sold ten prime acres to Angus to fund it."

"He does seem proud of his heritage."

She rolled her eyes. "Only the look of it."

"Hmm. Brandy over whisky."

"Sheep over cattle. Aye. He hasnae forced his crofters from their farms like some. But I suspect that's because he hasnae many left. Even the cottage he offered to Mrs. MacBean sits on MacPherson land." She shook her head. "Nah, he's a dafty. But he's nae vicious, ye ken? To do what was done to Broderick, a man would need to find satisfaction in cruelty. I cannae see it."

John nodded. "I agree. But that still leaves us with the question of who does possess such viciousness."

Her gaze slanted to the window then came back to him. "I have a suspicion. No proof, mind. Only a feelin'."

"Very well. Whom do you suspect?"

She nibbled her lip. "It mightn't make sense to ye. He doesnae have any tie to the glen or Skene or the MacPhersons. And Broderick has never met him, so far as I ken."

"Annie."

"I dinnae expect ye believe me. 'Tis just a—"

"Love. Tell me."

Her lips firmed and her chin tilted. "Lockhart." Eyes sliding away from his, she tucked Dunston's letter back inside his pocket then brushed at his lapel. Finally, she fussed with her skirt. "I think it's Lord Lockhart."

John sat back. Had she expected him to balk? Watching her nervously fidget, he could see she did. Because he hadn't believed her about Finlay, which, he now understood, had been his most critical error. That, along with his desire for proof rather than fanciful stories, made her doubt him.

He covered her hand as she began sorting her embroidery supplies. "I believe you."

She stilled. "Ye—ye do?"

"Yes."

"Ye havenae asked why I suspect him."

He angled his head to catch her eye. "It's enough that you do."

"Ye dinnae think me mad?"

A tiny thread of doubt in her eyes twisted his heart into a painful knot. "Annie Huxley, you are as sensible as an umbrella in a downpour."

She traced a finger over the spot on his collar where her teeth had dented the wool. "So, not mad, then."

"Not mad. I know it the way I know Highland rain makes better whisky and a Highland lass makes a better wife. Because only fools believe otherwise."

Her smile grew. "Bonnie, charmin' Englishman. Ye're not just sayin' that to get under my skirts, are ye?"

"Well, it's not the *only* reason," he teased. "Though I certainly wouldn't decline the offer."

She chuckled. Then kissed him. Then demonstrated how a Highland lass made her English husband an exceedingly happy man.

When Annie stood before her father and four brothers, attempting to explain why a Lord of Parliament none of them had ever met should be regarded with grave suspicion, her stomach quaked. She hadn't felt this nervous with the MacPhersons since she was a wee lassie.

"Ye saw him at the inn with Glenscannadoo," Angus said with a glower. "Were other men present, as well?"

Nodding, Annie squeezed John's hand and laced their fingers together. His firm grip gave her comfort. "A few. But if ye'd seen the way Lockhart handled his sister, Da—I cannae explain it. He looked pleased with himself."

Campbell and Rannoch, both standing with their arms crossed near the parlor fireplace, shot each other a look.

Reading their skepticism, Annie frowned. "Doubt me if ye like, but the fact is Lockhart was here in the glen last September visitin' the laird for a hunt. His sister, too. I saw them both in the square."

Alexander, sprawled beside Broderick on the sofa, rubbed the bridge of his nose with his thumb. "Broderick doesnae ken him, Annie. None of us do. What reason would Lockhart have to want him dead?"

It was an answer she simply didn't have. She was about to say as much when her husband spoke. "Whatever it is, you may be assured Annie's instincts are correct. She would not accuse someone without cause." Warm, hazel eyes found hers before shifting back to the MacPhersons. "Lockhart is well positioned in Edinburgh society, and his movements fit with what we know about Skene's backer. He was here in September. He was at the inn. He's exhibited cruel behavior toward his sister."

"Are we certain his sister didnae make a fuss over naught?" Alexander asked.

Annie glared. "Would ye handle me in such a fashion, Alexander MacPherson?"

"Nah." He grinned at her. "I'd fash about bein' brained with an iron pot."

"Quite right," she retorted. "I ken rough treatment when I see it."

John squeezed her hand. "The man who targeted Broderick wants him to suffer; his hatred burns hot, so it is very likely of a personal nature. Jealousy over a woman, perhaps. Or a transaction Lockhart regards as a personal slight. I've no doubt the blackguard will make another attempt."

"I never met Lockhart," Broderick said, his voice stronger than it had been a week ago, though still graveled. "Skene was the only name ever mentioned in the Bridewell."

"And we've laid a proper trap for the rat," Rannoch said. "Only a matter of time before he takes the bait."

Indeed, Campbell had explained how they'd stored Skene's cognac in a warehouse near Inverness, planted rumors among the rat's disbanded gang, and set men to watch for him. It was a sound plan, provided he behaved as predicted.

"Mayhap we should wait until we have Skene in hand, sister," Campbell suggested.

Annie looked to Angus. "Da?"

Angus glanced at each of his sons, lingering on Broderick. Then, he looked at John and finally came back to Annie. "Nothin' is certain. We havenae any proof."

Her heart began to shrivel.

"But if Annie believes him a threat, he's a threat."

And, just like that, her heart filled past its capacity. The first time Angus MacPherson had scooped her up and carried her into the kirk, she'd felt the same. Safe. Loved.

"Thank ye, Da," she whispered.

He nodded. "Sadly, we cannae take action against a lord without evidence of his crimes. We'll need proof."

John spoke up. "We have an idea about that. But first, we must ensure he comes here." John explained the plan he and Annie had discussed on the way home from Inverness. First, John would approach Laird Glenscannadoo to ensure he invited Lockhart to the Glenscannadoo Gathering. Then, Annie would write to Sabella Lockhart to encourage her and her brother to attend.

"If Lockhart is the man I think he is," Annie said softly, catching Broderick's gaze. "He'll want to see the damage he's wrought."

Half of Broderick's face consisted of a patched eye and a mass of raised scars. His mouth pulled tight at the corner, slashing down in a permanent scowl. His nose was flattened along the bridge and crooked in the middle. The other half of his face was also scarred, with long slashes through his brow and cheek and strong, square jaw. His good eye had returned to normal—dark and beautiful with thick lashes. She only wished her brother still lived there. Instead, the look in that eye broke her heart more than the scarring ever could.

He seemed to sense what she was going to ask before she spoke, for that eye smoldered with violence.

"I wouldnae ask it of ye—"

"I'll do it," he uttered, low and hoarse.

She swallowed. Nodded.

Sensing her distress, John pulled her tighter against his side. "First things first," he said calmly. "Let's get the blackguard here. Then, we'll see how a devil enjoys being caught in a trap of his own making."

CHAPTER TWENTY-TWO

Annie curtsied to Mrs. Baird a fourth time, wondering why it was so much harder than it looked. "Yer grace," she said, keeping her voice soft and dignified. "It is an honor to make yer acquaintance."

"Very good, Annie. Much better."

Annie shot her a wry grin. "Aye. At least this time, I didnae topple."

"Yer tone was perfect, as well." Mrs. Baird's bonnie yellow hair glistened in the light from the parlor window. "Respectful without subservience. Excellent."

Laughing, Annie blew upward to scatter the fringe of hair from her eyes. "Good thing subservience isnae required, else our Lady Lessons would be over before they'd begun."

For the past three Sundays, Mrs. Baird—or Eleanora, as she'd encouraged Annie to call her—had kindly traveled from Inverness to MacPherson House to give Annie lessons in everything from tea pouring to letter writing. She'd shown Annie how to curtsy without losing her balance, how to prioritize guest greetings, how to set a table with the proper number of spoons, and how to plan entertainments that wouldn't be spoiled by a wee bit of rain. She'd advised Annie on her hair and posture and speech. She'd explained the mysteries of polite conversation, offering such sage advice as, "If the topic is a body part ye'd ordinarily cover with clothing or a bodily function ye'd object to performin' in the market square, best ye consider it unmentionable." That ruled out so many things. But at least it was straightforward.

Annie appreciated straightforward. There were far too many rules. The jumble made her dizzy.

Mrs. Baird reached out to fuss with Annie's hair in a motherly fashion. "Remember, ye might have a lower rank, but ye aren't inferior. One day, ye'll be a countess. Won't that be grand?"

"Nah," Annie said, her stomach churning. "I wouldnae say grand. Though I do thank ye for yer kindness, Mrs. Baird."

"Eleanora," she corrected again. "Or simply Nora, if ye like."

Annie sighed and gave in. "Nora, then."

Nora Baird's smile beamed. "Now, have ye given any thought to the seating plan—"

"Annie!" Angus bellowed from his study.

Annie opened her mouth to shout a reply, but at Mrs. Baird's—or, rather, *Nora's*—admonishing look, she decided against it.

Which brought Angus stomping into the parlor seconds later. "Do ye intend to answer me, lass?" he grumbled.

"Aye, Da. At a sensible volume."

He grunted, scowled his displeasure, then held up a near-empty jar of liniment. "The auld woman promised she'd deliver a new batch."

"Mrs. MacBean will be here shortly. Are yer knees painin' ye, then?"

Another grunt. Angus's attention wandered past Annie's shoulder to Nora Baird. "Have ye bothered replacin' that useless trinket ye drive about, woman?"

"I have not," came the dressmaker's prim answer. "Nor do I intend to."

Angus stalked further into the room, darkening like a cloud. "If ye mean to come to my house every Sunday, ye'll find yerself a safer way to get here, or—"

"I thank ye for your concern, Mr. MacPherson—"

"I'll bluidy well come to Inverness and haul ye here, myself."

"—but your opinion of my vehicle is of little consequence."

As lightning flashed in Angus's eyes, Annie's brows arched. Oh, dear. She glanced behind her at Nora, who appeared surprisingly defiant. And surprisingly flushed.

"Er, Da? Mayhap ye should—"

"What did ye say to me, woman?"

"I said your opinion doesn't matter," Nora replied crisply, deepening the trench she seemed determined to dig for herself. "My visits here have naught to do with you."

"Is that so?"

"Aye."

Alarmed by the thick, inexplicable tension between her father and her dressmaker, Annie cleared her throat and used what Nora had taught her about keeping conversations polite.

The first step: tea.

"Da, why dinnae ye have a wee cup of tea, hmm?" She gestured to the tray Angus's new housekeeper had placed on the table. "I reckon there's a bit of laudanum somewhere about. I'll add a drop or two. And some whisky. Perhaps that will improve yer knees and yer temper."

"Are ye stayin' for dinner?" he growled.

Annie assumed he was still speaking to Nora, as he hadn't looked anywhere else.

"Annie has invited me, aye."

He glared with a ferocious scowl. "Bluidy hell. I'll have to follow ye home, then."

Swiveling her gaze between the two, Annie blinked, her mouth gaping. "Ah, Da?"

"Do as ye please, Mr. MacPherson," Nora replied, her expression a bit puckered. "I cannot stop you."

Annie was about to ask what the devil was wrong with both of them when the new housekeeper showed Mrs. MacBean into the parlor. The frazzled old woman wore one of the green tartan gowns Annie had made for her, along with her apron. She offered Angus his liniment.

Angus snatched up the jar, grumbling that it was about time, then stormed out of the room.

"Och, now, Nora," Mrs. MacBean said, digging inside her apron pocket. "I may have a wee bit of salve for that sunburn. Ye should wear a hat in this weather. Fair scorchin', it is."

"No need, Mary. I'm fine." A red-cheeked Nora turned away to pour herself tea.

Annie narrowed her eyes upon the dressmaker then glanced toward the doorway Angus had recently vacated. She opened her mouth to confirm her suspicions, but Mrs. MacBean dangled an oddly shaped wooden lump in front of Annie's eyes.

"'Tis a fertility charm, lass." The thing was strung upon a leather cord and roughly resembled a thumb. "Go on, then. Take it."

"What am I supposed to do with this?" Annie had her suspicions, and none of them were good.

"Wear it round yer neck. What did ye think?"

Not that, but she was relieved.

"'Tis a wee rabbit."

Annie squinted, turning the charm this way and that. She supposed the two carved lines that resembled buttocks *could* be ears. If she held it at a distance. And closed her eyes.

"Is this meant to help me conceive a lad?"

"Ye didnae specify a male." Mrs. MacBean accepted the cup Nora offered with a grateful nod. She took a sip then asked, "Have ye tried playin' a wee bit of ram and ewe, lass?"

Nora choked and spilled her tea on her skirt.

"Stag and doe? Farmer and wheelbarrow? Some say it improves yer odds," Mrs. MacBean continued calmly. "Though, I havenae found it particularly effective for aught but puttin' a smile on a man's face."

Annie crossed her arms and glared. "Ye ken I wish to have a son. And ye ken why."

The old woman's good eye slid away. She took another sip.

"What arenae ye sayin'?" Annie demanded.

"Nothin' at all."

"Nah, there's somethin'."

"'Tis only a wee suspicion."

Annie glared until Mrs. MacBean finished her sip. "Tell me what ye suspect, or those loaves I brought for ye will be goin' to Inverness with Mrs. Baird."

The old woman sighed. "Ghosties cannae be reborn."

"Wh-why would ye say—"

"I began to suspect somethin' was amiss when none of my remedies helped yer wee laddie."

Annie swallowed around a suddenly tight throat. No. The old woman must be wrong. Or daft. Yes, daft. That was it. "But ye *saw* him. Ye said ye did."

"Aye."

"And he … he told me who he was."

"He gave ye a name, aye."

"He said he …" Annie's hand automatically reached for the thistle charm in the wee pocket she kept sewn inside her petticoat. "He wants to return. It's his destiny."

"Is that what he said? Or is that what ye heard?"

Oh, God. Frantically, Annie searched her memory, clutching the thistle harder.

Sympathy shone in Mrs. MacBean's gaze. She set her cup on the table and took Annie's hand. "I didnae want to crush ye, Annie. I never wanted that."

Her breathing grew shallow. "No. Ye're wrong."

"Ghosts dinnae have a destiny. That's why they're ghosts. They're trapped in the crevices betwixt realms."

Annie shook her head.

"Listen, lass. No ghostie is capable of attachin' to a livin' person for nigh twenty years. It simply isnae possible. Most of 'em cannae travel far from where they died, else they wink out of existence. Ghosties are victims, ye ken? They're able to wreak a wee bit of havoc from time to time. Shakin' the lantern. Tappin' the window. Knockin' a book off a shelf." She snorted.

"Why do ye suppose I bury mine, eh? They're mischief makers. 'Tis all they have, the mad wee buggers. But no real power. Nae the sort yer laddie has."

She clawed at her ribs and clutched Mrs. MacBean's hand. "Wh-who is he, then? *What* is he?"

"Dinnae ken. He's nae like any creature I've heard about."

Annie's mouth worked over and over before she could force her whispered question from her throat. "Am I mad?"

Abruptly, the light in the room shifted, and for a moment, Mrs. MacBean's milky eye took on an eerie glow. "No, lass," she said, her voice sounding strange, as though it was layered with other voices. "Ye're protected."

"B-by what?"

A long, slow breath eased from Mrs. MacBean's chest. "What changes its form to suit its need?"

Annie shook her head. "Kelpies. Selkies." She paused. "Faeries."

Nora Baird's tea-stained skirt swayed into view. "Guardian spirits, perhaps," she said softly. Her eyes were wide and shining. "I—I saw one, I think. The night my husband died. I'd been ill with the same fever as he." She moved closer as Annie stared back at her. "I thought it was a dream. The next mornin' I awakened, and my fever had gone. There was a bird perched on my windowsill. An owl. Lit by the sun. 'Twas pure white."

Swallowing, Annie asked, "Ye believe it was yer husband?"

"No. An angel sent to take him, perhaps." A trembling smile touched her lips. "All I ken is that it was a spirit who watched over me until the night had passed."

"Aye," said Mrs. MacBean, her voice weaker now, her hand heavier inside Annie's. "He stayed to watch over ye."

Annie expected the old woman's gaze to be trained on Nora. But it wasn't. She was looking directly at Annie. "F-Finlay?" He'd appeared to her the day after her mam had died. He'd come right when she'd needed him most.

"He stayed as long as he could," Mrs. MacBean murmured.

Her heart squeezed until she gasped. *I stayed*, he'd said, *long as I could.*

"He stayed because he loves ye, lass. He left because he must."

I leave, he'd said, *because I must.*

Marry a lord, Annie. Destiny waiting.

Not his destiny. Not Finlay's. Hers.

John Huxley. Her husband. The father of her children.

Mrs. MacBean's milky eye briefly glowed brighter, caught in a shaft of light from the window. She clutched Annie's fingers until they hurt. Then, she pulled her closer, her voice a ragged, layered rasp.

And what she said sent a chill down Annie's spine.

"Dark is here, Annie. Mornin' hasnae yet come."

John heaved the monstrous caber with all his might. It toppled end-over-end, pausing briefly then landing at eleven o'clock. Not perfect. But not terrible.

Resting his hands on his hips, John tried to catch his breath in the dense heat. He'd come to the waterfall clearing every day since he and Annie had struck their bargain. He'd tossed the caber, thrown the hammer, heaved stones, sprinted, swam, and fought off midges. But every small misery would be worth it when Annie met his family. He grinned, imagining the look on her face when Meredith Huxley finally had a chance to embrace her new daughter-in-law. Mama would be over the moon, and Annie would have to concede he'd been right all along.

His wife was working hard, he knew. She'd begun by purchasing a dizzying quantity of household goods in Inverness. She'd filled their larder past its capacity. She'd hired additional maids and three more of Dougal's cousins. Then, every Sunday, she'd gone early to her father's house for Lady Lessons. He'd told her a thousand times they weren't necessary, but she was adamant. And proud. And determined "nae to disgrace ye in front of yer mother, John Huxley."

He'd also taught her a few new dances for the upcoming ball. She'd been nervous about that, too.

Her letters to Sabella Lockhart and his visits with Gilbert MacDonnell appeared to have borne fruit. Lockhart and his sister planned to attend the Glenscannadoo Gathering. Broderick was recovered enough to have moved back into his own house. The MacPhersons were increasing production at the distillery. Soon, they'd be hiring more men. John's training for the Games was progressing steadily. And, apart from the cracked tower window and a persistent rat problem in the cellar, the castle's repairs were all but complete. Most everything was falling into place.

He ran a hand over his face. God, he was bloody tired. It was the dreams, he thought. They'd disturbed his sleep for several nights in a row, always the same: He awakened in the dark with an overwhelming sense of doom. He searched the bed for Annie, but she was gone. Frantic, he rose from the bed and nearly fell sideways as the room wavered. Then, he saw the bird, a white raven perched on the foot of the bedframe. It stared at him until he walked toward it. Then it plucked up Annie's plaid from the bed and dropped the thing at John's feet. John wrapped himself in it. Watched the bird fly to the chest of drawers where his dirk lay. Picked up the dirk. The bird flew out of the room, and John followed. All the while, words chanted in his ears: *Dark is here. Dark is here. Dark is here.*

The dream was pure, heart-pounding panic. Confusion. His sense of loss and urgency coiled up into a knot, but he didn't know what he was supposed to do. Often, the bird led him to the tower then showed him the window he'd been unable to repair. It was always shattered. Blood always dripped from the jagged glass. And he always turned around to find Annie lying behind him, chest still, eyes blank, blood pooling on the floor from wounds in her belly. The seeping pool would reach his bare toes, and he would collapse to his knees with a roar of anguish.

That was where the dream always ended. For the last five mornings, he'd awakened in a sweat to find her lying beside him. He'd wrap her in his arms until she protested sleepily that she needed to breathe. Then, he'd love her until his heart felt capable of letting her leave his sight.

His training with the caber and hammer and stones helped release some of the tension, but he hadn't slept well in days. Now, he felt worn, his muscles sore. He cast off his kilt—a second, lighter one Annie had made for his training sessions—and waded into the pool beneath the fall. The water was a glorious chill on his skin, the cascade a brisk, much-needed pounding on his weary shoulders.

Through the curtain of falling water, he glimpsed a figure in shades of scarlet, cream, and lilac. She came toward him across grass and wildflowers, at first ambling. Then striding. Then running.

He waded toward her, his body going predictably hard. By the time the water was waist-deep, she'd reached the pool's edge and begun splashing toward him. He halted. "Love, wait. Your gown …"

She didn't seem to care. Lilac muslin ballooned around her as she strained to descend deeper and deeper. "I need ye, English."

He could see that she did. Cornflower eyes were fixed upon him, hungry and near-desperate. His wife usually fretted if a drop of rain landed on her skirts. He moved swiftly before she waded any deeper than her knees, taking her in his arms and cupping her nape as she clutched him around his ribs, her fingers digging into his back and her cheek settling over his heart. She was trembling, her skin hot and her breaths uneven.

Stroking her back, he rested his cheek upon her hair. "What's wrong, Annie?"

"I need ye," she repeated.

"You have me."

Her entire body began shaking.

He scooped her into his arms and climbed out of the water, going to where his kilt was laid out on a flat rock and settling down with her in his lap. Methodically, he ran his hands over her soft curves, reassuring himself she hadn't been injured. "Can you tell me what happened?"

For a long while, she said nothing. Then, she explained what had upset her—Mrs. MacBean's revelations about Finlay, how he'd misled Annie into believing he was a ghost. How she'd misled herself into believing they could be together again if she only married a lord. "I dinnae ken what's real anymore, English."

"We're real, love. You and I."

"I've lost him. And I miss him. And I have no way of bringin' him back to me."

"I know." He kissed her. Caressed her cheek. Stroked her hair.

"This doesnae mean ye're absolved of yer duty." She slid her hand to the center of his chest. "I mean to have yer bairns, English. Ye must still apply yerself."

He smiled. "Of course, love."

A sniff. "Ye're naked now."

"Indeed."

"I ruined my dress."

"It's only a bit damp."

She played with the hair on his chest. Nibbled at the skin of his throat. "Nah. I'll have to remove it."

He tugged at her skirt and slid his hand up her leg to her thigh. Then between her thighs. Then higher. "What if I did this, instead?"

She sighed and drew his mouth down to hers for a long, sweet kiss. "Clever Englishman," she whispered. "I kenned there was a reason I married ye."

CHAPTER TWENTY-THREE

The dream came again, as it had before. The white raven appeared to lead him to the tower. But the end was different this time.

This time, when John climbed the stairs to the uppermost story, a boy of perhaps six years stood in a shaft of moonlight. He had dark hair and blue eyes. His face was sweet and soft. He wore simple clothing—a white shirt and black breeches. No shoes. The boy stretched out a hand as John took the final stair and halted.

"Dark has come," the boy said. He turned and pointed toward the window, which had the web of cracks but no blood, no jagged glass. "She needs ye."

Frowning, John drifted forward, drawn by the boy's familiar face. His features were small yet hinted at strength. But he couldn't place them. Why did the boy look so familiar?

John moved toward him, reaching out for the small hand. When he touched the tiny fingers, he knew. A shockwave rippled through his body. "I saw you." He swallowed, his breathing short and tight. "That day in the haberdashery. You were playing with the Cleghorn boy. I *saw* you."

Blue eyes came back to him. For an instant, they flashed with the same warm, playful gleam he'd seen then. A crooked smile appeared.

John's heart turned inside out. He crouched down to the boy's level, gazing in wonderment. "Finlay."

The boy inclined his head.

John stroked his soft cheek with his fingertip. "I can scarcely believe it."

Finlay's grin gentled into understanding. Then, those sweet eyes turned solemn. "Ye must awaken, John. Ye must save her."

"Annie?"

Finlay clasped John's fingers and squeezed. He then turned his hand over, lifting it so John's palm lay open. A thistle appeared there. Wooden but recognizable. John had seen Annie worry at it with her fingers when she was missing her laddie. Finlay knelt and retrieved something from the shadows. It was John's dirk, the one with the stag blade. The boy held it out, handle first.

Reluctantly, John took it. "What am I to do with this?"

"Protect."

"From what?"

Before his eyes, the boy became a bird. The white raven flapped its wings and landed upon the windowsill.

"Finlay. What does this mean? What must I do?"

Blue eyes flashed again, this time turning white as the moon. And in his mind, he heard a single word in a thousand voices. "Awaken."

Annie's head hadn't ached this badly since she'd let Rannock fill her whisky glass one too many times, tripped on a crate of turnips, and slammed her nose into the sideboard. Presently, sound rushed in and out in loud whooshes while pain threatened to split her skull. Something was digging into her stomach. Something stank like sour sweat. Something was grunting and not letting her breathe.

Or, more rightly, someone.

She was being carried over a man's shoulder, she thought. Every step jostled her aching head and deflated her lungs. With an effort, she forced her eyes open. Darkness. Rough wool. Stink. Faint echoes of footsteps on wood. She blinked. After another jarring jostle, she sensed turning. But her hair was loose, so the slight light from passing windows shone through a curtain of red.

More grunting. Harsh panting. Her hands were numb, and now that she looked, she saw they'd been bound with twine similar to what she used in the kitchen.

Gray spots floated before her eyes. Sound disappeared.

They were moving toward a set of stairs now, she thought. The tower stairs.

Why the tower stairs? They only led down to the kitchen and the cellar. She swallowed, wondering if she'd be sick. Another turn. Starting down steps.

The cellar had a door to the garden, she recalled.

Someone was taking her to the cellar. Her head was thick, the light thin, and her mouth dry.

Someone was trying to take her from her husband. Her home.

He staggered and braced himself against the wall. Cursed in Gaelic. She recognized the voice. Skene. Though the pounding in her head made thinking near impossible, she tried to make sense of it.

Skene was in her house. Carrying her down the tower stairs. Had he been nearby all along? What did he want? She recalled the MacPhersons had laid a trap for him. Was he taking her to use against her brothers?

She didn't know. All she knew was that she must free herself.

Another jostling step sent pain stabbing behind her eyes.

Quickly, she took stock. Hands tied. Legs dangling. Skene gripped them around her knees, but he seemed distracted and off-balance, so his grip was loose.

No time. She had to get free now. Had to find John. Had to *run.*

At the final turn, just as she felt him start down a new flight, she reared up and slammed her bound fists into his ear. He howled and staggered. Fingers clawed painfully at her thigh, but she worked her body like a fish's, forcing their combined weight into a wide teeter.

The wood landing rushed toward her, slamming into her upper body. Her vision went black. Sound went muffled. Breathing came hard. Everything bloody hurt, especially her head. But she had to run.

No time, no time, no time.

Frantically, she rolled away from Skene's bruising grip, kicking blindly and striking flesh. She used the wall to brace her shoulder. Used her fear to drive her to her feet.

No time. She had to run.

She ran. Used her bound, numb hands to claw her way up the stairs. Screamed for her husband. "English!" Over and over, she screamed, though something told her she wasn't loud enough. Her lungs were flat and useless. And he was a hard sleeper. But, God, she needed him. Now. Bloody now.

If she could just make it back to the first floor, she'd sprint for the master bedchamber.

Skene wheezed behind her. She chanced a glimpse over her shoulder. Beady, malevolent rat eyes roiled with mad rage. Blood trickled from a rat nose. He wiped it away with his sleeve. He was right behind her.

She scrambled higher, kicking backward. He grasped her ankle, pulling her toward him. But she swung her hands into his damaged nose and broke free. Then scrambled away. Higher and higher. Toes slipping. Fabric tripping. Up and up.

Glancing back, she saw him close.

And in his hand was a blade, gleaming in the faint moonlight.

Only then did she realize, in her panic, she'd passed the doorway to the first floor.

A wave of sickening terror gripped her hard. There was no way past him. She could only go up. The tower was nothing but winding stairs and a series of empty bedchambers. The stairs led nowhere, but she hadn't any choice.

Up she went. Each step was too slow, almost dreamlike. Her shift tangled around her legs, her toes digging into stone. In her ears, blood and breath pounded.

"English!" she screamed again, hearing the echo spiral. Her voice was thin. Too thin. He'd never hear her from the other end of the house in the middle of the night.

Up and up. She took the steps at a frantic pace that still felt slow and clumsy, rounding each landing with a desperate glance behind her. Skene was there, following with the slow prowl of a predator that knew its prey was cornered.

His smile relished the chase.

Sweet Christ. He had her trapped. And he knew it.

Even if she reached the top of the stairs, there was nowhere to go. A window and an empty bedchamber. No weapons. No passage to another part of the house.

No way out.

"English!" she screamed again, hoping someone might hear her. If not John, then one of the MacDonnells. But they, too, slept in a different part of the castle. They, too, were unlikely to hear her.

Her feet slipped, and her shoulder slammed into the wall. She shoved with all her might and forced herself up onto the landing. More stairs. The last of them.

She reached the third story and searched for something—anything—she might use as a weapon. But there was only a long, low window, and a cracked one, at that.

Moonlight poured through the glass, making a prism of the webbed pattern. She gasped for more air— enough to scream louder and summon help. "English!"

The rat's head appeared on the landing below. He still wore his smile. "Ye're wastin' yer breath," he sneered. "They're all sleepin' sound. Wee bit of encouragement added to the cider casks took care of that."

He'd drugged them. That must be why she hadn't awakened when he'd taken her from her bed. Why she felt weak and dizzy and sick and like her head was splitting open.

Terror coiled like a serpent, squeezing until she wanted to whimper. But she refused to show this vile pestilence her fear. "They'll kill ye, Skene," she spat, her voice slurring and shakier than she'd like. "They'll tear yer ugly head from yer shoulders and drop it next to yer puny ballocks."

His gaze flattened into meanness. "No, lass. They'll return what belongs to me. And, if I'm feelin' generous, I'll return their sister to 'em." His smile stretched wide. He wiped his nose with his wrist. "A wee bit worse for wear, I grant ye. Recompense for my trouble, eh?" He climbed two more steps, taking them slowly. "The MacPhersons have caused me a *great deal* of trouble. Price for that will be steep."

She backed away, her elbow catching on stone.

Oh, God. She needed a weapon. Anything.

Light glittered in the corner of her eye. The window. Cracks. Ordinarily, she'd need a rock or a hammer to break glass this thick. But not now.

Now, she could use her kitchen-strong arms and numb, useless hands.

No sooner did she have the thought than she reeled back to take a wide, two-handed swing. The first one thudded hard and expanded the web.

Not enough.

The second swing shattered the glass into shards. One of them lay on the low sill, dotted with her blood. She forced her fingers to work. To pick it up.

With a nasty growl, the rat charged her, knocking her back into the wall. They struggled for control of the shard. Skene was stronger, but Annie was more determined.

"I will kill ye!" she screamed, aiming kicks at his ballocks and biting the hand that tried to grip her jaw. His knife flew, skidding across the floor to the chamber door. She sliced and jabbed at him with the glass, pleased with his grunts of pain. But she couldn't hold onto it. He managed to grasp her wrists and twist. Torturous agony weakened her grip and forced the shard from her fingers. He pushed her harder against the wall, flattening his body against her until she felt crushed.

Then the strangest thing happened. He reeled backward, screeching. Freeing her. White wings flapped on either side of his neck.

Annie blinked and tried to make sense of it. A bird had flown in through the shattered window. It had sunk its claws into Skene's nape and was presently using its beak to sever the top of his ear. He clawed and howled and tore at the bird.

A white raven.

She mustn't let Skene hurt the raven. She lunged to retrieve the knife, but her hands were slick and numb, and she couldn't grasp it properly. By the time she turned around, Skene had knocked the bird away. The bonnie white creature lay still near the stairs with one wing outstretched.

"No," she wailed. "Ye killed it!"

"I'll do the same to ye," he snarled. "MacPherson bitch!"

She gripped the knife harder, recalling what he'd done to Broderick. Pain disappeared. Light sharpened. Blood pounded and pounded. "My name is *Huxley*, ye putrid pile of shite! And if ye think the MacPhersons have done ye damage, wait 'til my Englishman gets hold of ye!"

She knew she was screaming nonsense, but she had nothing left. The knife was slipping. Her hands were weak. Cuts on her arms and wrists dripped blood in a steady stream. He had her cornered, and they both knew it.

Cold air gusted through the shattered window. A wave of dizziness assailed her. She slumped against the wall, her arms shaking.

Skene started toward her.

And that's when she heard the primal roar. "Annie!"

Like a Highland barbarian, her beloved Englishman topped the last stair wearing nothing but her plaid around his waist. He looked crazed. Ferocious.

Heavenly.

He charged Skene, who had spun to face him. The two men grappled for a moment before Skene leapt back and retrieved another knife from his boot.

Quickly, Annie slid down the wall and placed the blade she was holding between her knees. Then, she used it to saw at her bindings. If John needed her, she wanted her hands free. After a frustratingly long time, the twine gave way. Sharp prickles of returning sensation made her wince, but she had no time to waste.

John had a cut across his belly where Skene had gotten lucky with a slash. But Skene was much worse off. The rat's shoulder had two gashes, and his cheek was dripping from a long slice. The two men circled each other, both a bit unsteady.

She reckoned John was still feeling the effects of whatever Skene had used to drug them. How he'd managed to awaken and find her, she didn't know.

Suddenly, Skene lunged forward, his knife aiming for John's thigh. With another deep roar, John brought his dirk up into the rat's belly. Skene gave a wheezing mewl and staggered sideways. He tried again to stab John's leg, but his knife slid off the woolen plaid as though there were nothing beneath it.

John drove Skene backward. The rat wheezed and shook his head as John struck again, this time between the rat's ribs. With a final, desperate slash, Skene managed to cut John's forearm.

Annie gasped, shifting away from the two men and holding her own blade at the ready.

But she needn't have bothered. In the next instant, her Englishman whispered something to Skene and gave a mighty shove. Skene tumbled backward through the broken window, unable to catch himself. His momentum, oddly, seemed to increase as he clawed at the frame. Then, as though he'd been shoved again by an invisible hand, he fell. A heartbeat later, Annie heard a dull thud from the ground below. Then silence.

Breaths sawed in and out of her chest. She stumbled toward her husband, who stumbled toward her. He wrapped her up tight, whispering her name.

"English," she whimpered hoarsely. "Ah, God. Ye came."

"Always, love."

For long minutes, they held each other and breathed. Then, they began searching each other for serious wounds. Both of them had been fortunate, as the various slashes were thin and shallow. She explained why Skene had come for her, how he'd planned to use her against the MacPhersons. Gently, John asked what the blackguard had managed to do to her before he'd arrived. She set his mind at ease then explained how she'd escaped. How she'd fought. How she'd broken the window to give herself a weapon. Then, she remembered. She tugged away and rushed to the corner where she'd seen the bird lying still.

It was gone.

Frantically, she searched the shadows, kneeling and running her hands over the wooden floor. "Th-there was a bird," she murmured. "I swear, English. It flew through the window. It attacked Skene."

"A white raven."

She froze. Pushed to her feet and spun to face him.

"It was Finlay, love."

"H-how do ye—"

"I dreamt about him. He's how I knew to come here." John glanced down at himself then brushed the handle of the dirk he'd tucked between his waist and her plaid. "He's how I knew you needed me."

She wandered closer until she stood inches from her husband. "Ye spoke to him?"

He nodded. "I realized I'd seen him before, Annie. Last year, the day you and I spoke at the haberdashery. He was in the corner of the shop near the tartans, playing with the Cleghorn boy."

A tear coursed down her cheek. "He loved tartans. And wee Ronnie Cleghorn." She released a wet chuckle. "I cannae believe ye saw him."

"I thought he was one of the village lads. I had no idea …"

She wrapped herself around him, resting her cheek over his heart.

He soothed her with long strokes of her hair. "I was sorry before that I dismissed your stories about him, love. But let me say again how much I regret the hurt I must have caused you."

"Dinnae fash yerself, my bonnie Englishman. All that matters is that ye ken he's real, and so do I." She reached up to stroke his jaw. "After so many years of bein' the mad one, it's a pure pleasure to have company."

CHAPTER TWENTY-FOUR

A pre-dawn rainstorm followed by blazing August heat made the field west of the village a muggy stew. John wished he could blame his foul mood on the weather.

God, he hated losing.

"So ye lost the hammer throw." Rannoch clapped a giant hand upon John's shoulder. "Second place isnae so bad."

"This was my best event," John replied darkly, glaring at his youngest brother-in-law. "Your throw was longer by ten feet."

"Aye." Rannoch grinned. "'Twas a good day."

John snorted. He'd already lost the weight-over-bar event and the loch swim to Alexander, the stone put to Campbell, and the foot race to Rannoch. Only the caber toss remained, and given his performance thus far, he held out scant hope for winning his wager with Annie.

"Bloody hell," he muttered.

He'd already written the letter inviting his family to visit, though he'd waited to send it until after the

Glenscannadoo Games. Likely he'd be waiting a good deal longer. Possibly months. A year, even.

John peered across the vast green to where the spectators gathered. Locals, visitors from neighboring towns, and guests of the laird stood in groups or sat on blankets enjoying their luncheon. He scanned the crowd for a familiar head of banner-bright hair.

"To the left, near the bagpipers," Rannoch said. "She's speakin' with Lockhart's sister."

He found her. His glorious Highland lass. She wore a green, long-sleeved gown today with her tartan sash about her waist and blue silk ribbons on her straw bonnet. Her sleeves and gloves disguised the cuts that were still healing.

Thank God none of them had been deep. Thank God his wife was so strong.

He watched her laugh and converse with Miss Lockhart as though they were bosom friends. "She's quite convincing," John murmured, sliding his gaze several feet away to where Lord Lockhart stood with Laird Glenscannadoo.

"She's motivated," Rannoch replied. "If somethin' is a matter of will, I wouldnae bet against Annie."

John smiled. "No, indeed."

A week had passed since David Skene had tried to abduct Annie. Constable Munro had asked a few questions about the man's death, but not as many as John expected. Munro had appeared content to dispose of the rat and all the trouble he'd brought to the county.

Since then, John, Annie, and the MacPhersons had been preparing for the Gathering. Several times, Annie had ventured to Broderick's house in the east foothills of MacPherson land. She always returned home sadder and in need of John's comfort.

Broderick's injuries had largely healed—at least as much as they were likely to. But he was simmering with a bottomless rage, and his isolation wasn't helping. Annie didn't know what to do. She often questioned the wisdom of involving Broderick in their plans to confront Lockhart. "How can we ask this of him, English?" she'd whispered only last night.

They had little choice. If Lockhart was the man who had hired Skene to imprison and kill Broderick, he must be brought to justice. He must be made to pay.

Now, Rannoch distracted his glare away from Lockhart with another thump on John's back. "Best ye focus on the caber toss, Huxley. Campbell hasnae been defeated since he was a wee laddie."

Two hours later, Campbell still hadn't been defeated. But it wasn't over yet. John's first two tosses had been surprisingly good. Campbell's were better, of course. The man was a bloody monster made of pure muscle and bone. He hefted the two-hundred-pound log as though it were a twig.

Now, he threw the thing end-over-end in his third toss. It landed perhaps a degree shy of twelve o'clock. All of the man's tosses had been similarly excellent.

John's shoulder muscles ached. The heat was stifling. And the midges were relentless. He glanced to where he'd seen Annie earlier. She was there, cornflower blue eyes dancing like flowers in a midsummer field. He shaded his eyes to see her better.

She mouthed something. He thought it was *I love ye,* but it could easily have been *I'm winning.* Likelier it was the first one. Annie wasn't nearly as competitive as he was.

Finally, it was time for his third toss. He approached the caber that Campbell held propped and ready for him.

"Good luck to ye, Huxley," said Campbell in that deep, quiet rumble. "Win or lose, ye'll make a fine addition to the MacPherson tug-o-war team."

John chuckled, acknowledging his brother-in-law's compliment with a clap to that monstrous shoulder before accepting control of the caber. A breeze rolled through the glen, cooling his sweat and clearing his mind. He settled the caber against his shoulder, feeling it slide into the old, familiar spot along his bone. The MacDonnell officiating the event—one of Dougal's cousins—signaled he could begin and stepped back to give him room.

John breathed. Slid his hands down the wood to the bottom. Then gripped and lifted. At first, he thought he had it. But the weight shifted as he adjusted his laced fingers. He took a second to regain his grip.

Another breeze, cool and easy.

He calmed, remembering everything Annie had taught him. *Steady. Steady.* He started forward into his run. *Faster. There.* He planted his feet. Heaved skyward with a massive thrust of his arms and a barbaric roar.

The caber flipped in a perfect, vertical arc. The larger end planted. The tapered end toppled forward.

It landed with a *whump.*

John blinked. A breeze blew hard, playing with the pleats of his kilt. Campbell and the event judge wandered to where the caber lay, their hands on their hips as they examined its position. The event judge gave him a signal, and Campbell shook his head.

John couldn't believe it either.

Twelve o'clock. A perfect toss.

A grin took him. Then a burst of pure triumph. Bloody hell. He'd done it.

The only warning he had was a glimpse of scarlet from the corner of his eye. The next thing he knew, his wife was in his arms, clinging to his neck like a monkey, shouting, "Ye did it, John Huxley!" She kissed him madly. Clutched him tightly. Didn't seem to care a whit that she was making a spectacle of them both or that his sweat would stain her silk. Laughing, he heaved her higher against him and spun her around as she planted kisses all over his face.

"I did it, Annie," he said.

"Aye, English." Her eyes went liquid with tenderness. "I kenned ye would." She kissed him like the fiery hoyden he loved. "I kenned it all along."

Later that evening, as a band of MacDonnells fiddled away on the terrace, Annie entered Laird Glenscannadoo's ballroom on her husband's arm. The room was not particularly large, but it was a lovely, ornate space with cream walls, white plaster ornaments on the ceiling, three chandeliers, and gold draperies. Two sets of glass doors stood open. The local rabble danced outside while inside, swarms of landlords and a smattering of Lowland aristocrats sniffed and tittered in polite tones.

Annie cleared her throat twice, trying to dislodge the lump there. It didn't work.

"Love, you must stop fussing with your gown."

She glanced down to where her fingers were smoothing compulsively. The rich plum silk layered with an overskirt of spangled pink tulle needed no adjustment, but her nerves were zinging like a Highlander's fiddle string. She adjusted her light tartan shawl and dug her fingers into John's arm.

"You are stunning," he soothed. "Everything is set. I'm here with you. Always."

She nodded and drew a shuddering breath.

As they moved into the crowd, she gave polite smiles and nods to those who glanced her way. Which seemed to be everyone. And everyone seemed to be suffering from having a lemon shoved up their—

"Have I mentioned how magnificent your breasts look in that gown?"

She dug her elbow into her husband's side until she heard an *ooph*. "Have *I* mentioned how little ye'll see of 'em if ye dinnae stop sayin' such things to me right now?"

"You're too stiff. Relax," he whispered, calmly retrieving glasses of whisky from a nearby tray. "Have a drink."

She accepted gladly, tossing back the dram in a single swallow. "Fetch me another, English. I'm thirsty."

He chuckled and handed her his own glass before guiding her toward Angus. "Your father looks rather dashing in his finery, don't you think?"

"'Tis unnatural. Angus doesnae wear finery."

Except that this evening, he did. Thick iron hair gleamed half-silver in the candlelight. He wore his best kilt, a handsome black coat, a blue waistcoat, and the sporran she'd only seen him wear twice—once to his wedding to her mother, and once to a funeral for a friend.

Angus glowered as they approached. "Huxley, ye'll have yer hands full with Glenscannadoo. Wee tartan peacock's already sotted and rantin' all manner of nonsense."

Annie rolled her eyes. "The dancin' again."

"Aye."

John frowned. "What about the dancing?"

"He claims lasses shouldnae be permitted to enter the dancin' competition at the Games," Annie answered. "He's been tryin' to make it lads only for five years. Says that's traditional." She snorted. "He wouldnae ken Highland tradition if it leapt from his brandy glass and stabbed him with the wee butter knife he calls a dirk."

Her husband chuckled, rich and low. The sound warmed her, and she gave him a smile. Handsome, bonnie, delicious Englishman. He'd worn his good kilt this evening, along with all the accessories—even the dirk he'd used against Skene. How could a bit of tartan, leather, steel, and silver make her want him even more? She hadn't thought it possible, but there it was. He bent his head to kiss her, and the knot in her stomach unraveled.

Angus cleared his throat. "Lockhart is here. I'll gather the lads." He slipped out the glass doors into the garden.

Just like that, the knot returned.

"Easy, love," John breathed, stroking her lower back as he turned them both until Lockhart and his sister came into view.

The lord wore a sky-blue linen coat and gold waistcoat with buff breeches. He was handsome, she supposed, if one enjoyed a carp's mouth, small hands, and smugness. Sabella looked splendid, of course, in sea-green satin. Were those real emeralds?

She brushed her own naked throat and adjusted her shawl. She tried to sip her whisky, but there was none left.

John plucked the glass from her fingers and set it on a nearby table. "Just keep him focused on you. We only need ten minutes or so."

She swallowed. "Aye."

"Try to keep your temper."

"I ken."

"Do not attack him."

"I'm nae daft, John Huxley."

"I love you more than I've loved anything or anyone in my entire life, Annie Huxley."

That purely stole her breath. She didn't dare look at him. Rather, she stood there with heated shivers running through her veins in wee, sparkling streams.

"And, I suspect, were I ever granted another life and another and another—a thousand lifetimes in a thousand different places—I should still say the same."

"God Almighty, English." It took a few deep breaths before she gathered her overheated, love-softened senses enough to reply. "After we're done here, ye're going to have a *very* good night."

"Hmm. Is that so?"

"Aye. Now stop distractin' me. I've a job to do."

His hands stroked her arms with light, tingling touches. He whispered in her ear, "Nobody could do it better."

She nodded. "I'm ready."

They made their way back through the crowd to where the Lockharts stood between a potted plant and a garish settee.

Sabella's wide, brilliant smile suggested relief. "Lady Huxley! And Lord Huxley." She curtsied with perfect grace. "How lovely to see you both."

Annie reached for her hands, clasping them warmly. She bore no grudge against Sabella, who seemed blind to her brother's villainous nature. In truth, Annie pitied her. No woman should be trapped under the thumb of a man like Lockhart. "'Tis lovely to see you, as well."

Sabella took polite command of the conversation, performing introductions between her brother and John.

Lockhart's gaze sharpened. "Lord Huxley. Am I right in thinking your father is the Earl of Berne?"

John nodded. "Indeed."

The blond lord's eyes rested briefly on Annie's gown. "Here for the hunting, I take it?"

John's arm tensed beneath Annie's fingers, but he only replied, "Something like that."

Annie decided now was the moment to test her conversation skills. First step: tea. No tea? Ask about the day's activities. "So, Lord Lockhart," she ventured. "Have ye enjoyed the Glenscannadoo Games so far?"

Lockhart chuckled. "Very diverting, I must say. Although, I'm afraid it's all a bit rustic for Sabella." He gave his sister a condescending smile. "She has a delicate constitution."

"Oh, I wouldn't say that," Sabella demurred. "Some of the events were quite impressive. I very much enjoyed the bagpiping. And the footrace."

Annie had been standing next to her during the heavy events. She happened to know Sabella had enjoyed a good deal more than music and sprinting. "Have ye tried a bit of dancin' yet?" she asked. "The MacDonnells play a fine reel."

Third step in the Lady Lessons guide to polite conversation: Introduce new topics from the present environment. Mrs. Baird had used the examples of complimenting a guest's gown or commenting on the state of the weather.

But Annie had a mission, and she needed to move this conversation forward apace.

Sabella answered first. "No, I'm afraid not." She glanced toward the terrace, her expression faintly wistful. "We only arrived a short while ago."

John took the hint, bowing and offering, "Miss Lockhart, I should be honored if you would join me. The reel is one of my favorite dances."

Before Lockhart could say anything, Sabella accepted and John led her away.

As Annie had hoped, Lockhart focused upon her and, after a moment of frowning at Annie's hair, he grudgingly suggested, "Perhaps we should dance, as well."

"Och, no, m'lord," she retorted. "Why would I, a *viscountess*, dance with the likes of ye?"

Leaf-green eyes focused upon her with sudden alert intensity. "I beg your pardon?"

She gave an imperious sniff and brushed past him to lower herself gracefully onto the settee. As soon as he pivoted to face her, she raised a brow. "In England, ye'd be naught more than a baron. Scarcely titled at all."

A muscle twitched next to his eye. "Incredible," he murmured. "You've only just been plucked from a Highland scullery, and you're suggesting *I* am the inferior, here."

"Nae suggestin'. Sayin'." She gave him a grin. "Ye ken what they say." Her eyes fell to his gloves. "Wee hands, wee ... man."

His carp mouth twisted. "Your vulgarity should be shocking, I suppose, except for one thing." His head tilted. "I'd expect nothing less from a MacPherson."

Triumph surged like lightning. She had him. By God, she had him! But not entirely. There was much more to be done.

She pretended puzzlement. "Are ye speakin' of my brothers?"

"I'd rather not."

But she needed him to. "Aye. Only natural. Them bein' so much *larger*." Again, she eyed his hands. "A pure shame. Some men carry cabers. Some struggle to lift their teacups."

"I think this conversation has run its course."

"Did a MacPherson steal yer woman, then?" It was a guess, and a wild one at that. Annie had questioned Broderick extensively about any tie he might have to Lockhart, and he'd sworn there was none. But Lockhart's hatred was obviously a deep, personal fire. Which meant either the man was a wee bit peculiar and had wanted affection that Broderick refused to provide. Or Lockhart had lost a woman to Broderick.

Lockhart went utterly rigid, his eyes strangely serpentine. "Any woman I considered mine would remain so until *I* deemed otherwise."

Yes, that was it. Time to close the trap tighter. She grinned. "Unless she didnae. What happened? Bit of a problem hoistin' yer teacup?" She cast a pointed glance at his breeches. "Or perhaps she simply prefers Highland whisky to weak Lowland tea."

A flash of venom erupted as a snarl. "You're treading on dangerous ground, Lady Huxley."

"Like Broderick did?" She leaned forward and held his gaze. "I'd wager ye discovered yer lass fancied him. I'd wager ye werenae too pleased by her preference."

"I'd wager your brother is no longer the sort of man a lass fancies."

His low, cold words should have signified her victory. He'd all but admitted to damaging Broderick out of jealousy. But a wave of fury threatened to overtake her. Blood rushed in her ears. Shivers ran down her arms. The need to rise and claw the blackguard's eyes out fired her muscles.

She fought it. Repeated John's advice: *Try to keep your temper. Do not attack him.*

Do not. Attack. Lockhart.

With an effort, she riveted herself in place and kept her expression taunting. He was still too composed. After a few careful conversations with Sabella, Annie had gleaned more about his nature—mostly how he prized his own pride above all other things. So, poking that pride should enrage him.

She needed to generate more heat. "Oh, ye might be surprised," she said. "Sometimes, a lass favors the safety of a title."

No flicker. Not a prospective bride, then.

She tried again. "Or the luxury of a fortune."

A wee spark.

She chased it, adding fuel. "Other times, a lass wants more. Bein' a lord's mistress might seem a fine choice until she has somethin' to compare it to."

Thin nostrils flared.

Ah, yes. The flame had caught. Now for the stoking.

"How did ye ken ye'd lost her, eh? Did she stop botherin' to please ye? Stop doin' that wee trick with her smile that made ye believe she worshipped ye?"

His eyes narrowed while his carp mouth flattened. Aye, he wanted to shut her up. She could see it.

Time to press harder. "Here's the truth, Lockhart. I'll say it plain so ye cannae miss it. A woman can only pretend to love an empty bag of worthlessness so long. When she finds a real man with real substance, she kens what she's missin'. And no title or fortune can hold her."

Green eyes blazed with mad fury. He bent forward and braced his arm on the back of the settee. The position put his face within inches. "She didn't leave."

"Aye, she did. Mayhap ye kept her with ye. Mayhap she still lets ye wet yer teacup from time to time. But ye ken very well who she'd choose, had she the choice to make." Annie leaned closer until their noses nearly touched. "And it wouldnae be you."

His breathing quickened. His hand formed a claw then a fist. "It *was* me."

"Nah. 'Twas Broderick."

His arm flexed near her ear as he gripped the settee harder. "No."

"That's why ye had Skene set him up to take the fall for an exciseman's murder. That's why ye made certain he would die in the Bridewell."

His breaths roughened, his skin flushing. "He deserved his punishment."

"Ye couldnae bear the comparison. Couldnae bear thinkin' how she'd always want him more."

"Shut your mouth."

"A wee, empty man cannae hide his shortcomings when he's standin' next to a giant."

"Bloody harridan."

"His only hope is to bring the giant down."

Rage exploded. He pounded the back of the settee, narrowly missing her shoulder. "And down he fell," Lockhart snarled. "Like a great, bloody tower smashed into bloody ruins."

Pretending to be intimidated, she glanced past his shoulder. "'Twas a clever plan," she offered. "Very effective."

Satisfaction gleamed. "Aye. It was."

"Do ye wish to see those ruins, Lord Lockhart? Surely ye do."

A strange, hungry murmur emerged from the man's throat. "Aye."

"Turn round."

He straightened, the first inklings of the trap he'd landed in appearing on his face. He turned.

Behind him stood five MacPhersons and one bonnie Englishman. Broderick stood at the center. And to either side of him were two Lord Commissioners of the Justiciary, a Scottish duke, and a local magistrate for good measure. They'd heard everything.

Annie rose and moved to John's side, where he tucked her close.

But Lockhart barely seemed to notice. He'd frozen in place, all but shivering with savage satisfaction as he examined Broderick from head to toe.

For his part, Broderick returned the favor. He looked positively lethal. "I'm goin' to kill ye, Lockhart," he promised, his graveled voice cold as steel. "One way or another, I'll see it done."

Lockhart grinned. "Perhaps. But I've already killed you, haven't I? She'll never want you like this. Never again."

Angus gestured to two constables, who came to haul Lockhart away. The man didn't bother struggling until he lost sight of Broderick. Then, he writhed and twisted to keep his gaze fixed upon him.

Upon the tower he'd felled into ruins.

She reached for Broderick's hand, but he'd had enough. He spun away and stalked from the ballroom out into the night.

John cupped her waist and kissed her temple. "Let him go, love."

Her heart ached. "He—he needs me."

"He needs time. This is a battle you cannot wage for him."

During her conversation, John and the MacPhersons had quietly cleared the ballroom of all but the men they'd brought to be witnesses. John had invited the two High Court judges. Angus had invited the magistrate. And shockingly, the wee tartan peacock had managed to lure the Lowland duke here after promises that the Gathering offered a "true Highland experience."

Apparently, such things had captured the aristocracy's fancy of late.

It took some time after Lockhart was hauled away to explain everything to the witnesses, but once they understood what they'd overheard, there was little doubt Lockhart would be charged with conspiracy in the exciseman's murder.

Meanwhile, Annie went outside to tell Sabella what had happened. Upon hearing what her brother had done, the woman turned white as the moon and shook her head in disbelief.

"It cannot be true," Sabella whispered. "He—he wouldn't …"

"He confessed," Annie said gently. "There is no doubt. I'm sorry, Sabella." She offered the young woman a place at Glendasheen Castle until her brother's fate had been decided.

But Sabella stiffened until her face became a brittle shell. "No. I cannot … I shall conclude my visit here at the manor. Tomorrow, I shall return to Edinburgh." Her eyes, dazed and darting, dropped to her delicate hands. "My brother will need a solicitor at once."

Annie tried to comfort her, but Sabella pulled away. She couldn't blame her, really. Annie was the reason for Lockhart's detainment. And, as much as she regretted Sabella's pain and wished to help her, Annie wasn't the least bit sorry for exposing him. *Lockhart* had done this damage. He deserved all the humiliation that awaited him—and much worse.

When she returned to the ballroom, Angus and each of her remaining brothers came over to embrace her in turn.

"Ye did well, Annie," said Campbell, laying a kiss on her forehead.

"Aye," said Alexander, squeezing her shoulders. "I kenned ye would."

Annie raised a wry brow. "Did ye, now? I recall a slightly different prediction comin' from yer direction, Alexander MacPherson."

"Nah," he said. "When the occasion calls for pure aggravation, ye cannae do better than Annie Tulloch MacPherson Huxley."

Rannoch laughed then kissed her cheek, lifted her, and spun her around before setting her back on her feet. "Aye, if ye need someone to prick a man's pride or cook a meal straight from heaven, Annie is yer lass."

She swatted each of her brothers for their laughter, then laughed, herself. "Well, I did enjoy the bit about his hands, I must admit. Unnecessary, perhaps. But fun."

Angus wrapped his arm around her shoulders and kissed the top of her head. "I'm proud of ye, lass."

She hugged his waist and closed her eyes for a moment. "Thank ye, Da."

Before long, the MacPhersons joined the party out on the terrace. John tugged her outside, too, though she only really wanted to go home so she could show her Englishman how much she adored him.

He drew her past the lively fiddlers and milling dancers. He drew her around the outside of the manor house, through deep shadows and shafts of moonlight.

"Where are ye takin' me?" she demanded breathlessly.

"You'll see." He grinned over his shoulder and led her down the drive then onto the lane. Soon, they stood near the loch beneath a tall pine. He gathered her in front of him and pointed at a branch twenty feet up. "Look, love."

She squinted. It was hard to see in the dark. But something fluttered. Something white. She lost her breath. Another flutter, and a white feather fluttered down, whirling and twirling on a soft breeze. It landed in her open palm.

"Ah, God, English. How did ye ken?" She glanced back at her husband, who gazed at her with the most astonishing glow. "How did ye ken he'd be here?"

He kissed her softly. Sweetly. "The same way I know that Highland rain makes the best whisky and Highland lasses make the best wives."

She turned in his arms and cupped his jaw, then drew him down to whisper against his lips, "And there could be no better Highland husband than a bonnie Englishman."

&PILOGUE

September 14, 1826

Annie wiped sticky hands on her apron and ordered her kitchen maid to stop crying. "They're onions, for God's sake. Use yer handkerchief and keep choppin'!"

So much gravy. So many guests. She was dizzy and a wee bit nauseated, but at least she had enough bread left from yesterday. They hadn't eaten all twenty-four loaves yet. For that, she was thankful.

A lad skidded into the kitchen. "Mrs. MacDonnell said to tell ye we're out of bread," he announced.

Annie groaned. "Fetch me the flour." She shooed him toward the larder. "And find his lordship. Huxley, I mean. My husband." There were many "lordships" in the castle at present. And many Huxleys. So many, she'd had trouble remembering all the wee ones' names.

They'd all arrived at Glendasheen Castle the previous day. John's parents, Meredith and Stanton. His five sisters. Their husbands. Their children. So very many children.

Annie paused. "Will somebody open a bluidy window! It's stiflin' in here!"

The hearth was blazing, her new range hard at work stewing venison. Another wave of nausea started when the scent of onions drifted past her nose. She leaned against the table, closed her eyes, and waited for it to pass.

"May I be of help?"

Her eyes popped open. She spun. It was Maureen, a bonnie, soft-featured woman with sweet, golden-brown eyes and hair similar to John's.

Oh, God. Annie glanced down at her stained apron and dough-sticky hands. "L-lady Dunston." What was she doing in here?

Maureen waved a hand and moved deeper into the kitchen, glancing around with obvious curiosity. "Now, now. Maureen, if you please." She grinned, her cheeks displaying the most charming dimples. "Too many titles round here. Makes one dizzy."

Annie blinked as Maureen plucked another apron from the hook near the sideboard and tied it over her lovely yellow gown. "Er, Lady D—Maureen. Is there somethin' I can do for ye?"

"Hmm. No. I'll just make myself at home, shall I?" She plucked a bowl down from the sideboard and wandered toward the larder. "Oh! What a lovely arrangement of shelves." She wandered inside. "And you have cinnamon! Splendid."

Struggling to understand what was happening, Annie started toward the larder.

"Now, *this* is a proper kitchen."

Annie froze. Meredith Huxley bustled through the doorway. Annie's plump, round-faced, kindly mother-in-law cast a twinkling glance at the half-dozen maids working on dinner. "Such a delight to see a well-run household, dear."

"I—my lady, I—"

"Meredith," she insisted. "Or Mama, when you're comfortable."

The kitchen door opened again, and three more brown-haired Huxley sisters entered—sprightly, lovely Kate; wry, motherly Annabelle; and blunt, hat-loving Eugenia. They all surrounded Annie's table, chatting and arguing about feathers, flowers, Shakespearean plays, meals designed to either please or displease a husband, and whether tartan ribbon was sufficiently Scottish for a hat worn in the Highlands.

Maureen joined them and suggested she'd like to try haggis while she was visiting. All the other ladies groaned.

"Do you have any notion of what they put in there, Maureen?" asked Eugenia. "All the parts they should be tossing in the rubbish pile, that's what."

Maureen sniffed and raised her chin. "I've heard it's quite good, actually."

Annie cleared her throat and felt the weight of five sets of Huxley brown eyes settle upon her. "Haggis can be good, aye. When 'tis done well."

The fifth Huxley sister entered, peeking past the door through round spectacles. A warm smile wreathed her face, producing the dimples Annie had begun to associate with all Huxley females.

"My, this does appear to be the spot for tea and gossip," Jane said. The Duchess of Blackmore was not at all how Annie had pictured her. Despite John's many assurances to the contrary, Annie had imagined Jane as slender and swanlike with the remote sort of haughtiness bred into ladies who became duchesses.

She'd never been more wrong about anything. Jane was even shorter than Annie, plump and a wee bit plain with a fringe of dark, straight hair that brushed the silver rims of her spectacles. And she was shy. All yesterday, Annie had fretted that the duchess had taken a dislike to her. Then, John had gently explained, "Jane is shy. She's improved a bit over the years since her marriage, but it takes her a moment or two to feel comfortable with new people. Wait until tomorrow," he'd said. "She'll be boring you senseless about her favorite novel. I think I could recite the bloody thing from memory."

Now, the duchess came to stand beside Annie and covered her hand, squeezing. "Have you decided which chamber to turn into your nursery?"

Annie glanced around at all the other Huxley women, who wore similarly curious expressions. "Ah, I—I havenae given it much thought, no."

"Well, you'd do well to begin planning," commented Annabelle. "You have … what would you say, Mama? Eight months?"

"Seven," Meredith replied. "First babes do sometimes arrive early, but I'd say seven."

Annie glanced down at her middle then back up at her mother-in-law. "Y-ye reckon I'm …"

Maureen chuckled. "The way you went white as paper when you caught a whiff of those onions? Oh, yes."

"My stays have been a wee bit tight," Annie murmured. "I thought perhaps … but then, I couldnae be certain … It's been a distressin' time."

Jane patted her hand. "Best to choose a *sizable* chamber for the nursery, dearest."

Meredith, Maureen, Annabelle, and Eugenia all hummed their agreement.

Kate, whose slender features more resembled John's than her mother's, puckered her lips and rolled her eyes. "This again," the young woman muttered, crossing her arms. "Must we alarm her? It may not even happen."

"It is best she is aware, dearest," Meredith replied. "Forewarned is forearmed."

Alarm wound a wee spiral up her spine. "Forearmed for … what?"

They all chuckled. Meredith answered. "Huxleys are prolific, dear."

"We are absurdly fertile," said Annabelle. "One of Papa's cousins fathered eight children with his first wife and twelve with his second."

"To be fair," said Jane, "four of the twenty were twins."

"T-twins?"

"We haven't even mentioned Uncle Alfred."

Annie clutched her stomach. "Oh, God. How many? Ten?"

They all cast her sympathetic glances.

"Twelve?"

"Fourteen, at last count," answered Eugenia. "Aunt Phillis looked positively spent last time we saw her. Perhaps after this babe is born, she'll finally put her foot down."

Meredith sniffed. "I've told her how to gain a respite. She simply refuses."

Annie frowned as they all nodded. "How?"

"Feed them from your own breasts, dearest," Annabelle clarified. "Staves off conception for a time."

"How else would I feed a bairn?"

"A wet nurse," said Jane. "Many ladies have them. Mama refused. As have we."

"Sweet Christ and all his unicorns," Annie murmured. "Ye mean to say yer broods are the *smaller* ones amongst the Huxley clan?"

Maureen's smile was probably intended to be reassuring. "Well, yes. Also, we are Huxley females, not males, so … that helps, too."

Male Huxleys were *more* fertile? Oh, God.

Kate, who'd been listening with an occasional eyeroll, announced, "Well, I may be a Huxley, but that does not mean I am doomed to birth an army. And neither is Annie."

Meredith patted her youngest daughter's arm. "Of course not, dear."

"I intend to be the exception. One or two children is more than sufficient. Isn't that so, Annie?"

Annie glanced at Meredith, hesitant to support a notion Kate's mother did not appear to appreciate.

"Or even none at all," the young woman continued blithely.

Eugenia snorted. "What sort of eunuch are you planning to wed, Kate?"

"Perhaps I'm not planning to wed anyone."

"Don't be silly, dear. Of course you will," answered her mother. "You simply haven't found the right match yet."

"Because he doesn't exist, Mama. Besides, I'm going to become a playwright."

Another snort from Eugenia.

"Or perhaps a novelist."

This time, the snort came from Jane.

"Scoff if you like, Jane. But your favorite author is a lady."

"My favorite author is extraordinarily rare. Which is why she's my favorite."

Meredith intervened with a motherly tone. "Kate, there is no reason why you may not be both an author and a wife. Look at Annie."

Everyone did, and Annie wondered if she had flour on her face.

"Annie has many of her own interests, including cookery and embroidery."

Annie shrank a bit as she recalled the kitten pillow cover she'd embroidered for Meredith. The woman had hugged her for a good five minutes straight.

Meredith continued, "Yet, she has already begun her own family. An early start is best. One has more energy when one is young."

The Huxley women kept chattering on, but all Annie could think about was fourteen wee bairns who all looked like her Englishman. Grinned like her Englishman. Charmed and laughed like her Englishman.

Her hand settled upon her belly. Suddenly, even twenty seemed a paltry number.

As though she'd summoned him with her thoughts, he entered the kitchen looking so handsome, she wanted to leap upon him and demand he take her.

"Mama, I do hope you aren't frightening my bride with tales of Huxley eccentricity," he said with a twinkle.

His mother went immediately to embrace her son. She kissed his cheek and patted his shoulders. "No, my sweet boy. Merely tales of Huxley fecundity."

His eyebrows shot up. He glanced toward Annie. Then, his expression turned sheepish. "Did they mention Uncle Alfred?"

"And Aunt Phillis. Aye."

"Look, love. I know fourteen seems like a dreadfully large number."

"It is a large number, English. Very, very large."

"But nothing says we must have so many."

"Yer father's brother did."

"Well, yes."

"And yer father's cousin did."

"Right." He blew out a breath. "Twenty. That is rather a lot."

She crossed her arms and gave him a narrow look. "Ye're teasin' me."

A grin he'd evidently been disguising broke open. Hazel eyes danced as he laughed. "I promise you, it's all true. Uncle Alfred. Cousin George. Every word."

"Aye, but ye're pleased about it."

As he came to stand with her, those eyes flared again, this time with less amusement and more ardent longing. "I'm pleased you are my wife. I'm pleased our babes, whatever their number, will have you as their mother."

Six Huxley women all sighed in unison. Annie sighed with them. She supposed she was a Huxley woman, too.

She grinned up at her husband, who'd correctly predicted that his family would adore her, and she would adore them, and everything would be fine. Who'd chosen a Scottish hoyden above all the ladies he might have had to mother his brood. Who'd loved her and would continue to love her with everything he had.

"And I'm pleased ye're mine, John Huxley. Nothin' in a thousand lifetimes could please me more."

Watch for the next book in the
Midnight in Scotland series

COMING SOON!

MIDNIGHT IN SCOTLAND: BOOK TWO

THE TAMING OF A HIGHLANDER

BY

ELISA BRADEN

MORE FROM ELISA BRADEN

Be first to hear about new releases, price specials, and more—sign up for Elisa's free email newsletter at www.elisabraden.com so you don't miss a thing!

Midnight in Scotland Series

In the enchanting new Midnight in Scotland series, the unlikeliest matches generate the greatest heat. All it takes is a spark of Highland magic.

THE MAKING OF A HIGHLANDER (BOOK ONE)

Handsome adventurer John Huxley is locked in a land dispute in the Scottish Highlands with one way out: Win the Highland Games. When the local hoyden Mad Annie Tulloch offers to train him in exchange for "Lady Lessons," he agrees. But teaching the fiery, foul-mouthed, breeches-wearing lass how to land a lord seems impossible—especially when he starts dreaming of winning her for himself.

Rescued from Ruin Series

Discover the scandalous predicaments, emotional redemptions, and gripping love stories (with a dash of Lady Wallingham) in the scorching series that started it all!

EVER YOURS, ANNABELLE (PREQUEL)

As a girl, Annabelle Huxley chased Robert Conrad with reckless abandon, and he always rescued her when she pushed too far—until the accident that cost him everything. Seven years later, Robert discovers the girl with the habit of chasing trouble is now a siren he can't resist. But when a scandalous secret threatens her life, how far will he go to rescue her one last time?

THE MADNESS OF VISCOUNT ATHERBOURNE (BOOK ONE)

Victoria Lacey's life is perfect—perfectly boring. Agree to marry a lord who has yet to inspire a single, solitary tingle? It's all in a day's work for the oh-so-proper sister of the Duke of Blackmore. Surely no one suspects her secret longing for head-spinning passion. Except a dark stranger, on a terrace, at a ball where she should not be kissing a man she has just met. Especially one bent on revenge.

THE TRUTH ABOUT CADS AND DUKES (BOOK TWO)

Painfully shy Jane Huxley is in a most precarious position, thanks to dissolute charmer Colin Lacey's deceitful wager. Now, his brother, the icy Duke of Blackmore, must make it right, even if it means marrying her himself. Will their union end in frostbite? Perhaps. But after lingering glances and devastating kisses, Jane begins to suspect the truth: Her duke may not be as cold as he appears.

DESPERATELY SEEKING A SCOUNDREL (BOOK THREE)

Where Lord Colin Lacey goes, trouble follows. Tortured and hunted by a brutal criminal, he is rescued from death's door by the stubborn, fetching Sarah Battersby. In return, she asks one small favor: Pretend to be her fiancé. Temporarily, of course. With danger nipping his heels, he knows it is wrong to want her, wrong to agree to her terms. But when has Colin Lacey ever done the sensible thing?

THE DEVIL IS A MARQUESS (BOOK FOUR)

A walking scandal surviving on wits, whisky, and wicked skills in the bedchamber, Benedict Chatham must marry a fortune or risk ruin. Tall, redheaded disaster Charlotte Lancaster possesses such a fortune. The price? One year of fidelity and sobriety. Forced to end his libertine ways, Chatham proves he is more than the scandalous charmer she married, but will it be enough to keep his unwanted wife?

WHEN A GIRL LOVES AN EARL (BOOK FIVE)

Miss Viola Darling always gets what she wants, and what she wants most is to marry Lord Tannenbrook. James knows how determined the tiny beauty can be—she mangled his cravat at a perfectly respectable dinner before he escaped. But he has no desire to marry, less desire to be pursued, and will certainly not kiss her kissable lips until they are both breathless, no matter how tempted he may be.

TWELVE NIGHTS AS HIS MISTRESS (NOVELLA – BOOK SIX)

Charles Bainbridge, Lord Wallingham, spent two years wooing Julia Willoughby, yet she insists they are a dreadful match destined for misery. Now, rather than lose her, he makes a final offer: Spend twelve nights in his bed, and if she can deny they are perfect for each other, he will let her go. But not before tempting tidy, sensible Julia to trade predictability for the sweet chaos of true love.

CONFESSIONS OF A DANGEROUS LORD (BOOK SEVEN)

Known for flashy waistcoats and rapier wit, Henry Thorpe, the Earl of Dunston, is deadlier than he appears. For years, his sole focus has been hunting a ruthless killer through London's dark underworld. Then Maureen Huxley came along. To keep her safe, he must keep her at arm's length. But as she contemplates marrying another man, Henry's caught in the crossfire between his mission and his heart.

ANYTHING BUT A GENTLEMAN (BOOK EIGHT)

Augusta Widmore must force her sister's ne'er-do-well betrothed to the altar, or her sister will bear the consequences. She needs leverage only one man can provide—Sebastian Reaver. When she invades his office demanding a fortune in markers, he exacts a price a spinster will never pay—become the notorious club owner's mistress. And when she calls his bluff, a fiery battle for surrender begins.

A Marriage Made in Scandal (Book Nine)

As the most feared lord in London, the Earl of Holstoke is having a devil of a time landing a wife. When a series of vicious murders brings suspicion to his door, only one woman is bold enough to defend him—Eugenia Huxley. Her offer to be his alibi risks scandal, and marriage is the remedy. But as a poisonous enemy coils closer, Holstoke finds his love for her might be the greatest danger of all.

A Kiss from a Rogue (Book Ten)

A cruel past left Hannah Gray with one simple longing—a normal life with a safe, normal husband. Finding one would be easy if she weren't distracted by wolf-in-rogue's-clothing Jonas Hawthorn. He's tried to forget the haughty Miss Gray. But once he tastes the heat and longing hidden beneath her icy mask, the only mystery this Bow Street man burns to solve is how a rogue might make Hannah his own.

About the Author

Reading romance novels came easily to Elisa Braden. Writing them? That took a little longer. After graduating with degrees in creative writing and history, Elisa spent entirely too many years in "real" jobs writing T-shirt copy ... and other people's resumes ... and articles about giftware displays. But that was before she woke up and started dreaming about the very *unreal* job of being a romance novelist. Better late than never. Elisa lives in the gorgeous Pacific Northwest, where you're constitutionally required to like the colors green and gray. Good thing she does. Other items on the "like" list include cute dogs, strong coffee, and epic movies. Of course, her favorite thing of all is hearing from readers who love her characters as much as she does. If you're one of those, get in touch on Facebook and Twitter or visit **www.elisabraden.com**.

Printed in Great Britain
by Amazon

12497917R00236